THE REVENGE OF CAPTAIN PAINE

Also by Andrew Pepper

The Last Days of Newgate

The
REVENGE *of*
CAPTAIN PAINE

ANDREW PEPPER

Weidenfeld & Nicolson

LONDON

First published in Great Britain in 2007
by Weidenfeld & Nicolson

© Andrew Pepper 2007

A CIP catalogue record for this book is available
from the British Library

ISBN 978 0 297 85238 4 (hardback)
ISBN 978 0 297 85183 7 (trade paperback)

Typeset by Input Data Services Ltd, Frome

Printed in Great Britain by Clays Ltd, St Ives plc

Weidenfeld & Nicolson
An imprint of the Orion Publishing Group
Orion House, 5 Upper St Martin's Lane, London WC2H 9EA

www.orionbooks.co.uk

For Alison and David

Give to any man a million a year, and add thereto the power of creating and disposing of places, at the expense of a country, and the liberties of that country are no longer secure. What is called the splendor of a throne is no other than the corruption of the state. It is made up of a band of parasites, living in luxurious indolence, out of the public taxes.

TOM PAINE, *The Rights of Man*

AUTHOR'S NOTE

Much of this novel deals with different sums and denominations of money. In order to find the equivalence in today's terms, the usual advice is to multiply the 1835 figure by forty. Thus ten thousand pounds in 1835 would be worth approximately four hundred thousand pounds in today's terms.

PART I

*

The Ship of Fools

AUTUMN 1835

ONE

The brickbat whistled through the air as Pyke slammed it down on to the wooden stall, snapping the stall in half and sending its contents tumbling on to the cobblestones. Another lunge with the same weapon shattered a barrel filled with pickled cucumbers and herrings, the sour liquid spraying all those standing within a ten-yard radius. Drawing his sleeve across his mouth, Pyke stared into the hooded eyes of the man standing in front of him, ignoring the sea of sullen faces gathered in the walled pen at one end of Petticoat Lane.

His name was Gold.

Ever since Pyke's bank had started to court the burgeoning slop trade, Pyke had been at loggerheads with Petticoat Lane usurers like Gold: usurers who regarded the business of lending money to small businessmen – who, in turn, paid slave wages to growing numbers of workers in order to produce an ever-proliferating supply of underpriced goods – as their natural domain.

In his position as the bank's senior partner, Pyke had employed two former Bow Street Runners to collect debts in the vicinity of Spitalfields, and one of them, Bethell, had been attacked a few days earlier and been beaten with brickbats and pickaxe handles. In the subsequent melee, Bethell had lost an eye and a tooth. Investigating the matter himself, Pyke had discovered that the assailants were, or appeared to be, Jewish, and he knew that nothing happened in and around Petticoat Lane without Gold's approval.

Pyke's associate, Jem Nash, wielded a blunderbuss to keep the crowd from trying to help the unfortunate man at the end of Pyke's brickbat.

'If you ever harm one of my men again, or attempt to damage one of my places of business, I'll hunt you down and kill you. Is that understood?'

As he spoke, Pyke almost didn't see the figure moving out of the shadows and it wasn't until the man had slipped the wire around Jem Nash's neck that Pyke responded. In the blink of an eye, he had retrieved his knife and, in the same movement, thrust it against Gold's throat. It wasn't a manoeuvre he had had much use for in recent years but he had spent the best part of a decade as a Bow Street Runner and could still remember how to draw a pistol or turn a knife on an opponent.

For a moment, no one knew what to do. Nash's assailant swapped a panicky look with Gold.

'Let him go,' Pyke barked.

Gold's eyes darted between Nash and his assailant.

'*Let him go.*'

After what seemed like an eternity, Gold nodded his assent.

The man dropped the garrotte and Nash swung the blunderbuss around and fired, the ball-shot tearing his assailant in half and splattering the people gathered in the pen with blood, intestines and bone. The wounded man collapsed into a puddle of his blood, quivered and then died.

There was one shot left in the blunderbuss and thirty men unable to take their eyes off their slain friend.

'That just wouldn't have happened if your boy hadn't tried to choke my associate.' Pyke clenched his jaw and cursed Nash's rashness under his breath. He had brought the younger man because he'd needed someone who could keep the mob from retaliating but he hadn't, for a moment, imagined that Nash would be capable of turning the blunderbuss on someone and firing it in anger.

Gold stared at him, hollow eyed. 'You gemmen come down here like a couple of freebooters, pop the cull and expect to walk away?' There was a note of incredulity in his voice.

'You dealt the cards, you've got to play the hand.'

Gold nodded but didn't speak for a moment. 'Ever heard the phrase an eye for an eye, a tooth for a tooth?'

Pyke could feel the anger in the faces of those gathered around them. He glanced over at Nash, whose armpits were damp with sweat.

'Is it money you want?'

'I know this cully. I know his family. Who's going to put bread on their table now?'

4

Pyke let out a sigh. Gold was willing to negotiate. It meant they might escape with their lives. 'My man lost an eye, your man's dead. What do you think you're owed?'

Gold sneered. 'You think a few pieces of silver can buy a fellow's life?'

'What if the money folded?' Pyke asked.

Gold seemed to consider this for a short while and licked his lips. 'I give the word, there are thirty men here all wanting to pink you with two inches of cold iron.'

Pyke let Gold see the pistol in his belt and motioned at the blunderbuss Nash was aiming at the chests of the men surrounding them. 'Don't you reckon enough blood has been spilled already?'

Silence hung between them. In the distance, he heard a dog barking and someone laugh. More bodies appeared in the walled pen, eager to see what was happening. 'What kind of arrangement were you thinking of?'

Pyke took out his purse and tossed it on to the ground. 'There are thirty sovereigns in there,' he said, pausing. 'I'll pay you another fifty on top of that.'

'Thirty megs, eh?' Gold scratched his stubble and rubbed his eyes. 'And fifty more to come.'

There had to be forty men in the pen now and one word from Gold would see both of them engulfed by a wave of bodies and fists.

'Well?'

'It seems a little short to me. Man can hardly wet his beak with that.'

'A hundred. That's my final offer.'

'*Your* final offer? Are you the cock of the walk now?' Around Gold, a few of the gathered figures took a step forward as if to signal their intent.

'I'll send a man down with the rest of the money this afternoon.'

The blood was vivid in Gold's sunken cheeks. 'You need to put some reins on your colt. An unlicked cub goes out on the pad, he's axing to be hurt.'

Pyke nodded. It was a fair point. 'So do we have a deal?'

'I reckon I should put it to his family. Don't want 'em thinking they were gulled.'

'We're leaving now. I wouldn't want one of your men to do

anything rash.' Pyke nodded at Nash and they shuffled in unison towards the pen's only door. Nash's weapon was still trained on the mob.

'Maybe the matter's settled.' Gold smiled, half closing his eyes. 'But then again, maybe it ain't.'

Pyke kicked open the door and allowed Nash to hurry past him. 'Is that a threat?'

'Call it what you like, Pyke.'

The crowd of onlookers had cleared a narrow path for them but their glares hadn't softened.

'You'll have the rest of the money by nightfall.'

Gold looked down at his slain friend and muttered, 'I wouldn't like to be the cully who has to bring it.'

'In that case I'll do it.'

'You're braver than you look,' Gold said. 'Or more stupid.'

In the taproom of the Barley Mow on Upper Thames Street, Nash drank gin from the bottle, his Adam's apple bobbing up and down in his throat until he had to pause for breath. 'I killed a man,' he muttered, visibly trying to work out whether he abhorred the notion or felt some kind of pride at his actions.

With his dark blue swallow-tailed coat, checked trousers, crimped shirt, top hat and leather gloves, Jem Nash looked more like a dandy than the banking clerk – and more recently minor partner – that he was. Notwithstanding the fripperies of his outfit, people often commented that Nash and Pyke might have been brothers. Though Nash was a few inches shorter than Pyke and without his broad shoulders, they both had the same coarse black hair with trimmed mutton-chop sideburns and similar dark, olive-coloured skin. Pyke's waist had spread a little in recent years and the privileges of wealth had softened him to a degree, but he could still take the younger man in a fight, and when they stood next to each other in a public place, it was Pyke who turned the heads of the female passers-by. But Nash was not without his own attributes. In the short space of time he had worked at the bank, he had proven himself as one of the most ruthless operators Pyke had ever seen. Nash could foreclose on another man's livelihood without a thimbleful of sentimentality.

'What you did was stupid and, even worse, it was bad for

business.' Pyke drank from his pot and wiped foam from his mouth with his sleeve. 'We might have avoided an all-out war but a man like Gold won't forget what you did.'

'I killed him, didn't I?' The shock had subsided, but Nash's hands trembled as he picked up the gin bottle.

Pyke closed his eyes and tried to summon a memory that wouldn't quite come to him. 'The first time I killed a man it kept me awake for a week.'

That drew an astonished look. 'You've killed a man, too?'

'In spite of what you might think, I wasn't always a banker.' Pyke went to retrieve his greatcoat from the back of his chair. The morning had already taken its toll on him. In his former profession as a Bow Street Runner, he'd been kicked, punched, garrotted and attacked with a machete, and although he'd brought these survival instincts with him into his new career, it had been a while since he had fired a pistol or faced an imminent threat to his life. 'You owe me a hundred pounds: either you can pay me from your own account or I'll deduct it from your drawings.'

'What did you used to do?' Nash's eyes bulged with a boyish excitement.

Pyke tossed a few coins on to the table. 'That's for the gin. Drink it and you might actually sleep tonight.'

Outside, the wind had picked up and storm clouds were gathering on the horizon. Farther along the street, Pyke hailed a hackney coachman and climbed into the cab just before it started to rain.

TWO

'I regard the railways as central to the future well-being of our economy and our nation. Notwithstanding the competitive advantage the railways will afford our industries – I mean, just imagine being able to transport coal from the Tyne to London in less than a day – I think their impact will be far greater than anyone can presently imagine. You see, gentlemen, I was fortunate enough to be introduced to train travel earlier than most and I can say that once you've experienced the thrill of racing through the countryside at thirty miles an hour, sparks flying, smoke billowing from the engine, England's green and pleasant fields no more than a passing blur, once you've felt that intoxicating mixture of speed and freedom coursing through your blood, you can lay your hand on your heart and say, without a shadow of a doubt, the future has arrived.'

Sir Robert Peel sat down behind his desk, looking mightily pleased with himself. He had aged well in the intervening years since Pyke had last seen him. His reddish hair had retained much of its thickness and his robust figure and ruddy complexion suggested good health.

He carried himself with the air of someone who expected great things to happen to him. And, Pyke mused, ever since he had seized control of his party from the Tory Ultras and formed a credible opposition to Lord Melbourne's Liberals, this didn't seem like such an outlandish idea.

'That was a quite a speech, Sir Robert. Perhaps you should take a bow and allow us to applaud now?'

Peel shot him a sardonic look. 'If I hadn't already made your acquaintance, Pyke, I'd be rather offended by that remark.'

Pyke smiled easily. 'If you're offended then I accept the compliment.'

Peel chose to ignore him. 'I say this as preamble, to give you some context for our meeting.'

Pyke let out a brief yawn.

'I'm sorry. Am I boring you?'

Edward James Morris, who was sitting next to him in Peel's disappointingly bare office, chuckled more from embarrassment than humour.

Morris was a new customer to the bank and, though Pyke didn't know him well, he had already warmed to the older man. As a general rule, Pyke didn't like members of the landed gentry. It wasn't just a matter of their physical appearance – though it was true their general unattractiveness was almost guaranteed by their insistence on breeding with their own. Rather, Pyke didn't like their effete manners and private codes of behaviour, or the way they conveyed their privilege with a look or a sneer, as though it were a stick with which to beat others. Morris was not a good-looking man, with his big-boned face and pinkish, jowly cheeks, but he was sincere and well meaning and, though he was the firstborn son of a landed aristocrat, he had given up his claims on the family pile to pursue a career in business.

His demeanour and enthusiastic persona made him seem younger than he was, but his real age could be deduced from his choice of clothes. Preferring garish colours to the more sober hues that had come to dominate in recent years, he looked like a man better suited to Regency excess than the austere world of commerce he actually inhabited. His dark green coat and purple waistcoat were set against a pair of tan breeches and a bamboo cane.

Pyke listened while Morris and Peel talked enthusiastically about the prospects for the mammoth venture Morris had been charged with overseeing: building a 186-mile railway line that linked the capital and York via the cathedral cities of Cambridge, Ely and Lincoln. But he was a little perplexed by their behaviour and didn't fully understand the need exhibited by the great and the good to talk only in oblique terms about difficulties they faced. In the world of the tavern, if someone had a problem, they told you what it was and if you were the cause of it you could expect them to come at you with a knife or a pistol. Here Pyke could tell only from Morris's slightly awkward manner that something was amiss. If someone had been eavesdropping on their conversation, they might have been

9

forgiven for thinking that the railway's progress so far had been wholly positive.

In fact, the railway's problems had been well documented from the start. Disputes with landowners and an acrimonious fight for parliamentary approval had set the project back before a yard of track had been laid. More recently, progress had been hampered by various disagreements between subcontractors and suppliers, rows involving engineers and surveyors and disturbances involving crews of navvies. And rumours had now started to spread that the project's costs had spiralled out of control and that the company would soon need to go back to Parliament and investors to plead for additional money.

Nonetheless, it was only when Pyke interrupted and asked them *directly* about the problems facing the railway that the mood in the room changed.

Morris shot him a sheepish look. 'I knew that building a railway from London to York would be an arduous task but I thought everyone would pull together for the greater good. I didn't think I'd have to fight tooth and claw every step of the way.' He seemed relieved that he no longer had to pretend everything was fine.

'But at present, am I right in assuming that your task has been made a great deal more difficult by the presence of radicals stirring up trouble among your workers?' Peel asked him.

Morris nodded vehemently and Pyke thought, with sudden alarm, that it was as if they were putting on a performance for him.

'Perhaps you've heard about the activities of this rogue everyone's calling Captain Paine?' This time Peel was addressing Pyke. 'There are slogans bearing his name daubed across walls and gable-ends throughout the city.'

Pyke nodded but didn't say anything. Four years earlier, agricultural riots had broken out across much of southern England, apparently led by a mysterious figure known as Captain Swing. They had been easily crushed but Captain Swing had never been arrested, leading many to conclude that he did not actually exist and had been created by radicals in order to give a focus to their struggles. So when Pyke had first read newspaper reports about this new figure – he presumed he was named after the revolutionary writer and pamphleteer – apparently now agitating among the urban poor, he had assumed it was simply the same trick. He hadn't for a moment considered that Captain Paine might be a real figure or that someone of Peel's stature and astuteness might be sufficiently worried about him to call a meeting.

'Last year the coal-whippers went on strike demanding higher wages and a reduced working day. This month the tailors are going to strike. Next it'll be the bakers, the shoemakers, the carpenters, the bricklayers, the brass-founders, the cabinet-makers. I've been led to believe this Captain Paine has been instrumental in promoting all of these causes and that he's offering to support the strikers financially while they take their action. I've also been informed he's taken an interest in the navvies and that he's currently stirring up trouble among the men gathering in Huntingdon to begin work on the next section of the Grand Northern.' Peel glanced over at Morris for support.

'You believe he actually exists, then?' Pyke regarded him sceptically.

'Whether he exists or not, or whether he's the same figure who led the agricultural riots a few years ago, isn't the point. First, a workhouse in Bethnal Green was burnt to the ground. That was six months ago. Then a garment factory in Aldgate was broken into and ransacked. Finally last month – and this might concern you – a bank in Stepney that had lent some money to the so-called middlemen or sweaters working in the manufacturing of clothes and shoes was set alight with rags soaked with oil.' Peel studied Pyke's reaction carefully. 'But in answer to your question, yes, I do believe there is a particular individual posing as Captain Paine. I think he's personally wealthy or has a wealthy backer and that he's willing to use this wealth to support all manner of subversion.'

'Like encouraging people to join a union?' Pyke asked, trying to remember whether he'd heard anything about the bank in Stepney.

Peel reddened. 'I'm well aware the Combination Acts have been revoked.'

'But you still consider that encouraging other people to join a union is a criminal act?'

'No, I consider wanton damage to property to be a criminal act.'

'Tell that to the Tolpuddle labourers.'

A short silence hung between them. 'If you remember, it was Whig ministers and Whig magistrates who found them guilty, not my party.'

Ever since six Dorsetshire labourers had been transported to Australia two years earlier, having been found guilty of taking a pledge of loyalty to their union and thereby violating a law that had been brought in during the Napoleonic Wars to counter the threat of navy mutinies, huge pressure had been brought to bear on the government to quash their conviction.

'In which case, perhaps you could tell me why a former Tory prime minister would seem to be so keen to repeat their mistakes.'

Peel stared into the distance, his expression inscrutable. 'Notwithstanding the fact that I regard all radical activity to be unwelcome and detrimental to the long-term interests of this country, you could simply say that, in this particular case, I am merely assisting a friend.' Peel gave Morris a nod.

'You could say that but I wouldn't believe it.'

'That I wouldn't help a friend?' Peel seemed appalled by the insinuation but Pyke wondered how much of it was for Morris's benefit.

'Then go ahead and help him.' Pyke relaxed in his chair. 'But I still don't see what all this has to do with me.'

Morris cleared his throat, trying to draw their attention to his presence. 'Perhaps if I could say something, Sir Robert?'

'Go ahead, but I told you, he's stubborn and won't be talked around.'

'I was having dinner with Sir Robert last week,' Morris said. 'Your name came up in the conversation, Pyke. Sir Robert here is not an easy man to impress but he described you as a formidable figure. A fellow you'd want to have on your side, if it was humanly possible.' In the gloomy room, candlelight glinted off his shiny forehead. 'I have to travel up to Cambridge early next week and I'd very much like you to accompany me.'

Before Pyke had time to answer, Peel produced a copy of the *Morning Chronicle* and held up the front page. The headline required no further elaboration:

HEADLESS CORPSE DISCOVERED IN HUNTINGDON

'I thought it might appeal to your sense of the macabre.' Peel smiled weakly.

Like the rest of London, Pyke had read about the matter.

A headless, decomposing body had been found floating in the Ouse just outside Huntingdon, but no one seemed to know who the dead man was or why he had been killed. Perhaps unsurprisingly, the story had caused a sensation among the metropolitan populace, and rumours had already started to spread that an axe-wielding lunatic sent by Satan had been let loose on the countryside.

Pyke regarded him with a tight expression. 'So why is the leader of the opposition so concerned about a squalid murder that happened somewhere in the provinces? What is it you're not telling me?' From experience, he'd always found Peel a difficult man to read and this occasion was proving to be no exception.

'Not telling you? God, man, I know even less about this business than the person who wrote this report.' Peel held up the newspaper. 'But as someone who always has the best interests of this country at heart, it worries me greatly that a headless corpse has been unearthed just a few miles from the spot where radical types, possibly led by this Captain Paine, are busy organising themselves.'

'That still doesn't explain why it's any concern of yours,' Pyke said. 'In case you hadn't noticed, your administration only lasted for a hundred days before the electorate spoke.'

'I thank you for the reminder.'

A moment of silence passed between them. 'Even if *your* interest in this business is purely altruistic, Sir Robert, I fail to see how it has anything to do with me.'

Ignoring Pyke's mocking tone, Peel looked over at Morris. 'Perhaps you'll leave us for a moment, Edward?'

When Morris had pulled the door closed behind him, Peel stood up and walked to the window of his office. Outside was a view of the buttresses and passageways leading to the New Palace yard. A year earlier, a fire had ripped through the Palace of Westminster and destroyed the chamber used by the Commons as well as St Stephen's Chapel. The old House of Lords had survived the blaze and had now been colonised by the Commons, but the resulting pressure for space had meant that men as senior as Peel had been forced into accommodation far beneath their circumstances.

'I have been led to believe that a radical from the East End of London called Julian Jackman might know something about this Captain Paine.' His words were measured and his face composed. 'I'd like you to confirm or disprove this claim.'

Pyke drummed his fingers on the desk. 'And, short of killing my wife and framing me for the murder, how do you imagine that you're going to persuade me to accept such a poisoned chalice?'

That, finally, shattered the Tory leader's composure. Blood rose in his cheeks and, choked with indignation, he seemed unable to speak for a few moments. Six years earlier, Pyke's mistress had been stabbed in her bed while he slept with her, and he had been tried and convicted of her murder. Pyke had initially suspected Peel's involvement in the case and though his subsequent efforts to clear his name and find the killer had exonerated Peel of any blame, the accusation that the Tory leader could have orchestrated such an act still rankled.

Instead of exploding with anger, Peel became very quiet. 'A few hundred years ago, that kind of remark to a man in my position might have earned you a jail cell in the Tower.'

'Then I am fortunate to be living in more enlightened times.'

'But your rudeness is prescient all the same,' Peel said, returning from the window and taking his seat. 'For in this instance I do have a stick to wield ...'

'Oh?'

'It's come to my attention that you might be using your office as banker to further certain illicit practices.'

Pyke's jaw tightened. 'I'm presuming you have a specific charge in mind?'

'It is my understanding that money is brought to you by, how should I put it, less than salubrious figures, money I should add that has been acquired illegally, and that your generosity as a banker allows these figures to leave your premises with Bank of England notes that bear no trace of criminality.'

Pyke studied Peel's expression and tried to assess whether he was bluffing or not. 'I take it you can substantiate these claims?'

Peel's eyes wrinkled at the corners. 'Do I need to?' He cleared this throat. 'By that I mean, if the claims are entirely without validity, then you have nothing to worry about.'

Pyke waited and said nothing.

'But if there is more than a speck of truth in them, the last thing you want is your premises raided and your reputation, such as it is, tarnished.'

Quickly, Pyke weighed up his options, or lack of them. Peel

wasn't someone to be underestimated and, if Pyke refused to help him, the Tory leader could make his life very difficult.

'I'll give you one name. You can deduce from it whether I'm to be taken seriously or not.' Peel sat back in his chair and smiled. 'Ned Villums.'

Pyke kept his stare blank. 'Perhaps I can ask *you* a question, Sir Robert,' he said, wondering who might have given Peel his information. 'Why have I been singled out for this task?'

'You're a resourceful fellow.'

'And it has nothing to do with the fact that my wife is acquainted with many of the radicals?'

'Let's just say you're in the right place at the right time or the wrong place at the right time.'

Pyke bowed his head, not wanting the Tory leader to see the heat in his face. 'So let me ask another question. Why do you suspect this Captain Paine is mixed up with the business of the headless corpse?'

'I don't suspect anything of the kind.' Peel looked searchingly into his face. 'But the possibility that there *might* be a connection makes me nervous.' He held up a sealed envelope. 'Give this to the magistrate in Huntingdon. It might help to open doors.'

'If I accept the envelope, it doesn't mean I've agreed to do what you want me to do.'

'Take the damned thing and use it as bum fodder for all I care. But you'll do what I've asked you to do because it's in your own interest.' Peel paused, his stare losing some of its intensity. 'Just go to Cambridgeshire with Morris. Listen to him. Unlike me, he can offer you a positive inducement.'

'And if I find out that Julian Jackman and Captain Paine are the same person, will these unsubstantiated claims against my bank … disappear?'

Peel's brow was pricked with sweat. 'You're walking a fine tightrope, Pyke. Just do as you're asked and let everything else work itself out.'

'You're not offering me any guarantees then?'

'*Guarantees?*' Peel's laugh was without warmth. 'You, of all people, should know there are no such things.' But he followed it up with a flattering smile. 'Remember, too, that we're both on the same side this time.' He hesitated before adding, 'You're one of us, now.'

*

Outside in the New Palace yard, Pyke didn't notice the imposing figure of Ernest Augustus, Duke of Cumberland and the King's brother, striding towards him until they almost collided with each other. The duke, who sat in the Lords and had taken charge of the Tory Ultras (so called for their unwavering support of traditional values, the empire and the Protestant ascendancy), was deep in thought and looked up only at the last minute. He was a tall man dressed in military uniform and still bore the scars of battle on one side of his face. For a moment, Pyke didn't think the duke would recognise him – he had once humiliated the man in a courtroom before hundreds of spectators – but as their stares met, the duke's expression darkened and he pushed Pyke away, muttering, 'God, what are you doing here?'

But the duke had brushed past him before Pyke had time to answer and strode into the yard shaking his head.

It was a cold, wet afternoon and the wind was gusting off the choppy waters of the Thames. 'I have my carriage,' Morris said, choosing not to remark on Pyke's exchange with the King's brother. 'Perhaps I could offer you a ride back to Hambledon? As you might know, we're practically neighbours. My wife fell in love with Cranborne Park and insisted we snap it up. It came on to the market and she was suddenly desperate to move to the countryside.'

Pyke smiled non-committally but the idea that Morris should have moved to within a few miles of Hambledon at the same time as wanting Pyke's help in an unrelated matter seemed too coincidental.

They sat in silence as the carriage clattered out of the Palace yard and up Whitehall, finally crossing over on to St Martin's Lane after waiting for a collision between a wagon transporting barrels of Truman's ale and a costermonger's barrow to be cleared away. The air was laced with the scent of hops and a few scavengers were on their hands and knees, lapping up the beer from the gutters.

'Peel wouldn't tell me how the two of you became acquainted,' Morris said after a few moments.

'Before I married, I was a Bow Street Runner.' Pyke waited. 'An incident that I'd rather not talk about brought me into contact with Peel, who was then the Home Secretary under the Duke of

Wellington. Peel came to my rescue when his hand was forced, but he never warmed to me.'

Morris nodded awkwardly. 'He can be a cold fish on occasions, I'll grant you that. But when he's among those he knows well, he's a changed chap. He loves a bawdy tale as much as the next man.'

Pyke nodded blankly. They sat in silence for a while as they crawled their way up Charing Cross Road. In the past two years he had noticed an increase in the number of vehicles using the roads. Not just the drays, wagons and carts used to transport goods around the capital but also the brightly painted private carriages carrying well-fed men and women to and from their homes. There used to be a time when broughams and open-topped phaetons were the preserve of the very rich, but now it seemed that parvenus like him had decided en masse they couldn't get by without owning their own carriage.

'Do you miss it?' Morris wiped his forehead with his handkerchief. 'Being a Bow Street Runner?'

'Since the new police were set up, the job isn't what it used to be,' Pyke answered, still bridling from his encounter with Peel.

'But do you miss the *work*?'

'Sitting behind a desk hasn't been kind to my waistline but four years at the bank have made me a lot richer than ten years as a Bow Street Runner.'

It was as close as he'd come to admitting that he did sometimes miss it. Exploiting people's weaknesses and tilting events to suit his own circumstances were elements that applied just as well to banking as to policing, but it was hard not to remember the business of piecing together different scraps of information, pursuing suspects, questioning witnesses and forcing confessions out of people without some residual affection.

'Good answer,' Morris said, toying with his silk cravat. 'But perhaps I could ask you another question?'

Pyke shrugged, wondering what kind of inducement Morris might offer him and whether it would offset the bitter aftertaste his encounter with Peel had left.

'Don't look so worried, old chap. I'm not about to beg for money.' Smiling, Morris put on his spectacles and pulled out a watch from the fob pocket of his purple waistcoat. 'As I mentioned earlier, there's a meeting of the Grand Northern's Cambridge committee next week. I'd like you to accompany me and then travel onwards to Huntingdon, to see if there's any truth in these rumours about radicals stirring up trouble among the navvies.' He rubbed his eyes, sighing. 'Look, I'll be honest with you. I'm not against unionisation. I think men should be paid a fair wage for their labour and if they're not, they have a right to organise together in order to improve their circumstances. But I am very worried about worsening relations between the navvies and townfolk in Huntingdon. I suspect animosity is being stirred up by a local landowner who is absolutely opposed to the railway passing through his land. Sir Horsley Rockingham led a horrible campaign to kill off the railway while the Bill was being heard in the Commons.'

There was a short silence before Pyke said, 'I'm still not quite sure why you think I'm the right man to help you.' Outside a thin, yellow fog had enveloped the street and the figures on the pavements appeared fleetingly in the gloom, like marks on blotting paper, illuminated by the occasional gas lamp.

Morris coiled the chain of his fob-watch around his finger. 'Rockingham used to own a sugar plantation in Jamaica but he sold up and came home when Parliament finally outlawed slavery. Rumour has it he once raped a slave girl and when she gave birth to his child, strangled it in front of her. I also heard that after a slave rebellion a few years ago, he personally took charge of the reprisals. He whipped his slaves so hard you couldn't see skin for blood and he then rubbed hot pepper into their wounds.'

'He sounds like a despicable fellow but you haven't answered my question.'

That drew a pained sigh. 'Look, Pyke, I'm aware that we hardly know one another but I'd like to think I'm a good judge of character. You call things by their name and you seem to have a knack of imposing yourself on situations.'

Pyke didn't react, trying to make it clear he wouldn't be won over by such barefaced praise. But he was also intrigued. He was intrigued as to why Peel was so interested in a headless corpse discovered floating in a river near Huntingdon and what, if anything, this had to do with the problems Morris and the Grand Northern Railway were facing from the radicals.

'The Grand Northern's act of incorporation permits us to borrow a certain sum of money each year to facilitate our work and supplement the capital accrued from private investors. I'm in a position to offer your bank the exclusive contract for this business.'

Pyke digested what Morris had said and wondered, in turn, whether the older man already knew that Peel had him over a barrel. 'As you doubtless know, my bank has already invested heavily in your railway, misguidedly it seems, because the share price refuses to rise into double figures.' Two years earlier, Pyke had purchased a thousand shares with the bank's funds and had seen this investment plummet in value by more than half.

'I'm sorry about your losses, but you need to be patient. In the long run, those shares will be worth a lot more than you paid for them.'

'And in the meantime?'

'In the meantime I'm offering you a good deal. To put it in strict money terms, the figure we'll be looking to borrow – say, a hundred thousand pounds – will earn you interest payments of, let's say, eight thousand pounds in the first year alone, and because the whole enterprise is underwritten by the government, the risk to your bank is minimal.'

'I'll tell you what,' Pyke said, quickly. 'We'll toss a coin. If it lands on heads, you have yourself a deal.'

'And if it lands on tails?'

Pyke removed a sovereign from his purse and balanced it on his finger. 'If it lands on tails, you'll give me that watch you can't stop touching.'

'I couldn't possibly gamble this watch,' Morris said, appalled. 'It's a solid gold, English verge with a *champlevé* dial. There are diamonds on the case.' He took the watch out to show Pyke. 'It must be worth hundreds and it's a family heirloom.'

'Then we don't have an agreement.'

'God, you drive a hard bargain, don't you?' Morris stared at him through rheumy eyes.

'If you win, I'll come with you to Cambridge as you want me to.'

Morris seemed flummoxed and Pyke was about to return the coin to his purse when the older man relented. 'Heads I win?'

Pyke smiled. It told him that Morris knew nothing about Peel's successful attempt to blackmail him. The half-crown landed in the palm of his hand, the King's head facing upwards. Morris clapped his hands in obvious delight and relaxed back into the horsehair cushion.

'By way of recompense, perhaps you'll allow me the honour of inviting you to my home. I'm quite sure my wife would be delighted to make your acquaintance. She'd heard you were one of our new neighbours and asked if I'd ever met you before.'

Pyke felt his suspicion returning. 'Oh? Perhaps I know her. What's her name?'

'Marguerite.'

'Is she French?'

'No, but we met in France, while I was overseeing the construction of a waterway near Paris.'

'I don't know anyone by the name of Marguerite.' For some reason, this thought made Pyke feel better.

Morris winked conspiratorially. 'Actually, her name used to be plain old Margaret but she changed it to Marguerite after she moved to the Continent.'

'Margaret? As in Maggie?' Suddenly he could feel his heart beating a little quicker.

'I've only ever known her as Marguerite. But she's the most bewitching creature I've ever met in my life.'

Men had said the same thing about Maggie Shaw. Maggie, who'd left London to start a new life on the Continent ...

Pyke took a deep breath and struggled to get a grip of himself. It couldn't be her. But the thought that it *might* be her wouldn't go away, and half an hour later, when the carriage swept along the driveway and came to a halt at the front of the steps leading up to Morris' elegant Palladian villa, his stomach was iced with apprehension.

THREE

More than half of his life had passed since Pyke had last seen her. Then she had merely been plain old Maggie Shaw, daughter of hard-working costermonger parents, but it was clear even then that her efforts to scrape off the dirtiness associated with her family's job would find success. Maggie may have sworn, blasphemed and fucked like everyone else in the rookery, but even in the foulest conditions she'd glide through ankle-deep mud like a ballerina gracing the Parisian stage.

If she recognised Pyke, she did not show it. As she shook his hand, she could just have easily been looking at a butcher's boy delivering a tray of meat. 'I'm happy to make your acquaintance, sir,' she purred in an unrecognisably polished voice. Her hollow stare gave nothing away.

Time evaporated.

Fifteen years earlier, he'd watched from behind a flower stall as she had boarded a stagecoach bound for Dover, wondering with mounting panic whether he would ever see her again. Now, all these years later, he could still recall her face as she'd looked up and down the street, trying to conjure him out of thin air, using only the ferocity of her will. It had taken all of his self-control not to push the flower seller to one side and join her on the coach, and ever since then the scent of primroses conspired to induce feelings of such melancholy he could barely move his limbs.

She was as beautiful as he remembered, more so perhaps, if that was possible, but she no longer possessed the false naivety of the young girl he had once known. Standing there, he could admire her flawless complexion, her buxom, well-proportioned figure, her cool, intelligent eyes and her slender, creamy white arms, but he couldn't help mourning the girl he'd once known and a time in their lives that could never be recovered.

'Do come in, old chap,' Morris boomed, oblivious to his discomfort, leading them through an airy saloon that extended through the full height of the house. 'I'm delighted you accepted my invitation. Perhaps next time we might have the pleasure of your wife's company?'

Pyke bowed his head just low enough that he could continue to study Marguerite's expression.

'So you're married, Mr Pyke,' she whispered in a low, smoky voice that reminded him of an oboe.

'Pyke. It's always just been Pyke.' He met her stare but it slipped effortlessly from his face.

'And what's your wife's name, *Mr* Pyke?'

'Emily.'

'Delightful. How long have you been married?'

'Almost six years.' Instinctively he wrapped his fingers around a length of silver chain fixed to his belt with two keys attached to it. One of the keys opened the safe in the vault of his bank; the other, an old rusty object, had a more personal significance. During their courtship, Emily had risked her liberty by smuggling it to his cell in the condemned block at Newgate. Pyke had used the key to release his handcuffs and leg-irons and aid his escape from the prison. Even six years later, the sheer audaciousness and courage of her actions took his breath away, and he had carried it with him ever since as reminder of what she had done for him.

'Any children?'

'We have one boy.'

'A boy.' Her lips quivered as she stole a glance at her husband. 'And what, pray, is *his* name?'

'Felix. He's almost five.'

'Five?' For a moment Marguerite seemed to lose the thread of her own thoughts. 'A wonderful age.'

This torture was mercifully interrupted when a servant appeared carrying a shawl and handed it to Marguerite.

Taking it gratefully, she turned to face them. 'If you'll excuse me, I was about to take some air.' A lantern fixed to the wall illuminated her face and it struck Pyke that she may have been crying. The skin under her eyes looked sore and puffy and her eyes were bloodshot.

'Really, my dear. It's a beastly night. Can't it wait until the morning?' It was hard not to detect the tension in Morris's tone and briefly Pyke wondered whether 'it' simply referred to her desire to take the air.

'I'm quite sure you gentlemen have some pressing matters to discuss.' She turned on her heels and said, almost as an afterthought, 'It was nice to make your acquaintance, *Mr* Pyke. Please pass on my regards to your wife.'

Watching her depart, Pyke started to pick through the jumble of contrary thoughts her unexpected appearance had produced.

'She's had a rather hard time of it recently,' Morris confided after Marguerite had left. 'I'm just hoping she'll regain her *joie de vivre* soon.'

Pyke wanted to ask precisely what Morris was referring to but restricted himself to an innocuous question about their marriage.

After the butler had brought them champagne, Morris raised his flute and said, 'Yes, I suppose it's difficult to fathom why a woman like Marguerite would even notice, let alone agree to marry, a plain old man like me, isn't it?'

A rich old man, Pyke wanted to say, but held his tongue. He raised his glass and smiled. Maggie had always been attracted to rich men, just as she'd always been able to turn a hand of twos and threes into aces and kings.

Later, after Pyke had bid Morris goodnight, he instructed the coachman to pull in by the side of the driveway and wait there until he returned.

The rain had ceased and the clouds had cleared, the darkness lifted by an almost full moon that hung low and heavy in the sky. Pyke eventually found her standing alone in a field about half a mile from the house, not moving, the woollen shawl wrapped tightly around her shivering body.

She seemed to sense his presence before turning around to face him. 'I don't want you here, Pyke. Of all places I don't want you here.' Her voice was close to breaking.

His eyes had adjusted to the darkness now and he saw that she was standing next to what looked like an open grave.

He walked across and was about to peer into the hole when she pushed him away with her hands. 'Didn't you hear what I said? I don't want you here.'

'Is that why you insisted that your husband buy a country estate bordering on land belonging to my wife's family?' He glanced across at the hole. It wasn't large enough for a full-sized body.

This time her expression softened a little. 'It's eerie, isn't it, that we're both living off our respective wives and husbands.'

'I don't take a penny from my wife.'

'But you get to play the country gentleman.'

'Except I hate the countryside. I've always preferred the city.'

'But you're here, aren't you?'

He waited to see whether she was going to explain where 'here' was but she just threw her head back and laughed.

'What's so funny?'

'It's funny you're here with me. It's funny we're neighbours. It's funny because we're both such a long way from St Giles.'

'Neighbours,' he said, carefully. 'Except that isn't a coincidence, is it?'

She looked at the house in the distance, silhouetted against the starry sky. 'Do you sometimes think that people like us don't actually belong in places like this?'

'I don't know. You seem to have adapted well enough, Marguerite.'

'Think what you like, Pyke. I'm not the same person you once knew.'

He watched her face twitch in the darkness. 'I'm not sure I knew that person very well in the first place.' He waited for her to respond, and when she didn't, he added, 'But you've married a good man. That tells me something.'

A bitter laugh spilled from her. 'And I find out you're married, as well.' The moonlight played over her features. Her dimples vanished together with her smile. 'Perhaps we should all play happy families one of these days.'

'And I'm meant to think it's just a coincidence, you turning up here after all these years?'

'Work it out for yourself, Pyke. You never did trust other people's logic.'

'Are you going to tell your husband we knew each other in the old days?'

'Are you going to tell your wife?' When Pyke didn't answer her, she added, in the same tone, 'Eddy knows about my past. He's under no illusion about the kind of woman I am. I hope for your sake your wife is robust enough to take you for who you are.'

'And who's that?' he asked, feigning amusement.

Briefly their eyes met and a tiny spark of attraction passed between them.

'It's good to see you after all these years.' She wound her finger around a coil of her curly blonde hair. 'I was nervous when Eddy first mentioned your name and told me you lived close by. He said that he'd recently moved his account to your bank and that he planned to invite you for dinner. I knew I'd have to see you again and I didn't know how I might feel.'

'And how do you feel now you've seen me?'

'That's just it,' she said, turning around to face the house. 'I don't feel a thing.'

'Then nothing much has changed, has it?'

Pyke had never been able to tell what colour Marguerite's eyes were; they seemed to change with her mood. But when she turned to confront him they were as black as coal, and for a few moments she struggled to contain her indignation.

'You always did know how to make a lady feel good about herself.'

Pyke let her walk off towards the house but shouted after her, 'The Maggie Shaw I remember wasn't a lady.'

Pyke always woke early, a product of the many years he had lived in the vicinity of Smithfield Market, where the bleating and lowing of frightened creatures being herded through narrow streets by drove-boys and their dogs could have roused a dead man. For a while, he watched Emily while she slept next to him. Her skin was the smoothest he had ever seen and her cheekbones were prominent and finely crafted. Under her nightshirt, he could just about see a birthmark in the shape of a strawberry above her breast, and her silky chestnut hair fell around her face on the pillow. But as beautiful as she still was, it wasn't her looks he had fallen in love with. As the only child of a deceased aristocrat who claimed lineage as far back as Tudor times, she had inherited none of her father's traits: his cruelty, meanness, vanity and greed. Perhaps because she'd learnt to despise him from a young age, she'd wilfully set out to create a different life for herself and had succeeded in doing so, beyond her wildest imagination. Pyke could say that, without any doubt, she was the kindest, most intelligent woman he'd ever known. This didn't mean she was incapable of selfishness but rather that hers was a morality where the ends always justified the means. Having conspired with Pyke to see off her father, she'd used the income accrued from his estate to fund the charitable causes that she had devoted her life to supporting.

The previous night, after he had returned from Cranborne Park and they had eaten supper, he'd given her further instruction about how to load and fire a pistol. On the lawn, with only the light produced by the candles in the dining room to guide her, Emily had hit a tin sconce from twenty paces. Later, he had carried her upstairs to the bedroom and now he noticed that his fingers still smelled of powder and sex.

Quietly, Pyke left Emily sleeping and returned to his bedroom, where one of the housemaids had lit a fire and Royce, his valet and butler, had prepared his washstand and filled the basin with hot water. His razor and soap rested on a shelf above the basin and, in the corner of the room, a copper hip bath had also been filled with steaming hot water. Stirred by his presence, Royce appeared at the door and Pyke dismissed him with a few words of gratitude.

Like all of the servants, Royce hated him. They hated him because one of his first acts as the new master had been to cut the household staff in half; hated him because he didn't believe in tradition, because he'd closed down the old brew- and bakehouses and ordered the household bread and beer from suppliers in Edmonton; hated him because he wasn't Emily's father and didn't come from aristocratic lineage; because he came from the same stock as they did and because he knew their tricks, knew they fiddled the books to make a little extra for themselves. A few pennies here and a few pennies there, Royce and the housekeeper between them. They hated him and he despised them; despised them for mourning a petty tyrant like Emily's father, despised them for their small-mindedness and arcane country ways.

If Pyke had had his way, he would have closed down the hall and moved into the city, and they knew this – they had perhaps overheard his many arguments with Emily on the subject. Most of all they hated him because they feared him, feared that he would some day put an end to the only life they had ever known, a life that, under Emily's father, must have seemed so secure.

Before breakfast, Pyke found Royce sitting at his table in the butler's pantry and he spent half an hour going through the invoices. The expense of maintaining and running the hall never ceased to amaze him, and while the rents received from the tenant farmers just about covered the costs, more so now the costs had been scaled back, and left a little in reserve which Emily used as she saw fit (this had been one of the stipulations of the wedding contract), Pyke always baulked at the idea of spending so much money on things he barely noticed and didn't care about: veterinary bills, repairs to cracked windowpanes and chipped stone floors, the installation of new sashes, the replacement of old mattresses and rebinding of old books, payments to chimney sweeps, vermin removers, apothecaries, marble polishers, plasterers and picture gilders, as well as the usual moneys to the brewer, butcher, fish-man, grocer, laundrywoman, blacksmith, bell-hanger, post-boys, slaughter-men, charwoman and the dung and night-soil collector. This was without the wages of the permanent staff. The butler/valet (who also acted as the house steward), cook, coachman, under-butler (who also acted as footman), housekeeper, three housemaids, land steward, gardener, groom, stable-boy, and four gamekeepers. A permanent staff of sixteen, slashed from almost forty when Emily's father had still been alive: forty men and women serving one man.

There was one invoice in particular he queried. It was only for twenty pounds but twenty pounds to an apothecary for just a single month's supply of ointments, diuretics and emetics. Castor oil, camphor, spirits of lavender, blistering plasters, arsenic mixtures, liniments, leeches and, of course, his own supply of laudanum, which Emily knew nothing about.

'What are we running here? A sick house?' He surveyed the itemised list. 'Was it really necessary for Jones to visit ten times in a month?'

Royce bowed his head, showing off his bald scalp. 'I believe he had an abscess, sir. Mighty painful it was too, by all accounts.'

'And should I really be footing the bill for Mary's lip ointments?' Already hating himself for sounding so petty.

'I'm told these colder days make 'em terrible dry, sir.' Royce *despised* him. Pyke could hear it in his tone.

What he wanted to say was that he knew Royce was pilfering from him but in the end he held his tongue. He didn't necessarily mind that Royce was doing so – he expected it, in fact – but he didn't like the fact that the servant might be laughing at him behind his back.

When Emily appeared in the dining room later for breakfast she was wearing a white linen dress with an Empire waistline covered by a woollen shawl. She kissed him on the cheek and took her chair opposite him. Felix, their five-year-old son, had already taken his breakfast, Pyke informed her, and was being prepared by Jo, Emily's maid and Felix's nursemaid, for a walk.

'Will you be attending to your fatherly duties this morning, then, my lord?' Emily asked, in a mocking tone. She often teased him by addressing him this way because she knew it irritated him.

'The boy needs fresh air,' he said, not rising to the bait, glancing at the newspaper spread out on the table in front of him. There was nothing new about the headless corpse in Huntingdon.

Emily explained that she had some letters to write, or else she would have joined them. 'I'm organising a charity event in Coventry next month, for the weavers there, and I want to petition Thomas Wakley to table a question in the House about the exploits of the sweaters who've moved into the East End.'

Pyke didn't look up from the newspaper, but he thought about the money his bank had lent to such people.

'Pyke?'

This time he looked up and saw her eyes were shining. 'Yes?'

'We should try and do what we did last night more often,' she whispered, so none of the servants would hear her. Her pale skin reddened slightly.

'What? Practising with the pistol?'

That drew a throaty chuckle. 'It didn't seem like you needed much practice from where I was positioned.'

'Staring up at the ceiling counting the cracks in the paintwork?'

'I got to ten and lost count.' She was smiling now.

'You got as far as ten?'

'Don't get conceited.' She reached over and touched his hand. 'But I just wanted to say it was ... *nice*.'

'Nice?' he said, playfully. 'A puppy is nice.'

'I meant it just felt right. I hardly saw you in the last week.'

Royce entered the room with the morning post on a tray and

placed it on the table next to Emily. He departed with a bow of the head.

'Mrs Garner from the lodge wants to know whether we'll be hosting a midwinter ball this year,' Emily said, a few minutes later, looking up from the letter she had been reading.

That was another thing. Their neighbours hated Pyke, too, because, unlike Emily's father, he refused to throw open the doors of the hall for such social occasions.

'Tell that old harridan this year will be no different to last year or the year before that,' Pyke said, not looking up from the newspaper. 'If she wants a ball, she should host it on her own backside. It's large enough.'

Emily laughed out loud. 'Don't you think we should, one of these years? It might be fun.'

'What? A room full of gormless twits and giggling girls might be *fun*?' This time he glanced up from his paper, just in time to see Emily pulling a face at him. 'I saw that,' he added.

Despite the bantering of their morning, the hall had come between them during their six years of marriage. Since Emily's mother had died about a year earlier, Pyke had argued that a move into the city would give them more time together, but Emily couldn't bring herself to break up the household and claimed it was their duty to maintain the old hall until Felix came of age and decided for himself whether he wanted to take the place on and adopt her father's title. Anyway, Emily always said, making the one argument she knew he couldn't refute, the country air was much better for Felix than the dirty, smog-filled air in the city.

Their breakfast was interrupted again when Royce suddenly announced they had a visitor, and before Pyke could tell him they weren't receiving visitors, Reverend Cole had shuffled into the dining room, apologising for his unannounced visit.

Even before the curate had opened his pinched mouth, Pyke knew why the man had come. With Emily's blessing, Pyke had scrapped the practice of tithing on the estate. None of the farmers who rented their land was compelled to give anything to the church and, as a result, its income had plummeted and the church itself had fallen into disrepair. Pyke couldn't have cared less whether the building and its congregation sank into a deep bog but the murmurings of discontent among parishioners had reached a new high and various figures had been dispatched to the hall to plead with him for the reintroduction of tithing.

Reverend Cole was an odious creature with sharp, twitching features and ferret-like eyes. His humpback was the most obvious sign of his deformity but rumour had it that his feet were webbed. He was a pompous, self-regarding little man and had made a nasty habit of intruding on them at inconvenient times – deliberately so, Pyke had often thought.

Standing up, Pyke strode across to greet the diminutive curate and put a friendly arm around his shoulder. 'If you ever show your nasty, rat-like face at this hall without a prior invitation again,' he whispered, 'I'll come down to your church with a blunderbuss and shoot every single one of the stained-glass windows you're so proud of.' He gave the terrified man a final squeeze before releasing him. 'Is that understood?'

Ashen faced, the curate scurried from the room. Pyke looked across at Emily, who had raised her eyebrows.

'What? I didn't say anything.'

'Really? It looked to me like the man had just soiled his undergarments.'

'I just said I'd be happy to donate some money to the church's poor fund.'

She gave him a hard look. 'You've got to understand people are a little frightened of you.'

'Frightened of me?' Pyke tried to hide his delight at this prospect.

'Yes.'

He came up behind her and threaded his arm around her neck. 'I suppose I can be a very frightening person.' He kissed the whiteness of her neck.

'The servants, too. Jo tells me these things. ' Emily tried to push him away.

'The servants hate me because I'm not your father.' Surprised by her reticence, he put on a frown, adding, 'Are you saying you don't want to go back up the stairs and have me ravish you all over?'

'Jo's only just combed my hair,' Emily said, laughing. But her arm was peppered with gooseflesh.

'We could always fuck here on the table but I dread to think what Royce would do if he saw us.'

Emily giggled at this prospect and at Pyke's crude impression of the elderly butler, and when he next tried to embrace her, she looked around to make certain they were alone before kissing him back. 'Are you quite sure you've got enough powder left in your pistol?'

Pyke gave her a look of mock consternation. 'Enough to see off an invading army, my dear.'

'I told you, it's my lady, not my dear,' she said, as he carried up her the stairs in his arms.

As Pyke lay in her bed, the air thick with her perfume and his sweat, he closed his eyes and tried to remember when he had last been this happy. Then he recalled his brief conversation with Marguerite and the stranglehold Peel enjoyed over him and he felt his good mood begin to fade.

'A few weeks ago, you mentioned a meeting you were hoping to attend, bringing together different radical and trade union figures in the capital.'

She looked over at him, surprised. It wasn't often he asked about her work. 'What of it?'

'I was wondering when it was, that's all.'

'This Monday.' Wrinkles furrowed her brow. 'Why do you ask?'

'I thought I'd come and support you.'

Emily sat up in the bed. 'Why? You've not shown much interest in what I've been doing before.'

Pyke put on a hurt expression. 'Don't you want your capitalist husband there? Are you afraid I'll embarrass you in front of the mysterious Captain Paine?'

'Who said Captain Paine will be there?' This time there was a note of suspicion in her voice.

'So you think he actually exists?'

She gathered the sheet around her and stared out of the window. 'Where has all this suddenly come from?'

'I'm just trying to show an interest,' he said, playing up the hurt.

That seemed to placate her a little. 'Before the meeting, I have to visit the trustees of an orphanage in Hackney. Would you like to come with me?'

Pyke sank back into the mattress. 'I was just wondering whether you've met him, that's all.'

'Have I met Captain Paine?'

31

'Yes.'

She didn't answer him and continued to stare out of the window as though something outside had gripped her attention.

Later that morning, Pyke took Felix for a walk in the grounds of the Hambledon estate. In order to reach the starting point, they took the carriage to the outer fringes of the estate and from there walked briskly across open fields. It was a crisp autumnal day and above them the sky was a vast uninterrupted expanse of blue. Beneath their feet the mud track was hard and the verges were choked with blackberries and nettles.

Pyke had expected his own progeny to be fearless and hardy, rather than the frail specimen scampering along beside him. This frailty did not make him love the little boy any less – he felt a fierce protectiveness towards his son that meant he would do anything in his power to see that the lad came to no harm – but Pyke sometimes wondered how it had happened; how *he*, of all people, had fathered a child whose arms and legs were as thin as pipe cleaners and who was so prone to illness.

They walked for a while in silence.

'Nanny Jo read me a story last night but I fell asleep before the end,' Felix started. 'It was about a fox and a donkey and a lion.'

Pyke nodded his head. 'One of Aesop's fables.' He racked his brains to remember the story.

'Do you know what happens in the end?'

'The one where the donkey, fox and lion go hunting together and the fox makes a pact with the lion to give up the donkey?'

Felix took his hand. 'I think so.'

'Well, so the fox persuades the donkey to follow him and arranges that he should fall into a deep pit.'

'Why?'

'Because the fox thinks, wrongly as it turns out, he can save himself from the lion by giving up the donkey.'

'What happens next?'

'When the donkey has been pushed into the pit, the lion turns on the fox and eats him. Then he eats the donkey.'

Pyke looked down and noticed his son's terrified expression. 'So the lion kills the donkey *and* the fox?'

'Eats them, too.' There was no point in sugar-coating the tale.

'Why?'

'To teach the fox a lesson.'

'What lesson?'

'Don't trust anyone, especially not your natural enemies.' Pyke considered this for a moment. 'It's a useful lesson for business, too.'

Felix screwed up his tiny face. 'Is that what you do, Father? Business?'

'Indeed it is.' Pyke patted him gently on the head. 'But if I had been the fox, I wouldn't have turned my back on the lion.'

'Why not?'

'Because you always have to keep those stronger than you in full view.'

Felix thought about this. 'What if you were the lion?'

'If I was the lion, I'd make sure I was so fierce that the donkey and the fox would never dare to plot against me.'

'Why would they try and plot against you?' Felix seemed confused. 'What if they were your friends?'

'There are no friends in business. People will always try and cross other people to make money.'

'What's money?'

Pyke was momentarily startled by a magpie that landed on the path in front of them. Quickly he looked around for another. 'Money is freedom, Felix, but you can't have freedom without security. Security is like curling up inside your blanket. If you can't protect your family and loved ones from other donkeys and foxes, you're not a good husband or father. And you won't ever be free to do what you want.'

At some point they had crossed over into Morris's land, and though Pyke could just about see the outline of Morris's Palladian house in the distance, it took him another ten or fifteen minutes to locate the field where he had been the previous night.

They weren't alone, either. Marguerite and another gentleman, this time definitely not Morris, stood over the grave. Concealed behind an oak tree, Pyke watched them more closely. The man had a shovel in one hand and a dog leash in the other; at the other end of the leash, an enormous English mastiff was trying to peer down into the grave. Even from this distance Pyke could see that the man was not Marguerite's equal. His appearance and clothes were too scruffy and he stood a deferential distance away from the grave. Who or what had just been buried? he wondered. A family pet perhaps? Or a young child? But if a child had just been buried, why was Morris not there at the graveside? And why was there no clergyman presiding over the events?

Felix was becoming restless. 'What are they doing?'

Pyke pressed his finger to his lips and said, 'Ssshhh.'

He had been sufficiently intrigued by his encounter with Marguerite the previous night to return to the scene, but now he was there he felt uneasy, as though he had intruded on a private moment that he'd had no right to see. Later, he recalled Marguerite's willowy figure, her blonde locks pinned under a black lace bonnet, and it was hard not to be moved by her sadness.

'Come on,' he whispered to his son. 'The carriage is waiting for us. Your mother will be wondering where we've got to.'

Felix fell in beside him. 'What kind of dog was that?'

'A mastiff.'

'Oh.' He trotted happily along next to him. 'Who was the woman?'

'A neighbour.'

'Why didn't we go over and say hello?'

Pyke stopped and bent over to face his son. 'I want this to be our little secret. Can you keep a secret?'

'Of course I can.'

Smiling, Pyke patted him on the head. 'Because you know what happens to people who can't keep secrets?'

'No, what?' Felix stared at him.

Pyke raised his arms above his head and roared. 'The hungry lion eats them.' He started to chase Felix along the path.

But Felix tripped on a loose branch and fell on to his knees. He began to cry and Pyke felt a familiar shame washing over him. There was nothing he wouldn't do for the lad — throw himself in front of a pack of wild horses if it meant keeping Felix from harm — but he did sometimes worry about the boy's robustness and his worrying penchant for tears.

FOUR

On Monday, the flagstone pavements in the City of London were filled by eight in the morning: a mix of red-faced jobbers clutching sheaves of paper, bank clerks on their way to early morning meetings at the Baltic coffee house and the London corn exchange; street vendors trying to make themselves heard over the clanging of wheels and clattering of hoofs; old ladies selling hot pies from wooden stalls; dead-eyed men on street corners displaying their stocks of knives; petty thieves surreptitiously offering stolen trinkets; and costermongers selling fruit and fresh fish from rickety hand-pulled carts.

Blackwood's bank occupied the upper floors of a dilapidated Georgian town house on Sweeting's Alley, a narrow passageway that ran between Cornhill and Lombard Street. It was not a particularly auspicious home for a bank, and even their most loyal customers complained bitterly about having to climb up a steep, winding staircase to reach the main banking hall, which at one time had been someone's drawing room. For a while, Pyke had considered moving to better accommodation, but whereas the additional space and a more prestigious address would be welcome, he had grown fond of the old building, of its homely charm and low rent. It had everything he needed, and if it meant the customers had to walk up some stairs then so be it: to earn the high interest rate his bank was prepared to pay for their custom, most would doubtless be prepared to struggle all the way to the very top of the building.

At nine o'clock, Pyke swept into the boardroom only to find that his two partners, Jem Nash and William Blackwood, were already seated. Blackwood was leafing through some documents, while young Nash had his boots up on the table and was reading the personal advertisements on the front page of *The Times*, as he liked to do each morning. 'You know what it tells me?' he had said to

Pyke once. 'That the whole world is for sale. Everything, but everything, has a price. I wouldn't be surprised to see a child for sale.' Pyke had told Nash that he'd once seen a baby for sale at the annual Bartholomew's fair and that piece of information had seemed to delight him further. 'Isn't this a great time to live? Nothing is outside the market.' This time Nash put the paper away, to greet him, while Blackwood murmured 'Good morning' as Pyke took his usual seat by the fire and handed the clerk his coat and gloves, making it clear that he wanted them to be left alone.

'Gentlemen,' he said, before he'd even taken his seat, 'I have some exciting news to report.' He told them about the proposed deal with Morris and outlined the likely rates of return. 'In the first year alone, we'll earn as much as seven or eight thousand in interest payments.'

Nash smiled and nodded his head. Blackwood, unsurprisingly, seemed concerned. He reddened slightly and stared down at the polished grain of the table.

'Is there a problem, William?'

'I was just wondering about the wisdom of taking on yet more risk, especially at a time when we're already more exposed than I'd like to be.' Blackwood was a small, timid man with thinning hair and rotten teeth, who crept around the building like an old retainer.

Pyke chuckled bitterly. 'If you had your way, we'd simply lock up our customers' money in the vault and leave it there. This business is founded on risk.'

'The money we invested in General Steel has yet to pay a penny in dividends and, as I'm sure you know, the Grand Northern share price has fallen under ten pounds for the second time this month.'

'So?'

'The bank's most fundamental obligation is to pay cash to all of its customers on demand. If just a quarter of our customers demanded their money tomorrow, and gave us the necessary notice, we wouldn't be able to pay their balances.'

'Everyone gets their twice-yearly interest payments, don't they? People who want to close their accounts receive their full balances.' Pyke shook his head. 'Your problem is you've got no balls, William. No guts. No courage.'

Blackwood stared at him, aghast at being spoken to in such a frank manner. 'And you're nothing but a ... *gambler*, recklessly speculating with your customers' money to line your own pockets.'

'Don't forget your pockets, William. You earned what last year? One and a half thousand. That's almost a thousand more than you earned the previous year and the year before that. I didn't hear you complain then.'

Nash sat back in his chair, grinning. Since Pyke had given him a small percentage of the business, Nash supported him come what may in these meetings.

'All we need is for a handful of customers to demand their money and we'd be in trouble. This bank is teetering like a house of cards and to make matters worse you're proposing to take on more long-term debt; debt in a company whose share price has just dipped below ten pounds. It's sheer madness.'

'By my reckoning, we've currently got about a hundred thousand pounds' worth of discounted bills sitting in the vault earning three, maybe four, per cent. I'm instructing you to sell them so I can lend that money to the Grand Northern Railway. This way we'll more than double the return on our investment. Eight thousand per year instead of three. Is that understood?'

'But those bills are as good as cash. We need some funds at short notice in case of claims made against us.'

'Nonsense. We keep too much in reserve as it is. Dead money that's earning no interest for the bank.'

Blackwood's face reddened still further. 'It's my name above the bank's door. *My* name. People are willing to entrust us with their savings because of *my* reputation and *my* integrity.'

Smiling, Pyke heaved a sigh. 'That might have been true when you were running the four country banks in Norfolk but we both know that people here in London entrust us with their savings because we pay them a higher rate of interest than any other bank in the Square Mile.'

They were quickly getting to the nub of the matter. The four banks in question *had* been run by William Blackwood but only because his brother, Emily's father, the late Lord Edmonton, had shown no interest in getting involved, apart from greedily collecting any profits that had accrued. Edmonton had owned the banks, lock, stock and barrel, and after his death, the banks had passed into Pyke's hands as part of his wedding agreement with Emily, who, in turn, had inherited the Hambledon estate. In his new career as banker, Pyke had soon realised that William Blackwood was, indeed, a very competent figure and realised, too, that he'd need the man's help, if his plan of opening a branch in London was ever to be realised. In order to keep Blackwood at the helm, Pyke had given him a third of the bank's stock for nothing. Blackwood had always seemed to loathe his garrulous brother almost as much as Pyke did, but this didn't mean that he welcomed Pyke's takeover with open arms. In his rather traditionalist view of the world, banking was a risk-averse gentleman's profession in which bankers provided a service to respectable people and charged them an appropriate fee for doing so. It didn't involve sharp practices, brickbats and the whiff of violence. But since Pyke had retained two-thirds of the stock, his word was the one that mattered and it was this, more than anything else, which irked William Blackwood. At least Edmonton had never actually intervened in the day-to-day running of the banks, Pyke had once overheard him say. 'But now I have to listen to, and take orders from, someone who doesn't know an acceptance from an endorsement.' Pyke knew about money, though. He knew the difference between a farthing and a groat and, under their twin stewardship, the bank had flourished, but the disagreements and tension in the partnership had never gone away.

The door flew open and the meeting was interrupted by a dishevelled man dressed in tatty clothes who fell into the room, closely followed by the head clerk, who claimed he had been forcibly brushed aside by the interloper.

'Harry Cobb, at your service.' The man performed an elaborate bow, his velveteen coat touching the floor.

Amused, Pyke told the clerk to leave them alone for a minute and asked him what he wanted.

'I'm a humble shoemaker, sir, as was my father and his father, too. I remember a time when we were plump in the pocket but not any more. Not since the sweaters moved in and stole all of our business. It used to be that we'd get paid three shillings to make a pair of shoes, five for a pair of boots. But now there's this sweater by the name of Groat who's got all these wimmin and chirren, hundreds of 'em, mostly bilked from the workhouse, to make his shoes, working sixteen hours a day for almost nothing, and none of us folk can't compete with him, at least not on our own. Not after we've paid for our grindery, candles and tools.'

Pyke regarded him with curiosity. 'So what is it you want from us?'

'Just the chance to earn our bread.'

'Go on.'

'Well, sir, I ain't an unreasonable man, in spite of my barging in on your meeting. I knows youse all want to make a profit like the next man but I heard folk say Mr Pyke's a good man, not the kind who lends his arse and shits through his ribs, so that's why I'm here. Me and a few others have got together and we'd like you to lend us some Darby, so we can make our boots and shoes and show 'em direct to the public.'

Nash ran his fingers through his mane of black hair, swept back and held in place by a sticky unguent. 'Get out, you impertinent beggar.'

'Let the man finish his piece,' Pyke said, before turning back to face Cobb. 'How much do you want to borrow?'

'I reckon fifty megs should do it.' Sniffing, Cobb wiped his nose on the sleeve of his coat.

'And what security could you put up for the loan?'

'Security?' Cobb seemed flummoxed.

'Something to guarantee the loan. Some property perhaps?'

'If we owned property, sir, we wouldn't need to come to you cap in hand begging for Darby, would we?' He was puzzled more than angry.

'And unfortunately for you, we're a business and not a charity. If we were to lend you some money without any security, how could we stop you from pocketing it and then disappearing?'

'Why would we do that, sir? We're honest culls just wantin' a chance to earn our bread.'

Nash leaned back in his chair, resting the heels of his boots on the table. 'Listen to him. I don't know whether to pity the poor wretch or throw him out on his ear.'

Cobb looked perplexed. 'You mean you ain't gonna lend us a thing?' Suddenly he seemed on the verge of tears.

'Get out, you dirty little man.' Nash stood up and tried to push him out of the door.

'Jem, let the man be.' Pyke kept his tone flat and neutral. 'I'm sorry, Mr Cobb, but we require security.'

'Go and have a look for yeself. Groat has taken over the whole terrace on Granby Street. Rooms full of young chirren, kept in the dark, their little fingers worn down to the bone.'

'It won't make a difference.'

The wind seemed to leave Cobb's sail. His shoulders sagged forward and his head bowed to the floor. 'Thankee, sir, thankee. I won't hold you up any more.' He shuffled to the door and left without uttering another word.

Pyke watched his young assistant's face, as hard and unyielding as dried wax. It was one of Nash's attributes that he saw people only as entries in a ledger book, but while he would doubtless give Cobb no further consideration, Pyke was cursed or blessed by other thoughts. The old shoemaker might perhaps drown his disappointment with a few glasses of gin in a nearby tavern and then trudge home through dark, muddy streets to his lodging house in Bethnal Green, where there would be no food for his family to eat and precious little firewood to keep the room warm. As a younger man he had probably served a long apprenticeship learning the rudiments of his craft and had been assured that these skills would be sufficient to earn a living for the rest of his days, but in recent years the arrival of the sweaters and the hiring of non-apprenticed women and children to make inferior shoes had driven down prices, wages and conditions to such an extent that the old promises counted for nothing.

'What a pathetic old fellow,' Nash said, shaking his head. 'Now let's get back to this business of the loan to the Grand Northern ...'

Money was the only thing that counted, Pyke told himself. Not honour, not morals, not tradition. Men like Cobb couldn't feed their families because they had no money, not because they had no honour or morality. Money enabled people to live their lives as *they* wanted to, not according to the whims of others. Without money there could be no liberty or freedom.

Pyke closed his eyes and tried to clear his mind, but an image of Cobb's hunched figure and pleading face remained with him for the rest of the day.

There were many different ways to steal from people and many layers to the city's burgeoning criminal fraternity. At the bottom of the pile were the ferret-eyed pickpockets who trawled the markets, fairs, public houses and crowded pavements for easy marks, and the rampsmen who assaulted people at random with brickbats and cudgels and would kill or maim their victims without any compunction. Then came the mudlarks who scavenged the Thames near the wharves and docks in the East End for items deliberately discarded by their associates who loaded and unloaded the ships. Next were the rushers, who showed up en masse at someone's front door and forced their way into the home, taking whatever they could and disappearing before the police could be alerted. A little higher up the chain were the receivers and trainers who oversaw gangs of pickpockets from their flash houses and brothels, and the skilled housebreakers who broke into the upper floors of respectable homes and stole cash and jewellery. Near the top of the pile were the so-called cracksmen whose guile and equipment enabled them to break into apparently impregnable safes and strongboxes, and the flash Toms who ran brothels with iron fists and took a cut of all the illegal enterprises on their turf. But right at the top were a handful of figures who presided over a complex network of illicit buyers and sellers and who offered a service that no one else could provide: a way of transforming the proceeds of theft into untraceable notes and coins.

Ned Villums was such a figure, and every Monday afternoon without fail he was ushered up to Pyke's office, where he would deposit two sacks filled with stolen coins and notes. After they'd talked, Pyke would go downstairs to the vault, withdraw an equivalent sum of money, minus his commission, and return it to Villums.

Pyke had known Villums for a number of years and trusted the man unequivocally. It helped, too, that they both knew what the other was capable of and went out of their way to be fair minded. Pyke had once seen Villums feed a man he'd caught stealing from him to a bear tied up outside his tavern and used for sport.

'Does anyone else apart from you know about our arrangement?' Pyke asked him, as he prepared to leave.

That drew a sharp frown. 'I know the rules as well as you do, Pyke.' He shook his head, as though irritated he'd been asked the question. 'Has someone been blabbering?'

'Not that I know of.'

'But you suspect someone?'

Pyke shook his head. 'Not at this end.'

'But you suspect that someone knows? And you're fishing to see if one of my lads might have talked?'

Pyke shrugged. 'Is that a possibility?'

'No.'

They exchanged a cold stare. 'Then there's nothing to worry about.'

'Good.' Villums stood up and pulled his short, double-breasted jacket down over his belly. 'I'll show myself out.'

'Ned?'

Villums turned around at the door. 'Yeah?'

'Let's both try and be even more careful in the future.'

Villums left without saying a word. Pyke wondered whether he had unnecessarily antagonised a man with a history of and propensity for violence.

FIVE

The magistrates' court at Bow Street was located at the front of a tall, narrow, box-shaped building on the west side of the street, and by the time Pyke had pushed his way through the throng of law clerks, Bow Street Runners and lawyers assembled either on the steps at the front of the building or in the entrance hall and corridors, the hearing was about to start. Formerly the parlour in a private house, the room had long since abandoned any claims to respectability, and now the general air of dreariness, fostered by many years of neglect, had become institutionalised. Pyke knew it well, of course. As a Bow Street Runner, he had proffered testimony on many occasions from the witness stand, and it was the smell of the room, a musty odour of mildew, unwashed clothes, dried sweat and cheap tobacco, which carried him back to an earlier moment in his life. There were still one or two people he recognised from the old days but they either ignored him or refused to meet his stare: back then his reputation meant that few people had been willing to cross him and even fewer had sought him out as a friend or confidant.

Pyke's uncle, Godfrey, stood alone in the dock, an elevated platform in front of a large mirror with a wooden rail running around it, while the chief magistrate, Sir Henry Bellows, conferred with the man who would be presenting the evidence against Godfrey. The point of the hearing was to determine whether the charges against the accused – in this case, criminal libel and possibly also sedition – merited a trial in a higher court. Once the evidence had been presented by the Crown's barrister, Godfrey would be allowed to ask questions both about the evidence and the witness statements made against him in the hope of exposing contradictions and lies in the Crown's case. On the Crown's part, it was hoped that

Godfrey's testimony might be used against him if the case came to trial.

Wearing a blue, double-breasted Spencer coat with polished brass buttons over a cream embroidered waistcoat and frilly white shirt, his uncle did not look like a common criminal. He greeted Pyke with a hug and took a swig of gin from his flask before casting an eye across the crowded room. 'A sniff of scandal and the jackals come running. They could have charged on the door and still packed the room three times over.' He was a tall, broad-shouldered man approaching seventy years old, overweight, with a face as red as a beetroot and a shock of bone-white hair.

Pyke looked at the row of well-fed, smartly attired men sitting alongside Bellows on the bench. 'Which one is Conroy?'

'The silver fox with the coiled moustache. The bulldog next to him is his lawyer, Charles Frederick Williams, a King's bencher no less.' Godfrey took another swig from his flask and belched. 'I know this poison will kill me in the end but who would want to live in an age of moral propriety?' He shook his head with disgust. 'That's what I heard someone call it the other day.'

As a much younger man Godfrey had published provocative essays by the likes of Paine and Spence, risking imprisonment to do so, but his political idealism had waned in his middle years and he had found that salacious tales of criminal wrongdoing, sold to the working poor for a penny, were more lucrative than tiresome political pieties. Now in his old age, and with nothing left to lose, Godfrey had again become a thorn in the side of the authorities. A weekly scandal sheet, printed on cheap paper and sold for a penny, exposed the illicit sexual liaisons and misdemeanours of the cream of society, and an unstamped newspaper called the *Scourge* spread a hotchpotch of radical sentiment, though in Pyke's view it was often difficult to tell the two publications apart. It was also hard to determine which one enraged the authorities more.

One piece in particular had resulted in the charges being brought against Godfrey. Floridly entitled 'The Lady and the Scamp', the article had alleged that Sir John Conroy, comptroller of the Duchess of Kent's household, had been fucking the widowed duchess for some years. It also accused Conroy of procuring large sums of money from the public to line his own pocket and mismanaging the duchess's affairs to such an extent she would soon have to be declared bankrupt. The piece had caused quite a stir, both because Conroy enjoyed some important political connections and because the allegations necessarily implicated Princess Victoria, the duchess's sixteen-year-old daughter and heir to the British throne.

It was highly unusual for the evidence at a hearing for a libel case to be presented by a barrister acting for the Crown but, in the light of Conroy's elevated social status and fears that the claims might damage the young princess, palms had doubtless been greased and an exception had been made. Pyke suspected that the actual reason related not to the piece Godfrey had published about Conroy but rather to the fact that the authorities wanted to close down his publications once and for all.

Libel didn't carry a custodial sentence but if the damages awarded to Conroy were significant Godfrey could be bankrupted and sent to prison until he found sufficient funds to pay the debt.

'Once the Crown's barrister has presented the evidence against you, you'll have a chance to ask some questions,' Pyke whispered, across the rail. 'Call on me and ask what I've unearthed about Conroy's activities.'

'Good God, my boy, what have you found?' He grabbed Pyke's sleeve and looked pleadingly into his face.

'Just call me and follow my lead.'

But there wasn't time to explain. From the bench Bellows called the room to order and Pyke stepped back into the crowd.

The chief magistrate was a peculiar-looking man, with a V-shaped streak of ink-black hair that extended almost as far down his forehead as his eyebrows, a pointed, beak-like nose, sunken hooded eyes and teeth that looked as if they'd been sharpened on a knife grinder's stone. He sat back on the bench, rearranged his grey wig and glanced around the courtroom, not seeing Pyke in the faces amassed before him. This was a good thing as the surprise, when it came, would be far greater. Sir Henry Bellows had always disliked Pyke with a vehemence bordering on mania because he blamed him, rightly or wrongly, for the deaths of his two predecessors, Sir Richard Fox and Brownlow Vines.

To the palpable disappointment of those packed into the court-room expecting the exchanges to be laced with salacious details, the hearing lasted no more than five minutes. The Crown's barrister,

William Beresford, dismissed the article Godfrey had published as 'total fabrication' and called upon Godfrey to produce any evidence that could support his claims. Godfrey asserted that he *did* have a corroborating witness but that he had not been able to contact her for the hearing. This was lampooned by Beresford as another lie and in his summary Bellows ordered that Godfrey return to the courtroom in two weeks to stand trial for libel.

'If, by that time, you cannot produce this witness, it seems likely you will be found guilty and face the most serious reparations that can be levied against you under the terms of the law.' Bellows paused for breath. 'In my opinion, you are a loathsome creature who publishes wilful lies about eminent members of society with the sole intention of causing them shame and embarrassment. The sooner you are locked up, the better it will be for all of us.' Pushing his spectacles up his nose, he looked at Godfrey and added, 'Do you have anything else to add?'

'There was another matter I wished to draw the court's attention to, Your Honour.' Imploringly Godfrey looked around the room for Pyke.

'Yes?' Bellows said, both curious and irritated.

'It relates to the activities of the plaintiff, your honour.'

That drew a stern frown. 'I will not permit you to use this court to further slander an innocent man, sir. Now if there's no ...'

'Actually, Your Honour, I've employed an investigator to look into the plaintiff's affairs,' Godfrey said, thinking on his feet, 'and his discoveries are, indeed, pertinent to this case.'

'I've already ruled in this matter ...'

'But since these discoveries refer to your good self, Sir Henry, I think you should bear them in mind before reaching a decision,' Pyke called out from the floor.

Everyone turned to face him and an excited ripple of chatter spread throughout the room.

'Who has the gross impertinence to speak to me from the floor? C'mon. Identify yourself.' Bellows leaned forward on the bench and surveyed their faces.

Pyke raised his hand and waited for a space to be cleared around him. 'Last week I followed Sir John Conroy to the Travellers' Club on Pall Mall where, I believe, he dined as *your* guest, Sir Henry.'

The colour soared in Bellows's neck as he struggled to contain his embarrassment. The chief magistrate had clearly recognised Pyke, but was too affected by the accusation to formulate a coherent response.

'Since this lunch with the plaintiff, so close to the date of the hearing, effectively exposes your neutrality as a sham, it would be fair to reach the conclusion that your office has no jurisdiction in this matter.' Pyke turned to his uncle. 'Come on, Uncle. Let me take you for a drink.' Holding out his hand, he helped his visibly shaken uncle down from the dock and whispered, 'Just put your arm through mine, walk and don't turn around.'

'This is absolutely outrageous,' Bellows yelled from the bench, finding his voice. 'I will not be addressed in such an unpardonable manner by a guttersnipe.' He was standing up, his arms gesticulating like those of a police constable trying to control an unruly mob. 'You are both in contempt of this court and I order your immediate arrest. Officers, take them to the cells and let 'em think about their actions.'

'Just keep walking,' Pyke whispered to his uncle, as he strode confidently through the parting crowd.

'I said, Officers, arrest those men and throw 'em in the cells,' Bellows shouted, his face scarlet with rage.

As they approached the door, a man called Pierce, a Bow Street Runner from the old days, blocked their path. Perhaps he hadn't seen who it was and was just acting upon Bellows's command, but the moment their stares met, Pyke saw the uncertainty creep into the other man's eyes.

'Stop that bloody man,' Bellows spat from the bench, his neck swelling with rage.

Pyke stepped towards Pierce and whispered, 'We're leaving now and I don't want to cause a scene. I've nothing against you, Pierce, but if you try to prevent us from leaving this room, we'll have a problem.'

At first Pyke didn't think he'd move out of the way but at the last moment Pierce's resolve crumbled and seconds later they were gulping the air on the pavement outside the building, Bellows's threats still ringing in their ears.

As they wandered down Bow Street, Pyke could hear his heart hammering against his ribcage and realised his hands were trembling a little. It had been a long time since he had risked official sanction in this manner.

'That was bloody marvellous,' Godfrey said, before drinking his third straight gin in a row. 'But why didn't someone arrest us as Bellows was demanding?'

Pyke took a sip of beer. 'Bellows can rant and rave but men like Pierce have long memories.'

The glint in Godfrey's eyes indicated he understood. 'A warrant will be issued for our arrest, though.'

'Perhaps,' Pyke said. 'But my guess is that, when he's calmed down, Bellows will realise he's lost this one. He'll absent himself from the case, citing personal reasons. It'll go to another court and the same process will start all over again. We caught them out this time; next time they'll be ready for us and if you can't produce this witness, they'll throw everything they've got at you.'

Godfrey nodded, suddenly downcast. 'Kate Sutton was a kitchen hand who worked at Kensington Palace.'

'Was?'

'I made discreet enquiries about her at the palace. I was told she'd left her post for personal reasons but she didn't leave a forwarding address.'

'You don't know where she's gone?'

'No.'

Pyke sat forward and rested his elbows on the table. 'Did she approach you or did you seek her out?'

'The former, m'boy. She came to me, accompanied by a noxious, money-grabbing specimen called Johnny. I presumed they were copulating. They were both clear about the money they wanted. I'd say they were well suited to one another in that respect. We must have haggled for over an hour.'

'And did you give them anything?'

His uncle clenched his jaw. 'Fifty pounds.' He must have seen Pyke's face but he added, in a defensive tone, 'It was a good story. Apparently she walked in on Conroy and the duchess. He was fucking her in the arse.'

Pyke couldn't help but smile. 'I didn't read that in the piece I saw.'

Godfrey broke into a mischievous grin. 'Even I have standards, dear boy.'

'And you don't have any idea where she might be now?'

Godfrey shook his head. 'I paid a visit to her family's home in Spitalfields. The father pestered me for money. The mother hardly said a word.'

'But they didn't know where their daughter was?'

His uncle shook his head and stared down at his empty glass. 'I'm not very good at this kind of thing. Perhaps you could visit her family and ask them some questions? If they don't know where she is, they might know of someone who does.'

Nodding, Pyke checked his watch again. 'You could do something for me in return.'

'Anything, dear boy.' His uncle's smile revealed his stained, mossy teeth. 'Within reason, of course.'

'I'd like you to come with me to a meeting of radicals in the east end. Emily has been involved in setting it up.'

'If I must,' Godfrey said, with a dismissive yawn. 'I know I publish things for the poor to read, but actually spending time in their company is not my idea of an enjoyable evening.'

In Emily's position, it would have been easy to romanticise the working poor and turn them into exotic creatures waiting to be pitied and helped. In fact her view was much more complex, forged by a mixture of guilt, moral zeal and sympathy. Some middle-class charities sought to distance themselves from the people they were trying to help, finding the poor to be obnoxious, dirty, violent and blasphemous in a way they hadn't expected or counted upon. Emily suffered no such illusions. A year earlier, while organising an event at the Royal Opera House in Covent Garden in aid of the Spitalfield weavers, she'd travelled to the East End, where her carriage had been attacked. Two rampsmen robbed her of her rings and forced her to strip naked. No one had come to her rescue, doubtless enjoying the sight of a wealthy woman receiving her comeuppance at the hands of two ruffians. Later, after Pyke had tracked down the two rampsmen and retrieved the rings they'd stolen from her, he had asked whether the incident had shaken her commitment to her work. She had given him a puzzled look, as though the question were an irrelevant one, and told him she didn't blame the men for what they had done.

That was the thing about Emily.

Just when Pyke thought he had her figured out, she'd act in a way that made him alter his opinion of her. She wasn't a social chameleon, like Marguerite, a flibbertigibbet who changed her skin to suit her own desires. Rather, Emily was led by her convictions, and these changed according to circumstances over which she had no control. Two years earlier she had split from Elizabeth Fry's society of women, middle-class do-gooders and busybodies concerned primarily with temperance and for whom prison visits constituted the limits of their horizons. As a free agent, she'd used her financial independence to fund individuals agitating for workplace reform and to promote communitarian ideas borrowed from Robert Owen, the socialist. Recently she had turned her attention to the burgeoning trade union movement and had helped to organise and broker a meeting to find common ground between moderates and radicals who were agitating for wider disruption.

Pyke had expected that Emily's commitment to her work would have waned after the birth of their son but, strangely, it had intensified. In fact, he often felt that her zeal for her work had increased in direct proportion to his success as a banker: the more money he drew from the bank, the less she seemed to need or even ask for. He sometimes wondered whether her apparent selflessness – wilfully ignoring her own needs – was in fact another form of selfishness, a way of validating her own difference. He'd put this to her once and received a scornful reply.

The meeting was held in an upstairs room of the Standard of Liberty at one end of Brick Lane. As a Bow Street Runner, Pyke had once pursued a child rapist to the building across the street from the Standard. The man had made for the cellar, maybe hoping Pyke wouldn't follow him, but had lost his footing on the stairs and had fallen into a cess pool. Pyke could still remember the scene: the rapist floundering in the dark, viscous liquid, his arms and head covered in thick soil. Pyke had neither come to his rescue nor precipitated his death. At the time he hadn't known whether he had done the right thing, whether he'd robbed the mother of the injured child of the justice she and her child deserved, but when he had told her what had happened, she had thanked him and broken down in tears. The neighbourhood had not significantly changed in the intervening years: on the same side of the road as the Standard of Liberty, he counted a tavern, two ginneries, a brothel, a couple of pawnshops and a lodging house where donkeys and sheep roamed freely in and out of the door.

The meeting had already begun by the time they arrived, and having persuaded two men on the door that they weren't police spies, Pyke and his uncle took their seats at the back of the cramped room, just as the gathered men were applauding heartily. He saw Emily on the stage: she had clearly just addressed the meeting and had spoken well, for there was a jovial, enthusiastic atmosphere in the room. Some of the mob whistled their appreciation, at which Emily gave a mock curtsy. This drew further laughter. Pyke looked at his uncle and shrugged. He had no idea that Emily actually spoke at these meetings, and now that he had missed her speech he kicked himself for arriving late and wondered what she had said to the men. They seemed to have treated whatever it was with a degree of seriousness, or at least hadn't barracked her with a deluge of sexual innuendos. Emily bowed again and climbed down from the stage. Her place was taken by a white-haired speaker who didn't engage the audience in the same manner that Emily seemed to have done.

'That's James Munroe,' Godfrey whispered. 'He's a moderate voice together with chaps like Lovett and Cleave. They're part of the national trade union movement. On the whole, they're a respectable but tiresome bunch; the type that wash their faces, clean their teeth and fuck their wives in the dark.'

Pyke had once seen the renowned radical 'Orator' Hunt, who had died earlier in the year, whip up a crowd of working men into a frenzy with his plain-speaking approach. By comparison, Munroe's speech carried all the charge of a gobbet of rotting meat.

'We all know Peel and the Tories hate us but the present Liberal government has done nothing for us, will do nothing for us in the future and never wanted to do anything for us in the first place.' Pausing to receive the polite applause of the men packed into the room, Munroe nodded his head, seemingly pleased with his lacklustre performance.

Pyke felt like asking him whether anyone in the room believed that a government elected only by propertied voters would *ever* act in the interests of the working man.

'What we need, friends, is a wage that reflects the work we do. Today, more than ever, workmen do not receive a price for their labour that allows them to provide for their families. The devil-capitalist who has risen from our ranks and who lusts after money has become our enemy; he sits in his mansion revelling in his abundance while hard-working men are ground into the earth. These grubby money-mongers prey on our labour, require it to fill their pockets, exploit it and encourage others to exploit it, turn greed into a virtue, and in so doing make us not into slaves but machines, brethren of the very tools we use to do our work.'

This time the applause was more muted. Munroe seemed puzzled, unable to work out why he was not receiving more wholehearted support from the rambunctious mob.

From his vantage point at the back of the room, Pyke studied the gathered crowd, mostly shoemakers and tailors, he supposed, with a handful of labourers. The latter wore grubby shooting jackets and torn velveteen coats while the former were dressed in either smockfrocks or monkey jackets. He saw Emily right at the front of the room, having an animated talk with a young man sitting next to her. They looked to be sharing some kind of joke.

'Do you see Emily there? Who's she talking to?'

Godfrey put on his spectacles. '*Ah*, that's a chap called Julian Jackman.'

'Why do you say it like that?'

Up on the platform Munroe was trying to explain the merits of the Grand National Consolidated Trades Union.

'His mob is a different kettle of fish altogether. They might be a ragbag mixture of types but at least they've got some balls. They talk a good game but they're interested in the ordinary man, too.' Godfrey hesitated, his expression clouding over. 'In the current climate, I'd say that *any* association with Jackman and his lot is not going to be conducive to Emily's good health, though.'

Pyke felt the skin tighten across his cheek. 'What's that supposed to mean?' At that moment, his view of Emily and Jackman was obscured by someone sitting a few rows ahead of him.

'As far as I've heard, there's going to be a big clampdown on radical activity,' Godfrey whispered, 'and when it comes, the authorities won't concern themselves with someone's rank or station.'

'And has this information come from someone inside the government?' he asked, thinking about Peel's interest in Jackman.

'They're willing to tolerate the unions up to a point. But what they do not want is every Tom, Dick and Harry joining these organisations. Look around you, Pyke. Folk are rightfully angry. Reform hasn't changed a damned thing and they're disillusioned. That's why this figure Captain Paine has become something of a hero to them.'

'What do you know about him?'

'Who, Captain Paine?'

Pyke nodded.

'No more than anyone else.'

On the platform Munroe was starting to build towards a conclusion but there were already rumblings of discontent from the floor.

'Do you think he's flesh and blood?'

'You mean, do I think he's one man rather than an amalgam of people using the same name?'

'That's part of it,' Pyke whispered. 'But I was also wondering whether you'd heard the rumour that Jackman is Captain Paine?'

'Who did you hear that from?' The way Godfrey said it showed he was prepared to entertain the possibility.

Pyke ignored the question.

'Look, Pyke, whether Captain Paine is a fiction or not, he's someone the poor can cheer for. They see someone who acts rather than postulates. That's what makes him such a threat.' Godfrey hesitated, perhaps deciding whether to say what was on his mind. 'But there was something else ...'

'Yes?'

'This chap Jackman is rumoured to be something of a ladies' man. Apparently he's hung like a donkey.'

Pyke turned to his uncle. 'Why are you telling me this?'

Up on the platform Munroe was winding up his speech with an attack on vulgarity and drunkenness. 'Let us put into practice our democratic principles,' he shouted, his eyes fixed on something over their heads, 'by seeking the company of sober-minded, virtuous individuals.' Unsurprisingly, given that most of the people were drinking ale provided by the owner, this drew the first outward signs of dissent. Someone shouted, 'Give the man a drink,' and then added, 'Sit down, you old windbag.' This got the most raucous cheer of the evening. Then someone began chanting 'Captain Paine' and others followed, and soon everyone in the room had joined in, the chanting easily drowning out the end of Munroe's speech.

Someone jostled them from behind and at first Pyke put it down to an expression of high spirits. He heard some further mutterings and then someone threw some beer over the back of Godfrey's coat. Laughter ensued and it was only then Pyke realised they were being targeted because of their clothing: because someone had decided they didn't belong in such a gathering on account of Godfrey's blue double-breasted jacket and Pyke's knee-length cutaway coat.

Emily had climbed back on to the platform, together with Julian Jackman. Emily waited for the room to quieten before she said, in a deep, confident voice that surprised Pyke, 'And that's why you shouldn't allow us respectable, bourgeois types anywhere near these meetings.'

It was a direct rebuke to Munroe and it got the biggest cheer of the night.

Next to her, Jackman applauded her comments and commended Captain Paine to the mob.

'Death to the tyrant Whigs. Pestilence on the villainous Tories.' Jackman stepped to the front of the platform. 'Let the swinish multitude rise up and kick our fat masters in the teeth. Cut off their heads and stick them on pikes. What we need is revolution. While we're at it, let's throw Bentham and Malthus on the bonfire too. We should be striving for the betterment of the working man and *only* the working man: the middle classes can take care of themselves as they always have done.'

Those packed into the fetid room rose to their feet to hail his words, throwing their caps into the air.

Turning round, Pyke found himself staring at a fat, whiskered man of about forty wearing a monkey jacket that was too small for him and a stocking-cap pulled down over his forehead. 'Look at me again, cully,' he sneered, 'and I'll smite your costard.' He was cross eyed from drink. 'What are two rum culls like you doing mixing with the riff-raff? Didn't you hear the man? You ain't wanted.'

There were many ways in which Pyke could have answered the question, not least pointing to the fine work his uncle did riling the authorities with his unstamped paper the *Scourge*, but none of them seemed appropriate. So when the man started to pour the rest of his beer over Godfrey's head, Pyke snatched the bottle from his hand and, in the same movement, smashed it against his jaw, the bottle shattering into hundreds of tiny shards. The ruffian fell backwards into the crowd sitting behind him but someone else, obviously a friend of the injured man, came at Pyke with a knife. Pyke caught him by his lunging wrist and jerked it sharply down, the bone breaking with a clean, satisfying snap. The knife clattered harmlessly on to the floor and the assailant roared with agony, the veins in his neck swollen from the pain. Others might have waded into the dispute as well if someone hadn't fired a pistol up at the ceiling. The loudness of the blast brought the room to order, and when Pyke looked up, he saw his wife standing next to Jackman on the platform with a pistol in her hand, the acrid smell of blast powder filling the room. Stepping off the platform, Emily made her way through the mob, the men hurriedly clearing a path for her. Maybe she had already seen what had happened or perhaps she suspected that Pyke may have been involved in the rumpus because when she came upon them, surrounded by a mob spoiling for a fight, Emily's expression didn't noticeably change.

'You,' Emily barked, pointing the pistol at Pyke, and added, without changing her tone, 'You, too, old man.'

Once Emily had marched them out of the room at gunpoint, and they were out of sight and earshot of the crowd, she turned to Jackman and said, 'I'd like to introduce my husband, Pyke, and his uncle Godfrey.' She handed the pistol back to Jackman and added, 'Pyke, Godfrey, this is Julian Jackman.'

Jackman was a tall, slender, good-looking man with a trimmed beard, pouting lips and bright rosy cheeks. He asked Pyke whether he had found the meeting interesting.

'Illuminating might be a better description,' Pyke said.

'Oh?'

'See, I'm always intrigued by those who believe they can change the world with the might of their own rhetoric.'

'Do I detect a subtle rebuke in your words?'

Emily interrupted. 'Pyke thinks the current dispensation will carry on regardless of what we might or might not do.'

'Is that so?'

Pyke looked first at Emily and then at Jackman. It had been a while since she had challenged him in front of others and it told him that things between them had slipped more than he had perhaps imagined.

Interrupting them, Godfrey made his excuses and hurried out of the door, saying he needed to find somewhere to relieve himself.

'It's not all rhetoric,' Jackman said. 'We're currently attempting to unionise the coal-whippers and we have our sights set on other labouring men, too. In this context, our aims are less ambitious. Higher wages, shorter working hours. Straightforward issues that can make a difference to men's lives.'

Pyke noticed that Emily was nodding her head in approval, and wondered whether the radical might be attracted to his wife. Men usually were, Pyke thought grimly, but the attraction was not usually mutual.

'But if your wife is to be believed, you're suggesting even to *strive* for change is a futile yearning. Would that be a fair assessment of your position?'

'Man is a solitary animal.' Pyke shrugged, not really wanting to discuss the matter. 'It's in his nature to look after his own and his family's interests first.'

'And woman?' Jackman asked, almost mocking. He glanced across at Emily, who blushed, and Pyke had to rein in an urge to tear out his throat.

'In spite of your rhetoric about working-class solidarity and the evils of money, I think we both know what role my wife is performing here.'

Emily's face reddened. 'I don't think ...'

But Jackman cut her off with a laugh. 'You're correct, of course. We can't do all we need to do without some charitable assistance.' He nodded approvingly at Emily. 'But a few months ago, your wife stood up to a crew of mercenaries down at Cowgate wharf. They'd been sent there by the coal merchants to beat the coal-whippers into submission. A hundred and twenty-three men had just sworn their oaths and a strike had been called. Your wife was wearing a white dress, I recall. She pushed her way to the front of the mob and none of the hired ruffians knew what to do. No one dared attack. They left with their tails between their legs.'

Pyke nodded while Jackman told him the story, to suggest he'd already heard it, but inwardly felt aggrieved that Emily hadn't mentioned it. 'I don't need a lecture about my wife's courage.'

That seemed to chasten him slightly. 'Of course.' Crimson faced, Jackman stared down at his shoes.

A silence hung between them. Emily glanced from Pyke to Jackman, a quizzical look on her face. 'Why were they chanting Captain Paine's name?' Pyke asked, in the end.

'I don't know. You'd have to ask them.'

Pyke clenched his teeth. 'They're not here. You are.'

'You strike me as an educated man, Pyke. I'm sure you've read about the exploits of Odysseus and Jason. In troubled times, people look to heroes to do what they can't.'

'And that's what Captain Paine is? A mythical creation intended to give working people false hope?'

'Why would people's hopes be false?' Emily asked, stepping into the argument on Jackman's side.

'A lone individual bringing the capitalist order to its knees?' Pyke shook his head. 'That doesn't sound like a fantasy to you?'

'I think you're missing the point,' Emily said. Jackman was just looking at them, amused.

'And what is the point?'

Emily shrugged. 'That an individualist system where man looks out only for his interests has produced a world of such inequalities it cannot be sustained in perpetuity.'

Feeling uneasy about airing their differences in public, Pyke turned to the radical and said, 'I'd like you better if I felt you thought politics was the clash of opposing forces rather than some war of ideals.'

'But it's exactly what I do believe, that capital and labour are implacable enemies, fighting to the death.'

'Then the problem is that you infect others with your naive optimism so that they begin to see the world not as it really is but as you'd like it to be.'

Jackman seemed angry. 'Thank you, sir, but I can see the world well enough as it is. Men, women and children, sweating in hovels

57

and factories to earn less in a year than we might spend on dinner while the wealthy grow fat on the proceeds of their labour.' He shrugged. 'But I hope it won't always be this way.'

'That's exactly my point.' Pyke paused. 'Because if the world's as threatening as you admit it is, self-assertion is the only thing that will keep you alive.'

'But self-assertion and self-interest are different things entirely, Pyke,' Emily said, glancing nervously at Jackman.

Too late, Pyke realised that he'd become involved in an argument he couldn't win. 'Where I grew up, men and women had to fight tooth and nail for what they needed just to make it through the day.'

'But does it always have to be so?' Jackman's expression softened a little.

For a moment Pyke was lost for an answer. Emily stared at him, either willing him to say something or to remain silent.

'And what happens when men and women can't compete fairly in this struggle for survival because the authorities have stacked the deck so heavily in favour of the rich?' Jackman looked at him for an answer.

Pyke felt the skin tighten across his face. 'But the fact remains that in the struggle to put food on your table and clothes on your children's backs, it's down to you, and you alone. No one's going to offer you a helping hand.'

Jackman looked at him, almost pityingly, and said, 'In your world, perhaps, Pyke. In your world.'

It wasn't until later, as they prepared for bed on the top floor of the Islington town house Emily had also inherited from her father, that Emily and Pyke got around to talking about the events of the evening.

'I have to go to Cambridge tomorrow for business. I'll probably be away for a few nights.' He looked around the bedroom, embarrassed by its untidiness, piles of old clothes strewn across the floor. It was cold as well, the fire smouldering in the grate doing little to warm up the room.

'I'm planning to spend a couple of days at Hambledon,' Emily replied. 'It feels like weeks since I last spent any proper time with Felix.'

It had been Pyke's choice not to employ any domestic servants, and while the lack of warmth and tidiness didn't bother him when he stayed there on his own, he felt a little uncomfortable in Emily's presence. Not that she appeared to mind about the cold. She sat in her nightdress at the dressing table, brushing her hair in front of the looking glass. 'You know, there was a time when I might have been impressed by the sentiments you expressed tonight.'

'But now you're perfectly happy to take someone like Jackman's side over mine?' It was a more intemperate remark than Pyke had intended, but he was still rankled by his exchange with the radical.

'It's not a question of taking anyone's side.'

'What is it a question of, then?'

'You think I'm disloyal?' She laughed angrily. 'I told you before we married that I wouldn't be the kind of wife who'd slavishly attend to your every whim.' She shook her head, her anger ebbing away into disappointment.

'But you think it's all right that I'm compelled to watch as you hang off Captain Paine's every word?'

'Captain Paine?' She threw her chin up into the air. 'Whoever said that Julian was Captain Paine?'

'Well, isn't he?'

'Whether he is or isn't is not the point.' She stood up and hurried across the room to the bed. 'Anyway, why are you so interested in this Captain Paine all of a sudden?'

Pyke knelt down in front of the fire he'd tried to start and prodded it with a poker.

'Times have changed. Your ability to turn self-interest into a virtue is no longer as convincing as it was when you were poor.'

'And now I have a little money in my pocket, am I supposed to become a different person? More like you, perhaps?'

'What's that supposed to mean?' Emily sat up in the bed and stared at him, visibly angry now.

'It's easy for you to dismiss the importance of money because you've never been without it.'

That silenced her for a few moments. 'Once upon a time,' she started, 'you used to steal from men like my father.'

'And now I've turned into him? Is that what you mean?' This time it was his turn to show his irritation.

'You needn't worry about that,' Emily said, laughing. 'You'll never be my father.'

'But?'

'But you once had aspirations beyond merely wanting to be rich.'

'For you, money has always been a means to an end.' Pyke looked at her, shaking his head. 'Why don't you think the same applies to me?'

'It does. I *know*.' Emily sank back into her pillow, sighing. 'But what if those who most need your help are no longer those closest to you?'

Pyke left the fire alone and perched on the side of the bed, starting to take off his boots. 'There are always going to be people who need your help. Where do you draw the line?'

'For me, there isn't any line.'

He kicked off his boots and started to unbutton his shirt. 'In which case people will always take advantage of you.'

'So?'

'So what if someone like Jackman is just using you for your money?'

Emily pulled the blanket up around her body and watched him undress for a short while. 'It isn't about him or me, or even you. It's about something bigger, Pyke. Haven't you grasped that by now?'

Pyke finished undressing in silence and joined Emily under the sheets. 'I thought you handled that pistol quite well,' he said, quietly.

'Only quite well?'

'For a moment I thought you were going to shoot me.'

'I could have put one straight through your heart,' she said, playfully tapping his chest.

'You wouldn't have found it there.'

In the glow of the candle, he saw the faint trace of a smile on her face. 'It's bigger than you give it credit for.'

'A heart of gold, eh?'

She gave him a playful frown.

'Copper, then.'

'Brass.' Emily kissed him gently on the mouth. 'It's harder to shoot a hole in brass than copper.'

'So now I'm just a suit of armour to you?'

'Not just that.' She reached down and touched him.

'It would seem I've got a reputation to live up to.'

'Or down to.'

He began to laugh. 'Her ladyship would deign to have her way with a commoner then?'

'Is that what you are? A commoner?'

'A commoner, with very immediate needs.' Pyke straddled her and started to pull up her nightshirt.

'Then allow me to minister to the needy.' She blew out the candle and kissed him on the mouth.

SIX

Four whiskered men, all wearing tall-crowned top hats and black Macintosh coats, held lanterns aloft and formed a barricade across the sodden track. Above them, the sky was black and filled with a patchwork of heavy, swirling clouds. Rain had begun to fall shortly after they had departed Cambridge, where Morris had left him to make the onward journey to Huntingdon using a short-stop stage-coach. Now, two hours later, the surface of the road had become an unrecognisable river of mud. The driver had climbed down from his seat and was engaged in a heated conversation with the leader of the group, who had a rifle slung over his shoulder and was demanding that all the male passengers present themselves outside the carriage for inspection. In fact, this meant just Pyke and a nervous undertaker travelling on to King's Lynn. When the undertaker was allowed to retake his place in the carriage, Pyke stood alone in front of the man, wet gusts of wind buffeting the tail of his coat. Water dripped from the curled tip of the man's vein-riddled nose and the smell of gin on his breath was overpowering. Pyke was asked about his business in Huntingdon and when he refused to give an answer, the man took a step towards him and asked him whether he was a radical. Pyke absorbed the heat of his stare and the stink of his breath and explained that he was travelling on to Newark and hoped to break his journey in Huntingdon.

That seemed to confuse the man slightly. 'You sure you ain't a radical?'

'I wasn't the last time you asked, but if you leave me standing out here in the rain for too much longer I might turn into one.'

'How about a journalist? Are you a journalist? We hate journalists almost as much as we hate radicals.'

'Afraid of what they might write about your dreary little town?'

The man's eyes narrowed to slits. 'This is a good town, with fine, upstanding people. It's others have brought their troubles to us.'

'I've no interest in you or your town but if I catch a fever from standing out here in the rain I might take an interest.'

He let Pyke return to the coach with a curt nod and soon they were crossing over the River Ouse using the old bridge, the town appearing before them and a torrent of water gushing beneath them.

Before they had parted ways in Cambridge, Morris had told him again that he was less concerned about radicals than about Rockingham's attempts to thwart the progress of the Grand Northern beyond Cambridge and across his land. Apparently Rockingham enjoyed a great deal of support in Huntingdon, where the next phase of the construction work was about to begin because livelihoods like blacksmithing and innkeeping would be hit hard by the railway.

Pyke had told Morris to wait for him in his private carriage on the crossroads just to the south of Huntingdon at approximately eight the following evening. If he happened to make enemies in the town, Pyke didn't want to draw the older man into any possible repercussions.

Inside the stagecoach, a matronly woman said, with breathy excitement, 'I fancy the business with those men must have been related to the discovery of a headless body a few days ago.'

Directly across from her, the undertaker nodded. 'I heard there was a madman on the loose from an asylum near Cambridge. Either that, or one of the four horsemen of the acropolis,' he muttered, with a conspiratorial nod. 'I've dealt with bodies my whole life and I'll wager you don't know how much sweat it would take to hack through someone's neck with a knife.'

'Please, sir, I'd remind you there are ladies present,' the woman who'd started the conversation said, looking at Pyke for support.

'If someone knew what they were doing,' Pyke said, 'a few swings of a sharp axe ought to do it.'

'Aye, I suppose it would.' The undertaker scratched his chin. 'But so would a saw with a good blade.'

The matronly woman huffed but took no further part in the conversation.

When they finally pulled into the coaching yard, the carriage was surrounded by grooms and pot-boys wearing black aprons, offering to carry their bags to one of the inn's rooms. Stretching his limbs, Pyke watched as the grooms led the tired horses across to the stables on the far side of the yard, where they would be fed and rested.

Having changed out of his damp clothes, Pyke retraced his steps back to the taproom, where haggard women and dishevelled men huddled around a blazing fire. On the floor, a gnawed chop bone and some discarded oyster shells sat in a layer of wet butcher's sawdust.

When a pot-boy brought him a mug of frothy ale, Pyke asked about the two men playing cards next to the fireplace. The young lad explained that Septimus Yellowplush was the town's magistrate and Mr Burden the rector from All Saint's Church.

They were playing 'twenty-one' and it took Pyke just a few minutes to work out that Yellowplush, who had acquired a stack of coins, was cheating, by drawing the cards he needed either from up his sleeve or, more likely, from somewhere under the table. During each game, he would take his hand and inspect it under the table, ostensibly to shield it from his opponent. From this, Pyke concluded that duplicate playing cards must be fixed to the underside of the table.

With a hand of two jacks and an ace, the rector had just lost again, to an unlikely five-card trick, and he seemed to be on the verge of giving up. Seizing on his indecision, Pyke stepped forward and tossed five gold coins on to the table, considerably more money than they had been playing for. He patted the clergyman on the shoulder, consoling him for his luck, and asked whether he might play the next hand against his opponent. Yellowplush's eyes narrowed but his face remained composed. He looked at the coins and loosened his cravat. The rector didn't seem to mind and willingly gave up his seat, commenting only on his opponent's good fortune.

'And who might you be, friend?' Yellowplush said in a staccato voice that was far from friendly.

Pyke's initial impression of Septimus Yellowplush had been that of a schoolyard bully, the kind of man that he had once dealt with almost without having to think about it: a slap around the face, a few words of warning, perhaps even the flash of his blade to make his point. But having studied the man for a few moments – his hard, waxy skin that barely moved, even when he laughed or frowned, his grey eyes that looked like buttons drilled into his skull, and his small, pink tongue, which darted from his mouth as he spoke – Pyke saw a coldness in him and possibly even a propensity for violence. It was the curly wig which made him look ridiculous, but while misplaced vanity may have convinced him to don such a garment, the fact that no one had summoned sufficient courage to tell him about the folly of his choice told Pyke all he needed to know about the grip with which Yellowplush ruled his fiefdom.

'You can call me Pyke.' He eased into the chair, trying to seem more comfortable than he felt. It had been a long time since he had done this kind of work.

'And where are you from, Mr Pyke?'

'Just Pyke will do.'

'Just stopping here for the night?' Yellowplush picked up the cards and began to shuffle them.

Ignoring the question, Pyke took a swig of ale and wiped his mouth.

'Not the chatty type? Perhaps your luck will be better than your conversation.' A ripple of laughter spread across the room. 'It's a rich game you're asking for. You must feel lucky, sir.'

'Far from it,' Pyke said, staring down at the table. 'But any fool can see that luck like yours can't last for ever.'

Yellowplush's smile vanished. 'Would you have any objections to my dealing?'

Pyke took the pack, shuffled them and handed them back to his opponent. 'Be my guest.'

'A stranger in a strange town.' Yellowplush licked his lips. 'I'd be careful how you conduct yourself, sir.'

'Yes, I read in the newspapers this wasn't the most welcoming of places.'

'I'm guessing that you're referring to the headless corpse.' Yellowplush had dealt himself two eights and Pyke a ten and a seven. 'Or perhaps to the arrival of the navvies?'

'It's not every day a headless corpse is reported in the newspapers. I'd say it was the talk of London when I left.'

Yellowplush looked at him, unimpressed. 'Brutal murder may be commonplace in that city but it's thankfully rarer here in the provinces.' He smiled without warmth. 'What did you say your business was?'

'I didn't.' Pyke stared down at his hand and pushed the gold coins into the middle of the table. 'I'll have another card.'

The magistrate dealt him a card, face down. Leaving it on the table, Pyke turned over one of the corners and saw it was the four of clubs.

'Good card?'

Removing a purse from his coat, Pyke pulled out a ten-pound note. 'Just to make it interesting.'

There were gasps of astonishment around the table. It was more money than many of them would earn in two months.

'You're not one for small talk, are you?' Yellowplush looked down at the cards in front of him. Beneath his wig, he had started to sweat.

'As you said, a stranger should learn to hold his tongue.'

'Indeed.' The magistrate took some snuff on the tip of his finger, brought it up to his nose. 'I'll take the bet, sir.' It was what the whole room had wanted to hear.

'Perhaps you might allow me to see your money.'

This drew a hollow chuckle. 'You don't imagine I carry such a sum on my person, do you?'

'Then how am I to know you can actually afford to pay your debt?'

'Assuming I lose.'

Pyke nodded. 'Assuming I win.'

'Are you saying my word is somehow insufficient?' Yellowplush asked, smiling to conceal his threatening tone.

'Would you trust *my* word?'

'I'm the magistrate of this town.'

'I suppose someone has to be.' Pyke folded his arms and looked around the room dismissively. 'But I'll still need to see your money.'

Yellowplush licked his lips and studied Pyke's face. 'Perhaps you would allow me a few minutes to discuss terms with the landlord.'

'Be my guest.'

It took Yellowplush ten minutes to come up with the money; when he returned to the table, he emptied the coins out of his pockets on to the table. 'Count 'em if you like,' he said, taking another pinch of snuff.

Pyke leant across the table, whispering, 'How much does it cost to buy the law in a town like this? More than the price of a new wig?'

The outrage registered in the magistrate's dilated pupils.

'I'd be careful of loose talk in a town where folk are already twitchy and fearful of what might happen.'

'What might happen *when*?' Pyke stared at his opponent's leathery skin.

The magistrate shrugged and dealt himself another card.

As Yellowplush dealt it, Pyke again leaned over the table and whispered, 'That card remains on the table in full view of everyone here. If you try to swap it with one of those duplicate cards you've fixed to the underside of the table, I'll expose your squalid little scam. Nod once, to show me you understand.'

Colour drained from the magistrate's face and sweat leaked from beneath his wig.

'Was that a nod?'

Yellowplush didn't seem to know what to do. His curly wig slipped farther down his forehead but he didn't seem to have noticed.

A crowd of faces had gathered around the table, watching their every move with a keen interest.

'Did I just see a nod?' Pyke said, louder so others could hear him.

Yellowplush pushed his wig back up on top of his head and nodded. Pyke turned over his four of clubs. 'Twenty-one.' He smiled at the glowering magistrate. 'What? Has your luck finally run out?'

When Yellowplush neither answered him nor turned over his cards, Pyke added, 'Remember what I said about keeping your hands above the table.' Then he reached out, plucked the card from the magistrate's hand and tossed it on to the table. 'Makes nineteen, if I'm not mistaken.' Scooping up the coins and his own ten-pound note, he deliberately knocked over his ale glass, and watched as the brown liquid dripped on to the magistrate's lap. Before Yellowplush could stop him, Pyke swiped the curly wig from his head and began to mop up the mess. An awed silence fell across the room. Whistling, Pyke continued his mopping-up work, until the table was dry, and then rinsed out the wig and placed it back on the magistrate's head. Ale began to drip down on to Yellowplush's face. There were a few nervous twitters from the very back of the room. Otherwise, no one said a word. As he arranged the wig on the magistrate's head, Pyke added, 'Lay a finger on me in here and I'll make sure that every man and woman in this inn knows you cheat at cards.' Then he wiped both hands on his jacket and stood up. 'Now that's settled, perhaps you'll join me for some night air,' Pyke said, so that everyone in the room could hear him.

Insisting that Pyke go first, Yellowplush had prodded what felt like the end of his pistol into Pyke's back before they had even departed the inn. 'Tell me who you are and what you want right now,' he whispered, 'or I'll squeeze the trigger and you'll die a long, painful death.'

Outside, on the street, Pyke turned around to face Yellowplush, whose shining face was as large as a turnip, barely visible in the gloom. 'I'm an emissary from Sir Robert Peel. He's taken an interest in your corpse and he asked me to investigate the matter further.' Pyke expected that Yellowplush might be surprised by this revelation but the magistrate merely shrugged as though the matter were of no consequence. 'I have a letter confirming this,' he added, quickly, 'if you'll allow me to find it.'

Yellowplush poked the pistol into Pyke's chest. 'I can't understand why Peel's so interested in our body.'

'I don't know. Like I said, he asked me to look into the matter and report back to him.' Pyke waited, deciding not to say anything about Peel's interest in Captain Paine and the threat posed by radicals.

'Why didn't you introduce yourself at the outset?'

'Peel is a divisive figure,' Pyke said. 'In my experience, his name doesn't always open doors.'

'I know that, for a fact.' Yellowplush reached out his hand. 'Let me see the letter.'

Pyke retrieved it from his pocket and gave it to the magistrate, who surveyed the content without much interest. 'It doesn't mean I shouldn't kill you, leave you to bleed to death for what you did in the inn.'

'You think Peel wouldn't find out? Or that everyone in the inn who witnessed our card game loves you so much they wouldn't give you up, if and when Peel's men have to come looking for me?'

That seemed to register with Yellowplush. He put the pistol back into his belt and shrugged. 'You'd better come with me, then.'

It was a damp night and the air smelled of wet leaves. The street was deserted and they walked in silence as far as the watch-house where prison cells were visible from the street through iron grilles.

68

The watch-house was besieged, with men of all ages lining up in an orderly queue that snaked around the building. The magistrate explained they were waiting to be sworn in as special constables. Once this had been done, they would be allocated a weapon of their choice. The selection was a rich one. Lining the wall at the back of the watch-house were brickbats, muskets, shovels, swords, machetes, pick handles and even a few rifles. When Pyke likened the scene to an army preparing to go to war, Yellowplush looked at him and smiled.

'I take it you're expecting trouble,' Pyke said, as he followed the magistrate down a flight of stone steps to the cellar of the watch-house, where the headless body was being stored.

The flickering light given off by the magistrate's lantern barely illuminated the tomblike corridor.

Pyke smelled the corpse before he saw it, a ripe odour that filled the windowless room.

Yellowplush put the lantern down on the floor and said, 'I'll leave you the light. I don't imagine you're used to spending time with dead bodies.'

Pyke looked at him. 'And you are?' The air around them was cloying, fleshy and sickly.

'I used to serve in the army. The regiment was travelling to India when the ship caught fire in the Bay of Biscay. A casket of rum split open and one of the ship's officers dropped a lantern. The fire spread from the hold to the rest of the ship. I was tasked with the job of raising men from their cabins on the port side of the ship towards the stern but the fire spread too quickly for me. The screams of those men will live me with the rest of my days, sir. The next day, after the ship had finally blown up, we discovered the charred remains of a young child. I was there in the boat with his father when we came across it. The sound that came from the man's mouth was not one I ever want to hear again. So to answer your question, sir, the idea of spending some time in the presence of a dead body doesn't concern me in the slightest.'

The heels of Yellowplush's leather boots clicked against the stone as he ascended the stone steps.

The air in the cellar felt cool against Pyke's skin and it took him a few moments to adjust to his new surroundings. Holding his nose as best he could, Pyke pulled back the sheet, but the stench of rotting, decomposing flesh was too much and he snapped his head backwards, a hot spike of vomit spurting from his mouth. The next time, he whipped the sheet off with a single jerk. Underneath, the bloated corpse looked inhuman, a fatty torso already as stiff as a washboard and discoloured from decomposition, and just a bloody stump where the head had once been. Wiping bile from his mouth, he brought the lantern closer to the corpse and bent down to inspect it further. Pyke's eyes passed across the corpse's clammy skin but he couldn't see an obvious cause of death. There was no stab wound and no visible scars or bruises of any sort except for a cluster of what looked like burn marks at the top of his arm. Four or five reddish circles, no larger than a five-shilling coin. Pyke prodded them with his thumb, trying to work out what might have caused them.

He walked around the corpse a few times, taking note of the thickness of the arms and thighs and the hairiness of the chest and arms. He'd been a young man, Pyke decided, no more than thirty years of age, and physically active, with well-developed leg and arm muscles. There was a zigzag scar running down the length of his forearm and a birthmark on his chest. From the length of the torso and the thick hairs on his chest, Pyke guessed he would have been about six foot, with dark hair. He inspected the cluster of burn marks again, wondering what might have caused them and whether they had, in fact, been inflicted by the killer. Why bother to do this to a man whose head you were about to cut off?

Pyke brought the lantern up to the neck stump and inspected it, trying to work out what instrument had been used in the decapitation. The wound seemed remarkably clean, as though the man's head had indeed been removed with a couple of swings of an axe rather than hacked off in a less clinical manner. This suggested the act may have been premeditated, that the killer had *planned* to decapitate his victim, but it didn't begin to suggest why he'd chosen to do so in the first place. Pyke could rule out torture: he was reasonably confident that the decapitation had taken place after the man had died. There were no rope marks around the wrists or ankles, for example, and to cut off someone's head while they were still alive would definitely require restraints. This left the thorny question of motivation. Why had someone gone to the trouble of decapitating a man they had already murdered? The most obvious answer was that the killer or killers had wanted to conceal the victim's identity.

'Where was the body found?' Pyke asked, once he'd rejoined Yellowplush at the back of the watch-house.

'A farmer fished him out of the river just to the east of the town.'

Pyke considered this for a moment. 'Would I be correct in assuming the river flows from west to east?'

Yellowplush nodded.

'So the body was either dumped into the river where the farmer found it or, more likely, it ended up there having been discarded elsewhere.' Pyke rubbed his eyes. 'Who owns the land upstream from where the corpse was found?'

'Is that relevant?'

'It might be,' Pyke said. 'If you don't tell me I can always find out from someone else.'

'Sir Horsley Rockingham.'

'A friend of yours?'

The magistrate stared at him but declined to answer the question.

'Are you planning to leave the body down there until it rots?'

'The body belongs to a local lad. Word spreads slowly in the country. I'm waiting to see if someone decides to claim it.'

'You know it's a local lad for certain?'

Yellowplush shrugged.

Pyke nodded. 'So tell me something. How does an ex-soldier suddenly become a magistrate?'

The question seemed to take Yellowplush by surprise. 'I don't take kindly to your insinuation, sir. Remember, you're here as my guest and, as my guest, your invitation can easily be revoked.'

'Is that what happened to the dead man?' Pyke held the magistrate's stare. 'Was his invitation revoked, too?'

'You'd do as well to hold your tongue. The countryside isn't always the peaceful idyll city folk imagine it is.'

'I can see that well enough with my own eyes.' In the yard men were still queuing for weapons.

Yellowplush rearranged his wig and stared out into the darkness. 'Navvies can be a barbarous lot but we'll not tolerate their violence. If they try something, we'll be ready for them.'

'Why would they *try* something?' Pyke didn't bother to hide his scorn. 'What is it you're not telling me?'

'Despite that letter, I'm not obliged to tell you a thing.' Yellowplush waited for a few moments, his stare intensifying. 'And in answer to your question, do heathens need a reason to embrace violence?'

'I don't know,' Pyke said, staring directly into his dry eyes. 'Do they?'

'I think you've officially outstayed your welcome.' Yellowplush ran the tip of his pink tongue across his pale, flaky lips. 'I'll bid you goodnight, sir.'

'Goodnight *and* good riddance?'

'Country people don't much care for city types with their fancy clothes and slick ways.'

'I'm sure the feeling's mutual.'

'If you know what's good for you you'll go back to London and leave us to sort out our own troubles.'

'What if I don't want to go? What if I've taken an inexplicable liking to this dour town of yours?'

Yellowplush took out his pistol once again and thrust it into Pyke's face. 'Do you really want me to answer that question?'

Pyke stared down the barrel and said, 'Hasn't anyone ever told you that the wig makes you look like an overgrown spaniel?'

The very considerable wealth that Sir Horsley Rockingham had plundered from his sugar plantation and the exploitation of African slaves was on display from the moment Pyke entered the wrought-iron gates of his country estate and approached the huge Queen Anne mansion from the carefully manicured gardens. Beyond the mature oak trees, Pyke could see stables and a paddock where a young woman with blonde hair was riding a chestnut-coloured gelding. Straight ahead, the house, constructed from Portland stone and glistening in the midday sunlight, was four storeys high and twelve windows long. Pyke dismounted from his horse and tied it to a handrail. At the top of the steps, he passed through a pair of Ionic columns and swept uninvited into the entrance hall, where a flustered servant tried to enquire about his business. In the hall, oil paintings by Titian, Van Dyck, Rubens and Gainsborough hung on the walls alongside oriental tapestries.

Pyke found Rockingham eating lunch alone in the dining room. It was an opulent room with high ceilings, rich cornices and ornate gilding. The old man had a white napkin tucked into his collar and was slurping claret from a crystal glass. He greeted the intrusion by spluttering red wine on to his beefsteak.

One wouldn't have known from looking at him that Rockingham had spent much of his life in the West Indies. Wrinkled with age, his skin had developed a translucent hue that recalled a cadaver rather than a sun-kissed expatriate. Hunched over his food at one end of a long polished table, he cut a frail figure, eaten away from the inside by his own bile, and his eyes, as hard as acorns, darted nervously between Pyke and the servant who had followed him into the room.

'What's the meaning of this interruption?' He addressed the servant rather than Pyke. 'Can't you see I'm eating my lunch, boy?'

'I'm sorry, sir, but this gentleman wouldn't permit me to ask him his business ...'

'Stop bleating, man! Tell this blackguard to leave me in peace and learn some damned manners.'

Pyke wandered across to the polished table and spied the condiments. 'Perhaps I could pass you the pepper, Sir Horsley. I hear you enjoy smearing it into bloodied flesh.' Taking the ceramic shaker, he shoved it along the polished surface of the table in the old man's direction. He made no effort to stop it and the vessel flew off the end of the table, smashing on the wooden floor.

'Go and fetch the magistrate and his men,' Rockingham barked at the servant. 'Damnation, man, didn't you hear me?'

'Are you quite certain you want to be left alone in this man's company, m'lord?' The servant seemed puzzled, doubtless trying to work out whether Pyke's smart clothes indicated benevolent intentions.

'Do you imagine I'm intimidated by this *specimen*?' Rockingham shuffled across to where Pyke was standing. 'I lived for fifteen years among three-hundred-odd niggers, all of whom fantasised about killing me.' He rubbed his finger against Pyke's cheeks and peered down at it. 'I reckon you might have some nigger blood in you.'

Hesitating, the servant looked again at Pyke and turned to depart the room, afraid to disobey his master.

'Before the magistrate's men arrive and toss you out on your ear like a whipped dog, perhaps you might enlighten me as to the purpose of your unsolicited visit.'

Pyke wandered around to the other side of the table and filled a glass with claret from the decanter. Sitting down on one of the horsehair chairs, he took a sip of the wine and proffered an approving nod. 'I'm afraid we might be here for quite a while. It would appear that Yellowplush's ruffians are tied up in Huntingdon. Haven't you heard? There's going to be some trouble there involving the navvies.'

Rockingham gave him a peculiar smile. 'What do you expect if you permit hordes of barbarians to roam around the land on a whim?'

'I thought they were here to work.'

'More like piss their wages against the wall and infect our women with the French disease.'

'In my experience venereal diseases are the gift of the aristocracy.' Pyke stood up and walked over to the large Venetian window that looked out on to the lawn at the rear of the building. 'It explains why most of your lot are effete twits who can't tie their own shoelaces.'

That even drew a chuckle from the old man. 'I like you, boy. You're spirited. But a spirited horse won't always become a champion. That takes discipline and courage. I'd enjoy breaking you in, of course, but I don't think you possess those qualities. In the end, you'd end up in the slaughterhouse like the rest of the also-rans.'

'Since you seem to appreciate blunt talking, I'll try and make this as clear as I can. The Grand Northern Railway will be built across your land whether you like it or not.'

'You'll see to it personally?' Rockingham's voice was light, even mocking.

'Flatterers tried to convince Canute he could command the waves to go back but he only attempted to do so in order to ridicule them. You could learn a thing or two from him.'

'Is that so, boy? Perhaps you don't know as much as you seem to think.'

Rockingham shuffled over to the fireplace and stood there for a moment, his back to Pyke, while he fumbled at his breeches. Pyke heard the splashes and saw some steam rising from the fire before he realised what was happening. When he'd finished, the older man buttoned up his breeches and turned to face him.

It was an act designed to insult and shock but he let it pass without acknowledging it. Still, Pyke felt his long-held prejudices towards the aristocracy rise up inside him like a knotted ball.

'I'm guessing it was that old fool Morris who sent you here.' Rockingham belched loudly. 'Just imagine it, giving up your title to join the ranks of the plebeians. What right-thinking Englishman would contemplate such a prospect?'

'If a right-thinking Englishman would fuck a Negro woman and then, nine months later, strangle his own progeny in front of her, Morris might be better described as wrong-thinking.'

Rockingham regarded him coldly. 'I'd be very careful how you address me, boy.'

'If it was up to me, I'd make sure the railway cut through the middle of this house and then I'd build a station in the great hall.'

That drew a leering smile. 'You're actually quite an amusing sort.' He looked at Pyke, as though inspecting a slab of meat. 'Whatever Morris is paying you, I'll double it.'

'To do what?'

'Tempted, eh?' Rockingham grinned, blood rising in his wan cheeks. 'To leave me in peace so I can finish my lunch.'

'I'm waiting for you to tell me how a headless corpse came to be dumped in the river flowing directly through your land.'

This seemed to take Rockingham by surprise. 'It didn't have anything to do with me.'

'But it was found in the river just downstream from the edge of your estate.'

'So?'

'So it implies that you were somehow involved.'

'Did the magistrate tell you that?'

When Pyke declined to answer, Rockingham's mood seemed to improve. 'I didn't think so.' But it suggested that he wasn't as certain of Yellowplush's support as Pyke might have expected.

'It was just coincidence, then?'

'Dammit, boy, if I'd killed a man or paid someone else to do it, why would I have cut off his head and thrown him into a river near my own land?'

A moment passed between them. More on a whim than anything else, Pyke said, 'So what are you trying to hide?'

'Hide?' Rockingham spluttered, unable to contain his rage. 'I'm not trying to hide a damned thing.'

'It doesn't look that way from where I'm standing.'

Rockingham wiped spittle from his chin and waited until he was calm. 'It's time you left. This conversation is finished.'

'The young girl I saw outside in the paddock, riding one of your chestnut horses. Is she your daughter or granddaughter?'

Rockingham's outrage was confined to his trembling hand. 'I won't be talked to in such an outrageous manner in my own house, sir.'

'If you make any further attempts to impede the construction of the railway across your land, I'll smear the bloodied carcass of her favourite animal across the marbled floor of the entrance hall while she watches.'

'Are you threatening my family?' Rockingham asked, still trying to adjust himself to the shock.

Unbuttoning his trousers, Pyke relieved himself on the remains of Rockingham's steak while the old man looked on in horror.

'Do you really think you can come into my home and insult me?' Rockingham's eyes glowed with humiliation. 'I have powerful friends, in London as well as Huntingdon, and I won't stand for your impertinence. You hear me, boy? I'd watch your back if I was you.'

As he reached the front steps, Pyke looked up and saw two figures approaching the house across the lawn. The young woman with the blonde hair carried a riding hat. Her companion, a smartly dressed young man, walked by her side. He was leading a chestnut gelding.

In the morning sunlight, the whiteness of their clothes set against the manicured green lawn might have made for a pleasant sight and their happy demeanour, reinforced by the fact they were walking so close together, implied a blossoming romance. But Pyke could not bring himself to acknowledge them or their happiness. Perhaps they had no idea that their idyll had been purchased with the crack of a slaver's whip, but their innocence was not something he wished to contemplate.

Rockingham had followed Pyke outside, however, and approached him as he was preparing to leave. He called over the young couple, took the reins of the horse from the man and, without making any introductions or acknowledging Pyke's presence, asked them to leave.

'He's a beautiful animal, isn't he?' Rockingham said, gently

76

stroking the animal's head. 'But in a race at Newmarket last week he missed his footing and was beaten into third place.'

Pyke didn't see the pistol in the ex-slaver's shaking hand until it was too late. The first blast caught the startled beast between the eyes and the second hit him in the neck as he stumbled, the hind legs buckling first. On the ground, the stricken animal quivered and snorted in front of them, and then died.

'Perhaps now you know what kind of man you're dealing with,' Rockingham said, staring down at the slain animal without sentiment.

Hearing a noise from behind them, Pyke spun around and saw that Rockingham's daughter had witnessed the scene from the top of the stone steps, but her expression was composed and her stare was empty, as though the shooting had not happened or she had failed to see it.

SEVEN

In daylight, and now that it was no longer raining, Huntingdon might have looked like a pretty market town with its Norman church, well-proportioned houses and its lush meadows. In fact, for a few hours at least, the sun-dappled river, though it had broken its banks just past the old bridge, seemed almost peaceful. But it was also hard not to see the town in the light of its watch-house and jail, the workhouse that was being built, and the efforts of its inhabitants to arm themselves in the face of an enemy who had done them no wrong. Pyke had seen similar attitudes in other small provincial towns. Strangers were to be tolerated only if they did not stay, change was to be feared, tradition and superstition predominated, and men's fears were easily played upon by those with the power. It wasn't surprising that the coming of the railway had provoked unrest, especially as it threatened people's livelihoods. But Pyke suspected that some people were whipping up generalised anxieties for their own selfish interests.

Situated on the Godmanchester side of the old bridge, the navvy encampment was set back from the muddy track and partly hidden by a tall hedge that circled the field.

'Hey, fella, what do you want?' From the other side of the gate, a man peered at him and scowled. He was holding what looked like a musket.

'I want to talk to whoever's in charge.'

'Who are you?'

'The name's Pyke. I've been sent here by the chairman of the railway company in London.'

That drew an ironic laugh but the gate swung open and he was met on the other side by three burly men with muskets slung over their shoulders, wearing velveteen coats covered in mud.

'We'll need to search you,' one of them muttered. 'In light of the current situation, I expect you'll understand.'

Pyke nodded but wondered what situation they were referring to. Did they know that the townsmen were already preparing for trouble?

Although it was afternoon, there was a chill in the air and darkness had begun to gnaw at the edges of the sky, while giant pillars of dark forbidding cloud amassed on the horizon.

The word camp was perhaps too grand a description for what greeted Pyke. It was little more than a few canvas tarpaulins hoisted over low-lying tree branches and a single turf shanty built out of caked mud which sat on slightly higher ground away from the banks of the river. As he was led across the field, the stares of the navvies bore into him. He had to duck his head to enter the shanty and inside it took him a few moments to adjust to the gloom. One of the men introduced him as a company man from London. A fire burnt in a makeshift grate, the smoke drawn upwards by a small hole in the thatched roof.

There were three men sitting on tree stumps around the fire and Pyke realised he already knew one of them, though it took him a few moments to work out how and where from.

Julian Jackman looked as surprised as Pyke but tried to conceal it behind the same easy smile he had deployed in their first meeting at the Brick Lane beer shop. This time, Pyke scrutinised his features more closely – his smooth complexion, his piercing green eyes and his thick, bushy hair – and realised, to his disappointment, that the radical was indeed attractive.

'In what capacity are you here, Pyke? I take it not as your wife's keeper?'

Pyke stepped forward as if to strike him and watched, with pleasure, as Jackman flinched slightly.

'You know him, then?' Perched on a tree stump, a navvy took off his white felt hat and scratched his carrot-coloured hair.

Jackman nodded. 'I met him a few days ago in London. He's married to Emily Blackwood, the campaigner. Maybe you've heard of her?' It was odd to be described as Emily's husband and Pyke wasn't sure he liked it.

The redhead frowned. 'Can we trust him?'

Jackman stood up. 'I don't know, Pyke. Can we trust you?'

Turning to the navvy, he added, 'By profession, Pyke's a banker.'

The navvy seemed amused. 'A capitalist, eh? Is that right?' He looked up at Pyke for the first time.

'Who I am or what I do for a living doesn't matter. What I've come here to tell you does matter.'

'Well, sir, we tend to take folks as we find 'em.' The navvy broke into a grin. 'My name's Red and this here is Billygoat.' He pointed at the shaven-headed man next to him. 'It seems you already know our friend from London so I won't bother introducing him.' He put on his felt cap and turned up the brim. 'So what is it you've got to tell us?'

'Did you know that the magistrate has been swearing in some of the townsmen as special constables and arming them with machetes and brickbats?'

Red scratched his stubble, digesting this news, but his expression remained calm. 'And why d'you think we'd be interested to hear this?'

Pyke glanced across at Jackman. 'They say to be forewarned is to be forearmed.'

'Is that right?' Red broke into a smile. 'Is a gentleman banker such as yourself on our side now?'

'I came here to investigate claims that a landowner has been conspiring to obstruct the progress of the railway across his land.'

'Conspiring with whom?'

'That's what I'm here to find out.'

Red regarded him with interest but said nothing.

'You mean to tell us that you haven't been sent up here to keep an eye on radical activity?' Jackman shot Pyke a sceptical look.

'Personally I don't give a damn whether you join a union or drink yourselves into an early grave.' This time Pyke directed his remarks at Red.

'And does the central committee of the Grand Northern Railway company feel the same way?' Jackman asked, raising his eyebrows.

'I don't know.' Pyke folded his arms. 'I haven't asked them.'

Red glanced over at the radical. 'So you wouldn't have any objections to us taking these oaths and then, say, striking for higher wages and better workin' conditions?'

'If that's what you want to do, be my guest,' Pyke said carefully. 'Of course, if you took these oaths and declared a strike before other navvy crews had done likewise, it would put you in a weak position. That's the thing about labouring jobs. There are always men willing to take your places.'

Red seemed to enjoy this remark. 'I'd say you weren't accustomed to the toils of being a navvy. Fact of the matter is, there ain't too many folk are cut out for it.' But Pyke could see that he had already considered this point.

'Look,' Pyke said, impatiently, 'there are upwards of a hundred men waiting on the other side of the bridge with brickbats and pick handles and the magistrate seems to think you're about to attack their town. My question is, where has he got that idea from?'

'That would be because we are.' Red's expression was so calm that it took Pyke a few moments to comprehend what he'd said.

'You're going to attack the town?'

Jackman shot Red a worried look. 'You think it's wise to tell him about our plan?'

'He ain't going anywhere till we make our move, so what's the difference?'

'I still don't understand,' Pyke said, looking around the room. 'Why attack a place that you *know* is very well defended? Why attack it at all?'

'Come. I'll show you.' Red stood up and motioned for Pyke to follow him outside to the back of the shanty, where a body was laid out under a tarpaulin on a tatty hemp mat. It belonged to an old woman, and it looked as if she had been badly beaten before she died. Her neck was very much discoloured, as if her windpipe had been violently squeezed, and someone's fingernails had clawed the skin over her trachea. Her breasts were purple with bruises and her face looked as if it had been attacked with a hammer. These injuries alone marked it as one of the most brutal beatings Pyke had ever witnessed, but this wasn't even the worst of it: scarcely an inch of her body was free from contusions, but it was the marks around the old woman's vagina which turned Pyke's stomach and forced him to look away. He shared a brief look with Red. There didn't seem to be any other conclusion that could be drawn. Before she had died the woman had been raped.

'Our crew's been together for a year. Mary joined us at the start; she'd cook and clean and help out around the camp. Two nights ago, she was washing some pots yonder when this *thing* happened.'

His expression darkened and he spat the words out. 'Whoever did it must' a clamped his brutish hand around her mouth 'cos none of us heard a thing. Billygoat found her later, down by the river, all wet and dead, stripped naked and lying there like a piece of meat.' Red's hands were clenched so tight his knuckles had turned white.

'And you think someone in the town was responsible for this?' Pyke could barely bring himself to look at the body.

Red grabbed hold of his wrist. 'Apparently some fellow in the Fountain inn has been boastin' about it. We got a description. One of the lads saw someone matchin' this description loiterin' on the night it happened.'

'Can you describe him for me?'

'A hairy brute of a man. Whiskers all over his face. Close up, they reckon he has a glass eye, too.'

In the fading afternoon light, Pyke bent over to inspect the old woman's corpse, and it was only then he saw the marks on her breasts. Burn marks, exactly like the ones he'd found on the headless body.

'Have you seen these?' Pyke pointed at the round burn marks, trying to play down his excitement.

Nodding, Red rummaged around in his pocket. 'He might have used this. It was found next to the body.' There in his open palm was a half-smoked cigar.

'Can I have a look?'

Red hesitated and then thought better of it and handed the cigar to him. Pyke held it up to the light and inspected it. There wasn't much to identify the brand but a tobacconist might be able to tell him more. He asked the navvy whether he could keep it. Red shrugged and said he didn't see why not but added there were plenty of folk who liked to smoke cigars. But Pyke was already turning something else over in his mind. Now two bodies had come to light, within a few miles of each other, both with burns marks likely caused by the hot ash of a cigar.

What connected them?

Back inside the shanty, he sat down on a tree stump and looked over at Jackman. 'Can I make an observation?' Before either Red or Jackman could speak, he added, 'You know that Jackman wants you to attack the town. It's in his interest. If you march through the High Street looking for a brawl, there'll be some townsmen waiting for you. So when a few of your men get hurt, perhaps badly hurt, Jackman here can exploit the situation for his own political ends.'

For the first time, Pyke noted with satisfaction, Jackman looked genuinely angry. Blood rose in his neck. 'And if we do nothing, the company gets exactly what it wants. A nice, pliant workforce.' He nodded contemptuously in Pyke's direction. 'By his own admission, he's a company man. He just wants to smooth things over until the work has started.'

Red drummed his fingers on the makeshift table while he considered what to do. 'The thing is, Pyke, if we don't do a thing, then Mary's death goes unpunished. You see what I mean?' He waited for a moment, choosing his words. 'I went to see the magistrate yesterday to report what had happened.' His voice shook a little. 'The man told me to my face not to waste his time. *To my face*. You reckon we can turn the other cheek, not do a thing?'

Pyke glanced across at the radical. 'But it remains true that if the magistrate turns his militia and weapons on you, Jackman can exploit your likely injuries for propagandist purposes. He doesn't care about your well-being any more than I do.'

This time Pyke had pushed the radical too far and, without warning, Jackman took a swing at him. But it was a wild punch and Pyke easily ducked under it, leaving himself with time to take aim and land a clean blow on the radical's jaw. He put a little extra into the punch and felt a jolt of pleasure when Jackman went down.

Aroused by the disturbance, other men poured into the shanty and it took a blast of Red's musket to restore some semblance of calm.

'I've thought about what you said.' Red looked at Pyke and rubbed his chin. His stare was empty of sentiment. 'I've made my decision. We bury Mary and we march on the town.'

Cheers quickly spread through the camp. Gingerly climbing to his feet, Jackman nursed his cut lip. Only Red and Pyke seemed unmoved by what had happened, and when the furore abated the navvy turned to him and whispered, 'You may well be right but we don't have a choice.'

Later, when Pyke shut his eyes and pictured Mary's battered corpse, it was hard to disagree with Red's logic.

*

It was fully dark by the time they left the camp and the sky was once again laden with black clouds. It started to rain as they approached the bridge, a fine spray at first and then larger droplets of water buffeted their faces. A squally wind blew gold leaves from the branches and, deprived of sunlight, Huntingdon once again became a drab market town, grey smoke billowing out of red-brick chimneys. There were thirty-seven of them, including Pyke and Jackman, and their makeshift weaponry was no match for what Pyke had seen outside the town's watch-house.

They crossed the ancient bridge unopposed and marched three or four abreast up the deserted High Street, as anxious faces appeared and disappeared from behind drawn curtains. As they approached the Fountain inn, some of their number began to rattle their sticks and chant threats but, on closer inspection, both the inn itself and the adjoining taproom seemed deserted – certainly all the doors were locked and there were no signs of life anywhere inside the building.

It was raining harder and wet gusts of wind pummelled their unprotected faces. At the head of the mob, a breakaway group had decided to head for the square, and when they turned the corner into it, they were confronted by a row of well-armed men lined up to block their progress. The navvies were so obviously outnumbered it was a surprise that some chose to attack, but the whole crew was quickly forced back with brickbats and pick handles.

Pyke couldn't see what was happening at the front of the melee but he could hear the grunts and screams as blunt objects rained down on their heads, bones cracking under the onslaught. A gleeful townsman split open one of the navvy's heads with repeated swings of a brickbat, and just behind Pyke another navvy was pushed to the ground and kicked over and over in the stomach and head. On that occasion Pyke charged the lynch mob and managed to chase them off with a few lunges of his knife, long enough to pick up the stricken man and retreat with the rest of them towards the bridge. Some ran and others walked, turning only to check on the where-abouts of their pursuers. Pyke had lost sight of Jackman and Red but the man Pyke had rescued had recovered sufficiently to walk without help, even though he didn't appear to know where he was or what had just happened.

Ahead of them the bridge was just about visible through the

driving rain. Some of the townsmen were still pursuing them along the High Street, the sound of musket or rifle fire and the whiff of blast powder filling the damp air. From the size of their group, Pyke guessed that about half of the navvies had been left somewhere behind them, including perhaps Jackman, but he saw Red somewhere near the front, urging his wounded troops to retreat a little faster. It wasn't until they were halfway across the bridge that Pyke saw the men lined up on the *other* side of the bridge, the Godmanchester side, where they'd hoped to find sanctuary; townsmen carrying torches and sticks and waiting to ambush them.

Others had seen them, too, and they came to a halt in the middle of the bridge, caught between two advancing groups of townsmen. What happened next would live for a long time in Pyke's mind: the sounds of brickbats and pick handles raining down on their heads, cries of pain and anguish, blood splattered across his face, and splashes as terrified navvies jumped into the fast-moving river below to escape the onslaught. Later, he would be able to think back on what happened with greater clarity and determine what mistakes had been made and whether more could have been done to save those drowning men. But in the first moments on the bridge, he came as close to experiencing what a soldier might go through during an ambush as he would ever come, fighting to preserve one's life rather than win a victory.

One of the townsmen came at him swinging a pick handle. If he'd connected, the blow might have split Pyke's head open. Instead, he swayed out of the way, punched the man in the face and disarmed him of the stick. Turning it on someone else, he drove it hard into his attacker's stomach and watched as the man fell to his knees coughing up bile.

When they had finally broken through the ranks of the townsmen, who were tired of their victory, and made it back to the camp, Red embraced Pyke with both arms and whispered in his ear that he was a good man. Red's clothes were torn and muddy and his face was bruised purple from the blows he'd received at the hands of the townsmen. Pyke's injuries were slight in comparison. Others also offered their grateful thanks. From somewhere a horse was produced, its reins thrust into Pyke's hands. 'We need someone to tell folk what happened here tonight,' Red said, his voice bristling with emotion. 'We need someone to tell our story.'

Pyke checked his watch. It was barely seven o'clock. He still had time to make it to the rendezvous point with Morris by eight.

He looked out for the young radical but didn't see Jackman among the walking wounded.

Pyke had ridden a few hundred yards along the muddy track from Godmanchester when he saw them, a row of men in tall-crowned top hats carrying torches and blockading the road. The lashing rain and squally wind made it hard to tell how many of them he was facing. A clap of thunder shook the ground and a fork of lightning lit up the sky. He saw them better in the afterglow of the lightning. At first he thought the men had been placed there in order to protect the town from recriminatory attacks by the navvies. But when he pulled on the reins, dug his heels into the horse's midriff and tried to encourage the mare to turn around, this fallacy was exposed. A rifle shot exploded like the crack of a slaver's whip, closely followed by a second and a third shot. They weren't trying to stop or arrest the navvies. It was an assassination party and he was their target. Pressing his own horse into a gallop, Pyke lowered his head and held on to the beast as it clipped along the track. He didn't see the other men, advancing from the direction of the camp, until it was almost too late. They, too, had fanned out across the track, their rifles aimed at him. Pyke jerked on the reins and brought the snorting mare to a standstill, looking in both directions as the armed men closed in on him.

For a moment, Pyke cursed his own stupidity. He had under-estimated the threat posed by Yellowplush and Rockingham and had needlessly antagonised them for no gain other than to see them squirm. Worse still, he had become complacent, allowing himself to believe that his old skills would somehow carry him through, ignoring the fact that he hadn't fired a pistol in anger or ridden a horse in five years.

Kicking the horse in the ribs, he felt the beast surge forward and directed it from the track, the animal clearing the first ditch with an effortless leap, spewing up chunks of turf as it landed and throwing Pyke forward in the saddle. Ahead, through the rain, he saw a deeper ditch followed by a wooden fence. He didn't have any choice but to try to clear these two obstacles and had set about preparing the jittery animal for the jump when one of its hind legs seemed to give way, either because it had been hit by a bullet or because it had sunk too far into the mud. When he tried to make the jump, the mare toppled forward and threw him out of the saddle, catapulting him across the grass until he landed on his back with a thud.

Pyke felt a sense of weary resignation as he lay unmoving on the damp turf, and an acknowledgement that he had overplayed his hand and lost more than he could afford to lose. They found him in a matter of seconds, three or four of them gathering around him like hunters. The smell of whisky on their breath was unmistakable. He thought of his son, who would now grow up without a father, and of Emily. One of them poked him with the barrel of his rifle, while another asked, 'What do you want us to do with him?' As a Bow Street Runner he had once enjoyed the full sanction of the law, but here he was less than a nuisance, a nonentity who was expendable precisely because no one knew who he was. Then he heard the same voice say, 'Search and strip him.' Another voice muttered, 'Well, is it Cap'ain Paine or not?' Pyke looked up and saw the glint of a shovel. 'When you've done that, dig a deep hole, shoot him in the head and bury him.' The voice belonged to Septimus Yellowplush.

The magistrate bent down to address him. This time he wasn't wearing his wig and his bald head, as large as a pumpkin, glistened in the rain.

'No one does what you did to me and gets away with it.' He took aim and kicked Pyke on the side of his head with his boot.

When Pyke came to, he had been dragged deeper into the field and stripped of his clothes. Shaking violently, he felt the cold as he had never felt it before; it gnawed away at his toes and fingers and spread to the rest of the body. Trying not to panic, he looked up and saw two men, their backs turned to him, digging the hole that he would be buried in. If anything the rain was now falling harder than before. His wrists and legs had been bound with rope and he felt like a pig awaiting slaughter. There was nothing he could do except wait for the shot and hope it came quickly.

He had always hated the countryside.

When the first crack of a rifle sounded, he assumed it was one of the magistrate's men. The first shot was closely followed by another and then another and very quickly it became clear that it was the men digging the hole who were under fire and scrambling for cover.

Pyke had only managed to crawl a few yards when someone poked him from above with their rifle.

Jackman stood over him and produced a knife from his belt. His whiskers dripped with water. 'Here, hold out your hands.' Pyke did as he was told and the radical cut them free with a single jerk of his knife.

Pyke sat up, still dazed. 'What happened?'

'The bald one's dead. I shot him.' Jackman threw Pyke his clothes. There was a rifle slung over his shoulders.

It took Pyke a few moments to realise what Jackman had told him. Yellowplush was dead. 'And the others?'

'Didn't have the stomach for a fight.' Jackman hesitated, apparently choosing his words. 'Look, Pyke, I saw what you did on the bridge. It seems I was wrong about you.'

'I was wrong about you too.' Pyke stood up and put on his trousers. 'Yellowplush seemed to think *I* was Captain Paine.'

That seemed to amuse him. 'Must have seen you fight. It was an impressive sight, too.'

'Why would they think Captain Paine was here tonight?'

Jackman gave him a curious stare and laughed. 'Your guess is as good as mine.'

'What's so funny?'

But Jackman was already moving. 'We should get going. They might return with more men.'

Pyke pulled up his boots and reached for his soaking frock-coat. He looked across the field. In the distance, he could see men on horseback silhouetted against the branches of the trees.

On the other side of the field he joined up with Jackman and crossed a fence using the stile, taking cover behind a hedgerow. 'Follow this path. It'll bring you out on to the Cambridge road.' Jackman thrust the rifle into his hands. 'Take it. You'll need it. I have a feeling this isn't over yet.'

But as Pyke went to thank him again, Jackman had turned around and was moving in the opposite direction.

EIGHT

It took Pyke half an hour to reach the rendezvous point where the carriage, and Morris, were thankfully waiting for him: his assistant, Bledisloe, too, though he didn't get out of the carriage. When Morris tried to shake his hand, muttering about how relieved he was to see him, Pyke pushed him up against the side of the vehicle and shouted, 'I was almost killed. But others weren't so lucky. Navvies employed to build *your* railway were hounded into a quick-flowing river like they were rats.' It was still raining and Pyke felt the humiliation of lying naked in the field wash over him again. Morris seemed terrified by Pyke's outburst and listened like a beaten dog while Pyke tried to explain what had happened, words tumbling out of his mouth in an unstoppable torrent.

'What's that noise?' Something had interrupted his diatribe and Pyke stood there for a moment, looking back along the track he'd just run along.

Water dripped from Morris's nose. He was soaking wet as well. 'What noise?'

'Maybe it was just another rumble of thunder.' Pyke walked a little way along the track and stopped to listen.

The sound was more distinctive and it was getting louder. Sniffing the air, Pyke stared into the darkness and took the rifle in his hand. Inspecting the gun, he discovered it was loaded. This made him feel a little better, but without additional ammunition the rifle would be of only limited help. In the trees, he heard the twittering of an owl. With a jump, he started to run back towards the carriage, shouting at the driver to get going. When he caught up with it, the carriage was already moving, Bledisloe hauling them inside through the open door.

'What is it, Pyke?' Morris said, grabbing his arm. Bledisloe looked panicked as well.

'Men on horseback,' Pyke muttered, fighting for breath. 'And they're riding in our direction.'

'Shouldn't we take our chances and plead our innocence?' Morris asked. 'Perhaps we could hide you somewhere?'

'Where?'

They looked around the carriage. There were no obvious hiding places.

Pyke banged on the roof and ordered the coachman to make haste. Sliding the glass down, he leaned out of the window and looked behind them. The carriage was moving quickly now, bumping along the puddle-strewn track. Pyke could just about see them, six men on horseback riding in pursuit. But it was only when they had made up more ground that he saw their scarlet coats. They were soldiers, dragoons probably, skilled horsemen who were closing the gap on them with each passing moment. This time, Pyke opened the door and, clinging on to the iron rail that ran along the top of the carriage, hauled himself on to the roof, where Morris and Bledisloe's luggage was stowed. The carriage was rattling along at a fair speed, mud and water splashing around them, the crack of the coachman's whip urging on the team of straining horses. Behind them, the soldiers had closed the gap to a few hundred yards. Pyke took one of the suitcases fixed to the roof and hurled it up into the air. The contents of the case momentarily filled the sky before fluttering down on to the muddy track, the suitcase itself landing just where Pyke had intended.

The first of the horsemen swerved at the last minute to avoid the obstacle and buffeted the soldier right behind him, the collision sending both horses sprawling on to the track and dismounting their riders. Another two horses were downed in the melee but the two riders at the back managed to avoid the carnage and jump clear. A rifle shot whistled over Pyke's head. He could hear the panting of the horses, and the rattling of the wheels and harness. There was one suitcase left and he tried the same trick, but this time the riders were prepared for him and easily avoided the intended missile. The two soldiers were less than fifty yards behind them and Pyke could see their determined grimaces. Yellowplush had served in the army, he remembered. Perhaps they had come across his body and were hell-bent on avenging one of their own. But this didn't explain how they had mobilised so rapidly.

Pyke could see their crimson uniforms clearly and, with less weight to carry, one of the soldiers had almost caught up with the slower-moving carriage. But it was only at the last moment that Pyke saw the pistol in his hand, heard the blast and flattened himself against the roof of the carriage, narrowly avoiding the ball-shot as it whistled over his head. Rolling over on to his front, he retrieved the rifle Jackman had given him, steadied himself and took aim. It was an easy shot. The bullet struck the soldier in the chest and lifted him cleanly off the horse, sending him crashing to the track, dead before he'd even landed. The other soldier had seen what had happened but didn't stop to check on his fallen comrade as Pyke had hoped he might. This last remaining soldier had a pistol in his hand but this time the shot missed by some margin, and it gave Pyke a chance to hurl the rifle with both hands in his general direction. The weapon collided with the horse just as it was pulling alongside the carriage and as quickly as it had started the pursuit was over. Both horse and rider went down, and soon there was nothing behind them except trees and an empty track snaking its way across flat, barren terrain.

'You, shut up now,' Pyke spat at Chauncey Bledisloe, who had been panicking and shouting at Pyke ever since he had killed the soldier. Morris's assistant flicked his mop of greasy brown hair away from his eyes and folded his arms, sulking. He was the same age as Pyke but that was where the comparison ended: with his wan complexion, bony frame and hunched shoulders, he was every bit the runt of his particular litter. 'If I hear another word from you before we reach London, I swear, I'll throw you out of the carriage while it's still moving. Is that understood?' Turning to Morris, he added, without changing his tone, 'Did you know anything about the reception party waiting for me in Huntingdon? I want the truth.' Pyke wiped his mouth with his sleeve and sat back against the horsehair cushion. They were travelling at a more sedate speed and his nervous energy had abated into a hard, cold anger.

'I had no idea it would come to this. I'm so sorry, Pyke. You have to believe me. It's terrible, *terrible*.' Morris shook his head, colour draining from his cheeks.

'But you knew there was going to be trouble?'

'All I knew was what Peel told us in his office: that some radicals might try to agitate among the navvies.'

His response drew some of the sting from Pyke's anger. He closed his eyes and let out a sigh. 'I shot and killed a soldier. Injured five others. Do you think they'll just let me walk away from it?'

Morris stared down at the wet straw on the floor of the carriage. 'Perhaps the men who chased us weren't acting on official orders.'

It was a thought that had crossed Pyke's mind, too, but he looked up at Morris. 'What makes you say that?'

'After Peterloo, the military brass has been much more careful about turning their soldiers on the civilian population.'

'A man's dead. I killed him. The regiment won't let it go.'

For a while no one said anything, the clattering of the horses' hoofs and clanking of the harness filling the carriage.

Morris loosened his cravat and wiped the sweat from his forehead. 'How many of the navvies perished?'

'I don't know.' Pyke closed his eyes, his mind returning to the events on the bridge. 'Given the strength of the current, it can't have been easy for the ones who jumped off the bridge.'

'You have to believe I didn't know about any plans to attack the navvies, Pyke. I wouldn't have sent you there if I'd known. I'm not that kind of man.'

Pyke stared out of the window and thought about the old crone and the drowned navvies. He thought about the glass-eyed man whose assault on Mary had instigated the whole affair and the bloated, decomposing body he'd inspected in the cellar of the watch-house, too. Perhaps Morris was telling the truth. Perhaps he was just as surprised by what had happened as Pyke. But someone, somewhere had planned it, someone with the power or the contacts to call upon six armed dragoons, and when he found them, Pyke intended to make them suffer.

'What will happen to the railway construction now?' Pyke asked.

They had eaten supper at an inn south of Bishop's Stortford and were continuing their journey back to London.

'There will have to be an investigation, of course, and doubtless pressure will be brought to bear on all parties to blame the navvies.' Morris's face was haggard and drawn. 'That's the reality of the situation. And the construction work will be put back by months. If, that is, it happens at all.'

'Why wouldn't it happen?'

'I didn't tell you about the meeting, did I?' Morris shook his head. 'It would seem there's a growing feeling among the proprietors that we should terminate the railway at Cambridge.'

'Not go all the way to York?'

Morris shook his head glumly. 'It's become a straightforward question of money, Pyke. The proprietors are concerned about our stagnant share price, and who can blame them? They look at our competitor, the London and Birmingham Railway, and they see a spectacular success. The Birmingham railway was consolidated at the same time as us and they've already contracted eighty-six miles of track; they'll have the whole line under contract by the start of next year, as well. Meanwhile, we've only contracted thirty-eight miles of track — thirty-eight out of one hundred and eighty-six — and we've purchased less than a fifth of the land we'll need to get to York.'

Pyke could see that this failure weighed heavily on Morris's mind and decided not to push him.

'Whereas the Birmingham's shares have more than doubled in the last six months alone, ours are worth less than the proprietors have already paid in instalments. They're looking out for themselves.' He smiled ruefully. 'They couldn't care less about my tales of woe, the difficulties we've been having, problems with subcontractors and the battles with landowners like Rockingham. They just want a section of the railway to be completed as soon as possible so that we can begin to earn freight and passenger income; it's the only way our shares will ever become attractive to investors.'

Pyke struggled to grasp the implications of what Morris had told him. 'And that's why they want to focus efforts on getting the section of the line as far as Cambridge built before the rest of the work is attempted?'

'If only it were that straightforward. No, I think it's far worse than that. There's a faction in the company that would like to see us raise the white flag and make Cambridge our final terminus. Forget about Lincoln and York.'

'Why?'

'It's very simple. As soon as we start to earn money, they'll begin to receive their dividends.'

Pyke nodded. He understood the older man's dilemma. 'I take it you don't want to build a railway that terminates at Cambridge.'

Morris gave Pyke a hollow smile.

'Mr Morris was heroic,' Chauncey Bledisloe said, interrupting their conversation. '*Heroic* is the only word I can think of that comes close to describing it. The question of whether we should push on to Lincoln and York came to a vote and Mr Morris here stood and gave a speech that anyone who was lucky enough to hear it will be talking about for years, even *decades*, to come. What did you tell them, Mr Morris? That if we stopped at Cambridge, we'd miss out on the holiest of holy grails, a route linking London with the great factories and collieries of the Midlands and the North and perhaps one day even with Scotland.'

Pyke pointed at him. 'I thought I told you to keep your mouth closed.'

Turning crimson, Bledisloe flicked hair from his face and slunk to the far side of the carriage.

Pyke turned to Morris. 'What happened in the vote?'

'I carried the motion by a single vote.' Morris rubbed his eyes and yawned. He looked tired and old and his skin had assumed a wan, almost yellowy complexion. 'But the issue will be debated again in a week's time by the central committee in London and doubtless another vote will be taken and then another vote and then another vote until the jackals finally win the day.'

Pyke stared out of the window at the dark, featureless landscape. 'Of course, if the railway goes no farther than Cambridge, Rockingham will get what he wants.'

'I know.'

'So do you really think Rockingham could have pulled the strings of the soldiers, the townsmen and the magistrate?'

'I do know for a fact he's a ruthless bastard. On the face of it, I'm quite sure he'd be capable of *anything*.'

'But does his influence extend as far as your own board?' Pyke glanced across at Bledisloe.

'I don't know. I really don't know,' the older man said, sighing. 'But I wouldn't rule it out.'

*

94

Pyke's dreams were punctuated with images of decaying bodies and burning flesh and when he woke up his back and sides were drenched in sweat. Yawning, he stretched his limbs and looked out of the window. They were approaching the outskirts of the city: the flat, barren landscape had been replaced by red-brick houses, workshops, clay pits and tile kilns. Morris was fiddling with his watch and staring glumly out of the window while Bledisloe snored quietly in his seat.

'I was thinking ...' Morris hesitated. His skin was slick with perspiration. 'In the light of your experiences, I'd quite understand if you didn't want to have anything more to do with me.'

'Aren't you forgetting we have a business arrangement?'

'Of course I haven't forgotten,' Morris said indignantly. 'I just didn't want to drag you any farther into something you might later regret.'

'Someone tried to assassinate me last night. Don't you think I'm already part of it now, whatever it is?'

'I just didn't want you to feel obligated.'

Pyke cut him off. 'If you still need the money, the offer of the loan from my bank still stands.' He waited until Morris looked up at him. 'I might have walked away from it all but I tend to take it personally when someone tries to kill me and I don't know why.' Morris didn't need to know that Peel was holding something over him, too.

'Then we'll sign the contracts tomorrow afternoon at the railway's head office on Threadneedle Street.' Morris hesitated and rubbed his eyes. 'As one of the railway's chief creditors, you're also entitled to three votes whenever the committee votes on substantial issues. I hope I can count on your support.'

Nodding, Pyke wound the silver chain from his fob pocket around his thumb and played with the two keys attached to it.

'Actually, Pyke, there was something of a more sensitive nature I wanted to talk to you about.' Morris glanced across at Bledisloe, who was still fast asleep.

'I'm listening.'

Beads of sweat pricked the older man's temples. 'In addition to the company loan, I'd like to borrow a sum of money from your bank under a more personal arrangement.'

'What kind of sum?'

'Ten thousand pounds.'

Pyke whistled involuntarily. 'That's a lot of money. Do you mind me asking what you need it for?'

'I'm afraid I can't tell. As I said, it's a personal matter.'

'Personal as in you can't tell me or won't?'

'It's just personal,' the older man said, frustration getting the better of him.

'Tell me something, Edward. Are you in some kind of trouble?'

'Trouble? Of course I'm not in trouble.' Morris seemed unfazed by the question. 'I merely need to borrow a small sum of money in the short term and according to all the usual practices and procedures.'

'If you regard ten thousand to be a small sum then I truly take my hat off to you.'

Morris regarded him with a grimace. 'You don't wear a hat.'

'It was a figure of speech.'

A moment passed between them. 'So will your bank lend me the money or not?'

'What will you put up as security?'

'Cranborne Park. I own it free and clear.'

Pyke nodded, still turning over the older man's request in his mind. 'I assume this isn't something you've discussed with your wife?'

'Since when did men like you and I ever allow our wives to dictate the decisions we make?'

Pyke allowed himself a brief smile. 'So how soon do you need this money?'

'I'm afraid I'll need a decision at once. I'll need the money by tomorrow. In notes, if possible.'

'All right,' Pyke said, absent-mindedly fiddling with his two keys. 'Bring the deeds to the estate with you to the meeting tomorrow and you have a deal.'

They shook hands.

Morris's face brightened considerably but the strain was still evident. 'I'd prefer it if no one else knew about this.'

'We'll need someone to witness our signatures on the loan contracts.' Pyke waited and said, 'What about Nash?' He had first solicited Morris as a customer and they seemed to be on good terms.

'As long as it goes no farther than young Jem.' He looked across at Bledisloe who was beginning to stir. 'Look, old boy, I do appreciate what you've done for me. I'd really like to invite you and your family to tea at Cranborne Park. You clearly made quite an impression on my wife. She insisted that I ask you: insisted that you bring your family, as well. Perhaps after we've concluded our business tomorrow? We could pick up your wife and child on the way.'

Pyke assured him he would ask Emily and let him know at the meeting the next day. He asked, 'Do you ever think it odd that we've become neighbours and business partners at the same time?'

'Odd?'

'Coincidental.'

Morris shrugged. 'Like I told you before, it wasn't my idea to move to Cranborne Park.'

Pyke stared out of the window, declining to respond. But it was exactly this point which worried him.

NINE

Even by ten o'clock the next morning, barely a shard of daylight had managed to penetrate the asphyxiating miasma of soot and dirt that hung over the warren of narrow alleys and courts around Spitalfields. The stench, too, made Pyke's eyes water, a pungent odour of discarded, overripe fruit from the nearby market, human excrement and gobbets of putrid flesh from a nearby slaughterhouse where the walls were six inches thick with the blood and fat from slain animals. A long-tailed rat, as large as a small dog, scurried across the street, nimbly darting between ragged cobblestones to join others gnawing on the carcass of a dead cat. Pyke didn't bother to shoo them away; nor would the rats have taken any notice of him if he'd tried. It had been some time since he had ventured into this territory, and with each passing year it became more alien to him – the sight of out-of-work men dressed in filthy rags, teeth black from chewing tobacco, openly copulating with blowsy women while their bow-legged children ran freely in cess trenches. All of it took him back to his own childhood, but he was no longer able to remember what it had been like to actually *live* in such conditions. Money had softened him to such an extent that he now felt uncomfortable if he didn't bathe three or four times a week, eat fresh fish and vegetables off fine china, drink expensive French wines and sleep on good cotton sheets.

Strangely this anxiety had not prevented him from becoming nostalgic about his own past. A few weeks earlier, he'd walked past the ginnery he had once owned around the corner from Smithfield Market and had been seized by a feeling of such intense desire to be back in his old room that he had tried to gain entrance to the building. Once inside, he had been set upon by a gang of thieves who used it as a flash house and who tried and failed to strip him of his possessions. Afterwards he had attended a charity ball organised by Emily to raise funds for another of her causes, and it had struck him that, as much as he despised the rookeries, despised their dirtiness, their stink of misery and despair and the smoke-blackened rooms where ten or more men and women slept head to toe on flimsy hessian sacks, despised the ubiquity of violence and the imminence of death, he felt more comfortable there than he did attending events alongside the great and the good of society.

There was a time in Pyke's life when the Spitalfields weavers had been the blue-blood aristocrats of the artisan classes. The work had been secure and wage regulations had ensured that prices for their silk remained acceptable. More importantly the market for silk had been protected from foreign competition by government regulation. Indeed, as a child, Pyke could still remember visiting the homes of weavers and being astounded that they had gardens and summer houses. All that had changed when the government relaxed the ban on foreign imports, a move that flooded the market with cheap silk from France and Holland, and the combined effect of this and the influx of the sweaters who corralled women and children into slop shops and paid them pennies meant that the weavers had slipped from their position at the top of the working-class hierarchy to near the bottom.

Pyke had to ask a toothless old man for directions to the Sutton house, and when he eventually found it, the dwelling turned out to be no more than two small, windowless rooms on the ground floor of a cottage shared by a number of other weaving families. It was an airless morning, damp without being cold, and Pyke had to cover his mouth and nose with a handkerchief, to try to ward off the oppressive stink that clung to the entire neighbourhood.

The last thing he wanted to do was pick up a debilitating disease that he might pass on to his son.

Pyke pushed open the front door and stared into the room at an old man hunched over a loom. 'Are you Kate's father?'

Startled, the man looked up, two white eyes surrounded by skin that was so dirty it was hard to see him. Stepping into the room, Pyke saw it was lit by a solitary candle that three of them shared, the man and woman and a young girl. The man looked up from his loom and held up his hands to shield his eyes from the glare of the outside light. 'Who wants to know?'

As his eyes adjusted to the semi-darkness, Pyke realised the man wasn't nearly as old as he had initially thought. It was just that his skeletal figure and wan, sunken cheeks gave the impression of a much older person. He returned the handkerchief to his pocket.

'It's a gemmen,' the man croaked to his wife, springing to his feet and ushering Pyke into the spotlessly tidy room.

'I'm looking for your daughter Kate.' Pyke glanced over at the little girl, who gave him a toothy smile. She couldn't have been much older than Felix, he thought grimly, and already she had been put to work on a loom.

'Here, take a seat, sir,' the man said, offering Pyke the only chair in the room. 'That's a very fine coat, if I may say so. A very nice coat. Very expensive. Must have cost you a pretty penny.'

'Do you know where your daughter is? Has she been in contact recently?'

'Not for a while. Me and Missus Sutton are tryin' not to show our worry in front of the littl'un.' He came a little closer and whispered, 'But it's been mighty hard for all of us. That gal's always been my favourite. And between you and me, she always helped us with a few shillings from her wages.'

'My name's Pyke. I'm trying to find your daughter for my uncle. He visited you a week ago.'

The man took hold of Pyke's sleeve. 'Is that your uncle, sir? The publishing man? A gemmen he was, too. Gave us a few coins.'

'Do you have any idea where she might have gone?'

'Hear that, Missus Sutton?' he barked at his wife. 'This gemmen's gonna find our gal.'

'Don't be getting your hopes up, Freddie. You know as well as I do she's been gone nearly two weeks now.'

'Hush, woman. May wolves tear out your throat for speaking that way.' He turned back to Pyke. 'What was it you was asking?'

'Have you any idea where your daughter might have gone? She left her job at the palace last week without giving a forwarding address.'

Freddie shook his head. 'My gal wouldn't have left that job, not if wild horses had been dragging her. Mrs Sutton's cousin used to work in the palace, too, and she got our gal the job in the first place. Our Kate properly loved it. And it paid well, too. Enough to spare me a few groats at the end of the week.'

'Was she in any kind of trouble, at least that you knew of?'

'Our Kate?' He shook his head vehemently. 'Butter wouldn't melt in her mouth.' This didn't match Godfrey's description of her but Pyke let the opinion stand.

'And she never talked about resigning her post and going elsewhere?'

'Never once.' Freddie folded his arms.

Pyke studied his proud, leathery face. 'What about lovers?'

'Lovers? My gal ain't no cockish dell but she ain't a biter, neither. There might have been a gemmen. Not one like you, as well dressed and all, but a friend who liked her well enough.'

'Do you know his name? Where he lives?'

'I might do,' Freddie said, a disconcerting glint in his eye. 'But I might also need something to jog my memory.'

'Freddie, may the Lord forgive you, trying to profit when this gemmen just wants to find our gal,' his wife scolded.

'The way I see it,' the man replied, looking at Pyke rather than at her, 'he wants to find our gal for himself. He ain't doing it out of the goodness of his heart, is he?'

Pyke took out his purse, picked out a sovereign and handed it to the man.

'Gold. It's gold, Missus Sutton. I ain't see one of these in years. *Gold.*' He seemed beside himself with excitement.

'Kate's friend?'

'Ah, yes.' His expression became serious. 'Not a good sort. Johnny was his name. I always had him figgered as a bad apple. He wanted to be an actor and he expected our gal to keep him with her wages. I mean, that ain't right, is it? Taking Darby from a gal.'

'Do you know where I can find him?'

'Not where he lives but I remember him talking about a penny gaff on New Cut. He tried to get me to go and see him act. I never did but he told me it was the farther one from the Waterloo Road.'

Pyke looked down and saw that the young girl was standing next to him, hugging his leg. He bent down and patted her on the head. She seemed transfixed by the two keys on the chain and he let her play with them for a while.

'That's Milly, my youngest. Clever gal she is. A real magpie.'

'Is there anyone else Kate mentioned? An old friend? Someone she talked to at the palace?'

Freddie scratched his chin, straining to remember something.

'There was someone else, come to think of it ... another gal who worked at the palace, a proper lady, though ...'

'But let me guess,' Pyke said, retrieving his purse. 'Your memory requires further lubrication?'

'See, Missus Sutton?' Freddie said, turning to his wife. 'I said this was a gemmen, didn't I? As soon as I saw him, I said to myself this is not just a gemmen but a cock of the walk.'

Pyke wasn't sure when he had first become superstitious or even why he allowed such things to unsettle him. He harboured no religious sentiments, choosing instead to put his faith in rational thought and scientific discovery. But still, if a black cat ran out across the street in front of him, he felt somehow reassured, and if he saw one magpie, he would immediately look for another. Mostly he saw his burgeoning superstition in benign terms, as a product of his material well-being. If this was all he had to worry about, then his life must be fine and rosy. Nonetheless Pyke could never quite shake the feeling that he had prospered undeservedly and that everything he'd achieved could just as easily be snatched from him. Within the last year, ravens had taken to nesting in the roof of his bank and he had found their presence oddly reassuring. Rationally he knew such thinking was absurd: the presence of a few ugly birds had absolutely no bearing on the realities of his life. But each time he saw a raven out of his window, its black plumage set against the red tiles of the roof, it set his stomach at ease and he felt able to address his problems with renewed vigour.

Having returned to his bank from the Grand Northern's head offices and a lavish lunch of hot roast beef and plum pudding to officially mark the loan agreement between Blackwood's and the railway company, he made his way up to his office on the top floor of the building and looked out of the narrow window. There were two ravens perched on the sill.

While the evening newspapers had carried reports of the rioting in Huntingdon, none had mentioned the use of soldiers to quell the disturbances. No mention had been made of any loss of life suffered by the navvies, but one paper in particular had no doubt where the blame lay. It was just as Morris had predicted. '*This peaceful market town was thrown into the utmost consternation in consequence of one of those disgraceful outrages taking place amongst the navvymen arising out of an apparent disagreement with the good men of Huntingdon,*' the report had claimed. '*They then commenced a bloodthirsty, indiscriminate attack on the town and rioting of such magnitude ensued that special constables had to be sworn in to uphold the peace.*' The blatant untruthfulness of the piece made him want to find the journalist and ram the paper down his throat.

One of the clerks downstairs had told him that Jem Nash was processing bills in the main office, a large room at the back of the building on the floor below him where a hierarchy of rank and seniority determined who sat closest to the fire. But when he looked into the room, past the rows of clerks sitting at individual desks hunched over their ledger books copying invoices or fingering tall stacks of bills payable, he didn't see his younger assistant. It was barely two in the afternoon and already it seemed dark, the only light in the room produced by individual candles that burned on each of their desks, alongside the inkwells and goose feathers. A year ago, Pyke had tried to introduce oil and gas lamps but the clerks had objected to the foul smell. Aside from the cashiers who manned the tills in the banking hall, the main business of the bank was undertaken in this room, and whereas his partner, William Blackwood, knew all the clerks by name, Pyke didn't know a soul and found the room sombre and depressing. They hated him and loved Blackwood.

Nash was down a further flight of stairs in the banking hall and greeted Pyke with evident sheepishness. His boyish face was bruised and swollen, a purple welt the size of a grapefruit bulging from his cheek and making it hard for him to see out of one of his eyes. When he saw Pyke, he grinned as though it were of no consequence, and asked him what he wanted.

Pyke told him that Morris was coming in an hour and needed him to witness their signatures.

'Signatures for what?'

'A loan.' Pyke waited, and added, 'He wants to borrow some money but he wants it to go no farther than the two of us.'

Pyke started to walk away but turned around, anger rising within him like a gusty wind billowing into an unfurled sail.

Eighteen months earlier, Nash had visited Pyke in his office – he was then a lowly clerk at Lister's, another private bank in the city – with news that his bank was preparing to pass on or rediscount to

Blackwood's some seemingly sound bills of exchange that would quickly become worthless. Needing to bolster their own cash reserves Lister's had bought a rediscounted bill that was due to expire in two months; whereupon a Lancashire spinner was due to pay the bill's bearer twenty-five thousand pounds. Nash had informed him that his superiors were seeking to 'sell' on the bill to another bank because they had been told that the spinner was about to go out of business and wouldn't be able to meet his debt. (In which case, the bank or institution that had last endorsed the bill would be liable for the full debt.) Even then Pyke had been able to smell Nash's ambition and they struck a deal. If Nash could somehow gain access to the bank's vault and find a way of smuggling Pyke into the building, he would reward him with a five per cent stake in Blackwood's. Two months later, Nash had returned with a set of duplicate keys and the following night they had broken into the Lister's vault. Though bold, sometimes foolhardily so, Nash had little sense of why Pyke had wanted to gain access to the bank's safe. Certainly he had seemed confused when Pyke had spent much of the night counting money, rifling through bills of exchange and scribbling down information about outstanding loans.

'You mean we're not actually going to take a *thing*?' Nash had asked, bewildered, doubtless wondering why he'd gone to so much effort to procure wax imprints of the keys they'd needed to gain entry to the vault. He had already started to pack his leather satchel with coins.

'Why would I risk being caught with a few bags of stolen coins? I could be hung by the neck, and for what? The possibility of making a few hundred pounds.'

'There must be thousands here, not just a few hundred.'

It had been like watching a starving man enter a patisserie, only to be told that he couldn't touch a thing.

'We're going to put everything back exactly as we found it.'

'Then why did you make me go to the effort of stealing all those keys?' That had been further evidence of his petulance, though in fairness Pyke had already decided there was more he liked about Nash than disliked: even then it had felt as if he'd found a man whose ambition, determination, courage and flexible morality reminded Pyke of himself.

'Because we're not just going to steal a few coins and some

notes,' Pyke had said. 'We're going to steal the whole bank.'

He had enjoyed the younger man's reaction: the delicious truth finally dawning on him.

Pyke's inventory of the vault's contents had confirmed what he had suspected ever since Nash's initial revelations: Lister's had borrowed short, lent long (where the money was tied up in speculative investments) and kept too little in reserve.

A month later, and with some help from Pyke, Lister's closed its doors for the last time. Pyke had picked up the pieces, assimilating what remained of it into Blackwood's. A week after that, and in spite of concerns about Nash's inexperience, he'd come good on his promise and offered Nash a small stake in his business.

Still, it was Nash's gambling, rather than his inexperience, which had caused Pyke most worry and, though he had quickly displayed an acute aptitude for business and had rapidly learnt the rudiments of banking, his recklessness at the roulette tables had earned him an altogether less favourable reputation.

'So how much did you lose this time?' Pyke's booming voice echoed around the hall. They were closed for business but the cashiers were counting up inside their booths.

'I was *this* close to the biggest win of my life.' He held his thumb and index finger together until they almost touched and grinned.

'One hundred?'

Licking his lips, Nash looked around the hall. 'Couldn't we perhaps talk about this somewhere more private?'

'Did other people at the gaming house see you lose your money?'

Nash bowed his head and didn't answer.

'Then it's not a private matter, is it?' Pyke felt the blood rising in his neck. 'Was it more than a hundred?'

When Nash didn't answer him, Pyke slapped him on his bruised cheek.

The younger man winced and his eyes glowed with indignation. 'It's my business, not yours.'

'You're a partner in this bank. That means if you can't pay your debts, the person you owe money to can come after us.' He hit Nash again, this time on the other cheek and harder, his knuckles closed. 'More than this, you owe money to someone you're beholden to. It makes you weak and other people will sniff out your weakness and exploit it.'

In the booths the cashiers had stopped counting their coins and were watching the exchange.

'I'll settle my debts.'

This time Pyke almost lifted him by the throat and marched him across to one of the cashiers. 'Before you gamble away your own money, you can settle your debt with me.' Turning him around, Pyke pressed Nash's face against the iron grille of the booth and said, 'This gentleman here would like to withdraw a hundred pounds from his account. If he doesn't have the funds, I authorise you to take it out of his next quarterly drawings.'

Terrified, the cashier gathered up the money and, with trembling hands, passed the notes through the grille.

'That's for the business with Gold.' Pyke pocketed the money and wiped the palm of his hand on his coat. 'I want you to greet Morris here in the hall at three and show him up to my office.'

Glowering and humiliated, Nash nodded but said nothing.

TEN

They didn't make it back to Hambledon until five and it took a further half-hour to gather Emily, Felix and Jo together in order to make the short journey to Cranborne Park where, Morris assured Pyke, Marguerite and another guest, Abraham Gore, awaited them. Pyke knew Gore only by reputation and was curious to meet the man. During the journey from London, Morris had explained that Gore was one of his oldest friends; they'd known one another for thirty years.

To say that Gore was already a legend in London's world of business would have been a gross understatement. His story was one that fathers told their children in the hope of instilling in them grand ambitions and a hard-work ethic. As a younger man, Gore had inherited a country bank in Warwickshire; by the time he was thirty he'd opened a further ten branches throughout the West Midlands; by forty, he had extended his banking empire into Lancashire as well as moving his headquarters to one of the grandest addresses in the City. Nowadays, Gore's was not only the largest private bank in London, larger even than Rothschild's or Coutts: Gore had also opened subsidiary branches in Edinburgh, Brussels and Dublin.

The most curious detail about Gore's career, however, related to his personal life, or rather his lack of personal life. For years, he had been touted by society columns and gossip magazines as one of London's most eligible bachelors – he was said, by some, to be the nation's wealthiest businessman – but he had never taken a wife, nor shown any inclination to do so. Furthermore, throughout his time in the capital Gore had lived in comfortable, but by no means extravagant, circumstances, in a suite of chambers at the Richmond Hotel, paying just a hundred pounds a year for the privilege. He also owned a large estate in the Warwickshire countryside but his modest, even ascetic tastes and his apparent lack of interest in settling down with a wife had, rightly or wrongly, earned Gore a reputation as an eccentric.

Morris had greeted Emily and Felix warmly and told them he hoped they wouldn't be too uncomfortable in his rickety old carriage. In fact there was more than enough room for all of them and when the carriage came to a halt at the front steps of Morris's Palladian mansion, Felix was first out of the door, closely followed by Jo. Pyke and Morris alighted last and Pyke looked up towards the portico, where Marguerite had gathered Felix up into her arms. Next to her, an older man, whom Pyke presumed was Gore, smiled amiably and patted Felix gently on the head. When Pyke and Morris joined the party in the entrance hall, Marguerite had already introduced herself to Emily and only reluctantly passed Felix on to Jo. 'He's such a sweet, delightful boy,' Pyke heard her gush to Emily. He was uncomfortable about the whole idea of Emily meeting and perhaps even befriending his old flame, and vice versa. While Emily was formally introduced to Abraham Gore, Pyke took a moment to compare the two women in his mind. With her tall, slim figure and clear, unblemished skin, Emily was unquestionably beautiful, but in a natural way that stood in contrast with Marguerite's preened sophistication. And while Emily's preference for Empire waistlines and simple, loose-fitting dresses made her seem wilfully anachronistic, Marguerite's pale pink dress, laced tightly around the waist to accentuate her figure, reflected the very latest Parisian fashion.

When it was his turn, Pyke shook Marguerite's outstretched hand, neither of them meeting the other's stare, and then greeted Gore, who took both of his hands and squeezed them as though they were old friends. Gore's ruddy cheeks and beaming smile put Pyke in mind of his uncle, and he had something of Godfrey's warmth. The main difference between the men was that Gore's shiny head was apparently almost devoid of hair and perhaps to conceal or indeed to compensate for this, he wore a black top hat even inside the house. It matched his black frock-coat and black trousers. He looked even more like a banker than Pyke's partner, William Blackwood.

From the entrance hall, Morris led them into the drawing room, where a fire was burning in the grate and a collection of china cups and saucers had already been laid out on the polished mahogany table. Marguerite and Emily complimented each other on their dresses, while Morris, Gore and Pyke hovered at the threshold of the room. Felix, in the meantime, had raced up the main staircase and was being carried back down by Jo, trying to free himself from her grip. 'A spirited lad,' Gore said, smiling. 'I like to see young lads with spirit.'

'Your dress is so lovely and ... simple,' Marguerite was saying to Emily.

Taking Morris to one side, Pyke asked him very quietly whether everything was all right.

'Of course. Why shouldn't it be?' Morris said, glaring.

'You left my bank this afternoon with ten thousand pounds. Perhaps I have a right to be nervous.'

Morris gave him a hard stare and whispered, 'It ceased being your money when I signed those documents.' His look told Pyke he didn't want to discuss the matter any further and they both rejoined the group.

'Why are you wearing a hat inside the house?' Felix had just asked Gore, once Jo had put him down.

Laughing, Gore removed the hat and self-consciously arranged his few strands of hair. He handed it to Felix, who tried to put it on his own head, only to discover it was too large. Morris joined in the laughter and Felix, enjoying the attention, proceeded to repeat the trick.

Emily went across to rescue Gore from the attention of their son. As she did so, Pyke shared a brief glance with Marguerite and wondered whether she would let anything slip about their shared past. He also wondered why he hadn't said anything to Emily and whether Marguerite might exploit his silence in this regard, to try to embarrass him. He wondered, too, whether she had said anything to Morris about their past, deciding that she probably wouldn't have, and probably wouldn't allude to their liaison. Morris seemed to think she had fallen in love with the house and estate on their own merits and Marguerite wouldn't want to disabuse him of this notion. No, he was safe for the time being, but this thought didn't make him feel any more comfortable about the prospect of the next hour or two.

'Who would have thought it, eh?' Marguerite whispered, beside

Pyke. 'The two of us taking afternoon tea and pretending to behave like members of the aristocracy.'

'Is that all this is to you? A pretence?' Pyke muttered, without turning to face her.

'Why? Are you worried I'll say something out of turn?'

'It's not the time and place for this conversation,' he said, still not looking around at her.

'Doesn't your wife know that we used to fuck?'

'Her name's Emily.'

'A nice, proper, wholesome name.'

'And if Morris found out you had another motive for wanting this particular house and estate,' Pyke whispered, 'would he be so understanding?'

'Don't flatter yourself, Pyke.' Briefly Marguerite turned her head in his direction. 'I had other reasons for wanting to move here.'

Emily had gathered Felix up in her arms and was giving him an exaggerated kiss, the kind that unfailingly made him squeal and giggle, and for a moment they all watched the performance, Pyke feeling a brief moment of pride that he was Emily's husband and Felix's father. He glanced across at Marguerite and noticed that her eyes were fixed on Emily and Felix with a peculiar intensity and that her fists were tightened into small round balls. Having put Felix down, Emily started to chase after him and, squealing with delight, for this was one of his favourite games, he hared across the room, straight into Marguerite's arms. She tried to scoop him up and offer the boy the same kiss that Emily had given him, although with rather less success. In the process of trying to free himself from her grip his little fist accidentally caught her in the mouth and she let go of him. Felix landed awkwardly on the marble floor. For a moment, Pyke was certain the lad would burst into tears, and went to try to comfort him, but after a stunned silence Felix stood up a little gingerly and looked up at Marguerite, who was still trying to recover from the inadvertent punch she'd received. 'I'm sorry,' Felix said, almost in a whisper. 'Did I hurt you?' That was enough to take the sting out of the situation and Marguerite bent down, gave Felix a hug and said of course he hadn't hurt her. Soon Felix was running around the room, pursued by an out-of-breath, laughing Marguerite. By this point Emily was chatting with Morris and Gore and Pyke couldn't tell how she felt about being usurped, in their son's eyes at least, by another woman.

'I was just teasing Eddy here that, as a natural-born aristocrat, he can never quite know the *extent* of the pleasure that one experiences as a self-made man.' Gore turned to Pyke and gave him a good-natured wink. 'Perhaps you know a little of what I mean, sir.' They were standing in a semicircle around the blazing log fire.

'I'm always telling Emily that she doesn't know the value of money because she's never been without it.' Pyke had meant it as a joke but saw her thunderous expression and realised, too late, that he had revealed too much.

'I understand only too well the value that some men attach to the contents of their bank accounts.' Emily's tone was light and breezy but there was an edge to it as well.

'You disapprove of such a state of affairs?' Gore asked her, his eyebrows raised, a note of scepticism in his voice.

'I disapprove of excessive wealth being hoarded away in dusty old vaults by the lucky few while ordinary men and women barely have enough to feed and clothe their families.'

'Admirable sentiments but what might you consider to be … *excessive*? A hundred pounds? A thousand or perhaps even ten thousand pounds?' Gore asked, with a smile.

This time she turned to face him. 'If I told you I consider the wealth that one class derives from the toils of another to be parasitic in nature, you might be able to guess my answer.'

Morris chuckled, more from nerves, Pyke sensed, than because he found what she had just said amusing. 'Surely you can't object to the basic principle of risk and reward? The more a man risks, the more he deserves to be rewarded.'

Emily turned to him. 'Perhaps you'll agree that the most a man can risk is his own life.'

'Of course,' Morris said, quickly.

'Then what of the men who risk their lives every day to dig the tunnels through which the London-to-Birmingham trains will eventually run?' Emily looked over at Gore and folded her arms.

Silently Pyke kicked himself for not having remembered, until that moment, that Abraham Gore was also the chairman of the London and Birmingham Railway. Evidently, Emily had not been as slow on the uptake: from the first moment they'd been introduced, she had known who Gore was and what he did. Briefly he wondered *how* she'd known it and whether this knowledge had anything to do with her dealings with Julian Jackman.

'Are you suggesting that the navvy men are somehow unfairly rewarded for their labour?' Gore asked carefully.

'In comparison to the proprietors who have seen their investments *quadruple* in the last six months, yes, I am.' Emily paused for breath. 'I read in the newspaper that a tunnel near Watford collapsed last week. Ten men lost their lives.' She turned to Morris. 'Using your risk–reward model, and given the extreme risks these men faced, without complaint or fear, how much do you imagine they were rewarded?'

For a moment no one spoke. Marguerite, Felix and Jo had disappeared to another part of the house. Around the fireplace, Gore and Morris exchanged an awkward look and Pyke both felt for their discomfort and admired the way in which Emily had turned their words against them.

'Two shillings a day. Meanwhile, a moderately well-off clerk who has invested a small proportion of his savings, let's say ten pounds, in London and Birmingham stock – someone whose risk is, in relative terms, quite small – would've seen, in the space of this last month, his ten-pound investment double in value. In other words he has made a profit of ten pounds for doing very little while the workers who continue to risk their lives make only a miserly two shillings a day. To me, that doesn't seem fair. But perhaps I've missed something here that your more enlightened minds can put me right on?'

Pyke couldn't help but smile. She'd posed a question that couldn't be answered, at least not without Gore revealing his rapaciousness or hypocrisy.

Gore cleared his throat. 'If I told you of the sleepless nights I've had since those poor men tragically lost their lives, would it make a difference?' The sorrow and humility in his voice sounded genuine enough. 'Or that I've done my very best to ensure that all of the dead men enjoy, though it's probably the wrong word to use, proper funerals and that their families receive a full month of their wages?' It was as good a response as he could have made in the circumstances.

'I think you miss my point, sir,' Emily said, gently. 'I am not trying to berate you personally and I'm sure the arrangements you made were greatly appreciated.'

'Your point was a more general one, then?' Gore replied. 'You, perhaps, believe labour should be the sole parent of wealth?'

'I believe labour should receive its due reward and that workers have the right to the full product of their labours.'

'Turning Ricardo, the economic philosopher of industrial capitalism, against his own, eh?' Gore seemed to be enjoying the exchange now.

'If Ricardo is happy to concede that capital is little more than accumulated labour, then who am I to argue?'

Gore nodded, almost as though he agreed with the point. 'Perhaps I could ask you another question, my dear. Do you think the railways that Eddy and I are trying to build are, per se, a bad thing?'

Pyke could see where Gore intended to go with this and wondered whether Emily would be able to stand her ground.

'Properly funded by the state, I don't believe they would bring *harm* to the nation, if that's what you mean.'

'So you believe they should be paid for out of general taxation?'

Emily nodded, and glanced across at Pyke.

'Then what should the exchequer sacrifice in order that we should be able to pay for the railways? Or perhaps taxes should be raised for everyone?'

'If the well-off paid more, would that be such a terrible thing?'

Gore shrugged. 'Did you know that more than twenty million pounds has already been invested in the construction of a railway network in this country? That figure would represent almost a quarter of our government's total yearly expenditure. Think of the cuts that would have to be made elsewhere to come up with that sum. I don't believe the state can afford to pay for the railways. Which leaves us with a dilemma, because unless we can persuade private individuals to dip into their own pockets, then it stands to reason that we won't have a railway. And to do this requires a system of inducements. To put it bluntly, my dear, without the risk-and-reward model Eddy mentioned a few moments ago, nothing at all would get built or manufactured. And we, as a country, would quickly return to the Stone Age.'

'But you're assuming, are you not, that railways, or anything else for that matter, are given life to by capital, when in fact these things, in reality, are created by the hands of men and women.'

It was an admirable response and one that left Gore struggling for something more to say. In the end, he started to laugh, a great, booming laugh that carried across the room, and said, 'My God, you're a formidable woman. *Formidable*. You've more than met your match here I'd wager,' he added, looking at Pyke. When no one rushed in to say anything, he continued, 'But isn't this exactly what makes this country so great? That we can freely and without fear of repercussion air our differences?'

'You believe we should be able to say what we like about whoever we like?' Pyke asked.

'Within reason. I mean, if someone deliberately set out to cause offence to someone else, that person's rights would be to have protected too.'

'Perhaps you've heard of my uncle, the publisher Godfrey Bond?'

Gore scratched his chin and thought for a moment. 'I don't believe I have. What kind of things does he publish?'

'A scandal sheet and an unstamped newspaper. He's currently being hounded by the law because, and I'm guessing here, he poses a threat to the reputations of the upper classes.'

'Ah.' Gore's eyes narrowed slightly. He glanced across at Morris and wetted his lips.

'Not the kind of free speech you'd be comfortable defending?'

That appeared to offend Gore. 'You jump to the wrong con-clusion, sir. I wouldn't rush to celebrate such low publications, but I would always defend their right to exist in the first place.'

'And a worker's right to form a union and takes oaths of allegiance to that union?' Emily asked quickly.

That brought a lid down on the conversation and, for a short while, no one seemed to know what to say.

'Tea, anyone?' Morris interrupted.

'That would be splendid,' Gore said, evidently relieved that someone had changed the subject.

'And I was going to say,' Morris added, while he poured out the tea, 'I'm hosting a charity ball at the Colosseum in Regent's Park in honour of Marguerite's birthday tomorrow evening. I know it's short notice, but I'd love it if all of you could be there to celebrate with us.'

He looked at Pyke and Gore but it was Emily who answered

him first. 'I'm afraid I'll be away from the capital.' She hesitated and looked at Gore. 'There's an event I have to attend in Birmingham.'

Gore remained silent but Morris piped up, 'Really, my dear? What kind of event?'

'To speak at a meeting organised by the GNCTU.'

'Eh?' Morris handed her a cup of tea, not having really heard what she'd said.

'The Grand National Consolidated Trades Union of Great Britain and Ireland.'

'You actually speak at such events?' Gore asked, apparently surprised, a note of caution in his tone.

'I heard her address a similar meeting in the East End,' Pyke said. 'She had the men cheering on their feet.' Out of the corner of his eye, he saw Emily blush with gratitude and felt his pride swell further. A pulse of desire rose within him and he fought to keep his expression neutral.

'And the men don't mind, being addressed by a ...?'

'A woman?' Emily offered. 'The daughter of an aristocrat?'

Gore smiled at her remark and asked them all to excuse him for a few moments, while he visited the necessary house.

They talked about inconsequential matters while they took their tea, but when after a further ten minutes there was still no sign of Marguerite, Jo and Felix, Emily proposed that, since it was nearing Felix's bedtime and it would take them a good half-hour to ride back to Hambledon, someone should perhaps go and find them. She volunteered herself but Morris wouldn't hear of it and assured her he would retrieve them at once. But when he returned five minutes later, a look of unease on his face, saying that he hadn't managed to locate them as yet, Pyke and Emily exchanged a worried glance, Pyke saying he would look for them outside, Emily that she would join Morris in searching for them inside the house. For his part, Morris seemed embarrassed more than worried, that Marguerite had disappeared for such a long time, and taken two of their guests. As he put on his coat and headed into the garden, Pyke thought about the scene he'd witnessed a few weeks earlier, the burial, and wondered again just how stable Marguerite was. But he didn't believe, for a moment, that she would try to harm their son.

He didn't find them in the garden, though, and didn't think Marguerite would have taken them farther afield into the estate.

Not with Jo there, too. Jo knew that Felix wasn't dressed for such a venture.

Back in the house, Pyke traced his path to the drawing room, where a now clearly agitated Emily was pacing up and down while Morris and Gore tried to reassure her that the women and the boy would appear from some 'nook' or 'cranny' at any minute.

'No sign of them?' he asked.

Emily shook her head. 'Nor in the garden?'

'I'm afraid not.'

'They will be here somewhere,' Morris said, sounding simultaneously angry and embarrassed.

'Where could they be?' Emily stared at Pyke. 'They've been gone for almost an hour now, haven't they? And Felix has only just recovered from a dreadful cold. If she's taken him outside ...' She paused and added, 'Why would a complete stranger insist on throwing herself at our child?'

'She isn't a complete stranger,' Pyke replied, trying not to show his concern. 'And remember Jo is with them.'

'I'm sure my wife hasn't *thrown* herself at your lad,' Morris said, sounding a little hurt. 'And, to be quite frank, he would be perfectly safe whether your nursemaid was with them or not.'

'If they're not in the house,' Emily said, ignoring Morris's intervention, 'and not in the garden either, then where are they?'

Morris didn't know what to say and muttered something under his breath.

Gore heard something first and sprang up from his armchair. 'There; that'll be them.' He sounded as relieved as any of them.

They looked around and from a door at the other end of the room Felix appeared, closely followed by Marguerite and finally Jo, who immediately gave Emily an awkward, apologetic look. Felix ran across the room to greet Emily, who lifted him up into her arms, Felix explaining that Marguerite had taken them up to the attic, where there were all these toys and games. Pyke exchanged a brief look with Marguerite, who seemed, as far as Pyke could tell, almost pleased by the worry she'd caused. Morris shot her the dirtiest of looks and once again apologised for delaying their departure. The carriage was waiting for them at the front, he assured them, and it was ready to leave as soon as they were.

Having said their farewells, and having made a point of not taking up the matter in front of their hosts, Emily turned on Jo once they were safely ensconced in the carriage.

'I tried to insist we rejoin the rest of you in the drawing room,' Jo said, almost in tears, 'but she wouldn't have it. And Felix was so happy playing with all of the toys ...'

'Didn't you suppose I'd be worried?' Emily said, shaking her head. 'After all, you were gone for almost an hour.'

Reddening, Jo stared down at her shoes and mumbled another apology.

'And that's another thing,' Emily snapped. 'Why does *she* have all these children's toys and what are they doing in the attic?'

Felix was sitting on Pyke's lap and had started to doze off. He was exhausted and Pyke kissed him on the top of his head.

'I don't know if you noticed it too,' Emily said, this time to Pyke, 'but she kept on staring at you. That is, when she wasn't fawning over my son.'

'I didn't notice.'

'Well, I did.' She turned to Jo. 'Did you get that sense, too?'

'She seemed very determined to keep us up there in the attic.'

Emily shook her head, as though Jo's innocuous remark confirmed her suspicion. 'You had a brief conversation just after we arrived, Pyke. What did she say to you then?'

'I don't remember having a *conversation*.' He looked at Emily and shrugged. 'She might have said something about the cold weather and the fact that the nights are drawing in.'

'Well, I can't go to her party,' Emily said, folding her arms, 'and I hope you don't go, either.'

'I hadn't given the matter any thought.'

'Well, I don't want you to go. I can't stop you, of course, but there's something about that woman I don't trust ...'

'You don't trust her or you don't trust me?'

Jo looked away, embarrassed that they were talking this way in front of her, and Emily stared out of the window, making a point of not answering his question.

Pyke woke up while it was still dark outside, the treetops swaying in the wind and rain beating against the windowpanes. His body was lathered with sweat and his heart was pumping. He sat upright and was considering returning to his own bed when Emily asked him what the matter was.

'What did you make of Abraham Gore?' Pyke said, still puzzling over something in his mind. When she didn't answer him straight away, he added, 'You knew right away he was chairman of the Birmingham railway, didn't you?'

Emily pulled the blanket over her shoulders. 'Is that why you've been tossing and turning all night?'

'How did you recognise him so quickly?'

'He's a well-known figure. I've seen him at charity events.'

'And it's got nothing to do with your association with Julian Jackman?'

'Why bring Julian into this?' Emily waited for a moment. 'You didn't tell me you fought alongside the navvies in Huntingdon.' She was sitting up and ran her finger across the side of his cheek. 'Is that how you got this bruise?'

'The fact you know means Jackman's returned to London,' he said, not bothering to temper his indignation.

The silence hung between them like an invisible barrier.

'It's obtuse and a little sad,' Emily said, eventually, 'that I have to learn about my husband's exploits from another man.'

'And that I have to learn about my wife's fortitude in the face of a crew of strike-breakers from the same source.'

Briefly they lay there in silence, listening to the wind buffeting the windows. 'So what was Jackman doing in Huntingdon?' Pyke asked.

'What were *you* doing there? You told me you were attending a business meeting in Cambridge.'

'The disturbances you read about were orchestrated. Until now I suspected a local landowner, Sir Horsley Rockingham. He's dead set against the railway crossing his land. But it suddenly struck me that Gore has also got a good reason for wanting to damage the prospects of the Grand Northern.'

Emily was quiet for a moment. 'Because he's in charge of a rival venture?'

'If the Grand Northern fails to reach York, or has its terminus at, say, Cambridge, it'll leave the London and Birmingham Railway with a monopoly on freight and passenger traffic between the capital and all of the Midlands and the North.'

'That could be worth a lot of money.'

'I know.'

A while later, just before she drifted back to sleep, Emily whispered, 'Pyke?' And when he turned over to face her, she added, 'Does this mean we're on the same side?'

Lying on his back, Pyke stared up at the ceiling and listened as the rain continued to beat against the windowpanes, thinking about the question she had just asked and what side, if any, he was on. Soon he could hear her quiet snores, but Pyke knew that sleep was beyond him and after a few minutes he slid out from under the sheets without waking her up and went to retrieve the laudanum that he kept hidden in a cabinet next to his own bed.

ELEVEN

At a quarter past seven the following evening, Pyke met Jem Nash in the banking hall. Having apparently put their altercation of the previous afternoon behind them, they had agreed to share a hackney carriage to the Colosseum in Regent's Park where Morris was hosting his charity ball.

While Pyke hadn't bothered to change his frock-coat and trousers – he had always disliked evening wear and a shirt with a frilly front was the only concession he'd made – Nash's outfit was typically extravagant: a knee-length grey woollen coat with shiny brass buttons over an embroidered waistcoat made of white cotton and a matching white linen neckcloth wrapped several times around his throat and tied in a loose knot.

'Tell me. How's William seemed these last few days?' Pyke asked as they left the building.

'He sulked a bit after the last meeting but he seemed all right when I talked to him this morning. I think he's still worried about the scale of our debt, though.' He waited for a moment. 'You don't think we're in trouble, do you?'

'Of course not.'

They'd walked through Sweeting's Alley to Cornhill, the Royal Exchange directly in front of them. Pyke was looking for a cab to hail and didn't see the elderly woman until the last moment, by which time she'd taken his hand and stripped off his glove. He tried to shoo her away but her grasp was surprisingly strong and she seemed intrigued by what she'd seen in his palm. Under the hissing gas lamp, he could only see her beak and jaw, since the rest of her face and head was covered with a black lace bonnet, but her features looked foreign. Perhaps she was some kind of gypsy. While Pyke wanted to push her away and find a cab, when she finally looked up at him, there was something in her eyes which unsettled him.

'I can see you're a powerful fellow, sir, and you've achieved great things but the signs ...'

Pyke tugged his hand away and went to put on his glove. 'Move out of the way, you dishclout.'

'I fear a terrible tragedy lies ahead.'

That stopped him dead. She'd hooked him and she knew it. 'What do you mean, a tragedy?'

'If you'll cross my palm with silver ...'

Pyke felt himself relax. She was just a con artist, someone trying to trick him out of a few coins.

'I can see you've a beautiful wife and a young son, five years old.' Her accent was indistinct but it had a lilting, almost hypnotic quality.

'How did you know that?' Pyke stared down into her wizened face.

Next to him, Nash tried to shove her to one side, but Pyke held out his arm. 'What about my wife and child?'

'Come on, Pyke. She made a lucky guess. That's how these harridans make their money.'

'You live in a big house in the country,' she said, closing her eyes, perhaps trying to conjure an image of it.

'She knew Felix's age.' Pyke held her by the wrist. 'How did you know his age?'

'Leave her be, Pyke,' Nash said, stepping between them and giving her the chance to wriggle free. 'The old hag's just playing with you. It's the oldest trick in the book.'

'What tragedy?' he called out, as she darted behind them into Sweeting's Alley. A few passers-by stopped to look at him.

The old woman disappeared into the darkness, moving quickly in spite of a limp. But later, as they rode in silence, Pyke couldn't shake the feeling that the old woman had known more than he'd allowed her to say, and that he'd just been afforded a glimpse of his own unpleasant future.

A gargantuan edifice overlooking Regent's Park, the Royal Colosseum was less a gladiatorial arena in the Roman sense of the word than a modern pleasure palace where the middle classes could go and wonder at the 'Panorama of London', which occupied an acre of canvas and stretched around the inside of the central rotunda. Morris's charity ball was held on the ground floor under a tent-like roof that prevented people from seeing the panorama but partygoers could either walk up to the viewing promenade using a spiral staircase or take the 'ascending room', an iron cage powered by steam that transported them up to the spectacle without any physical exertion. Pyke left Nash in the rotunda and walked up the circular staircase to the viewing promenade, where Morris was greeting his guests.

Immediately Pyke could tell that Morris was inebriated. His eyes were bloodshot and unfocused and his hands were shaking more than Pyke remembered. He didn't know the older man well enough to tell whether this was in character or not, but he had to wait a full five minutes for Morris to acknowledge him and another five before he came to greet him. Briefly Pyke wondered whether the older man was still smarting from Emily's implied criticisms of Marguerite.

'I'm glad you could make it,' Morris said, formally. 'And I'm just sorry your wife couldn't be here with us, too.'

Pyke acknowledged Morris's conciliatory remark. He had argued again with Emily before she had left for the Midlands earlier that morning. He hadn't wanted her to travel on her own but had been powerless to stop her.

'I had a thought about what happened in Huntingdon.'

That drew a weary groan. 'Can't you leave it for tonight?'

'If the Grand Northern terminates at Cambridge, it means the Birmingham railway will have a monopoly on freight and passenger traffic between London, the Midlands and the North. That could be worth a huge amount of money.'

Morris removed his spectacles and rubbed his eyes. 'I hope you're not suggesting Abraham had anything to do with that terrible business.'

'Why not? He's the chairman of the Birmingham railway, isn't he?'

'As I told you yesterday, Pyke, he's also my oldest and best friend,' Morris said, with a scowl.

Pyke looked around at the promenade, still thinking about the old gypsy who had approached him outside the bank. 'Friend or not friend, Gore will stand to make a small fortune if your railway goes no farther than Cambridge.'

Morris shook his head angrily. 'As you know, I've invited Abraham to the ball. I don't want you peppering him with awkward questions, either.' With inebriation came a belligerence that Pyke hadn't seen before.

He waited for a moment, looking into Morris's rheumy eyes. 'When someone tried to kill me, the business in Huntingdon ceased to be just your problem. I'll do what I think is necessary.'

They were the last words he'd spoken to Morris that evening.

The 360-degree panorama replicated the view from the top of St Paul's in painstaking detail and was an impressive feat in its own right. Apparently the artist, Thomas Homer, had spent weeks in a cabin above the dome at St Paul's, sketching the view in preparation. But Pyke couldn't work out why people would pay money to see a painting of a view that they could witness for themselves, just by scaling Wren's mighty dome.

'Look, over there you can see the market where my parents once plied their trade.' Pyke turned around suddenly, surprised to see Marguerite next to him. She was pointing towards New Cut on the panorama. She stared at him with her cool eyes, her shimmering crêpe dress nearly filling up the cramped promenade with its puffed sleeves and flounced skirt.

'As a child, I used to love the sight of that market at night, the candles and tallow dips twinkling among the fruit and vegetables.' She wound her little finger around a coil of strawberry-blonde hair that had fallen on to her face. 'But I can also remember the stink just as well. I like to think it taught me not to be nostalgic, to see things for what they are.'

They were standing at the end of the viewing promenade and beneath them was a sheer drop of a hundred feet on to the tented roof that hid the panorama from the guests on the ground floor.

'You always did have a knack for stripping away other people's pretensions.'

Marguerite joined him at the railing. 'Your wife was angry at me for taking your son away from her yesterday, wasn't she?'

'I think she was surprised you were gone for as long as you were.'

'And you? Were you angry with me, too?' she asked, flirtatiously.

'What do you want me to say, Maggie? That I lay awake last night thinking about you?'

'You're here, aren't you? Without your wife, who I'm told is off somewhere trying to help the needy.'

'She sends her apologies.'

'And her best wishes?' Marguerite asked, mocking.

'Is it so wrong that she cares about more than her appearance and what clothes she wears?'

But instead of responding angrily, Marguerite chuckled. 'Not all of us are cut out for sainthood. I would have thought you'd have appreciated that more than anyone. Just as I'm guessing you don't *really* believe in her attempts to improve the lot of the working man.'

'And why's that?' Pyke asked, gritting his teeth.

'Because, like me, you're a selfish bastard when it comes to it.'

'When it comes to what?'

Marguerite smiled, apparently pleased that she'd rattled him.

Pyke looked around for some sign of Morris. 'Did you know Edward's more than halfway to being drunk?'

'Yes, he's upset about something.'

'As in?'

'Is that any of your business?' she snapped at him. 'Look,' she added with a sigh, 'it's just difficult for Eddy to see the world as it really is; how ugly, cruel and deceptive people can be.'

'You make it sound like a weakness.' Pyke looked out at the panorama but could see the creaminess of her slender neck out of the corner of his eye.

'My first years in Paris weren't happy ones. I despised every man I slept with and I slept with a lot of men. Then I met Eddy. By then, my reputation, such as it was, was beyond salvation and I was past caring about it or myself. But Eddy didn't seem worried in the slightest by what I'd done and what other people said about me behind my back. It didn't matter to him because he only saw what he wanted to see. So you see, Pyke, I'm not suggesting his idealism is a weakness; just that I'd never known such unconditional acceptance, such gentleness and such goodness in a man.'

'Then why doesn't it sound like you're paying him a compliment?'

'I'm not sure what you mean. Unlike my younger self, I've come to value a good heart more than good looks.'

'Then I hope it's made you happy.' Turning to face her, he felt a jolt of excitement in his stomach.

'Can't you see it? I'm delirious.' Even as she said it, he could see the lines crease around her eyes.

Pyke was going to say something else but managed to bite his tongue. He gave her a nondescript shrug. 'For someone who no longer cares about looks, you appear to be attracting rather a lot of them this evening.'

Marguerite allowed a smile to settle on her lips as she gazed out at the panorama. 'You know as well as I do, this is a gathering of waifs and strays. Society types wouldn't come to anything as vulgar as a ball to celebrate my birthday, even if Eddy is a very well-respected businessman and the cause is a charitable one.' Her stare drifted back towards him. 'People like you and I will never be invited into the private homes of Park Lane and Mayfair.'

'Is that such a loss?'

She shrugged. 'I speak fluent French and can read Plato's *Republic* in Greek and yet some women still get up and leave when I walk into a room.' As she turned to go, her arm brushed against his sleeve and he smelled her; an earthy, intoxicating scent that took him back to his adolescence. 'Do you know something, Pyke?' she added, under her breath. 'I might have been unfaithful to my husband but I'll never leave him.'

Downstairs the ball was in full swing; the mini-orchestra were playing a piece by Mozart and the supper room had just been opened.

After helping himself to some food, Pyke looked around the room and his glance fell upon a slobbering, tawny-coloured mastiff straining at its leash. It was unusual, to say the least, that such an animal should be allowed into the building, especially at a formal function, and the dog's owner didn't seem ill dressed for the occasion in his cutaway coat, tan breeches and elastic-sided leather boots. There was something familiar about the man but it was the squat, muscular mastiff which first jogged Pyke's memory.

Both man and beast had been with Marguerite at the graveside in the grounds of Morris's estate.

And while he held the dog tightly on its leash, the man was amiably chatting with Abraham Gore.

'It's good to see you, Pyke,' Gore said, shaking Pyke's hand with a warmness he found disarming. Then he turned to his companion and said, 'Do forgive me, sir, but I've forgotten your name ...' He winced with embarrassment but the man didn't seem to mind. 'Jake Bolter,' he said, making a mock bow, 'and this here is Copper, a proper rum dog. Say hello to the nice gentl'man, Copper.'

The animal was an enormous creature with a square head, a short muzzle, a light fawn coat and a black mask around the eyes and nose. As it growled, a string of drool fell from its jaws, but it remained at Bolter's side.

Bolter was horribly disfigured, to the extent that it was hard to tell what age he might be or what he might have looked like before he was burnt. Instead of eyebrows, he had two slight dents above his bulging eyes, and what remained of the skin around his cheeks was raw and blistered, a thatch of scar tissue with the rough-hewn texture of pork rind.

'Mr Bolter was just educating me in the proper usage of cant,' Gore said, winking at Pyke. 'He's an ex-soldier, you see. He was just telling me his story. Actually it's rather tragic. His one real aim in life was to kill someone in the heat of battle. He claims he was something of a sharpshooter with the rifle. But he sustained a serious leg injury and even though his eyesight was perfectly fine they decided to give him an honourable discharge.'

Bolter grinned idiotically. 'I'm a hearty old cock. Mr Gore is quite correct – I did yearn to serve in His Majesty's infantry and get the chance to shoot some infidels – but I ain't never allowed injuries to damage my prospects.' His snuff-blackened nostrils flared with pride.

'Indeed,' Gore said dubiously, staring down at the mastiff. 'Where was it you said you worked?'

'Prosser's school for stray and homeless children in Tooting,' he said, proudly. 'I ain't shot the cat once since I started there.'

'Very good, *very* good,' Gore said, as though he were talking to a pet. 'And if I may be so bold, what is shooting the cat?'

'Vomiting through drunkenness,' Pyke said.

They both looked at him, surprised, but it was Gore who said, 'You understand this cant?'

Pyke glanced across at Bolter. 'If I heard someone referring to this man as a freebooter, I'd know what they were talking about.'

Bolter absorbed the insult silently. 'Then you'll also know that to "pike" means to run away.'

Pyke looked down at the mastiff, wondering again why it had been allowed into the Colosseum.

'See? That's stopped the cull's blubber, ain't it?' Bolter said, more to the dog than Gore.

Gore seemed unhappy about the sudden air of tension and tried to laugh. 'I find it all delightful and very inventive. If I wanted to indicate I was hungry, I'd say my guts are beginning to think my throat's been cut. Is that right?'

'And if you were cheating a friend,' Pyke said, trying to catch Gore's stare, 'you'd be gulling him.'

Gore turned to Bolter. 'It was really delightful to make your acquaintance, sir. But perhaps you could leave us for a moment?'

Bolter cleared his throat and bowed his head. 'Of course, cock. My cup is dry and I need some grog to meller the red lane.' He nodded at Pyke and said, 'Gemmen,' before leading the mastiff away.

'It's quite beyond me why our gracious host would permit such a ghastly creature to join the celebrations,' Gore said, shaking his head, leaving Pyke to wonder whether he was referring to Bolter or the dog. 'But it's good to see you again, Pyke. In fact, there was something I wanted to tell you, but from the look on your face I'd say you have something to say to me first.'

Pyke looked into his genial face. 'I travelled with Morris to Cambridge and on to Huntingdon.'

'I know. I hope you don't mind. Edward told me about the trouble and, of course, I read about it in the newspapers. Terrible business.'

'What's terrible? The fact the townsmen acted like lawless vigilantes? Or that a handful of navvies were forced to jump from a bridge into the Ouse and probably didn't survive?'

'All loss of life is unfortunate but disregard for the law in this age is unacceptable, too.'

'In this age or any age?'

'The law and the market are the bedrocks of our civilisation. The law governs our actions and the market allocates resources. If either one fails, the whole of society fails. It may be a simple view of the world but it's one I ascribe to.'

An uneasy silence hung between them.

'But the problems facing the Grand Northern in Huntingdon will directly benefit the Birmingham railway, won't they?'

Gore seemed puzzled. 'I'm not sure I follow your logic.'

'If the Grand Northern terminates at Cambridge, as now seems possible, it'll leave your railway with a monopoly on passenger and freight traffic between London and all points north.'

Gore stared at him for a moment, trying to comprehend what he'd just suggested. 'And you think I might have had something to do with the trouble in Huntingdon?'

'I'm looking into *everyone* who may or may not be involved.'

That seemed to placate him a little. 'If this business is permitted to go unchecked, it'll undermine the Birmingham railway just as surely as the Grand Northern.' He waited for a moment, unsure what to say next.

'But the violence in Huntingdon didn't just happen. The navvies were deliberately provoked and the townsmen were waiting for them to attack.'

'Then I deplore what happened and would encourage you to take whatever actions you can to bring the culprits to book.'

'And if I need your co-operation in this task, you'll give it to me?' Pyke asked.

'If the law's been flouted, and it would seem from your assessment of the situation that it has, then I'll do everything in my power to help bring the malefactors to punishment. Remember, Edward is one of my oldest friends and, while we might represent competing interests, I would never do anything to compromise our friendship. I hope you understand that.'

While Pyke assessed Gore's response in his mind, the older man added, 'I'm not saying I support these radicals. That would be obtuse. If you'll excuse me for saying so, I think their ideas pose a real threat to the stability of our country, but if they protest within the law, I am content to give them their dues.'

'As the Tolpuddle six recently found out, the law isn't as impartial as you seem to imagine.'

Gore nodded, acknowledging the point. 'You seem like an educated man. Perhaps you've heard of an artist called Hieronymous Bosch.'

'Indeed I have.'

'You know his work?' Gore asked, seemingly delighted by this prospect. 'I think the two of us have more in common than we'd like to admit. Self-made men with a liking for gloomy art.'

Pyke couldn't help but smile. There was something infectious about Gore's good-natured enthusiasm. 'Were you thinking about a particular painting?'

'*The Ship of Fools*. Perhaps you know it?'

Nodding, Pyke said that he was aware of the painting.

'It's how I see this alliance between the radicals and the working man. Everyone trapped on a rudderless boat, no work ethic, no hope, just drifting slowly, inexorably, into oblivion.'

'I thought it better described the experience of being a shareholder,' Pyke replied. 'Stupid, greedy people, condemned by their own self-delusion to chase after something that'll always lie beyond their grubby reaches.'

But then Gore surprised him. Instead of taking offence, he broke into a hearty laugh and slapped Pyke on the back. 'That's a good one.' He continued to laugh. 'I like it. I like it a lot.'

Pyke waited until his smile had disappeared before he said, 'At the risk of causing offence, perhaps I should ask you a more direct question.'

Gore took out a handkerchief and started to mop his face. 'You don't strike me as the kind of fellow who cares whether he causes offence or not.' He stopped what he was doing and looked up at Pyke. 'But to pre-empt what might be an awkward moment, can I just repeat what I said earlier. Edward is my friend.'

'I didn't think there were any friends in business,' Pyke said, warming to the older man, in spite of his suspicions.

'I'm a simple man with a simple philosophy of life. I do what I do because it will hopefully make me richer but I also hope that my activities will benefit others. Take the railway, as an example. I expect to profit from the venture, of course, but so will the proprietors who have risked their savings and who will, I hope, see a favourable return on their investment. And if they benefit, so too will the butcher, the baker and the candlestick maker who depend on their custom. And let us not forget the navvies who get paid for the work they perform and who spend their wages in the public house, thereby benefiting the landlord. And most important of all is the railway itself. A safe, fast and reliable mode of travel; even the flintiest of hearts would be hard pressed to deny the general utility of such an enterprise.'

'My wife certainly wouldn't agree with those sentiments,' Pyke said, still trying to determine what he thought about Gore and whether his last comment had been disloyal to Emily.

'But you, as a businessman, can appreciate them?'

Pyke shrugged but said nothing.

'I'm pleased we've had this conversation, Pyke. I've admired what you've done at Blackwood's for a while now and I felt we got off on the wrong foot yesterday.' He held up his hand. 'I didn't take offence but you seemed to imply that my defence of the right to free speech was somehow calculated.'

'I didn't mean to cause offence,' Pyke said, choosing his words carefully. 'But it's rare to find someone in your position willing to defend *everyone*'s right to the freedom of speech.'

Gore bowed his head, accepting the explanation. 'I don't know exactly why but I felt it necessary to prove myself to you. I'm a man with a few political connections and I put them to good use today.' His eyes were shining and his lips moist. 'Your uncle's legal problems have been taken care of.'

This was the last thing that Pyke expected him to say and for a moment he was too stunned to respond. 'Just like that?' was all he managed in the end.

'I had a few sharp words with the magistrate in question ...'

'Bellows?'

Nodding, Gore broke into a smile; clearly the memory of this exchange gratified him. 'A nasty piece of work, I'll grant you, but with a few political connections, in spite of his pompous, self-aggrandising ways. The request to drop the matter, which I presented to him, was signed by Russell, the Home Secretary.' Gore began to chuckle. 'In fact, it wasn't really a request. The chief magistrate huffed and puffed for a while but in the end he knew he was a beaten man. It would seem he's desperate to ingratiate himself to men like Russell: men who will decide whether he assumes charge of the bench of the Central Criminal Court at Old Bailey when the Right Honourable Charles Lord Tenterden retires at the end of this year.'

'I'm still not sure why you felt the need to do it,' Pyke stammered, trying to work it out for himself, 'but I'm certainly grateful to you.'

'I did it because I like you, Pyke. I see a little of myself in you. And I didn't want you to think badly of me. I wanted you to know I put my money where my mouth is. Who knows? One day you might be in a position to return the favour.' He smiled kindly at him and added, 'Now if you'll excuse me, I should pay my respects to the host and hostess.'

As Gore moved off to join Morris, Pyke thought about their encounter and what, if anything, it told him about the man's real character.

But that was not Pyke's final interaction with Gore that night. A little later in the evening, requiring a place to urinate, Pyke followed a well-worn path to a row of huts at the rear of the building. His tug on one of the doors was perhaps stronger than it needed to be, because the flimsy lock gave way, and he found himself staring at Gore, breeches around his ankles, ruddy cheeked, straddling one of the young serving girls from behind. Gore's hips wiggled in an ungainly fashion as he thrust himself at the woman's arse, her face bowed towards the stinking cess pool beneath them. Her eyes were shut and barely registered the interruption. But Gore looked up, saw who it was and offered Pyke a subtle wink, before carrying on with his business as though nothing had happened. Pyke closed the door and left them to their respective fates.

He found Bolter by the table of food in the supper room, feeding a boiled egg to his dog.

'How do you know the hosts?'

Bolter licked his fingers and patted the mastiff on its head. 'Is that any business of yours?'

'You're an acquaintance of the wife rather than the husband.'

Bolter seemed surprised Pyke knew this but his face remained composed. 'She's a generous lady. Mr Prosser's school couldn't do without her and the like.'

Pyke nodded, a moment's silence passing between them. 'How did you get your burns?'

Bolter's eyes narrowed. He tugged the mastiff's leash and muttered, 'Copper here needs the necessary house. You'll have to excuse me.'

Pyke was thinking about going after him when he noticed Jem Nash slip into the room through a door used by the servants. He smoothed his hair back using the palms of his hands and helped himself to some food from the table. Marguerite walked through the same door a few moments later, arranging her hair. She looked flushed, the colour rising in her cheeks.

Pyke joined his assistant at the table and, for a while, they watched Marguerite in silence.

'She's quite a specimen, isn't she?'

'Who?' Nash looked at him, frowning.

'Morris's wife.'

Nash sniffed. 'A bit old for me.' But he seemed flustered, and Pyke wondered whether something had taken place between him and Marguerite.

'I knew her when we were both much younger.'

A shimmer of interest passed over Nash's otherwise dull stare.

'Back then she was just plain old Maggie Shaw, except there was nothing plain or old about her.'

'Did you fuck her?'

Pyke looked at his assistant and smiled. 'Straight to the point, eh?'

'I can see why you might have wanted to …' Nash paused, as though not sure what else to say.

'But?'

'But nothing.'

Pyke didn't believe Nash held grudges but wondered whether he was still secretly rankled by their encounter in the banking hall. 'I was young and selfish. I used her, in a way I'm not proud of. But I found out she was a cold fish, too.'

Nash regarded him sceptically. 'Why are you telling me this?'

'Just be careful, Jem. That's all I'm saying.'

'Be careful of what?'

Pyke was about to answer him when he reached down to touch his chain and keys and discovered they were missing.

Nash must have seen his expression change because he asked what the matter was. 'Someone's palmed my keys.'

'What keys?'

'The key to the bank vault and …' Pyke hesitated and kicked himself. He couldn't possibly explain the worth of the other. Nor could he ever replace it.

'Are you certain someone took it?'

'As opposed to me losing it?'

Nash shrugged. 'If someone was going to try and break into our vault, they'd need at least five different keys.'

Pyke nodded and felt himself start to relax. Nash was right. But still, the idea that someone had picked his pocket upset him. He thought about the ravens. The tiny key that Emily had given him in the condemned cell at Newgate all those years ago was part of the same thing. Somehow not having it made Pyke feel exposed, vulnerable. He tried to think who might have stolen it. He'd had the keys when he arrived back in London, that was for certain. The old gypsy perhaps? Then he remembered what Freddie Sutton had said about his young daughter. A real magpie. The same little girl who had hugged his leg ...

'Say goodnight to Morris for me,' Pyke said, already moving towards the rotunda, wondering whether Sutton's daughter had really palmed his keys.

'Do you want me to check on the vault?' Nash called out.

Turning around, he shook his head. 'That won't be necessary. But thanks for the offer.'

Outside, Pyke strode down the steps from the Doric portico, looking for a hackney coachman. He saw Marguerite standing with her back to him, staring out into the park.

'Maggie?'

She spun around with a start and tried to hide the fact that she'd been crying. Her arms were covered with gooseflesh.

'What's the matter?' he asked, gently.

Sniffing, Marguerite stared out into the darkness. 'I had a blazing row with Eddy. He's drunk as a lord. I have to leave him alone when he gets like this. He won't listen to reason.'

'I did try and warn you.'

She looked away and shrugged, her face streaked with the traces of her own tears. 'People aren't always who you think they are.'

'And does that apply to your husband ...' Pyke waited for a moment and added, 'Or me?'

The tip of her tongue brushed against her bottom lip. 'Why didn't you come with me to France all those years ago?'

Pyke stared at her and sighed, not sure what to say. 'It would never have worked out, Maggie.'

She smiled at his use of her old name. 'Perhaps.' She took a step towards him and stopped. 'The fact I won't ever leave Eddy doesn't mean I don't desire other men.'

Pyke felt his throat tighten. 'Why are you telling me this?'

This time she didn't answer but took another step towards him.

He could smell her, a sharp tangy scent that reminded him of lemons. 'Eddy and I haven't shared a bed in three years.'

Pyke looked around for a hackney coachman. 'I'm going home to my wife.'

A look of disappointment, even bewilderment, registered on her face, and then she gathered up her shawl and started to walk back towards the portico.

'Why did you insist to your husband that you wanted to live at Cranborne Park?' he called out after her.

But she continued on her way as though he hadn't spoken or she hadn't heard him.

TWELVE

It was late, well after ten o'clock, by the time the carriage pulled up in front of the cottage shared by Freddie Sutton and his family. The coachman hadn't wanted to venture into Spitalfields and had been persuaded only by the offer of a guinea. Pyke instructed the coachman to wait and banged on the front door. When there was no reply, he repeated the act, but still no one answered. It had started to rain and in the night sky the yellow moon, suddenly visible though a mass of low clouds, shone like a gargoyle. Pyke walked around to the window and peered into the room. In the neighbouring cottage he could hear a man and a woman arguing. There were no candles burning in the room and it was difficult to see anything through the broken, smeared pane. He tapped lightly on the window but nothing and no one stirred inside. A dog barked, and in the bushes he heard something move, but then it went silent.

Walking back to the front door, he knocked again, only louder this time, and then tried the handle, to see whether it was unlocked. The door swung open and he called out Sutton's name. Still no one answered. Treading carefully, he stepped into the room and waited for his eyes to adjust to the darkness, but he didn't have to see anything to know what had happened. The smell was enough. On certain occasions, as a Bow Street Runner, he had visited the underground slaughterhouses in the vicinity of Smithfield and the sweet, putrid stench of fresh blood and ripe flesh had imprinted itself on his memory. Taking a box of matches from his pocket, he took one and struck it against the wall. The match exploded, temporarily filling the room with light. That was when he saw them, Freddie Sutton and his wife, propped up against an overturned ale barrel. Their throats had been cut and the floor around them had turned crimson with their blood. Pyke tried to cover his nose and mouth with a handkerchief, but too late. He felt the revulsion build in his stomach and then rise up to his throat until he could taste it in the back of his throat. The match died in his hand but not before he saw blood glistening on the toes of his leather boots. He retched but nothing came up.

Another match confirmed what he had just seen. Freddie Sutton and his wife had been murdered, their throats slit with a sharp knife. Their bodies were warm too, indicating they hadn't been long dead.

That was when he heard the noise. At first he had thought it was a rat scurrying over the floor or possibly a small dog or cat. It came from under the table, and when Pyke bent down, the tip of the match still burning in his hand, and peered under the tablecloth, the little girl gasped and backed away, her eyes wide with fear. Crab-walking back to the wall, she stared at him, her lips ever so slightly parted, assessing him as a cat might regard a much larger dog.

'Here.' Pyke knelt down and held out his hand. 'It's Milly, isn't it?'

Her pale, liquid eyes widened further, as though trying to make sense of what was happening, and then she nodded.

'Do you remember me from earlier today?'

She remained rooted to the spot, her unblinking eyes never leaving his, even for a second. Had she seen what had taken place? Did she know that her parents were dead?

'Milly, I want you to come with me. Can you do that?' He extended his hand out a little farther. One thing was certain. He couldn't leave her there.

But she didn't budge.

'Did a man come and visit earlier this evening?' As he said it, he wondered whether she could understand him.

The match had died but he could see that her expression was blank.

'Here, girl, give me your hand.' He was practically under the table with her, their hands almost touching.

'Did you steal those two keys from a chain attached to my pocket earlier today?' His missing keys seemed trivial by comparison but he still needed to ask her the question.

She gave her head an indignant shake.

'Did you see what happened in here?' He lowered his voice to a whisper.

Her stare glazed over but her eyes remained fixed on him.

'Here, Milly.' He took her hand and pulled her gently towards him. She didn't try to resist.

'I don't know what Emily'll say,' Jo fretted, as Pyke emerged from the room next to the nursery where he'd just tucked Milly up in bed. Milly still hadn't spoken a word to him, but when he'd said goodnight and made to leave the room, she'd whimpered in a way that suggested an attachment had already been formed. The poor little girl had shivered in his arms throughout the entire journey back to the hall. Pyke had woken Jo up, to explain the girl's presence in the room next to Felix's, but Emily wasn't expected back from Coventry for a couple of days. Gently Pyke closed the door and turned to Jo.

'We'll cross that bridge when we come to it,' he said, quietly. What he wanted to say was, *What other choice did I have? Her parents were murdered. Their throats had been slit. I saw them with my own eyes. Their blood is on my boots.* But even though he knew Jo well, and liked her, he didn't think it appropriate to share his thoughts with her. He looked away and tried to swallow. His throat felt dry and scratchy.

Once Jo had returned to her room, Pyke crept into the nursery and watched Felix sleep for a while. He liked to do this, if work had kept him late and he hadn't seen his son for a while. After a few minutes, Felix stirred, rolled over and looked up. 'Father?' He sounded alarmed.

Pyke told him not to worry and to go back to sleep. He had always wanted a sister or brother for Felix but somehow it had never happened. Now when Felix woke up, there would be a girl, a few years older than him, in the room next door. Briefly Pyke wondered how the lad would react to this development, whether he would welcome it or not.

Leaning down, Pyke kissed him on the head.

He thought about telling the boy that he loved him but the words wouldn't come.

*

There were three police constables and a sergeant, from H Division in Stepney, all wearing their dark blue, swallow-tailed coats, matching trousers and black stovepipe hats. The sergeant, a ferret-faced man, cleanly shaven with pimples on his chin, took charge of the situation, banging on the door of the cottage with the end of his truncheon and, when no one answered, gingerly opening the door with his hand. The other policemen followed him, leaving Pyke to bring up the rear. The sergeant, who had treated his revelation about corpses with weary scepticism, turned to him, arms folded, as if to affirm the rightness of his initial suspicions.

'No bodies here, sir.'

Disbelieving, Pyke looked down at the spot where he had seen Freddie Sutton and his wife the night before. The sergeant was right. The bodies had been moved.

'But you can see the blood,' Pyke said, bending down to indicate where the marks were. The floorboards had been scrubbed clean but some of the blood had seeped into the wood, staining it a darker colour.

'It could've been blood.' The sergeant looked around the room and sniffed. 'Could've been any number of things.'

Pyke wanted to grab his lapels and shake him. 'Two people were killed here last night. Freddie Sutton and his wife. I *saw* them. Their throats had been cut. I want to know what you're going to do.'

'Anyone else see the bodies?'

'Is that relevant?'

'Perhaps you'd like to tell me again what you were doing in the neighbourhood last night, sir.'

Pyke removed one of his boots and held up the toe to the sergeant's face. 'That's their dried blood. I trod in it by accident.'

The sergeant glanced at it, unimpressed. 'I'll make a file of your claim. Leave me your name and address and I'll get back in touch.'

Struggling to control his anger, Pyke pushed his way past the other constables and stepped outside. A small crowd of onlookers had gathered to see what all the fuss was about.

'Two people were murdered last night. Did any of you see anything?'

He heard a few gasps and some frightened looks and then one by one they turned their backs and walked away, until he was left staring at a black-and-white dog that wagged its tail and barked at him.

But Pyke's morning didn't improve when he finally turned up at the bank. In fact what awaited him there left him dazed and disoriented.

William Blackwood met him in the banking hall, his expression pale and sombre. 'Have you heard the news?'

For a moment Pyke thought Blackwood was talking about the two murders and he was about to shoo his partner away when he realised he had to be talking about something else.

'What news?' The skin tightened across his face.

'The whole of the city's talking about it.'

'Talking about *what?*'

'Edward James Morris threw himself off the viewing promenade at the Colosseum last night. He's dead, Pyke. Morris is dead. He killed himself.'

Pyke had to steady himself on his partner's shoulder. It felt as if he'd been hit over the head with a cudgel.

Morris, dead. The words wouldn't cohere with images in his head. He could hear the old man's voice booming in his ear; and if he closed his eyes, Pyke could still see his grinning, big-boned face.

'Of course, this will have implications with regard both to our investments in the Grand Northern and the loan you recently agreed with the company.' Blackwood stared at him without blinking.

Pyke grabbed Blackwood by the throat and pinned him to the wall. 'A good man has died. Can't you leave it at that for the moment?'

But as soon as he'd thought about it, Pyke knew that Blackwood was right. He let him go and wiped his hand on his coat sleeve. There was the small matter of ten thousand pounds. *And* the missing key.

Suddenly Pyke felt nauseous, searing panic seizing his entire body until he could hardly breathe. The key, the loan, Morris. A pattern was emerging and it didn't look good for him.

'Go and get your key to the safe and meet me downstairs in the vault,' he shouted at his apparently bewildered partner.

Five minutes later, Blackwood joined him in the vault, holding his key. 'Where's yours?' he asked, frowning.

But Pyke's heart was beating too fast to take any notice of what his partner was saying. He took the key and inserted it into the safe's door, twisting it a full rotation until the lock had opened.

Pulling open the heavy iron door, he quickly scanned the contents of the safe and felt his tension ease a little. It didn't appear that anything had been disturbed. But he still wanted to check the documents he'd placed there the previous afternoon. He'd put them at the back of the safe and he had to reach in almost with his entire arm. Behind him, his partner was holding aloft the lantern, curious to know what Pyke was looking for. As far as Pyke was aware, Blackwood knew nothing about the ten-thousand-pound loan he had made privately to Morris. Kneeling down, he peered into the safe, his heart quickening. The documents, including the contracts and the deeds to Cranborne Park, were not where he'd left them.

A solitary drop of sweat leaked from his armpit and snaked its way down his side, as it dawned on him what was happening.

Pyke searched some more but the documents weren't there. Someone had taken them.

When he staggered to his feet, his head was spinning. He blinked, closed his eyes and tried to focus. If the documents were missing, and the ten thousand pounds he'd lent Morris couldn't be traced, he would be liable for the full amount of the loan. The thought terrified as much as it enraged him. He could stand to lose *everything*.

'Who else has been down here since yesterday afternoon?' His voice teetered on the precipice of rage.

'No one, as far as I know.'

'Have *you* been here?' Pyke stared at him; there was no one else who had a key.

Blackwood sensed something was wrong but didn't appear to know what it was. 'I brought the money taken by the cashiers down here as usual . . .'

'I put some documents in here yesterday at close of business. They're now gone. Do you understand what I'm saying?'

'I hope you're not insinuating I had anything to do with it,' Blackwood replied in a rush.

'There are only two keys that open this safe. Yours, and one that was stolen from me yesterday.'

Sweat had broken out around Blackwood's temples.

'Yesterday I made a private loan to Morris of ten thousand pounds.'

Blackwood looked at him, open mouthed. Finally the seriousness of the situation was beginning to dawn on him. 'I take it there was a witness.'

'Nash.'

'Then you've covered yourself, haven't you? We can always recover the money from Morris's estate.'

Pyke nodded but he couldn't shake the feeling of unease that lurked in the pit of his stomach.

'Of course, if Nash doesn't verify your story then we might have a very serious problem,' Blackwood added.

Pyke's punch landed squarely on Blackwood's nose, knocking him backwards, blood spurting freely from his nostrils. 'Why wouldn't Nash verify it?' Pyke lifted him up by his collar. It was like picking up a skeleton. 'I said, the documents were stolen. Didn't you hear me?'

Blood glistened on the end of Blackwood's nose. He was too nonplussed to speak but his eyes burned like hot coals behind glass, as though he couldn't quite put a name to the humiliation he felt.

The entrance to Moor's Yard was blocked by two policemen and when Pyke tried to push past them, the taller of the two men held out his arm and told him that no one was allowed to enter the yard. Other people wanted to know why both ends of the yard had been blocked and what the policemen had found there. The mere sight of the police made Pyke even more jumpy than he'd been before. He tried to explain that he had important business with one of the residents, business that couldn't possibly wait.

'You ain't going in there, squire,' the policeman said, squinting at him.

A small crowd had gathered on the pavement around him, forcing passers-by on to the road. The midday bells of St Martin's began to chime. Pyke couldn't wait. The worry was eating him up. He had to find Nash. Seeing his chance, he shoved the other officer to one side and broke into a run. Behind, he heard shouts and cheers but he didn't look back. He ran along the narrow alley until it opened up into a yard. Nash lodged at number eight, above the farrier, an apartment on the first floor that overlooked the horse pond. But there were more policemen in the yard and, alerted by the shouts of their colleagues, they were ready for him.

'Nash. I need to talk to Jem Nash. He lives at number eight.'

A few of them exchanged looks.

'What is it?' Panic iced Pyke's stomach.

'I don't think you want to see him, the state he's in, sir.' The policeman was blocking the doorway leading up to Nash's apartment.

'Is he dead?' Pyke felt his throat tighten.

'Dead?' The policeman laughed. 'If you can survive without a head, then I'd like to know how.'

Pyke's legs buckled.

The policeman nodded. 'That's right, cully. When word starts to spread, as it will, there'll be panic on the streets.'

With a sudden movement, Pyke shoved past him and bolted up the stairs ignoring the shouts of the policemen behind him. At the top of the stairs, he pushed open the door to Nash's apartment and stepped inside. He didn't get beyond the entrance hall. Nash's body lay there on the floor, still dressed in the outfit he'd worn to the ball. The air smelled cloying. The stump where Jem Nash's head had been was bloody and raw. Pyke tried to get a better look at the body, but policemen had chased up the stairs and dragged him out of the apartment.

Were there burn marks on the body? That was what he wanted to know. And was the head there? Had the killer taken the head?

It took six of them to drag him down the stairs. One of them tried to arrest him for disturbing the peace. Outside it had started to rain but Pyke hardly noticed it. Everything he'd done, everything he'd achieved, everything he'd earned since he'd taken over at the bank, was hanging by a thread. He thought about the old crone, the dead navvies, Freddie Sutton and his wife, and now Morris and Nash. Were they all part of the same thing? All that blood spilt and for what?

The policemen left him alone. Doubling up, he spat bile on to his boots. He could still see Freddie Sutton's dried blood on them.

He would find out who had done this and make them pay. Someone, somewhere, would pay dearly for what had happened. Staring up at the rain, he repeated these words like a mantra.

PART II

*

The Eminence of Thieves

THIRTEEN

In the days after the discovery of Nash's mutilated corpse, the mood in the capital was anxious and expectant. The murderer had struck once in Cambridgeshire and again in London, and many seemed to think it was only a matter of time before he murdered again. The theories most often repeated were the absurd ones: that the murders were the work of an escaped Bedlamite unable to control his impulses or else that they had been committed by devil worshippers. To Pyke's surprise, no one had thought to connect the first headless corpse, pulled out of a river near Huntingdon, with the brutal clashes that had taken place between the navvies and special constables in the town itself. But then again no one apart from Pyke knew that the same burn marks had been found on the first victim and the old woman whose senseless rape and murder had sparked the navvies' anger. Pyke didn't yet know whether Nash's body had been afflicted with the same marks and couldn't begin to think how his death might be linked to the body found in a river near Huntingdon. For a start, the coincidence seemed too glaring. Just a week after he had been asked by Peel to investigate the first headless corpse, his assistant had been murdered in exactly the same fashion.

Perhaps more perplexing were the circumstances linking Nash's murder, the death of Edward James Morris and the sudden disappearance of the loan papers from the bank's vault, and it was this matter which constituted Pyke's most immediate concern. For without a witness or any supporting documentation, there was no evidence that a loan had indeed been made. Pyke had arranged for one of the cashiers to bring ten thousand pounds up to his office and, as such, the missing sum could be traced back to him. All of which meant that his partner, William Blackwood, would be within his legal rights to demand that the money be paid back to the bank

146

in full. *Ten thousand pounds*. His savings, which he had struggled to build up for the past fifteen years, didn't even meet this figure. If he failed to recover the stolen papers or indeed the money, then his financial future looked bleak. The moment Blackwood demanded the money be repaid, Pyke would be sunk. But at the same time, he knew that even if he did have the money in his bank account, he wouldn't give it up without a fight. He had to get back what had been stolen from him. What he needed to do was work out how someone had gained access to the safe; whether they had used the key purloined from him, possibly by the gypsy, or Blackwood's duplicate key, and whether his partner had played any role in the burglary.

On the same afternoon he had learnt about Nash's death and the stolen documents, Pyke gathered together the watchmen who had been guarding the bank the previous night. But to his consternation and irritation, it transpired that no one had seen or heard a thing. Pyke believed them, too. The watchmen he'd employed didn't have the wit or the courage to lie to him.

'I want to know who's stolen from me and I want you to help me,' he'd told them at the meeting. 'And if I find out that one of you was involved or knows something and is covering up for someone else, I'll make you wish that you'd never taken a job at this bank.'

If Nash's murder was linked to the corpses discovered in Huntingdon it suggested that the suppression of the navvies and the rape of the old woman were in turn connected to the internal politics of his bank. But in spite of his investigative prowess Pyke couldn't determine what the connection might be. In his eyes, the only way Nash's murder and the riots in Huntingdon *were* linked was by the slavering interest shown in both events by journalists and news editors. It was perhaps inevitable that a gruesome murder would find favour with hacks who could exploit its sensationalist appeal to promote their names and sell newspapers, but Pyke was surprised by the extent of the coverage on the riots and the obvious bias shown towards the townsmen. Even the apparently liberal *Chronicle* and *The Times*, though regretting the still-unconfirmed loss of life suffered by the navvies, placed all blame for the disturbances on the navvies and the radicals who'd infiltrated their ranks and incited them to violence.

To counter this view, the unstamped newspapers like Godfrey's the *Scourge* had started to circulate an alternative account of the events in Huntingdon among the city's poorest neighbourhoods, producing a groundswell of sympathy for the navvies and anger at the perceived vigilante behaviour of the special constables who'd been appointed without due process and who'd taken the law into their own hands. Many of the trade unions had already convened impromptu meetings to plan their response, something that in turn had prompted the government to fill up the barracks on Birdcage Walk with detachments of cavalry from Hounslow and Croydon and regiments of infantry from Woolwich and Chatham. There were also two thousand uniformed police officers making their presence felt on the city's streets.

Unlike Nash's murder, Morris's apparent suicide merited only a very brief mention in *The Times'* City Intelligence column and was deemed to be significant only insofar as it affected the already flagging fortunes of the Grand Northern Railway. The *Chronicle* ran a slightly longer account of his 'unfortunate demise' and speculated that the difficulties facing the railway and boardroom tussles regarding the future direction of the venture had driven him to 'tragically' take his own life. Unsurprisingly, since no corpses had yet been unearthed, no mention had been made of the two Spitalfields weavers, Freddie Sutton and his wife, whose deaths Pyke had stumbled across. Nor, in spite of his personal intervention, had anyone at Scotland Yard treated his claims seriously; Pyke had been shooed from the assistant commissioner's office and warned not to waste police time with his 'groundless scaremongering'.

As Gore had intimated, Bellows was the kind of man whose apparent commitment to public service concealed a burning private ambition to succeed the Right Honourable Charles Lord Tenterden on the bench of the Criminal Court at Old Bailey. As such, his liberal contributions to the royal commission on capital crimes and his proximity to the Home Office were not principled stances but rather appropriate ways of currying favour with those who might be able to influence the appointment of the next Lord Chief Justice. As the chief magistrate at Bow Street he had sought to foster a reputation as a thoughtful, fair-minded figure, liberal in his dealings with the poor but hard on all forms of political radicalism. In public, he liked to believe that his efforts were part of a larger project to reform the entire judicial system according to Benthamite principles; in private he was a cruel, vindictive man who beat his servants and used his office to punish those who had personally crossed him.

Pyke had heard a rumour that Bellows had once set up a man who had cuckolded him on a false theft charge and sentenced him to hang.

On the morning of the coroner's inquest, Pyke met the chief magistrate outside the King's Head tavern, the first time he had encountered the man since walking out of his courtroom with Godfrey on his arm. It was an awkward moment but Bellows made no mention of that incident and pushed past him without uttering a word, indicating to Pyke that he had no desire to discuss the fact that all the charges against Godfrey had now been dropped. His bristling, self-righteous air suggested that he hadn't adjusted to his humiliation very well.

The stink from the filth-blackened north bank of the Thames at low tide had filled the upstairs room of the King's Head. Filthy remains washed up from the tanneries and glue factories on the Surrey side of the river mixed with slaughterhouse offal and human excrement to produce dark pools of slime whose eye-watering smell easily penetrated the closed windows and overpowered the rosemary and lavender that had been sprinkled over the floor.

It was the only room that the coroner, Daniel Day, had been able to requisition at such short notice that was large enough to accommodate the twelve jurors and the various witnesses he intended to call upon. Still, his timid apologies regarding the foulness of the air and the grubbiness of their surroundings did little to appease Bellows, who bewailed having to run the gauntlet of the rambunctious mob gathered downstairs in the taproom, where, Pyke knew, ratting contests sometimes took place.

It was highly unusual that such an important legal figure should attend or present evidence at a coroner's inquest, even more so because the chief magistrate had no connection with the deceased. This didn't stop him complaining bitterly about the vile stink and the drunken behaviour he had witnessed downstairs. Briefly Pyke thought about explaining to him that public houses always did brisk business on the day of inquests but decided that he would be wasting his time. How could Bellows ever be made to see that the working men and women weren't drinking to celebrate someone else's death but rather to affirm the fact they were still alive? He would never imagine that survival was a sufficient cause for revelry.

Including the twelve men of the jury, there were twenty or so people squeezed around the two adjoining tables. Bellows sat at one end and a space had been reserved for Day at the other end. A few others rested on spittoons and window ledges and perched on top of the old piano. But pride of place had been reserved for Morris's corpse, laid out in the middle of the two tables and covered with a dirty sheet. Pyke could just about make out Morris's features under the sheet and felt a mixture of sadness and anguish wash over him.

'Thankee kindly for helping a crippled man.' Jake Bolter hobbled into the room with the grace of a man wearing leg-irons and collapsed into the Windsor chair reserved for the coroner. Behind him, his mastiff stood panting, a wet string of saliva hanging from its powerful jaws.

When Bolter sat down, he let rip with a fart that seemed to go on for minutes and which produced a stink much worse than the odours emanating from the river. 'That's what they call letting a brewer's fart, grains and all.' Bolter grinned as he looked around at the others. 'Must be the meat pie I ate playing with my digestion.'

Those who were sitting nearest to him edged away, perhaps because of the smell but also on account of his mastiff, which had taken its place at Bolter's feet and growled at anyone who looked at it.

Day, who had helped Bolter up the staircase, looked around for a chair, now that his had been taken.

'Can anyone fetch me a pot of ale?' Bolter said, trying to get comfortable in his chair. 'I've a powerful terrible thirst and I need a drop to meller the throat.'

'I'll go,' Pyke offered, having given up his chair for the coroner. 'Would a pot of Barclay's ale suffice?'

Bolter looked up at him, unable to hide his surprise. Bellows seemed confounded, too. 'That would hit the spot perfect, sir. Much obliged to you.' Bolter doffed his cap and smiled awkwardly, doubtless still trying to make sense of Pyke's generous offer.

Downstairs in the taproom, Pyke pushed past a gang of coal-whippers to the zinc-topped counter and waited until he'd caught the landlord's eyes. He took out a sovereign and pushed it across the counter. 'There'll be another one for you, if you bring me one of your ugliest sewer rats, in a box, within the next few minutes.' When the landlord didn't move, he added, 'Oh, and I'll have a Barclay's ale, too.'

When Pyke returned to the upstairs room, he placed the pot of ale on the table in front of Bolter, who thanked him profusely, and kept the small wooden box on the floor. No one paid it any attention.

Bellows' jurisdiction as chief magistrate at Bow Street extended only as far north as St Martin's Lane, and the Colosseum in Regent's Park, where Morris had died, fell under the auspices of the Marylebone police office. Nonetheless it was Bellows, rather than Day, who began the proceedings and as soon as he'd done so, Pyke asked on what or under whose authority he was there. Bellows smiled thinly and told the jury he'd been asked by his 'good friend' and the 'barrister-at-law' at Marylebone to attend the meeting. Attend but not take charge of? Pyke asked. This drew another frosty stare, by which time the coroner had developed enough of a backbone to impose himself on the meeting. 'It's stuffy in here,' he said, looking at Bolter and his dog. 'Perhaps we could allow a little air into the room? At present it resembles a garden of earthy delights.' He looked around him to see whether anyone had picked up on his reference.

'Or a ship of fools,' Pyke said, looking at Bellows.

Bellows was up on his feet. 'I object to this man's impertinence.'

Day waved his hand in a fey manner. 'Good Lord, man, pipe down. We were just sharing a private joke. He meant no offence and I'd hope none was taken.' He looked at Pyke and smiled, revealing a set of perfectly straight teeth. 'The air will have to do. After all, this is the Thames and not Lake Windermere.'

Bellows glared but said nothing. Pyke found himself warming to the coroner.

'Well?' Day folded his arms and looked at the chief magistrate. 'Don't you have some evidence to present, sir?'

Bolter took a few sips of ale and put the pot down on the floor for his dog. Copper slurped from the pot and nuzzled against Bolter's leg.

Bellows stood up and addressed the room. His chest puffed out, he said it was his belief that Edward James Morris had tragically taken his own life on the second night in November, 1835, and that he had done so by jumping off the viewing promenade, a raised platform some two hundred feet above the ground floor of the Colosseum, at the end of a charity function held there to celebrate the birthday of his wife Marguerite.

Pyke interrupted and asked how he knew that Morris jumped and wasn't pushed. 'That's what we're here to determine, isn't it? I'd hate to think the chief magistrate was trying to sway the minds of the jurors even before any evidence has been heard.'

Pyke didn't know for a fact that Morris *hadn't* killed himself, but he was intrigued that Bellows seemed so keen to rule out foul play.

'Whether Morris jumped of his own volition or was pushed,' Bellows muttered, 'you surely don't deny he fell two hundred feet from the viewing platform to the ground beneath him and that this fall caused his death?' Everyone looked at the corpse that lay in front of them on the tables.

Day cleared his throat and told the inquest that Morris had almost certainly died from injuries sustained from the fall. But from his examination of the body there was one anomaly that he couldn't fully explain. Morris's backbone and pelvis had been shattered in many places, indicating that this part of the body had borne the brunt of the initial impact, but there was also a contusion and a partial fracturing of the skull. These injuries were most likely sustained as a result of the fall, Day explained, but he hadn't yet determined how they were consistent with those sustained in his lower back area.

What if he'd been hit over the head with a blunt object first and *then* thrown over the railings? Pyke asked.

This drew a howl of derision from Bellows. There was no physical evidence to suggest foul play, he said, and all the circumstantial evidence pointed towards suicide. With some skill, Pyke had to admit, Bellows laid out the various pieces of information at his disposal and called upon the assembled witnesses to corroborate them. In doing so, he gradually built up a picture of what had happened prior to Morris's death. At a quarter to midnight, Jake Bolter had come across Morris up on the viewing platform. According to Bolter, Morris had been incoherently drunk, and when Bolter had tried to help him, he had pushed him away, repeatedly referring to himself as a 'dirty monster'.

'I like the grog as much as the next man but Mr Morris, God rest his soul, was in the gun and obstropulous. That's the truth. I'll take an Alfred David if I have to.' Bolter then coughed up a lump of black phlegm in his handkerchief and gave it to the dog. The mastiff greedily licked it off the handkerchief and those jurors who had seen this winced with horror.

Jake Bolter, Pyke had already concluded, was there to corroborate Bellows' ironclad belief that Morris had taken his own life. It was time to disbar him as a witness. Pyke nudged the wooden box towards the mastiff and waited until the animal noticed him and growled. At this point, he kicked the box over and watched as the long-tailed rat scurried from beneath it directly in front of the mastiff's giant paws. The effect was instantaneous. Letting out an excited yelp, the creature went for the fast-moving rat, a sudden movement that wrenched the lead from Bolter's grip. So focused was the dog on the scuttling vermin that it didn't look to see where it was going: the result of which was chaos on a level that even Pyke couldn't have imagined. The lumbering beast tore through, rather than past, the chief magistrate, upending him from his chair and sending him sprawling gracelessly on to the floor. The dog also ploughed through the entire row of jurors sitting along one side of the table, and in its efforts to catch up with the escaping rat, it banged against one of the table legs, which had the effect of destabilising the table to such an extent that Morris's corpse rolled from its precarious resting place on to the floor. The jurors' screams fell on deaf ears, as far as the mastiff was concerned, for the snarling animal, realising the rat was darting back across the floor in the direction it had just come from, suddenly doubled back on itself and collided head-on with Bellows, who had just picked himself up off the floor. At first it was difficult to tell who had come off in a worse state, Bellows or the dog, but when Pyke next looked, the resourceful beast had somehow managed to ensnare the wriggling vermin in its mouth and was shaking its head and gnashing its jaws to kill it. By this point Bolter had recovered sufficiently to try to bring the situation back under control, but his clumsy efforts to restrain the dog had the opposite effect, and as the animal tried to shake off his attentions the half-dead rat flew from its mouth and struck one of the jurors squarely in the face. His screams, Pyke guessed, could be heard on the Surrey side of the Thames.

Once some semblance of calm had returned to the proceedings and everyone had returned to their seats, Bellows turned on Bolter, who had pacified his dog and recovered the leash, and spluttered, 'Get that ugly stinking creature out of my sight this instant.'

'But if I tie him up downstairs someone'll bilk him for certain. This here is a rum burgher.'

'*Get that beast out of here now*,' Bellows yelled, his face turning a violent shade of crimson.

Interrupting, Pyke said they could probably do without Bolter's testimony. After all, he added, was a man like Bolter really the best person to comment on the deceased's state of mind?

That drew some chuckles from the jurors and the blood rose in Bolter's neck. He yanked on the leash and the dog growled and, this time, bared its teeth.

As Bolter trudged disconsolately out of the room, with his mastiff, he gave Pyke a sour grimace. Even Bellows, who had calmed down considerably, appeared sorry that he was going.

Pyke had won the first skirmish but Bellows was in no mood to concede the battle to him.

As Bellows went on to explain, Morris had last been seen alive, on the viewing promenade, by a pot-boy from the Crown and Anchor tavern in Camden Town, who had been charged with clearing-up duties, just *after* midnight. The caretaker of the Colosseum stood up and testified that he had 'personally' toured the platform at half-past midnight and hadn't seen Morris, or anyone else, there. He told the jurors that when he had locked the building up at half-past one, Morris was nowhere to be seen. He had discovered Morris's body only the following morning, when he'd opened up the building. The caretaker explained that he didn't know exactly *when* Morris had fallen to his death, and Bellows speculated that Morris must have hidden himself in the building and jumped later, when no one was around.

'If, indeed, he jumped,' Pyke interjected, 'rather than being pushed. As far as I'm aware, the jurors haven't yet reached their verdict.'

Bellows muttered an apology and tried to assure the jurors that he hadn't intended to influence them.

'Placing a pistol to their heads might have been more subtle,' Pyke replied.

Bellows chose to ignore that comment.

Day, the coroner, had then posed the question that had been at the forefront of everyone's mind. Was it likely or even possible that Morris had been of a suicidal frame of mind?

On this note, Bellows tried to convince the jurors that, by all accounts, Morris had been upset about *something*.

'But the one person who might have upheld this claim has now left this meeting,' Pyke said, 'so clearly this assertion should be struck from the record.'

'Morris was as drunk as a sailor. I hope you don't dispute that,' Bellows retorted bitterly.

'And that's supposed to confirm his suicidal state of mind? If that were so, every man and woman downstairs enjoying a drink might very soon be expected to throw themselves into the Thames.'

That drew a further ripple of nervous laughter.

Pyke didn't doubt that Morris was both severely drunk and perhaps deeply troubled by something that had happened to him. But he didn't believe Morris was suicidal. In his experience, men like Morris killed themselves for two reasons: acute money worries or intolerable inner turmoil, neither of which seemed to apply to Morris. Still, he couldn't help but think about the large sum of money Morris had borrowed from Blackwood's and about his inebriated rant to Bolter: if true, what had Morris meant when he'd described himself as a 'dirty monster'?

The last witness to give evidence was Bellows himself. Apparently he had spoken to Marguerite Morris – 'the deceased's wife' – to break the news to her, and he proceeded to offer a description of their conversation. He explained that, for obvious reasons, she had been too upset to attend the inquest in person but that she had talked openly and freely with him. The jurors were told that, on the night of the ball, Marguerite had argued with Morris about his drunkenness – this much chimed with what she'd told Pyke – and had left the Colosseum at half-past ten. Servants at Cranborne Park confirmed that Marguerite had arrived back there just before midnight. The chief magistrate went on to point out that Marguerite had clearly loved her husband very much and said that she had described him as a virtuous, good-natured man who was nonetheless prone to bouts of depression and secretiveness. To his credit, Bellows didn't claim Marguerite had described her husband as suicidal but he also said she hadn't ruled it out as a cause of death.

All in all, he made a very convincing witness.

Drawing the inquest to a close, Daniel Day asked whether anyone else had something to add that might have a bearing on the jury's decision.

Pyke coughed. 'What happened to Morris's watch?' He waved the piece of paper that listed the items retrieved from the dead body. The watch hadn't been listed. 'I saw it in his pocket a few hours before he died. The watch must have been worth hundreds. Its case was encrusted with diamonds. It was a family heirloom. He was never without it.'

Bellows looked at Day and the Colosseum's caretaker. 'Did either of you come across a gold watch?'

Day just shrugged but the caretaker rose to his feet and stammered, 'I hope you ain't accusing me of bilking it, sir.'

Bellows told him to calm down and that no one was accusing him of anything. He shot Pyke an angry stare. 'An antique watch has gone missing,' Bellows added, this time to the jurors, 'but I don't think we need to concern ourselves about it. You have sufficient evidence to reach a verdict on the cause of death.'

'Why are you so concerned to rule Morris's death as a suicide, Bellows?' This time Pyke stood up, to directly confront him. 'What is it that you're trying to prove or trying to hide?'

'Your belligerent tone and sharp tongue will land you in serious trouble, if you're not careful.'

'I still don't understand why you're even here in the first place.' Pyke pointed at his chest. 'Morris's death has got nothing to do with you or your office.'

'You've flouted my authority once and, to my intense dismay, seem to have gotten away with it. Do it again and I'll see you're locked up for a year without trial. Don't think I can't do it, either.'

'I think you're a fraud and a liar and I also think you've unfairly used your office to sway the outcome of this meeting.'

Bellows sprang to his feet and gesticulated angrily. 'Someone arrest this man.' Of course, there were none of his officers, and no policemen, in the room, and no one reacted to his demand. When he realised that he'd made himself seem vaguely ridiculous, he went an even deeper shade of crimson and ordered the jury to arrive at a verdict without further delay.

It took them just a few minutes to reach their decision. It was unanimously agreed that Morris had committed suicide by jumping to his death on the second night of November from the Colosseum's viewing promenade. His voice still trembling from Pyke's insult, Bellows then congratulated them for their eminently sensible verdict.

If that had been the end of it, the meeting would have been deeply depressing, but as the jurors stood up and stretched their legs, the door was flung open and a panting, red-faced Abraham Gore stumbled into the room and muttered, 'Am I too late? Please tell me I'm not too late.'

'What do *you* want?' Bellows muttered, clearly recognising Gore and not relishing the intrusion, even though the meeting had, for him, reached a favourable conclusion.

'I'm here to throw my shilling's worth into the pot. I knew the deceased, Edward James Morris, for more than thirty years,' Gore spluttered at the jurors, still recovering from ascending the stairs too rapidly, 'and I can lay my hands on my heart and swear to you that he would never, *ever* have taken his own life.'

'This is the eminent banker and industrialist Abraham Gore,' Pyke told the jurors. A few of them recognised the name and seemed stricken by the dilemma he'd presented them with.

'I'm afraid the evidence has already been heard and a verdict, a most reasonable verdict, agreed. You, sir, should learn to be more punctual.' Bellows glanced nervously at the jurors, some of whom had sat back down, and licked his lips.

'Has this imbecile presided over a verdict of death by suicide?' Gore asked Pyke, shaking his head.

Pyke nodded. 'I tried to warn the jurors about the folly of delivering such a verdict but they wouldn't listen to me.'

'More like they were too cowed by this bully to reach a more considered decision. No, my evidence will be heard. My good friend of thirty years would never have taken his own life.' Gore turned on the jurors. 'Which can mean only one thing. He was murdered. Do you hear me? *Murdered.*'

'You might have connections far beyond the reaches of this meeting, sir, but here at least they count for little. The jurors reached a verdict and that decision has to stand.'

'Balderdash,' Gore said, training his stare on the chief magistrate. 'Complete and utter balderdash.'

'I'll ask you one final time to refrain from insulting me and the jurors, sir. After that, even a reputation such as yours cannot save you.' Sweating profusely, Bellows had lost all his former poise.

Gore looked around the room. 'Who's the coroner? Let me make an appeal to the coroner.'

Timidly Day coughed and raised his hand.

'Will you reconsider, sir? I'm sorry I was late but my carriage was held up on the Strand.' Gore took another step into the room. 'Good God, man, don't you understand the terrible stain you're placing on my friend's reputation? Only cowards and Bedlamites kill themselves.'

'A verdict of suicide perfectly suits Morris's killer or killers,' Pyke added, quickly. 'It means his death won't be investigated and their crime will go unpunished. Is that what you want on your consciences?' He looked at each juror in turn; some of them had visibly whitened.

'I will not stand for this talk,' Bellows screamed, cowing the jurors still further. 'A decision has been reached. I am the only arbiter of the law here and if I am happy that procedures have been adhered to and the law upheld, then that, sirs, should be the end of the matter.' Red eyed and hands trembling, he turned on Gore and pointed at him. 'And if you, sir, should dare to challenge my authority one more time, then I will have no choice but to hold you in contempt, and issue a warrant for your arrest, which I promise you *will* be served.'

Outside, Gore pulled Pyke to one side and took his arm. 'I'm so sorry I was late. I feel I've let my friend down terribly. I know you did what you could, Pyke. I also know for a fact that Eddy would never have taken his own life. I'm aware this verdict makes an official investigation unlikely, if not impossible. But I'm also told that you've had certain experience in this area and I was wondering whether I could employ your services to try and determine what really happened to him. I know you're probably far too busy to even think about committing to such an undertaking but I also know Eddy thought a great deal of you and, it goes without saying, I would remunerate you handsomely for your services, whether you found Eddy's killer or killers or not.'

'I'll do what I can,' Pyke said, having considered the proposal for a short while. He looked up at the giant herring gulls circling above him, no doubt drawn by the leftover scraps to be had at the nearby fish market, and felt a biting anger that rose up from the pit of his stomach until he could taste it at the back of his throat.

On the wall opposite someone had daubed the words 'Captain Paine' in red paint, and when Gore noticed it and saw how fresh the paint was he shook his head, muttering, 'I don't suppose you heard about the latest outrage? One of the warehouses belonging to our subcontractors, near Kilsby, was attacked and set on fire. The brigand calling himself Captain Paine claimed responsibility. They lost everything.' He shook his head sadly and shrugged.

Pyke returned the expression, not sure what to say. On the other side of the street, he noticed Bolter and the dog lurking with intent.

Gore patted him gently on the arm and said that if there was anything he could do to help, anything at all, Pyke had only to ask. His shoulders hunched, Gore trudged along the narrow street to his waiting carriage.

'Can I have a quick word, Pyke?' The coroner, Day, had sidled up next to him and was smiling awkwardly. 'I believe the chap who was found beheaded in his apartment in Moor's Yard was a friend of yours.'

'Jem Nash. He was my assistant at Blackwood's.' Out of the corner of his eye, he saw Bolter and Bellows reconcile. 'Actually there was something unusual I wanted to ask you.'

Day squinted suspiciously at him. 'Oh?'

'Have you inspected the body yet?'

'Cursorily,' Day said, clearly embarrassed by something.

'But you'd know if the corpse had been marked with red welts?' Pyke paused for a moment. 'The kind you might get if someone pressed a hot cigar into your flesh.'

This drew a sharp frown from the coroner. 'I don't recall seeing any such marks.' He hesitated and gave Pyke an awkward stare. 'Listen, Pyke, as you might know, I was to have conducted the inquest into his death later today, even though there doesn't appear to be much doubt as to what actually caused his death.'

Across the street, the giant mastiff tugged on Bolter's leash, having seen something intriguing farther down the hill towards the river.

'Nash's body was taken to the Turk's Head in Holborn. But his death has attracted so much print and interest ...'

'What happened?' The skin tightened across Pyke's face.

'Resurrectionists broke in late last night and stole his corpse. I'm afraid there'll be no inquest after all.'

'You know for certain it was the resurrectionists?' Pyke asked, shaking his head. He knew there was a trade in dead bodies and that unscrupulous surgeons sometimes paid as much as ten guineas for a fresh corpse.

'Who else would want it?'

Across the street a wiry greyhound trotted around the corner and came face to face with Copper. It froze to the spot and then tried to retreat, its hackles raised and its belly scraping the ground. Without any hesitation, Bolter let go of the leash and the mastiff tore after the terrified greyhound and caught up with it in a few bounds. It was over in a matter of seconds. The mastiff's jaws clamped around the smaller dog's throat and its body went limp. Blood on its mouth, the mastiff shook the greyhound like a rag doll and dropped it on to the ground. It then rejoined Bolter and the two of them ambled up the hill towards St Paul's.

'Can I ask you a question?' Day asked, looking down at the greyhound's mangled carcass. 'Do you really think Morris was murdered and Bellows tried to force the jurors to declare his death as a suicide?'

Later Pyke thought some more about Day's question. Why had Bellows been so insistent that Morris had committed suicide? Or rather, why did it matter to him?

In the end he could think of just one answer.

It mattered because Morris hadn't actually committed suicide.

Which, in turn, suggested that someone had instructed Bellows to cajole the jury; someone whose interests might be damaged by an investigation into Morris's affairs.

Who had wanted Morris dead? And what had happened at the Colosseum after the guests had left?

FOURTEEN

Marguerite's cheeks were streaked with tears and her breath carried the sour traces of claret. The fact she'd made no effort with her clothes, nor with her blonde hair, which fell untidily to her shoulders, made her seem unusually vulnerable. She had greeted Pyke on the steps of the house and had fallen into his arms, burrowing her head deep into his neck and clinging to him while she sobbed. This had lasted for what seemed like minutes, her whole frame shaking violently. Finally she peeled herself from him and stared up at him through cloudy eyes.

He could taste the salt of her tears on his lips.

They were alone in the drawing room, the same room they had taken tea in just a few days earlier. She walked over to the full-length Venetian window and watched as the afternoon skies darkened and rain began to fall. 'It's beautiful here, with this view of the garden.'

Pyke contemplated the view with her. 'Is it why you persuaded Edward to buy the house?'

Marguerite didn't answer. Instead she pressed her face right up against the steamy pane and sniffed.

'You must have known I'd be your neighbour.' Pyke took a step towards her.

Again Marguerite stared out of the window at the landscaped gardens. He reached out and wiped away a solitary tear that was rolling down her cheek. 'Edward's death was ruled as suicide.'

She nodded, as though she'd been expecting it. 'But you don't believe he killed himself, do you?'

'Do you?'

'In spite of what you might think, Pyke, I loved him. Maybe not ...' She hesitated, fresh tears forming in the corners of her eyes.

'Maybe not?' Briefly their eyes met but she looked away first.

'But I wouldn't have left him.'

Though Marguerite's skin was mottled from her tears and her hair was ragged and unkempt, she was still one of the most beautiful women he had ever met.

'Most people only saw his naturally gregarious side but Eddy was a troubled man in lots of ways.'

'In what way was he troubled?'

'What man could possibly live up to the ideals he set himself?' she said, suddenly angry.

Pyke nodded. 'I presume Edward left everything to you.' As far as he knew there hadn't been any children.

'After we married, Eddy told me he'd changed his will.' Marguerite wiped her eyes. 'We didn't discuss the matter again.'

'Have you actually seen his will?'

'He kept it with his lawyer.'

'But there will be a copy of it in the house. In a safe perhaps?'

They were standing just a few feet from one another. He could smell her powerful, earthy scent.

'There's a safe in Eddy's study.'

'If you felt able to, we could have a look.'

This time Marguerite looked up at him. 'Why are you so interested in the terms of his will?'

Pyke took a breath. 'Did Edward mention that on the day he died he borrowed a large sum of money?'

'From you?'

'The bank.'

'How much?'

Pyke shrugged.

Something changed in her expression. 'And that's why you're here? To check on your investment?'

'He walked out of our offices with a lot of money in a satchel. If it was stolen, it might begin to explain his state of mind.'

She nodded but didn't speak for a few moments. 'When I saw a carriage coming up the drive, I hoped it might be you. For some reason, yours was the shoulder I wanted to cry on.'

'I'm sorry for my intrusion. I shouldn't have come.'

'Eddy's barely been dead for a day and already vultures are circling above his carcass. I didn't think you'd be one of them.'

Pyke could see the heat in her cheeks. 'In spite of what you might think, I liked him and if someone did kill him, then I'll find them.'

'And then?'

'Of all people, Maggie, you know what I am.' He looked into her eyes. 'And what I do.'

That evening at Hambledon, Pyke went to check on Milly after dinner. According to Jo, she still hadn't eaten anything or spoken a word and had spurned all efforts to lure her out of the room.

Pyke closed the door behind him and set his lantern down on the table next to her bed. She was sitting across the bed, her back leaning against the wall, staring blankly out of the small window.

'Milly?'

She didn't look at him or even acknowledge his presence.

Tentatively Pyke perched himself at the end of the bed, but still she didn't look at him. 'Milly, I want to help you. I want to find the people who hurt your parents but to do that, I'll need your help.'

Ignoring him, the little girl started to hum.

'Can I bring you some food? Or something to drink perhaps? Lemonade? Ginger beer?' As he said it, he wondered whether she'd ever tasted lemonade or ginger beer.

Gingerly Pyke reached out to touch her, if only to disturb her from her torpor, but she flinched and shuffled to the very far end of the bed, still humming quietly to herself.

In the neighbouring room, he noticed that Felix was still awake and went in to see him.

'Why won't that girl say anything?' Felix asked, sitting up in his bed.

'She's still frightened. She saw some bad things, things no child should be forced to witness.'

'What kind of things?'

Pyke reached down and touched his son's forehead. 'Nothing that need worry you, my boy.' He knelt down beside the bed. 'But I want you to be especially nice to her. Can you do that for me?'

'I already asked if she wanted to play with my toys,' Felix said, indignantly, as though Pyke had accused him of something he hadn't done.

'That's very good, Felix, but you need to persevere. Talk to her.

Try and get her to talk to you. We need to make her feel welcome.'

'What should I talk to her about?'

'Her name, what she likes to do, her parents . . .'

Felix screwed up his face. 'Why's she staying with us? Where are her parents?'

Pyke kissed him on the head and stood up. 'It's time to go to sleep now.'

'Father?'

From the doorway, Pyke looked around and said, 'What is it, Felix?'

'She scares me. The way she looks at me . . .'

Pyke put down the lantern and returned to Felix's bedside. 'We all need to learn how to overcome our fears.'

Felix stared up at him, wide eyed. 'What are you afraid of, Father?'

Losing you, Pyke thought, as he asked whether Felix wanted the lantern to be left in the room.

'We can't have her stay with us indefinitely,' Emily said, as they sat across from one another in the living room.

She had returned from the Midlands that afternoon sporting a large bruise on her forehead, the product of a violent scuffle that had broken out at the meeting she had been addressing, but when Pyke started to claim that she shouldn't be attending such events, if her safety was at risk, she turned away from him and refused to discuss the matter further.

'What other choice did I have? Her parents were murdered. Their throats had been cut. I saw them with my own eyes. Their blood is probably still on my boots.' Pyke tried to swallow but his throat felt dry and scratchy.

'Then you need to get the police involved. Have you even contacted the police?'

'Did you contact the police over the fight that's left you scarred and bruised?'

'It was nothing. More an accident, really.' But she wouldn't meet his stare.

'I went back to the home with the police the following day. The bodies had been removed.'

That got Emily's attention. 'By whom?' When Pyke shrugged, she asked, 'What were you doing there in the first place?'

'I was trying to find their daughter – Milly's sister – as a favour for Godfrey.'

'What does Godfrey want with the daughter?'

'She was going to take the stand in a libel trial that Godfrey was facing.'

'Was?'

'The case against him has been dismissed.' Pyke saw her frown and added, 'It's a long story.'

Emily watched him, her expression inscrutable. 'Milly's scaring Felix and none of the servants know what to do. She won't eat any food and they're worried she might pass away.'

'Would you prefer that I throw her out on to the streets?'

Emily sighed. 'No, of course not . . .'

'But?'

'But I'm worried about you, Pyke.' She came and sat next to him on the sofa and touched his face. 'I'm worried you might have got yourself into something . . .'

'I told you. I was trying to find the girl's sister for Godfrey.' He waited, not sure what else to say.

'And you don't have any idea who might have killed the parents or why?'

Pyke looked over at the fire blazing in the grate. Emily stroked his cheek, adding, 'You just looked tired, that's all. Is anything else wrong?'

Yawning, Pyke told her that everything was fine, even though it was obvious that everything was not fine. Why couldn't he look her in the eye and admit that he could lose his entire fortune? That someone was conspiring against him? Why were these things so hard to admit even to someone he loved?

'Sometimes I feel you don't know how to talk to me, Pyke. I'm worried about you and the girl upstairs. I don't know what to think but I'm guessing there's more to this than you're telling me.'

'Just like there's more to your bruise than you're telling me.' He waited until she was looked at him before adding, 'You didn't just get pushed over at a meeting. Someone attacked you, didn't they?'

Emily laughed, though not particularly convincingly. 'If someone had attacked me, do you really think I would have walked away from it with just a bruise to my forehead?'

Later that night, as they lay next to one another in bed, Pyke asked, 'Have you heard about a sweater called Groat? He owns a whole terrace on Granby Street in the East End.'

In the darkness, a puzzled frown appeared on her face. 'Why is it that just when I think you've lost the capacity to do it, you go ahead and surprise me?'

Morris's funeral was an intimate affair held in the Church of St Edmund the King on Lombard Street, near the Grand Northern's head office. After many clergymen in the city had politely refused to host the funeral on the grounds that Morris had taken his own life and thereby committed a mortal sin in the eyes of God, the vicar at St Edmund's had taken pity on Marguerite and agreed to accommodate her wishes for a Christian funeral. It later transpired that Abraham Gore had made a large donation to the church's coffers on the condition that they perform Morris's funeral.

Most of the Grand Northern's central committee attended the short service, as did all the clerks and under-clerks His assistant, Bledisloe, wept openly in the second row. Other than that, the congregation mostly comprised family and friends. Gore was there and so was Jake Bolter. His dog had been tied to the railings at the front of the church. Peel had come, too, and indicated that he wanted to talk at the end of the service. Earlier Pyke had seen Bolter chatting quietly with Marguerite and, again, he wondered about the basis of their friendship.

Pyke sat with Emily five or six rows back from the front of the gloomy church. He had made eye contact with Marguerite once, when they had first arrived, but he hadn't tried to approach her.

As the service started, Emily whispered, 'There's something about her I still don't trust but she's very beautiful, isn't she?'

'Who?'

'Marguerite. Morris's widow.'

Pyke put on a non-committal face.

The vicar stepped up to the pulpit to give the eulogy. He spoke quietly and blandly for five minutes about God's grace, hardly mentioning Morris once. It was Abraham Gore who finally decided enough was enough, striding down the aisle and relieving the stricken vicar of his place on the pulpit.

'What my friend here meant to say was this is a sad, sad day for those of us who respected and loved dear Edward and at this very sad time our thoughts and prayers are with Marguerite, his beloved wife, whose gentle care and fierce support sustained Edward through good and bad times.' He looked up at the congregation and took a few moments to gather his thoughts.

'We stand on the precipice of a new era. This great city of ours is changing before our eyes. Within a generation, the broken city we inherited from our Georgian ancestors, with its fetid slums and gin-addled paupers, will be swept away for ever. And in its place will rise up a city of magnificent sweeping avenues, elegant buildings and open spaces for all to enjoy, a beacon for the entire civilised world, a veritable new Jerusalem. A city built in *our* image, reflecting *our* values: no longer a dark place where crime and disease are rife, infecting young and old alike, but a clean, enlightened city where men and women, inspired by their wonderful surroundings, can better strive to do God's work and remake themselves in his image. Open your eyes. Look at the buildings, the squares, the circuses. Even as I speak, railways are cutting a welcome swath through the damp, derelict slums; verminous places abandoned both by God and our ancestors. Our dear, departed friend committed his life to such good works, and now, as we look back at his achievements, and give thanks for his life, we might all pause for a moment to reflect on his example.'

There were a few sobs from the hushed congregation. Pyke, however, was puzzled by the speech. He hadn't considered Gore to be a religious man.

'Edward James Morris stood, nearly alone, while lesser men – men of an artistic sensibility – rushed to attack what they perceived to be the destruction of what William Blake called our green and pleasant land by the dark satanic mills of commerce. Edward saw this posturing for what it is and was: empty rhetoric. While blind men of letters could see only the deadening impact of money, Edward believed in its virtue: what could be achieved if men were allowed to pursue their interests and freely participate in the market without interference from government. Could the railways, so dear to Edward's heart and which are now spreading out across this great country of ours like arteries carrying blood to all parts of the body politic, have even been contemplated without this freedom? Could Edward have realised his dream of building a railway across our great land without this freedom? Could he have improved the lives of men currently toiling to build his railway without this freedom? Of course not.' Gore bowed his head and stepped down from the pulpit to murmurs of approval.

'Could Abraham Gore have lined his own pockets to the tune he has done without this freedom?' Emily whispered.

'Of course not.'

Emily nudged him playfully in the ribs and they both shared a smile.

After the pall-bearers had carried the coffin up the aisle, followed by a procession of horsemen with black ribbons tied around their arms and feathermen carrying trays of black plumes, the rest of the congregation filed out of the building.

'That was quite a eulogy,' Pyke said to Abraham Gore on the steps of the church.

'Thank you, Pyke. I'm most touched by your kind words.' Gore bowed his head at Emily. 'Mrs Blackwood.'

'I'm afraid I found your eulogy rather self-congratulatory,' Emily said, pulling her woollen shawl around her shoulders. 'I thought it revealed more about yourself and your own ambitions than about the deceased.'

Gore seemed amused rather than hurt. 'And you knew Edward well?'

When Emily didn't answer, Gore bowed his head again and turned to greet some of the other mourners. As they filed past him, Pyke whispered, 'Why did you have to say that?'

Emily's laugh was coruscating. 'Don't tell me you actually *like* the man now?'

Pyke didn't answer her – he didn't know whether he liked Gore or not, but he *did* believe that Gore was genuinely upset by Morris's death. What else could have explained his laudable actions at the coroner's meeting? They walked on in silence, neither wanting to cede ground.

It wasn't difficult to spot Peel's brougham. It was the largest and shiniest on the street and was attended to by four liveried footmen. Pyke asked Emily whether she'd wait for him in their carriage and went across to join Peel, who was standing on his own, watching someone in the crowd.

'Why did you want me to go to Huntingdon?'

Peel regarded him with an amused look. 'Straight to the point, eh? I wouldn't have expected anything less.'

'Someone tried to kill me. I think that gives me a right to be blunt.' His sharp tone cut through Peel's feigned bonhomie.

'Perhaps we should talk in the carriage,' the Tory leader said, pointing at the door. 'There might be more privacy.'

Once they were both settled inside, Peel nodded and the footman pushed the door closed. The mahogany interior gleamed in the fading afternoon light.

'Well?' Pyke kept his stare fixed on the leader of the opposition. 'Did you know there was going to be a riot?'

'You think too much of me.' Peel's smile was devoid of warmth. 'I have a certain talent for oratory but I'm afraid I can't predict the future.'

'But you suspected something might happen?'

'As I told you before, I'd heard some rumours about an increase in radical activity in the area,' Peel said, watching him carefully. 'Who tried to kill you?'

'Townsmen who'd been sworn in as special constables. And soldiers ...' Dangling this revelation in front of him.

Peel took the bait. 'Soldiers were used to put down the rioting?'

'Dragoons.' Pyke wondered whether Peel had heard about the shooting of one of them or not.

'How many of them?'

'Six, perhaps.'

'In uniform?'

Pyke nodded. Peel didn't *seem* to know anything about the use of soldiers but that didn't necessarily mean anything. He was a canny operator who hid his feelings well. 'The magistrate had it in mind that I was Captain Paine.'

The Tory leader didn't know whether to be surprised or amused. 'Why would he have thought that?'

'You'll have to ask him,' Pyke said, wanting to see whether Peel had heard about Yellowplush or not.

'Perhaps I will.'

Pyke looked searchingly into his face. 'Why were you so interested in the headless corpse?'

'I explained all that to you before.'

'Try again. I'm a slow learner. I don't pick things up very quickly.'

169

There was a disconcerting glint in Peel's eyes. 'Why do I get the sense that you're not telling me something?'

'You think *I'm* the one who's lying to you?'

'I'm aware of your skills as an investigator. Given our last chat, I don't think you would have returned from Huntingdon empty handed.'

'People were trying to kill me. Forgive me for not caring about your problems.' Pyke rearranged himself on the horsehair seat. 'Tell me why you're so interested in this Captain Paine and Julian Jackman?'

Peel gave him a sardonic look. 'Did you find out whether they were one and the same?'

'With the benefit of hindsight, and in spite of your efforts to blackmail me, I can't see why you're so interested in Jackman.'

'Blackmail is a very impolitic description.' Peel shook his head, his lips pinched together. 'But in the light of the price you've already paid, what would you say if I gave you certain guarantees that your liaison with undesirable figures like Villums will remain our secret?'

'Just like that?'

Peel nodded but didn't say anything.

'Do you want to know what I really think?' Pyke asked, again wondering how the Tory leader had known about his dealings with Villums in the first place. 'For a start, and in spite of your claims to be merely helping a friend, I don't think you give a damn about the navvies or about the progress, of lack thereof, of the Grand Northern Railway. I think you were hoping to use the radical protests for your own ends.'

'Those are serious allegations.'

Pyke waited for a few moments. He'd wanted to try to draw Peel out of himself but the Tory leader's defences were impregnable. 'How well do you know a landowner called Sir Horsley Rockingham?'

'He made his fortune from sugar in the West Indies and from what I've heard he's an obstinate bugger and rather full of himself.'

'You don't make him sound like much of a threat.'

'Should I?'

'I think he was responsible for orchestrating the disturbances in Huntingdon.'

'Go on.'

'He didn't want the railway to run across his land. And now the construction work has ground to a halt in Cambridgeshire and Morris is dead, it doesn't appear likely that it will.'

By reputation Peel was a scrupulously moral person but virtue, for him and others like him, was defined by its consequences, and Pyke didn't doubt, for a moment, that he would roll up his sleeves and dirty his hands if it might result in a perceived good.

'What if I told you I didn't believe Morris committed suicide?'

This time, Peel's interest was unmistakable. He leaned forward and said, 'I'd ask you to justify your claim.' In the fading afternoon light, his skin glowed with a peculiar intensity.

'You'd be prepared to entertain such a notion?'

'I would want his death to be properly investigated.'

'I attended the coroner's inquest earlier. Under pressure from Sir Henry Bellows, he declared it to be suicide.'

'Bellows?' The news was clearly a surprise; he stared out of the window, turning it over in his mind. 'You're saying the verdict was rigged?'

'I'm saying it's strange the chief magistrate took time out of his busy day to give evidence at a corner's inquest when he didn't know the deceased and had no jurisdiction over the death.'

'But your suspicions are based only on gut instinct?' Peel sounded disappointed. 'By that I mean, you don't have any evidence to refute the verdict returned at the inquest?'

'Only a sense that people like Rockingham have profited from Morris's death.'

'People *like* Rockingham or just Rockingham?'

'Are you suggesting I should think about other suspects?' Pyke asked, detecting something in Peel's voice.

But Peel would not be drawn on this subject. A long, awkward silence followed.

'Since you refuse to disclose your own interests in all of this,' Pyke said, finally, 'you force me to speculate.'

'About *my* intentions?'

'You've seized control of the party from Tory Ultras like Eldon and the Duke of Cumberland. Now it's a question of taking power back from the Liberals.'

'You make it sound like a despicable ambition.'

'Melbourne's second ministry is already teetering on the brink. The King doesn't like him. Nor does the Church, the bar, much of the landed gentry and a sizeable minority in the Commons. He was only able to form a government with the support of the radicals and the industrial North.'

'Don't forget O'Connell.'

'Of course,' Pyke conceded. 'But the radicals are starting to turn on their former allies: what happened in Huntingdon is likely to drive a further wedge between the two factions. It's my guess you're trying to exploit the situation for your own gain.'

'One could just as easily claim the Liberals are being quite successful at guiding the radicals down manageable paths.'

Later, when Pyke thought about the conversation, he was struck by the deft way in which Peel had steered it away from awkward subjects.

'I'd say Bellows is worth keeping an eye on,' Peel said, trying to sound as though the issue wasn't an important one.

'Why's that?'

Peel tapped on the glass and the footmen hurried around to open the door. 'You're the investigator. But I'm told he's recently purchased rather a lot of land in the vicinity of the New Road just along from Battle Bridge near Somers Town.' He smiled coldly. 'You might want to look into that.'

As Pyke threaded his way through the phaetons, broughams and cabs on Lombard Street, he looked around and noticed Gore at his side. His smiling face was covered in sweat. 'All these damned people wanting to shower me with their religious homilies and fake piety.'

'I would have guessed from your eulogy that you claimed a Christian belief, too.'

'Oh, that?' Gore chuckled. 'Isn't that the kind of thing one is supposed to say at a funeral?' He must have seen Pyke's expression because he added, quickly, 'Don't get me wrong, Pyke. I meant every word of what I said about Morris. But I threw in the religious sentiments as a sop to the congregation. Personally I find the idea of praying to some kind of God a little mystifying.'

Pyke couldn't help but smile. Such an admission was rare in an age when people used the church to secure their social standing.

They came to a halt, Gore turning to face him, his top hat balancing precariously on his head. 'I wanted to ask you whether you'd thought any more about the offer I made after that blasted coroner's meeting.'

'I told you then that I'd do what I could.'

Gore nodded genially. 'Quite, quite. I don't mean to put any pressure on you ...'

'But?'

'But I thought you might take a closer look at that odd fellow with the burnt face and the dog. For a start, I've no idea what he was doing at the ball.'

'He was invited by Morris's wife.'

'Yes, well, I found him to be a shifty sort of fellow. Untrustworthy and capable of violence, I'd say.'

Gore's assessment tallied with Pyke's own view of Bolter but he kept this thought to himself.

'I couldn't help but notice you get out of the carriage belonging to Sir Robert Peel. I have to admit I'm intrigued.' Gore swung his arms from side to side as though the issue he'd just raised were unimportant.

Pyke let Gore's remark pass without comment.

'Do you know him well?'

'We're acquainted,' Pyke said, nonchalantly. 'Why? Is he a friend of yours?'

'A friend?' Gore laughed. 'No, I'm afraid I'm something of an old Whig. I'm sure Sir Robert would regard me as a dinosaur.'

'You're too modest,' Pyke said, trying to read Gore's opaque expression. 'As your intervention in my uncle's trial demonstrates, your influence would seem to extend right to the top of government.'

'Well, like all businessmen I have my contacts, I suppose. And come election time they expect me to make a generous donation to the party coffers.'

'Pigs at the trough?'

This time Gore's laugh came from his belly. 'I couldn't have put it better myself.' He glanced up at the seagulls circling above them. 'But you're right. I do have some political connections and from time to time they tell me things.'

'About?'

'Take Sir Robert, for example. I'm told he's become obsessed by a headless body that was found near Huntingdon.'

'Obsessed in what sense?'

'Do you know he even visited Huntingdon in person?'

Pyke tried to assimilate this information without giving too much away but such was his shock that he may not have been successful. *Peel, in Huntingdon.* Pyke thought back to his conversation with the magistrate. What had Yellowplush said, when Pyke had told him about Peel's interest in the body? Something like: *I can't understand why Peel's so interested in it.* And another thing: Yellowplush hadn't seemed surprised when Pyke mentioned Peel's involvement. *I can't understand.* Yellowplush knew about it already because Peel had been to see him.

'Why are you telling me this?' Pyke waited for a moment. 'Is it something you just *guessed* I'd be interested to hear?'

Gore shrugged. 'I told you because it's the only morsel of information I've heard about the Tory leader in a while.'

'From where I'm standing, it looks very much like you're trying to smear him.'

'Whatever you might think, Pyke, it's the truth. I'm not the kind of man who tells lies about other people.'

'Judicious editing of the truth can sometimes be more effective than blatant lies.'

'Can I be more honest with you? I fear that Sir Robert suspects my involvement in inciting the navvies in Huntingdon to violence. Just as you did and, for all I know, maybe still do. I also fear that he's trying to do what you just accused me of. Smear me with the taint of association.'

Pyke had wondered about Peel's motivations all along and this finally made some kind of sense.

The fact that Gore, when pushed, had been honest with him in a way that Peel still hadn't suggested the banker's innocence. And Pyke knew that Peel wasn't above stirring up rumours to besmirch those who threatened him.

'And you had nothing to do with what happened in Huntingdon?'

Gore stared pleadingly into his eyes. 'As I've said before, Eddy was my friend, my best and oldest friend, and I would never have done *anything* to harm him or his interests. If nothing else, you have to believe *that*, Pyke.'

Through the thinning crowd, Pyke saw Marguerite chatting to Emily. They were standing on the pavement next to his carriage, their heads nodding as they listened to one another talk. Briefly Pyke paused, more in horror than fascination, to look at both women and try to assess their mood.

Emily noticed him first. Her expression was unreadable but she didn't break into a smile. 'I was just passing on our condolences to Marguerite.'

'Thank you so much, my dear.' Marguerite trained her stare at Pyke. 'I'm so glad that you and your husband could come. I can't tell you what it means having a friendly face from the old days here.'

Just for a moment Pyke thought – hoped – that Emily had missed the implication of Marguerite's deliberate attempt at sabotage. She looked between them, Marguerite and him, and frowned. 'I'm sorry, but do the two of you know each other?'

Marguerite tried to appear contrite and muttered, 'Oh? Didn't he mention it? Well, we didn't know each other well but we certainly knew each other.' She didn't look across at him. 'Before a few weeks ago, we hadn't laid eyes on one another for, perhaps, fifteen years.'

Pyke laughed, trying to make light of it. He wanted to wring Marguerite's neck, of course, but that would draw further unwanted attention to their former attachment. 'Yes, I almost didn't recognise her.'

'I suppose we've both come a long way since those days.' Marguerite put on a sad smile and added, 'If you'll excuse me I have other people to greet.' She looked across at the funeral cortège and shook her head. 'When you called at the house the other day,' she said, looking directly at Pyke, 'I wasn't doing very well, but perhaps once today is out of the way I'll feel more like facing up to my responsibilities.'

Pyke said nothing as she disappeared into the crowd, but when he turned around to look for Emily she had already taken her place inside their carriage.

FIFTEEN

They were very quiet in the carriage as it crossed over on to Fenchurch Street, the noise of horses' hoofs clattering against cobblestones somehow amplified by the silence that grew between them.

Earlier in the day, Emily had made arrangements to show Pyke the row of terraced houses on Granby Street where Horace Groat employed up to a hundred children, some as young as six, to stitch together boots and shoes in near-darkness, working them for fifteen or sixteen hours and paying them as little as a shilling a day.

'You lied to me,' Emily said, eventually, in a menacing tone.

'It didn't seem important.'

Emily nodded, as though she'd expected him to say this. 'If it wasn't important, why go to the effort of lying?'

'Because I didn't want you to think what you're no doubt already thinking.'

'And what am I no doubt thinking?' This time there was a trace of real anger in her voice.

Pyke stared out of the window, not wanting to answer her question.

'We went to her house. *All* of us. Felix, too. And you didn't think it necessary to let me know she was an old friend?'

'She was an acquaintance, not a friend.'

'I don't care *what* she was,' Emily shouted. 'But you deliberately kept something from me.' Before he had a chance to respond, she had thought of something else. 'What am I? Stupid? Am I supposed to believe that her arrival in our neck of the woods is just a coincidence?'

'I had nothing to do with that. I was as surprised as you were.'

'But you went to see her without letting me know. *After* Morris had died.'

'I had some pressing business, relating to a loan Morris has taken out, to discuss with her.'

'*Business.*' Emily shook her head. 'So how well were the two of you acquainted?'

'We knew some of the same people.'

'Did you fuck?' The word sounded even more shocking coming from her mouth.

'No.' The lie was more instinctive than anything else.

'Did you want to fuck her?' Emily asked, not changing her tone. 'After all, she's a very beautiful woman.'

This time he looked directly at her. 'I don't expect you to tell me about all the men you find attractive. I just expect you not to act on your impulses.'

'*My* impulses? Why is this suddenly all about me? You were the one who lied to me, Pyke.'

He fell silent, knowing he was beaten.

But Emily hadn't quite finished. 'I take it you haven't yet acted on your impulses.'

She waited for a moment. 'Yet.'

'What's that supposed to mean?'

'Now she's a widow and doubtless a very rich one at that ...'

'You're a very rich woman, too,' Pyke said, gently. 'And you're the one I chose to marry.'

'Except she's more beautiful than me, isn't she?'

'She's a peacock. All feathers and plumage.'

Emily's scowl started to crack. 'If she's a peacock, what am I, then?'

'You're my very own bird of prey.'

'And that's supposed to make me feel better? Being compared to a buzzard?'

'In a fight, who would you put your money on? A peacock or a buzzard?'

'So now you expect the two of us to fight for you?' A small smile appeared on her lips.

Pyke edged towards her and kissed her gently on the cheek. 'Of course, if you did fight, you'd win by a mile.'

Emily punched him on the arm. 'You'd better believe it, sir.' But she still wasn't mollified. Pyke could tell that he was a very long way from being let off by his wife.

In the first room, once the drab, mildewed parlour of a private dwelling, he counted twenty children, all under ten years old, hunched over their work, either cutting out pieces of material for the lining or sole or stitching the lining and sole together. Each child sat on a wooden stool, a candle burning on the floor by their feet to guide their work. Emily and Pyke watched them from the doorway, noting their emaciated hands and dead stares, and listened for any signs of the master who lived upstairs and apparently ruled with an iron fist. Their guide, a mute, cadaverous man of fifty with a limp and two tufts of hair sprouting from an otherwise bald head, waved them into the next room, where the ceilings were so low Pyke could not stand straight. It was a smaller room but it housed the same number of children, all occupied with similarly numbing tasks. The first thing Pyke noticed was the near-total silence – no one uttered a word and the only sounds were the occasional coughing fit and shouting from the street outside. The second thing he noticed was the concentration fixed on their faces. There were other things he would remember later on – the icy temperature, the choking air, the eye-watering stench of overcooked food, and the dirt-encrusted walls and ceilings – but what stood out most of all was the atmosphere of fear, which assumed an almost tangible presence. The silence and the concentration were the undoubted products of the master's reign of terror. Pyke had tried to talk to one of the youngest, a boy barely older than Felix, but his efforts to strike up a conversation had come to nothing. The boy had been too terrified to speak.

Outside, Emily said, 'There are ten houses on this side of the street, all owned by Groat. That's ten houses with as many as twenty young children crammed into each of the rooms. Four hundred children. Upstairs belong to the masters. They rule their houses with an iron fist. You saw how frightened the children were.' She shook her head. 'All of this means that Groat can sell his shoes for sixpence a pair and still make a tidy profit. People want cheap shoes, after all. Everyone suffers apart from Groat and his henchmen. Most of all the children, but also the shoe- and bootmakers who can't compete with Groat's prices. And the shoes people buy fall apart within a few months because the children who make them haven't been properly apprenticed.'

The odour of fried fish was pungent in the stiff breeze. 'Where do all the children come from?'

'Workhouses, the street, orphanages.' Emily's eyes were blazing. 'It's a profitable business, the trade in children. Groat might have paid a few pounds for each of those kids. That's a few pounds multiplied by four hundred.' She pulled her shawl tighter around her shoulders. 'Government legislation forces people into workhouses, workhouses then farm those same people off to middlemen because they can't afford to feed and clothe them and the middlemen sell them on to private enterprises like Groat's for profit. It's all part of the same grubby system.'

And banks like Blackwoods' lent sweaters like Groat the money to start up their businesses in the first place, Pyke thought grimly.

'So what is it you're trying to do here?'

Emily looked up at the terrace and said, 'A year ago, when I was still a member of the Society of Women, I would have said lobby government to change the legislation and raise money for charities working to help the poor and dispossessed.'

'And now?'

At the end of the terrace, someone had daubed the words 'Captain Paine' in white paint on one of the gable-ends. Emily pointed to it and shrugged. 'If a Liberal government has allied itself with the Malthusians who want to turn the country into a workhouse, what hope is there?'

Pyke could hear the ire in her voice. For some reason, he hadn't noticed it before, at least not to the extent he did now. 'So what's changed?'

'I've woken up. Others, too. Paine said as much forty years ago and we thanked him by forcing him out of the country.'

'Said what?'

'Give a man or a band of men too much power, too much money, and the liberty of the nation is threatened.'

'And that's what you think has happened?'

Emily stared at him through her long lashes. 'Perhaps this isn't a talk we should be having.'

'Why not?'

'As you indicated the other night, we might see that our respective positions aren't as compatible as we might have once hoped.'

'Perhaps they're closer than we might have imagined, too.'

'In what sense?'

'Captain Paine is an advocate of direct action, isn't he?' Pyke looked at the words daubed on the gable-end in white paint. 'It's what I've always said. You want to make an impression, you don't reason with someone. You take out a pistol and press it against the man's head.'

They had travelled a few hundred yards along the cobbled street in their carriage when Pyke banged on the roof and ordered the driver to stop.

'Where are you going? What are you doing?' Emily called out as he opened the door and took off back down the street. '*Pyke.*'

He found one of the masters in an upstairs room, shaving with a razor over a pail of hot water.

The man wore a black monkey coat with knee breeches, wool stockings and lace-up boots. Standing up, his whiskers lathered with soap, he held out the razor. 'You want, I can walk the blue dog with you, cully.'

Pyke went for his throat and the master managed only one wild swipe of the razor, catching Pyke's forearm and slicing through his coat and jacket, before Pyke had landed a clean blow on his nose, breaking the bone, blood and sinew exploding from his nostrils. Clutching his nose, the man fell backwards, the razor clattering harmlessly to the floor, as Pyke scooped him up by the collar and dragged him over to the half-open window. 'As of now, your employment here is terminated.' Pyke rammed his head through the gap, forcing the rest of the man's body out of the window but making sure he held on to the legs. Soon the master was dangling precariously from the upstairs window, people gathering in the street below to watch. 'It takes a big man to keep children in line, doesn't it?' From somewhere out of the window he heard the master scream for help. But he was heavier than Pyke had realised and his boots were slippery, too, and soon Pyke knew he wouldn't be able to hold him.

Later, when the children Pyke had rescued from the first house gathered cautiously around the man's motionless body, hardly daring to get any closer, Pyke suspected the fall might have killed him, but then he saw the man's limbs twitch and heard him gasping for air and realised that he was just very badly injured. But the ensuing pandemonium had roused the masters from the other houses on the terrace and, when they saw what had happened, they tried to round up as many of the stray children as possible. Some of the children were still too dazed to take evasive action; others had seized the chance and had already made their escape. The masters were armed with pistols and sticks and there were too many of them for Pyke to take on without support. Retreating along the street, he came across one of the youngest boys he'd seen in the first room huddled in a fetid alley. Pyke hadn't stopped to think what might become of the children, assuming that a life on the street was preferable to another minute in Horace Groat's employment, but now it struck him that he'd rushed into something, more to appease his own conscience than to help the children, and created a whole new set of problems.

Where would this child sleep tonight? What would he eat? How would he survive on his own?

If Pyke didn't do anything, the lad would be back stitching together Groat's shoes before nightfall.

'Do you have anywhere to go? Any family?'

The boy stared up at him though large, liquid eyes.

'Who brought you here?'

The boy shrugged. 'A man. Before, I went to a school in the country.'

'What kind of a man?'

'A man with a dog.'

'A big, fighting dog with copper-coloured fur?'

'Aye, that's the one.'

Pyke tried to sound calm. 'You went to Prosser's school in Tooting?'

The boy nodded. 'My family all died last year.'

A moment passed. 'What are you going to do now?'

'I don't know.'

Pyke thrust a few coins into his hand and said, 'There's this basement shop in St Paul's Yard, number seventy-two, in the shadow of the cathedral. Present yourself there today and tell the white-haired man I sent you. My name's Pyke. He'll pay you to deliver a newspaper. It's not much but it might keep you alive. Do you think you can remember all that?'

The boy gave him a confused, bewildered stare and later, when Pyke was lying in his own bed unable to sleep, it struck him that the young lad might not have the necessary toughness and guile to make it through the night.

'I want you to call in all of Horace Groat's outstanding loans. Everything we've lent him.'

William Blackwood flicked through an oversized ledger on the table in front of him and frowned. 'He's a very good customer. He hasn't missed a single payment.'

'I don't care,' Pyke said firmly. 'In addition, I don't want us to lend another penny to the slop trade in the East End.'

Blackwood removed his spectacles and rubbed his eyes. 'Can I ask what's brought this on?'

'No, you cannot. I've made my decision. I don't want to talk about it.'

'But those are some of our most reliable customers,' Blackwood said, frowning. 'And in the light of your questionable decision to loan such a large sum to the Grand Northern, we need to set our liabilities against more reliable forms of income.'

They were sitting around a table in the boardroom, just the two of them. They had begun the meeting at nine o'clock as usual, without acknowledging what had happened to Nash or even mentioning the matter of the loan and the missing contracts. They had taken their usual places around the table, Pyke nearest to the fire, but their efforts to continue as normal quickly seemed misplaced.

Someone – a good man, no less – had died and a proper reckoning of the situation was required.

'Just do it. I want the notices served on him by the end of today.'

There was a loud rap on the door, but it was William Blackwood, rather than Pyke, who called out, 'Enter.' Tiny beads of sweat had appeared around his temples.

'And you are?' Pyke asked, barely looking up from the table.

A smartly dressed grey-haired man wearing a full-length velveteen coat and a white piqué waistcoat buttoned all the way to the top stood there, his top hat cradled in his hand.

But Blackwood had clearly been expecting him and shook the man's hand, before showing him to one of the empty chairs at the other end of the table.

'Allow me to introduce Mr James Herries,' he said for Pyke's benefit. 'Mr Herries is currently the solicitor to the committee of bankers for protection against forgers and fraud.'

This time Pyke had a proper look as the man shuffled to his chair. Herries was a strange, elfin-looking individual with long, pointy ears, sharp canine teeth and an unctuous manner that immediately irritated him. Grinning, Herries assured Pyke that there was nothing to worry about and that the whole matter had doubtless been a terrible misunderstanding that could now be cleared up.

There wasn't too much difference between him and the eels they pulled out of the Thames.

Clenching his fists until the knuckles had turned white, Pyke stared at his partner. 'This is your doing, I presume.'

'Let's try and move beyond attributing blame.' Herries smiled. 'Suffice to say, an audit was conducted yesterday afternoon that I oversaw, and it's come to light that a sum of ten thousand pounds of the bank's money cannot be accounted in terms of the existing documentation.'

Still ignoring the lawyer, Pyke said, to Blackwood, 'I told you I lent that money to Morris according to the standard procedures of this bank.'

'Ah, indeed, very good, sir,' Herries said, interrupting. 'Then perhaps you would be so good as to provide me with the attending documentation and this unfortunate matter can be resolved.'

'You know me and what I'm capable of and yet you still decided to humiliate me in this way.' Pyke waited for his partner to look up at him but his eyes remained rooted to the floor. 'That either tells me you're stupid or you know something I don't. Which one is it?'

But it was the lawyer who answered him. 'If the documents aren't forthcoming in, say, ten days – after all, we don't mean to be unfair – it's my unpleasant duty to inform you that a warrant for your arrest will be served and you will be sanctioned by the courts to repay the ten thousand pounds from your own pocket or face a lengthy sentence in one of His Majesty's prisons.'

Finally Pyke turned to him and licked his lips. 'If you haven't left this building by the time I've counted to thirty, I'll tear you apart with my own hands and happily face the scaffold.'

But Herries wasn't cowed. 'I was warned about your questionable reputation and I should just add that if something *untoward* was to happen either to Mr Blackwood here or myself the charges against you would still be pursued right the way to the highest court in the land.' Gathering up his papers, he stood up and smiled. 'Good day, gentlemen.'

But when Pyke stood up at the same time, the lawyer's composure finally cracked and he bolted for the door.

As the dust settled, Pyke had to hold in the urge to stamp on his partner's head, but the feeling passed quickly. This time he knew that a different approach was needed. For a start, there was no conceivable way Blackwood would have initiated such a bold move on his own, which meant that someone else was pulling his strings. Someone with sufficient status and power to afford Blackwood the protection he would undoubtedly need.

'William?'

Blackwood was trying to slip out of the room without a confrontation and seemed to freeze as Pyke barked his name. 'Yes?' But he couldn't bring himself to actually look at Pyke.

'You do know you won't get away with it.' Pyke shook his head, feigning sadness rather than anger. 'That's to say, you do know I'll do everything in my power to stop you ruining my name.'

Blackwood licked his lips. He looked like an unarmed man trapped in front of a cavalry charge.

'Ten thousand has effectively been stolen from under my nose.' Pyke slammed his fist down on the table so hard that Blackwood jumped. '*Ten thousand.* I don't even have that amount in my own account.'

'I don't know what you expect me to say,' Blackwood mumbled.

'I don't expect you to say anything. But I want you to know I'll strangle you with my bare hands before I give up a penny of my own money,' Pyke added, calming down. 'Nod, if you think I'm capable of it.'

Dumbstruck, Blackwood scurried from the room, his face noticeably whiter than it had been at the start of the meeting.

Pyke had thought that if he traced the missing ten thousand pounds, he would find Jem Nash's killer; but equally, if he found out who had killed Jem Nash, he would surely be led to the stolen papers and the missing money. And what he discovered from Ned Villums later that afternoon, though not throwing any direct light on the issue of who may have killed Nash, certainly revealed Pyke's assistant in a new light.

Villums was waiting in his office. A coal fire had been burning in the grate since early morning and the room was comfortably warm. An oil lamp on his desk produced a greasy yellow flame.

Pyke sat down behind his mahogany desk and poured them both a glass of whisky from a crystal decanter. 'I wasn't expecting you for another couple of days.' He'd already seen that Villums hadn't brought anything with him: no case, no money to deposit.

Villums took a drink of the amber liquid. 'The chat we had the other day made me nervous. Then I happened to read that your assistant at the bank had his head cut off.'

'Are you saying you want to terminate our arrangement?'

Villums shook his head. 'I just want to give you a few weeks to get your house in order.' He pulled up his chair closer to Pyke's desk and added, 'And I thought you'd like to know something about the lad.'

'Nash?' The skin tightened around Pyke's eyes.

Villums nodded. 'He lost seven thousand on the roulette table at Barnaby Hodges' gaming house in a single night.' He must have seen Pyke's expression because he added, without changing his tone, 'Suffice to say, he couldn't pay his debt.'

'He told me he lost money on the tables. But I had no idea it was as much as that.' Pyke finished his whisky and poured himself another. The fiery liquid tasted good against his throat. 'It would have been the night before he died. The next day at work, it looked as if he'd been in a prize fight.'

'Hodges told me that his men gave your lad a reminder of what might await him if he didn't settle his debt.'

'But you don't think they killed him?'

'Why would they? What good would Nash be to them dead? Hodges is still owed the seven thousand.'

Pyke tried to turn this information over in his mind but he could see that Villums hadn't quite finished. 'There's something else, isn't there?'

'Hodges also told me your lad liked to frequent a place called the Bluebell Club on Windmill Street in Soho. You know it?'

Pyke shook his head.

'It's a club for mollies.'

'Mollies?'

'Mollies, mandrakes, she-shirts.' Villums winced. 'You know.'

He must have stared at Villums for some time, unable to assimilate or make sense of this revelation, because the next thing he was aware of was Villums preparing to depart.

'Does he know for a fact that Nash was ...'

'A molly?' Villums put his coat on and shrugged. 'Hodges told me he'd heard it on very good authority.'

Later, Pyke tried to reconcile what Villums had told him with his own knowledge of his assistant. He had always imagined Nash to be a ladies' man, someone who had shown no inclination to settle down because he was happy playing the field. In addition, Pyke had always thought himself a good judge of character and an exemplary reader of people's thoughts, but armed with this new information, he felt foolish and short sighted, and wondered what else he might have missed about his young assistant.

'Before you go, Ned, I was hoping there was something else you might be able to help me with.'

'Oh?' Villums turned around in the doorway.

'I'm looking for a man.'

'Go on.'

'A heavily whiskered man with a glass eye. A nasty sort. The kind capable of rape and murder. He likes to burns people with cigars.'

'And you reckon I might know him?'

'Of him.' Pyke stared into his associate's unflinching face. 'Just like you know of everyone else who steals, cheats and kills in this city.'

That drew a hint of a smile. 'I don't have any doubts that you'll get to the bottom of this whole mess, Pyke, but I want to make it clear to you that I don't want to get drawn into it.'

'I just want a name.'

Villums nodded and said he would see what he could do. 'And Pyke?'

He looked up from behind his desk.

Villums tapped his head. 'Remember, there are times when this works just as well as a loaded blunderbuss.'

After Villums had gone, Pyke went over to the window and looked out at the vista of tiles, steeples and chimneys. The ravens were no longer there.

*

It had been a few years since Pyke had last seen Townsend and he was shocked by the much diminished figure that shuffled into his office. They had once served together as Bow Street Runners and Pyke remembered Townsend as a barrel-chested man with hands as large as grapefruits, knuckles like sovereigns and forearms that resembled the branches of a mature oak tree. He had once seen his former associate lift two fully grown pigs, one under each arm, without breaking into a sweat. Pyke had heard that Townsend had suffered some kind of fever but he hadn't expected the dismal sight that greeted him. His head had been given a prison-crop shave, his shoulders and limbs had lost much of their power, his clothes were tatty, and his skin was dotted with pockmarks, the kind that suggested smallpox.

They chatted for a few minutes about the old days, but it quickly became apparent that any rapport they'd once shared had now been eroded by the strictures of money and class. Out of shame or perhaps resentment, Townsend could hardly bear to meet his stare, and it took Pyke's act of passing an envelope containing money across the table to lighten the atmosphere. That cleared up a lot of the problems. Townsend realised Pyke was about to offer him some work and, on that basis, he appeared happy enough to remain where he was.

'I'd like you to do a couple of things for me.' He looked up and tried to assess his former associate's reaction.

Townsend had made no effort to retrieve the envelope from the desk.

'First, I'd like you to find out everything you can about a man called Jake Bolter. He works, in some capacity, at Prosser's school in Tooting, and he never goes anywhere without a giant mastiff called Copper. I know he used to serve in the army and his face is horribly scarred. I want to know which regiment he served in, what he did after he left the army, who he associates with.'

Townsend scribbled some details down on a pad of paper Pyke had left for him on the desk.

'And the other thing?'

'I'd also like you to keep an eye out on my partner, William Blackwood.'

'What's he done?'

'He may have stolen from me. I'm not sure.'

'So what am I looking for?'

'What he does when he leaves this building. Who he talks to and where he goes.'

'Is that it?' This time, Townsend picked up the envelope and opened it. His face remained composed.

A sharp knock on the door interrupted them and one of the clerks from the banking hall peered sheepishly around the door, holding out a letter. 'This was left for you, sir,' he said, taking a gulp of air.

Pyke beckoned him into the office, relieved him of the letter and read it. It simply said: '*Rockingham expected in the capital today. Coach due to arrive at Swan with Two Necks at six*'.

'Who delivered it?'

The clerk shrugged. 'No one saw. It was left on one of the tables, with your name on the front.'

Pyke thanked him and surveyed the note again to see whether he could glean any further information from the looped handwriting.

SIXTEEN

The Swan with Two Necks was an enormous coaching inn across the road from the General Post Office in St Martin's-le-Grand. Between the Swan, as it was more often called, and the next-door Bull and Mouth, there was underground stabling for more than a thousand horses and the two establishments employed well over three thousand men and boys to groom the horses, prepare the coaches, attend to the passengers and carry luggage to and from the upstairs rooms. The scene may have appeared chaotic to some but Pyke knew it was a well-drilled operation: passengers would take their seats in the yards of the Swan or the Bull and Mouth and the coaches would then cross the road to the post office, where porters and liveried guards would load sacks of mail on to their roofs. To travel on the mail coaches was the quickest and most reliable form of transportation and passengers paid a premium for it. As a result the yard at the Swan was one of those rare places where the working poor rubbed shoulders with the very rich and, as such, attracted every type of petty criminal. Indeed, while it may have been a colourful sight to some, a riot of motion and noise as pot-boys, ostlers, grooms, coachmen and passengers jostled past one another, Pyke's view took in only the pickpockets, footpads, rampsmen and prostitutes, each intent on scavenging from the other, inhaling the foul air and thrashing around like goldfish cast off into a puddle of water.

Pyke had no attachment to coaches and their yards and disliked the stink produced by the horses, the endless streams of dung that even the collectors could not keep up with, but he wondered whether he would miss them when they were gone. Railway mania was sweeping the country and within a few months the first line, from London to Greenwich, would be opened. Further lines would link London with Birmingham, the West Country, Brighton and (though this was becoming a dwindling possibility) York. That autumn had seen an additional seven companies consolidated by Acts of Parliament, and within five or ten years railway travel would be the norm, turning vibrant enterprises like the Swan into ghost towns. Pyke did not object to the coming of the railways per se, and in the hands of men like Morris he could see how they might transform the country and the world for the better, but the mania had also unleashed a tidal wave of greed and get-rich-quick schemes, many of which would doubtless come to nothing and leave people destitute and homeless. Not that Pyke cared about people who couldn't look after their own concerns, but the idea that the naked pursuit of material betterment should become the sole ambition of people's lives made even him feel queasy.

On the dot of six, four different coaches arrived almost at the same time, and Pyke almost didn't see Sir Horsley Rockingham being helped out of one of them by the guard. As soon as he was back on terra firma, Rockingham barked some kind of unpleasantness to the guard and two pot-boys immediately appeared, one to carry his overnight case and the other to hail a Hackney coachman. Pyke had to act quickly to make sure that he'd be able to follow the landowner by carriage if necessary, and only just managed to find a cab in time to pursue Rockingham's vehicle out of the yard. He settled down in the back of the carriage and, ignoring the smell of damp straw and stale tobacco, thought again about the note and why someone might have wanted to alert him to Rockingham's arrival in the capital.

It didn't take him long to find out. As Rockingham's carriage pulled up in front of the Athenaeum club on Pall Mall, it was greeted by two porters who helped him out of the cab and took his case. There, too, was the unmistakable figure of Jake Bolter and his dog Copper. At first, Pyke couldn't work out what was happening. Rockingham followed the porters into the Athenaeum while Bolter and the dog hopped into the waiting cab. Pyke remained where he was, about fifty yards farther back along Pall Mall on the same side of the street, and told the coachmen to wait. The cab ahead of them didn't move and in a few minutes Rockingham emerged from the club with one of the porters, this time without his case, and was helped into the waiting carriage. As it turned around in the street and rattled past them, Pyke concealed his face and told his driver to follow it, if possible at a discreet distance.

The journey across the city to their eventual destination, a public house on Tooley Street in Bermondsey on the south side of the Thames, took just over an hour, a stop-start trip during which they had to inch their way through streets and thoroughfares choked with other vehicles and pedestrians spilling off the pavements. To pass the time Pyke perused a copy of the *Public Ledger* and waded through further vitriol directed at the radicals and navvies who had instigated the riots in Huntingdon. Only briefly did it mention that two Members of Parliament, Joseph Hume and Thomas Wakley, had both asked questions in the House about the illegal use of untrained citizens as special constables. The report also mentioned that a march in support of the navvies was being planned by the two national trade union movements after which a petition demanding an enquiry into the deaths of three navvies would be delivered to the prime minister's Whitehall residence. There was no further mention of Nash's murder and nothing about the brutal killing of Freddie Sutton and his wife at their home in Spitalfields. Outside, he noticed, it had started to rain. It would turn the mud and manure that coated the surfaces of the streets into a stinking brown slush, and for the time being Pyke was glad to be protected from the elements. On such a night, with winter fast approaching and a yellow fog rolling off the Thames, London could be a truly miserable place.

In spite of the rain, the yard at the back of the Jolly Sailor public house on Tooley Street was teeming with people: smudge-faced dockers with their unkempt whiskers and crushed billycock caps, market traders dressed in velveteen coats, silk neckerchiefs and beaver-knapped hats, prostitutes wearing heavy cotton print dresses and brightly coloured ribbons in their lace bonnets, and farm labourers in soiled smock-frocks, all attracted by the likelihood of seeing someone or something's blood spilled. The air around them was thick with the stink from the nearby tanneries, and though it was dark, the plumes of black smoke that belched out of the chimneys of the Barclay's brewery were just visible in the night sky.

For the time being Pyke had lost sight of Bolter – he had disappeared into one of the stables adjoining the yard – but

Rockingham was standing across from him, his small, quick eyes focused on the gladiatorial ring. The ring was no larger than a good-sized pig pen and was surrounded by a waist-high wooden fence. A generous covering of straw had been laid over the mud. Pyke had no idea what kind of sport they had all come to witness, whether it would involve dogs, cocks, bears, rats or bulls, but the betting was furious and the mood expectant.

The bull was first to appear, a hulking brute of a creature with long, pointed horns and hoofs that clattered against the cobblestones as four burly men dragged it, head first, towards the ring. Pyke couldn't tell whether the beast was terrified or angry but its nostrils were flayed and raw. Once the snorting bull had been shoved into the ring, a path was cleared and the first dog appeared, a squat bulldog slavering at the end of its leash, held by a man wearing braided kerseymere. Bolter was next, the giant mastiff straining on his leash in a similar demented fashion, closely followed by what looked like a Great Dane as large as a pony, its fur peppered with bite marks. The three owners conferred with one another for a few moments, before, to the roar of the crowd, the dogs were released into the ring, where the bull waited.

It was raining heavily and despite the thick covering of straw the bull was having difficulties manoeuvring on the cobbles, giving an advantage to the dogs. But it was the bull who attacked first, its head down and horns ready as it charged first at the Great Dane, which nimbly skipped out of the way, and then at the bulldog, which only just managed to avoid being mauled. Meanwhile Copper, Bolter's mastiff, had circled around the back and lunged with its powerful jaws at the bull's hind legs, ripping out some flesh and ligament before retreating backwards just as the enraged beast spun around and tried to impale him on the end of its horn. The other two dogs followed the mastiff's lead and pounced on the bull from behind, the bulldog tearing a strip of skin from its back and drawing first blood and the Great Dane going for the beast's injured hind leg. Shrieking with pain or anger or both, the bull spun around in a second and speared the Great Dane with one of its horns, a cheer from the crowd drowning out the groans, the bull lifting the giant dog up into the air on its horn, shaking its head and hurling the limp, stricken hound into the mob standing on the other side of the ring. The flying beast narrowly missed Rockingham but his face was splattered, along with others standing by the rail, with the dog's blood and entrails, as the animal itself flattened ten or fifteen men, as though they were no more substantial than a few skittles.

For a moment Pyke watched Rockingham rather than the contest. He might have expected the country landowner to be appalled by what had just happened and uneasy at being among such a rough crowd. But though specks of blood peppered the older man's face, he couldn't tear his eyes off the carnage in the ring, his caked lips glistening with his own saliva – and Pyke remembered the unblinking way in which he had shot his own horse.

A gutsy cheer erupted around the ring as the tawny mastiff clawed its way up on to the bull's back and sunk its jaws into flesh, while the snarling bulldog attacked one of its front legs. The bull's hind legs kicked viciously upwards, sending the mastiff crashing back to the ground, apparently uninjured, but the bulldog had managed to lock its teeth around the bull's leg and crunched down until its jaw touched bone. Pyke was certain that the bull's shrieks could be heard as far away as Rotherhithe, making a mockery of the law passed by Parliament banning blood sports in public places. Tottering on one good front leg, the bull turned on the bulldog but couldn't keep its footing and toppled over on to the straw. It hit the ground with a thud that shuddered the foundations of the pub and which Pyke could feel in his stomach. Then the two remaining beasts were on top of it, the scent of blood thick in their nostrils. But the bull wasn't finished yet and managed to haul itself up on to its three good legs, one of its hind legs kicking the bulldog in its jaw and sending the stunned dog to ground. Turning around, the bull charged and the stricken dog couldn't limp out of the way, and while most of the gathered mob had to look away at the moment when the bull's hoofs punctured the bulldog's chest, Rockingham's eyes glistened with evident delight.

Now the odds had shifted firmly in the bull's favour, a fact that was underscored by a glimpse of Bolter's anxious face. The two beasts circled one another warily, the bull still only able to use three of its legs. The mastiff seemed much less sure of itself, now its companions lay dead, and the bull perhaps sensed this, lowering its head and charging at the dog. Copper just managed to get out of the way, but in the charge the bull's horns had become skewered in one of the wooden posts and, as violently as the bull shook its neck, its horns wouldn't come free. No one knew what to do; no one apart from Bolter's mastiff, which doubled back on the bull, now it was incapacitated, and attacked its hind legs with a flash of teeth. What followed sickened Pyke to his pit of his stomach. Sensing the kill, the mastiff tore apart the hind end of the paralysed creature, blood and entrails dripping from its jaws. But it wasn't a quick death and no one came to the bull's rescue. Instead, as the mastiff tugged at the dying beast's insides, the faces of those closest to the ring seemed to reflect the ugliness of what they were watching. Rockingham's expression was especially disturbing: it was as if he was experiencing some kind of sexual thrill from the sight of the carnage. It took the mastiff a further ten minutes to finally slay the bull, by which time the bookmakers had already paid out to those who had bet on the dogs and some of the crowd had started to drift back into the pub.

Farther along Tooley Street, Pyke found a small grocer's store that sold bottles of laudanum and imbibed most of the tincture to settle his stomach. He had not taken laudanum in a while and its effect was almost instantaneous, a numbing calm spreading throughout his body.

When he returned to the Jolly Sailor, it took him a few minutes to find Bolter and Rockingham. They were alone in the games room playing billiards. The dog was nowhere to be seen.

In his time as a Bow Street Runner, Pyke had been knifed, garrotted, shot, kicked and assaulted with everything from a cudgel to a machete. He had killed people, too, and even though he didn't consider himself to be violent by nature, he had done so seemingly without a burden on his conscience. But at times he would lie awake, listening to the trees outside the window swaying in the wind, and think about his ex-mistress, Lizzie, who had been slain in the bed while he slept next to her, and about the men, for they were all men, whose lives he had cut short, and wonder whether he wasn't drawn to blood and violence like a moth to a candle.

The mood in the games room was a jolly one, as Bolter chatted happily about his dog's achievements and attributes. They didn't seem to notice Pyke at first or, if they did, it didn't puncture their high spirits. It was Rockingham who saw him first, a peculiar smile appearing on his cadaverous face, as though the surprise was a pleasant one. Bolter lifted up his cue and moved around to the other side of the billiards table, his eyes never leaving Pyke for a moment.

Later Pyke would try to convince himself that the young lad he had rescued from Groat's sweat houses was at the forefront of his thoughts as he strode across the room and picked out a wooden cue from the holder. In fact he just felt numb, the laudanum infusing his insides with a deadening warmth.

Holding the cue with the tapered end, he swung it through the air and struck Bolter on the side of his face, his cheek splitting open from the blow, his eyeballs bulging from their sockets. A streak of crimson arced across the green baize. Bolter went down, his legs buckling as if they were made of paper, and Pyke bent over him, holding the cue at either end and pressing the middle part down against Bolter's neck. For a moment he thought he might throttle him.

'How do you know Rockingham?'

He lifted the cue, enough for Bolter to croak, 'He's involved with the regiment.'

Immediately Pyke remembered a story that had been told to him by the magistrate in Huntingdon. 'You were on the *Kent* when it caught fire and sunk in the Bay of Biscay, weren't you?'

Bolter's eyes bulged as Pyke pressed down on the cue but he managed a desperate nod.

'Did you kill Morris?'

Bolter shook his head.

'I said, did you kill Morris?'

'No.'

He released the cue and Bolter rolled over and retched, his whole body convulsing through lack of air.

Standing up, Pyke turned to face Rockingham, who had sought neither to intervene nor call for help. Rather the older man had stood there, rooted to the spot, and watched as Pyke had struck his companion with a wooden billiards cue, as though it had been a form of entertainment put on only for his benefit. Others had drifted into the room, attracted by the whiff of trouble, but as Pyke walked past Rockingham, the old man opened his mouth, a blast of fetid breath leaking from it, and whispered, 'I'll see you in hell.'

And it was this, more than what he had done to Bolter, which made Pyke contemplate what he had done and wonder whether he was as damned as he felt.

The following morning, as he walked through Regent's Park, Pyke could still smell traces of blood on his clothes. It was a beautiful November day and, away from the choking miasma of dust and smoke that hung over much of the city, Pyke could see the cornflower blue of the sky and feel the pleasant crispness of the air against his skin. It was the kind of day that should have made him feel happy to be alive, but as the giant portico and rotunda of the Colosseum loomed in the distance, above the line of trees, he couldn't rid his mind of an image of Morris plummeting to his death.

It was only half-past eight and the attractions weren't yet open to the public, but he found the caretaker mopping the floor in the central rotunda. His figure looked as if it had been bent out of shape and he needed the mop to prop him up. He watched Pyke cross the floor towards him, his paintbrush moustache twitching and his armpits already dark with sweat.

Perhaps he recognised Pyke from the coroner's inquest or perhaps he didn't. But it was only when Pyke asked the question that a trace of caution, even concern, appeared in his face.

'If you toured the building at one, before you locked up, and didn't see Morris or his body anywhere, how is it possible that you found it lying here on the floor when you opened the building the following morning?'

The caretaker pulled himself up straight and shrugged. 'Like the man said, maybe the cully that died hid himself in the building and then jumped after I'd done my rounds.'

'That would be one explanation.'

'And the other?' The caretaker seemed amused by something.

'You waited until all the guests and workers had gone and then turned a blind eye while someone dragged Morris's drink-addled body over to the edge of the promenade and hauled him up over the railing. Perhaps you even helped.'

'The man's death was ruled as suicide. You'd do as well to remember that, before spreading your lies.'

'How much did someone pay you to keep your mouth shut? Ten guineas? Maybe twenty?'

'I've got work to do. If you'll excuse me.' He started to walk off in the direction of the entrance.

'Who killed him? Was it Bolter? Or perhaps a man with a glass eye?'

But the caretaker didn't turn around and Pyke caught up with him only on the very edge of the main floor. 'Did you see anything unusual or strange that night, sir? Please, it could be important.'

His unexpected politeness softened the caretaker's indignation. 'Now you mention it, I did see the gentl'man who died arguing with a cull up on the promenade. There were still a few guests left but none up there. Well-dressed cull, black hair, same as yours. I'd say he was younger than you, mind.'

'You didn't hear what the argument was about?'

The caretaker scratched his head. 'No, I don't reckon I did.'

Pyke described Jem Nash as best he could and asked whether this was the man he'd seen arguing with Morris.

'Aye, it could have been.' The caretaker looked towards the entrance. 'You'd better go. My supervisor catches me chinwagging, I'll be shown the door faster than you can say Jack Robinson.'

Outside something had disturbed the jackdaws from their treetop perches and the sky was momentarily turned black by a flapping of wings. Pyke thought about the man's claim to have seen Morris and Nash arguing and wondered whether it had been true and, if so, what it indicated.

From the outside, Bartholomew Prosser's pauper's 'school' looked like any other genteel residence on the outskirts of the metropolis, a well-maintained Palladian mansion with a plain stucco façade and Regency bow windows concealed behind a sturdy wrought-iron fence. But inside was a different story. All the effort and money had been spent on maintaining the exterior of the building and keeping the lawns spruce. Inside was a rabbit warren of damp, gloomy rooms connected by long passageways that put Pyke in mind of a prison. In fact the carceral analogy was entirely appropriate because upstairs Pyke found out that the boys were kept under lock and key, with as many as ten shivering, emaciated bodies crammed into rooms that were barely larger than a privy. In all he counted twenty such rooms, meaning the school or, rather, juvenile prison housed more than two hundred boys aged between five and fifteen. Pyke could not find Prosser himself, nor Jake Bolter, who apparently hadn't been seen since the day before, but at gunpoint he forced an elderly matron figure to unlock all the doors and allow the boys to roam freely in the corridors and rooms.

From her, and his own intuition, Pyke gleaned how the establishment operated. In light of the recent Poor Law amendment, Prosser had written to the workhouse managers telling them about his 'school' and requesting that they send him any unwanted boys, for which he would charge a fee of three shillings and six pence a week, which represented a small saving on what it cost to keep a boy at the workhouse. Instead of feeding and educating the boys as he'd promised, however, Prosser then sold them on to various sweaters in the East End and continued to claim the money from the workhouse managers who'd sent him the boys in the first place. It was a lucrative operation that might have earned Prosser as much as five hundred or even a thousand pounds a year.

Pyke was walking back towards the main gate when he looked behind him and saw Jake Bolter appear from one of the outbuildings, his mastiff Copper choking on the end of its leash. Even at a distance of a hundred yards, he could see the man's injuries as a result of his assault. Bending down, Bolter took off the leash and suddenly the giant mastiff was tearing towards him across the lawn, barking and growling, his paws chewing up chunks of turf. Pyke just managed to climb over the painted fence before the dog took a piece out of his ankles but it didn't stop the beast from pressing its nose up against the wrought-iron railings and baring its teeth.

Bolter ambled down to the fence and patted the mastiff on the head. 'Not so brave now, are we?' Up close, Pyke saw that the gash around his left eye hadn't properly healed and a flap of skin hung down, surrounded by congealed blood.

'Tell Prosser that I'm going to close this place down and throw him on to the street where he belongs.'

'Is that right?' Bolter was grinning now. 'A blackguard like yourself, caught up in an apron-string hold.'

Pyke stared at Bolter through the wrought-iron fence, his jaw clenched. 'What did you just say?'

'I heard you was living on Queen's Street. Do you want me to be more plain still, sir? I'm saying your piece wears the breeches.'

Pyke absorbed the insult but he could feel the heat in his own face. 'I talked to the man at the Colosseum. He admitted he lied at the coroner's inquest.'

'Now why would the cull go and do a thing like that?' Bolter regarded Pyke with scepticism. Down at his feet, the dog was still barking and baring its teeth.

'He named you.'

'Named me in what?'

'The conspiracy to kill Edward James Morris.'

This time Bolter's grin broadened. 'I see your plan, sir. You're putting your line in the water and hoping the fishes bite. Reckon you got it worked out. Except this little fishy ain't hungry.' Reaching down, he patted Copper on the head.

'Who or what did you bury in the grounds of Cranborne Park a few weeks ago in the company of Marguerite Morris?'

For a moment Pyke thought he saw something register in Bolter's eyes but it was gone as quickly as it had appeared, replaced by a bland expression that suggested Bolter regarded Pyke merely as a nuisance.

'You want to know about the lady's business, ask the lady herself.' With that, he turned around and walked back across the lawn towards the old house, the mastiff trotting happily at his side.

The hack-chaise dropped Pyke at Cheapside, just as the shopkeepers were pulling up their wooden shutters for the night and the lamplighters were working their way along the street, the greasy flame of the lamps hissing in their wake. It was a miserable evening, and the rain had turned the dung and mud into a slushy liquid that coated the trousers and breeches of pedestrians. Sweeping past them and spraying more of this foul brown mulch on to the pavements were the omnibuses, Shillibeer's originals recognisable by their green markings and others belonging to different operators, all packed, the knife-boards on their roofs filled with back-to-back passengers shivering under tarpaulins.

Pyke had walked perhaps fifty yards along Cheapside in the direction of St Paul's Cathedral when he realised that someone was following him. At first it was just a feeling, an intuitive sense gained from years of experience as a Bow Street Runner following other people: even among the throng of pedestrians, when he stopped, he could sense someone stopping behind him, even without turning around to check. At the corner of Wood Street, he waited until the last moment and ducked into a bazaar, following a narrow passageway until it opened up into a room adjoined by a myriad of smaller shops set in alcoves, with a refreshment counter at the back. Hiding behind a collection of exotic plants, he waited to see whether someone had followed him into the bazaar, the twittering of parrots and cockatoos drowning out the buzz of voices and the cries of vendors seeking to advertise their wares. Through the green foliage, he surveyed the faces of those entering and leaving the room but didn't see anything or anyone acting in an unduly suspicious manner. Relaxing a little, he retraced his path to the passageway.

They saw one another and froze. Pyke was close enough to see his glass eye and smell the gin on his breath. Just for a moment it wasn't clear who was the hunter and who was the hunted. He was a lithe, wiry man, his face covered by a ragged beard and a bushy untrimmed moustache that ran into each other and covered his mouth completely. It was Pyke who moved first, lunging for the man's arm, but he was quicker than Pyke had expected and had spun around before Pyke could grab him. Barging shoppers to one side, the glass-eyed man set off along the passageway back towards Cheapside, Pyke following him outside on to the street. There the man turned right and stepped out on to the road, just missing a phaeton that swept past at a canter, arms pumping as he broke into a full sprint. Ducking out of the way of a costermonger's barrow, Pyke kept up with the man in pursuit and shouted, 'Stop, thief,' hoping that someone might intervene and bring the man down for him.

Further cries of 'stop, thief' reverberated ahead of Pyke, but to avoid being tackled by a random passer-by, the glass-eyed man had swerved on to the road, narrowly avoiding a dung sweeper, weaved his way through the traffic to the end of Cheapside and then crossed over on to St Paul's Yard, the mighty dome casting its vast shadow over the entire area. But the man was quick and Pyke was able to make up only a few yards, not enough to prevent him racing around the side of the cathedral and entering it through the doors on the west side.

Pyke followed him into the cathedral through the main entrance and stopped for a moment: the evening service had just started and the glass-eyed man had pushed his way through a procession of godly men wearing ceremonial robes, gasps of astonishment and shock accompanying his actions. Pyke took the less populated route along the north aisle and managed to cut the glass-eyed man off on the main floor just under the dome, forcing him to take refuge behind the table, where a visibly frightened canon was preparing the communion Eucharist. By this point the choir had stopped singing and the procession had come to a halt farther down the aisle, no one quite knowing what to do or how to address the disruption.

But though cornered, the glass-eyed man was, by no means, finished. Taking out a knife from his monkey coat, he pulled the shaking canon towards him and held the blade to his throat. Behind the ink-black tangle of hair, his one good eye shone with a peculiar malevolence. Someone had seen what was happening and screamed for assistance. Other anguished cries followed. Pyke held up the palms of his hands and took a stride towards the table.

'Stay there, cully,' the glass-eyed man barked, 'or the priest gets cut.' He started to back away towards the entrance down to the crypt, dragging the canon along with him. As he did so, he picked up the communion cup with his one free hand and took a swig of the wine, streaks of the claret liquid spilling down the sides of his mouth into his tangle of hair. He let out a burp and grinned. 'Tell that bitch of yours to watch her back,' he said in a low, gruff voice that sounded almost animalistic in its tone. Around them, the air was thick with the smell of candle wax.

Hot with anger, Pyke started to follow him but the glass-eyed man dug the sharp point of the blade into the canon's throat and ordered to him to stay where he was. At the top of the stairs that led down to the crypt, a good twenty or thirty yards from where Pyke was standing, he drew the blade across the canon's throat in a single motion, let the stricken man fall to his feet and turned and disappeared down the steps. But by the time Pyke had covered the ground across to the top of the stairs, checked to see that the canon could not be saved, blood pouring from his neck where the jugular had been severed, and descended the stone steps three at a time, the glass-eyed man had left the building through one of the many side doors and was nowhere to be seen. Above him, Pyke could hear wails of grief and outrage, and rather than trudge back up the stairs and face the combined wrath of the clergy and the congregation, he slipped out of the same door the glass-eyed man had used and closed it behind him.

SEVENTEEN

It was just a short step from the cathedral to his uncle's shop in St Paul's Yard and Pyke decided to take refuge there, rather than attempt to run the gauntlet of the massed ranks of police constables who would doubtless be summoned to the cathedral and would soon be looking for the priest's assassin. In the deserted yard, a squally wind had whipped the sodden pages of a discarded newspaper into the air. Digging his shaking hands into his pockets, Pyke thought of the priest who had been killed for no other reason than that of being in the wrong place and wondered what kind of human being would kill a man of the cloth without pausing for thought, as though the act of taking a life were akin to having a piss or discarding a half-eaten pie. He also thought about the threat he'd made against Emily and decided that, having seen his uncle, he would return to Hambledon to make sure she was safe.

The stone steps that led down to Godfrey's basement shop were wet from the rain and at the bottom Pyke was surprised to see that the door was ajar. Godfrey liked to complain bitterly about the ill effects of the cold weather. It wasn't just raining, though. A fog had rolled up the river from the east and made it difficult to see the top of Wren's dome, even though the cathedral was just a few yards away.

Peering through the door, Pyke shouted out his uncle's name, his eyes straining to see through the darkness.

He heard Godfrey's cry before he saw the state of the shop; even in the dim light produced by half a dozen candles, the chaos was evident. Books had been torn apart, piles of manuscripts had been riffled through and strewn on the floor, and bundles of letters had been cut open and discarded.

At the back of the shop, two men wearing tailored swallow-tailed coats over knee-length breeches and wellington boots had pinned

Godfrey against the wall. With knife in his hand, Pyke steadied himself and took aim, sending the weapon corkscrewing through the air. The blade tore into one of the men's flesh, embedding itself deep into the leg. The wounded man screamed in agony and fell to the floor, giving Pyke time to move carefully through the shop. The other man looked up, visibly startled. He wasn't physically favoured, by any stretch of the imagination, but his quick, darting movements and powerful forearms made him someone to be reckoned with. But Pyke didn't stop to take stock of the situation and assess the threat posed by the two men. Rather he sprinted through the shop and threw himself at the larger man, driving him backwards into the wall and winding him in the process. He landed a clean blow on his jaw and watched as he collapsed.

Godfrey had slumped to the floor and was wheezing like an injured hog, clutching his chest. Pyke knelt beside him and asked whether he was all right. Godfrey tried to whisper a few words but they wouldn't form on his tongue.

But the two attackers hadn't finished with him. The larger man, the uninjured one, had retrieved a broken table leg and was advancing towards him, swinging it wildly in the air like a machete. The first swing missed Pyke's cheek by a whisker but the follow-up swipe caught him a little off balance and gave his attacker enough time to push past him and run for the door.

Rather than setting after him in pursuit, Pyke decided to concentrate his efforts on apprehending his companion, who, by this stage, had managed to haul himself up on to his legs and hobble to the back of the shop, where a door opened out on to a small court. In the doorway, and just in time, Pyke saw the glint of a gun barrel and fell to the ground before a blast of powder sent ball-shot fizzing over his head.

Pyke moved after the wounded man with more caution. Outside in the courtyard, he followed the trail of blood along a high-walled alleyway, catching sight of the man as he turned the corner into another alleyway, which led to Ludgate Hill. The injured man was moving slowly but Pyke opted to keep his distance, in case the pistol contained another shot.

Ludgate Hill was deserted apart from a street sweeper and a costermonger pulling his barrow by hand. From the entrance to the alleyway, Pyke looked across the street and saw what the wounded man clearly hadn't: a two-wheeled phaeton pulled by a couple of strapping mares bearing down on him out of the swirling fog. The driver saw the man too late to change his course but tried to pull on the horses' reins. For his part, the wounded man saw what was about to happen and held up the palms of his hands, a final, pitiful act of defiance before he was trampled under the hoofs of the terrified horses, run over by the wheels of the carriage and impaled on the axle, which had snapped in two as a result of the collision.

First at the scene of the accident, Pyke checked to see that the driver of the phaeton would live and then turned his attention to the dead man, who, minutes earlier, had tried to attack Godfrey in his shop. Pulling the knife from the man's leg, Pyke wiped the blade on what seemed to be an expensive coat and briefly rummaged through his pockets. The only thing of interest that he found was a brass cravat pin supporting some kind of military coat of arms. The police would have to deal with yet another dead body, Pyke thought grimly as he wandered back to Godfrey's shop. Two in a night, both within a few hundred yards of each other. Perhaps they would try to connect the two. Perhaps they *were* connected, he mused.

Back in the shop, his uncle was sprawled out on the floor. He wasn't moving and when Pyke tried to rouse him, he groaned slightly and clutched his chest, wincing with evident pain. 'It's my heart, dear boy,' he wheezed. 'I don't know if I'll make it.' His eyelids fluttered and closed.

But Godfrey did not pass away that night or, indeed, the following day, and by the next evening he had rallied sufficiently to take a few sips of water and two mouthfuls of bread. Pyke had paid for a room in St Bartholomew's, and also for Sir Henry Halford, the well-respected royal physician, to attend to him around the clock. Pyke hardly slept at all on the first night and remained with his uncle throughout the following day. Emily visited in the evening with victuals and they sat across from one another, each holding one of Godfrey's withered hands, their thoughts drowned out by the terrified grunts and squeals of animals being herded into the market outside.

'You know, it was Godfrey who taught me how to read,' Pyke said, on the second night.

Emily smiled warmly and took Pyke's other hand in hers.

Pyke looked at her but his mind was elsewhere. The previous night it had struck him, maybe for the first time, that his uncle might die, and he realised how unprepared he was for this eventuality. 'I still remember the first thing he ever read to me.'

'Yes?' Emily looked up at him.

'*The Life and Times of Sawney Beane.*'

'Who's that?' One side of her face was lit up by the candlelight.

'Sawney Beane.' He met her gaze across the bed. 'He robbed people and ate their flesh.'

That drew a knowing smile. 'And how old were you at the time?'

'A little older than Felix.'

'I was going to say it hasn't done you any harm.'

Pyke smiled. 'Godfrey always reckoned you could do more damage than good by trying to shield young minds from the less palatable aspects of life.'

Emily regarded him with a thoughtful expression. 'It sounds very different from our son's upbringing.'

Pyke reached out and stroked his uncle on the forehead. 'I'm just saying he never felt the need to censor. Good, bad, gruesome, uplifting. He read them all and let me come to my own conclusions.'

Pyke watched her from the other side of the bed. It was at moments such as these, he mused, that you realised what people meant to you. He had experienced a similar blind panic when Emily had almost died while giving birth to Felix. She had lost consciousness for a few days and Pyke had remained at her bedside for the entire time, trying to keep her alive with the strength of his will.

In the intervening years, he had often wondered why she hadn't conceived again. The first time, it had happened quite quickly, within a year of the marriage, allaying fears carried over from a former attachment that he might be barren. But Emily's recovery had been long and slow and it had taken a full year before she had been ready to try for more children. The physician who had treated her said there was no reason why this shouldn't happen, but for some reason it never had and, in recent months, they had stopped talking about it as a possibility.

Pyke looked down at his uncle's sleeping face. 'Apart from Felix, the only people that matter to me are right here in this room.'

Emily squeezed his hand and smiled gently. 'Do I detect a subtle rebuke in your tone?'

'Captain Paine may want to improve the lot of the poor and destitute. I just want to keep my family safe.'

It seemed to amuse her. 'Is that what you were doing the other afternoon when we visited Granby Street?' She hesitated, licking her lips. 'Or why that little girl is in one of the rooms at Hambledon?'

Pyke took her hand and waited for a few moments. 'The other night, just before I found Godfrey in his shop, I turned the tables on this man who'd been following me. I chased him into St Paul's where he killed one of the priests. You might have read about it in the newspaper. Just before he escaped – he was holding a knife to the priest's throat at the time – he made a threat against you.'

'What kind of a threat?'

'His exact words were, "Tell that bitch of yours to watch her back." Pyke stared at her across the bed. 'Why would he say something like that?'

Emily shrugged. 'You don't know who he was and why he was following you?'

'No.' He didn't want to tell her about the glass-eyed man's apparent brutality and unnecessarily scare her but he wanted her to know that his threat was a serious one.

'Then I don't see what I can do about it.'

Pyke let go of her hand and glanced down at his uncle. 'Perhaps you should think twice about maintaining such a public presence.'

'You want me to stop doing what I do?' A hardness had entered her voice.

'I don't know what you've been doing,' Pyke said, losing his patience. 'That's my point. If I did, I could judge the potential threat to your safety.'

'And how about what *you* do? Have you thought to tell me about the problems you seem to be facing?'

'We can talk about this another time,' Pyke said, noticing that Godfrey had stirred ever so slightly. 'But for now, promise me you'll take extra precautions. I'm being deadly serious, Emily. This man was not someone to be taken lightly. I just think you should lay low for the next week or so, while I see if I can turn up any information.'

Emily left shortly after that, saying she wanted to get back to

Hambledon in time to say goodnight to Felix. Pyke asked her to send Felix his love and make sure that Milly was all right.

It was only on the third day after the attack that Godfrey rallied sufficiently for the physician to declare that he was 'out of immediate danger'. That afternoon, after Halford had departed, his pockets loaded with money, Pyke helped his uncle to a few sips of beer he'd smuggled into the hospital from the Old Red Lion.

'It's not gin but I suppose it'll have to do,' Godfrey said, as streaks of the brown liquid dribbled down his chin.

Pyke wanted to tell Godfrey how much he meant to him and how scared he'd been at the thought of the old man's death but somehow the words wouldn't come. Instead, he explained to Godfrey that the libel charges against him had been dropped. That seemed to cheer him up no end.

'That's bloody marvellous news,' Godfrey said, taking another swig of ale. 'How did it happen? They seemed to have the bit between their teeth this time.'

Pyke told him about his dealings with Abraham Gore and Gore's intervention on Godfrey's behalf.

'The banker?' Godfrey didn't bother to conceal his surprise. 'Why would he want to help me?'

'I think he wants me to like him.'

'And do you?'

'I don't know. He's always been very open and honest with me.' Quickly he told the story of Gore's arrival at the coroner's meeting and the invectives he'd heaped on Sir Henry Bellows.

'A man after my own heart,' Godfrey said, laughing. 'Do you think Bellows knew about his intervention in my case?'

'Yes, I'm sure he did.' Pyke thought about it some more. 'But he was wary around Gore in a way that he wasn't with me.'

Godfrey nodded. 'That would seem about right. If I were you, my boy, I wouldn't underestimate Gore's influence. I've heard he's a generous man, gives a lot of his money to charity, but he didn't get to where he is now without cracking a few eggs.'

Pyke absorbed the warning and steered the conversation back to the incident in the shop. Who had the men been, for example?

'Never seen the blighters before in my life,' Godfrey said, with clear indignation.

'But you know who might have sent them or what they wanted?'

'They kept asking me for the letters, as though I'd know precisely what they were talking about.'

'What letters?'

'I don't know for certain, dear boy.' Godfrey ruffled his mane of bone-white hair. 'I think it might have had something to do with the missing girl and the court case.'

He must have seen Pyke's jaw clench because almost at once he asked, 'What is it, dear boy?'

Pyke told him about finding Freddie Sutton and his wife in their Spitalfields shack, their throats cut. He also mentioned the young daughter, now recuperating at Hambledon, and explained how, when he had returned to Spitalfields with the police, the dead bodies had been removed. The police, he added, didn't seem to believe a crime had actually been committed.

Godfrey took the news very badly, as Pyke suspected he might, but the shock was not sufficient to induce further chest problems. 'And you think the two men who attacked me might have done for the parents?' He seemed aghast and genuinely frightened by this prospect.

'Perhaps,' Pyke said, adjusting his position on the hard wooden chair. 'I found this on the one who fell under the phaeton,' he added, retrieving the cravat pin from his pocket and showing it to his uncle.

The silver object glinted in the candlelight as Godfrey sat up in the bed to inspect it. 'I wouldn't mind wagering it's the coat of arms for one of the military regiments. Can I hold on to it for a few days?'

'By all means,' Pyke said, thinking about the six dragoons who had chased him on horseback in Cambridgeshire and wondering whether there might be a connection. Certainly Jake Bolter, Septimus Yellowplush and Sir Horsley Rockingham were either affiliated with or had once served in the same regiment: the 31st, which was barracked somewhere near Huntingdon.

Bolter and Yellowplush were brothers in arms, having gone down in the same ship in the Bay of Biscay and lived to tell the tale, and their apparent closeness seemed to shed light on an important aspect of the conspiracy to halt the northward progress of the Grand Northern Railway. They had perhaps acted together to stir up the navvies and hence retard the construction work north of

Cambridge, but had they conspired to kill Morris and make it look like a suicide? And, as Peel seemed to believe, was there any connection between their machinations and the headless corpse that had turned up in the River Ouse?

Pyke stood up and stretched his legs. 'You don't have any idea what these letters might refer to or be about?'

'From what I could grasp, the men in my shop seemed to believe Kate Sutton had stolen them from Kensington Palace and had passed them on to me.'

'Or left them with her parents,' Pyke added, grimly.

Godfrey considered this for a short while. 'Do you think Conroy might have sent them?'

'Let's assume for a minute that Kate Sutton really did steal some letters from him, letters of great significance, letters he desperately needed to get back ...'

'Desperate enough to kill for?'

Pyke studied his uncle's jaundiced face. 'What else do you know about him?'

'Conroy?'

Pyke nodded.

'He's originally from Ireland, County Roscommon, I think. He served in the Royal Artillery before becoming the Duke of Kent's private equerry. After the duke perished, he slipped into the dead man's shoes in more ways than one. Became the duchess's lover and comptroller, if Kate Sutton's to be believed. I'm told he's handsome, charming and totally unscrupulous. And quite a hothead, if his reputation is to go by. Perhaps he reckons that when Victoria becomes queen, as she soon will do, he'll be the puppet-master pulling the strings of the young woman and her mother.'

Pyke rubbed his chin. 'Perhaps there's something in the letters that threatens this possibility.'

Godfrey fell back on to his flimsy mattress. 'I feel I've brought this whole situation about myself. After all, I gave encouragement to the girl's attempts to sell her information regarding Conroy. She seemed desperate for money.'

'Don't blame yourself for other people's cruelty. You didn't put a knife to Freddie Sutton's throat.'

This did little to improve his uncle's mood. 'Actually, now I think of it, there was something else. Something one of them said.'

'In the shop?'

Godfrey nodded. 'I'm fairly sure I heard the taller, burlier one tell the other one, "He won't be happy," when it became evident I didn't have the letters. Except he didn't say *he*.'

'So what did he say?'

'I don't know,' Godfrey said, scratching his head. 'To be honest, it sounded like he said H.'

'As in the letter?'

'Exactly.'

'So whose name begins with the letter H?'

'I've racked my brains and I can't come up with a soul.'

They talked in this roundabout manner for another few minutes before reaching a dead end. To fill the silence, Pyke asked Godfrey whether a young lad had come to the shop asking for work as a delivery boy. Godfrey shook his head, said, no, he didn't think so, and forced Pyke to tell him about the circumstances surrounding the lad's escape from the sweatshop. When he'd finished, there was a glint in his uncle's eye. Changing the subject, Pyke asked him whether he'd heard any rumours about Sir Henry Bellows buying up land in the vicinity of New Road.

Godfrey shook his head but said that he would look into the matter. Gloomily, he added that, even though the libel charges against him had been dropped, he still felt duty bound to keep looking for Kate Sutton.

'We know Bellows is friendly with Conroy,' Pyke said, thinking out loud. 'But we also know that he has, or rather had, an interest in declaring Morris's death a suicide. Is there a connection?'

Godfrey looked up at him frowning. 'What sort of a connection?'

Shrugging, Pyke told his uncle about his suspicions about a conspiracy involving Bolter, Yellowplush and Rockingham, and then about the anonymous note he'd received warning him of Rockingham's arrival in the capital.

'So someone wanted you to follow him and perhaps see who he met and what he did?'

Pyke nodded. It had already crossed his mind that someone had *meant* him to see Rockingham in Bolter's company. It also struck him that he hadn't managed to determine why the landowner had visited London: the visit to the gaming tavern had surely just been a brief diversion.

'You have any ideas who might have wanted this?'

Pyke shook his head.

'I've heard of this Rockingham chap. An ex-slaver from the West Indies, made his fortune from a sugar plantation and has, subsequently, tried to buy respectability with the proceeds.'

Nodding, Pyke told him about Rockingham's Queen Anne mansion and thousand-acre estate.

'You want to get under this fellow's skin, you hit him where it hurts.' Godfrey sat up, grinning. 'What does he most like doing? What gives him the respectability he seems to crave?'

Pyke considered this for a moment. 'He has a stable of thoroughbred racehorses.'

'And you say his estate is just north of Huntingdon? Then he'll be a member of the Jockey Club at Newmarket.'

Shrugging, Pyke said he didn't know this for certain.

'If he owns and breeds racehorses, he will. Trust me.' Godfrey's cheeks glistened with excitement. 'What we do is knock up some handbills that make certain humiliating claims about the fellow, and then pay someone to circulate them in and around Newmarket.'

'What kind of claims?'

'I don't know, dear boy. Use your imagination. Perhaps he fucks his grooms or his horses or his daughter. Take your pick.'

'And if the allegations are entirely false?'

Godfrey shook his head vigorously, as if Pyke had missed the point. 'That's never stopped me in the past. Listen, am I right in thinking this blackguard had something to do with Morris's death?' When Pyke muttered, 'I think so,' Godfrey added, without changing his tone, 'So rattle his cage, hit him where it hurts and see what he does. You unsettle him enough, he'll make a mistake. Smoke the rabbit out of his hole and wait around to mop up the mess.'

EIGHTEEN

As he walked along the Waterloo Road, Pyke was stopped at almost every street corner by women with painted faces propositioning him. Some did so from the steps of their ramshackle dwellings, others called out to him through broken windowpanes. It was early evening and the air had turned so cold he could see his breath in front of him. This was one of the grimmest streets in London with its open cess trenches and pervasive stink of poverty and despair. But worse still was New Cut, a street that ran perpendicular to Waterloo Road, where the daily market left a stink of such immense magnitude that it was hard to negotiate its pavements without being sick. In one short stretch, Pyke counted five ginneries, a beer shop, four brothels, three slop shops and a dozen doss houses. In front of each, dishevelled men and women guzzled home-brewed gin straight from the bottle and would do so until the early hours, because the alternative, lying on open floors while rats nibbled their frostbitten fingers, was too unattractive a prospect. Above them, the smoke from the breweries and factories that clung to the south bank of the river had turned the skies black.

This was also the street where Maggie Shaw had grown up and where her parents had once tended a barrow in the market.

Looking at the piles of rotting vegetables and offal lining the gutters, it was hard to believe that Maggie had once graced this street. It was hard to believe she had really moved among the rickety barrows stacked with cagmag, oilskin caps, rancid fish, soiled clothes, mildewed boots and second-hand corduroy coats, and hard to believe that she had once belonged to the same tribe of people Pyke now passed – drunken, toothless creatures who would slit your throat in a minute if they believed you had money and they could get away with it. Perhaps Maggie was right. Perhaps she had never really belonged there, just as he had never really belonged in

St Giles. Having lifted themselves out of poverty, they had found security and prosperity in their middle years, but this wealth did not necessarily breed a sense of entitlement and, for Pyke at least, the feeling that it might at any point be snatched from his grip remained with him constantly. Maybe it was the same for Maggie, he mused.

If the opera and ballet represented the most rarefied 'arts' experience in the capital, attracting a predominantly aristocratic audience who would clap politely and share gossip in the intervals, the theatre was a generally more rambunctious affair. This didn't include venues like the Theatre Royal in Covent Garden and those on Drury Lane and Haymarket: these establishments still catered to gormless gentlemen and their ugly wives. But throughout the capital, there were hundreds of smaller venues staging bastardised versions of *Hamlet* or loose adaptations of popular novels and fables, and at any of these actors could expect to be abused and harangued from the pit by members of the public who might be sodden with drink. At such establishments the actors were rarely if ever professional, in the sense that they earned money from their craft. Rather they were clerks, shop boys and milliners who trod the boards in order to escape from the grim tedium of their everyday existences. Kate Sutton's beau, Johnny, was apparently such a figure, but his domain was a good deal less salubrious even than these 'low' venues. The so-called 'penny gaffs', which tended to be situated in the poorest parts of the capital, represented the grubbiest, bawdiest and least refined stage experience of all. It was not unusual to be mugged or robbed in such venues, often at the behest of the management, and children as young as twelve copulated in their dark corners.

There were four penny gaffs on New Cut, and when he eventually found the right one, having followed directions given to him by Freddie Sutton, it turned out to be little more than a warehouse, an empty shell of a building with exposed joists and damp walls. The stage, if it could be called that, comprised a few planks of wood nailed to a collection of overturned wooden beer barrels, and the only lighting was provided by an assortment of tallow candles, haphazardly arranged at the back of the stage in different-shaped wooden holders.

Pyke found the performers sitting on wooden crates at the back of the stage. They were drinking gin from the bottle and one of them, a tall, brutish man dressed to resemble a monarch or prince, was smoking a pipe. They looked up in response to his question and the king told him to get lost.

'I asked where I could find Johnny,' Pyke repeated, this time putting some metal into his tone.

The three of them continued to stare at him blankly.

'I was under the impression Johnny worked here.'

'Johnny, you say? Ain't shown his ugly face here for more 'n a month now.' The king stood up and rearranged his faux velvet cloak. He was a brute of a man with grazed knuckles, broad shoulders, cauliflower ears and a nose that had been broken in more than two places.

'Do you know where I can find him?'

'Johnny?' He stole a glance at the other two. 'You could always try the Theatre Royal.' They all guffawed loudly.

'Why do I get the sense that I'm not likely to find him there?'

'Look around you, cully. This ain't exactly Drury Lane.' The king picked up his paper crown from the floor and placed it on his head. 'Now beat it. The show's about to start.'

'Perhaps I didn't make myself clear,' Pyke said, removing the pistol from his belt and poking the end of the barrel into the man's chin. 'I asked where I could find Johnny.'

The king regarded him coolly but the other two sprang to their feet and sought to appease him. 'One day he was here and the next day he wasn't. Didn't give no explanation, neither.' The man who'd spoken was also dressed to resemble a king or an aristocrat but in a much more grotesque manner; there was a pillow stuffed under his coat to make him look fatter and he wore shoes decorated with hair to resemble animals' feet. 'This whole thing was Johnny's idea. When he was around, he'd play my role. I reckon he liked the reaction he got from the crowd.'

'Is that right?' Pyke jabbed the barrel of his pistol into the cleft of the taller man's chin. 'Is your friend suggesting Johnny had the talent?'

'Johnny liked to think so.' But the king did not seem unsettled by the pistol.

A bell rang and the three actors looked at one another. One of them explained that the show was about to begin but assured him they would answer his questions once it was finished. Pyke knew he was keeping something back but decided to let them go because the crowd was starting to get restless. Putting the pistol back in his belt, he took his place among the noisy crowd, trying to ignore the stink of unwashed bodies, and waited for the performance to begin.

'Enter our glorious, beloved monarch, William IV, King of England, Scotland and Ireland,' one of the actors bellowed from behind the makeshift stage.

'What about Wales?' someone shouted from the back of the room.

'Who gives a fuck about those leek-eating noddies?' someone else yelled in reply. This got the loudest cheer of the night.

The king climbed up on to the stage, the paper crown resting uneasily on his head. He too now had a pillow strapped around his waist, still visible under his torn velveteen coat. As he strutted around the small stage, his regal waves were absurdly fey but the mob didn't seem to mind; though they mocked him more than they applauded him, their mood was generally good natured.

'Now enter the King's conniving brother, Ernest Augustus, Duke of Cumberland and Earl of Armagh.'

The mood of the crowd changed at once, and as soon as the actor playing the duke had climbed up the rickety ladder on to the stage, he was pelted with rotten vegetables and roundly jeered. In addition to numerous pillows crammed under his bulging jacket and his cloven shoes and tail, dark hair sprouted from every part of his body and his head sported a pair of cuckold's horns. A Tory Ultra, Cumberland was unpopular among liberals and reform-minded figures for his conservative views, and satirists had taken to representing him in bestial terms.

The actor playing Cumberland strutted around the tiny stage but the heckling reached a climax only when he assaulted the king; what seemed to be a playful scuffle quickly turning into a full-blown punching match. Pyke wasn't certain whether the fight was real or staged – certainly both actors, to the delight of the audience, didn't seem to be holding back – but when the thuggish king was caught by a blow that lifted him clean off his feet and knocked him from the stage, no one knew whether to applaud the actor for his skilful fall or continue to rail against the unpopular duke.

Moments later, another actor appeared on the stage and carefully placed an orange sash around Cumberland's bulging neck, briefly getting the material caught on the tips of his horns. More vociferous booing ensued. In booming voices, the two men congratulated each other over the king's death and made plans to mobilise every man in their order to seize the crown, repeal the Reform Act and further enslave the poor. There followed a few hammy soliloquies, the best of which saw the duke reminisce about how he'd once slit his valet's throat and later forced himself on his sister Sophia. These confessions drew gasps of astonishment from the crowd. At one point, one of the crew had to prevent an enraged costermonger from climbing up on to the stage and assaulting the duke himself.

The final act saw a tall, sneering figure introduced as Sir John Conroy conspiring with Cumberland to murder young Princess Victoria, played by a ripe-looking girl who, much to the crowd's delight, took every chance to show off her ample cleavage, which was barely hidden under a flimsy muslin dress. The climactic scene featured Cumberland atop a ladder, his shadow covering much of the stage, rubbing his hands together while Conroy administered droplets of poison to the princess. As she weakened, Cumberland climbed down from his vantage point and seized the tattered crown from her head. Pandemonium followed his triumph and a shower of vitriol, and a few rotten carrots, rained down on the stage. At some point, this segued into applause, as the actor who had played the duke took off the crown and basked in the limelight.

At first, Pyke didn't hear the shouts from the front of the room but it soon became apparent that something was wrong: the door had been flung open and a stiff breeze filled the fetid room. Then he saw them, their tall stovepipe hats above the bobbing heads of the crowd, a dozen or more police constables forcing their way into the room, wielding rattles and leather truncheons. One of them fought his way up on to the stage and announced that the show was being closed until further notice and the management and actors were being pursued on charges of sedition. If apprehended, Pyke supposed the key players might even face the scaffold.

The actors seemed to realise their predicament even before the police sergeant had spoken and, having discarded their costumes, they bolted for the exits, along with the rest of the crowd. Pyke followed the one who had played Cumberland down an alleyway that ran along the side of the building and caught up with him in a small court. Others flooded past them but Pyke kept a steely grip on the man's coat and forced him up against one of the walls. The yard was cluttered with disused costermongers' carts and a trough for pigs and sheep to feed from.

'Please don't hurt me, mister.' His back was facing the wall and his hands were raised to protect his face.

'I just want to talk,' Pyke said, keeping his tone measured as he opened his hands out in front of him.

'That's what the other bruiser said, before he did this to me.' The actor tore open his shirt and let Pyke see three circular burn marks on his left shoulder.

They were identical to the marks he'd found on the bodies of the headless man and the old crone in Huntingdon.

Pyke didn't try to hide his shock. 'Did he burn you with a cigar?'

That drew a puzzled expression. 'How did you know?'

Pyke gave a description of the man – heavily whiskered and sporting a glass eye. 'Did he do this to you?'

The actor seemed nonplussed. 'He wanted to know where he could find Johnny. I told him I didn't know but he didn't believe me.'

Pyke felt his mind unravel with the confusion. How was it possible that the same man had been hunting for letters stolen from Conroy as well as inciting the navvies to violence in Huntingdon?

'When was this?'

The actor seemed taken aback by the urgency in his voice. 'I'd say a month ago.' The burn marks had faded in the intervening period.

'Can you be more exact?'

The actor scratched his chin. 'The show here had just started. It would've been the first week in October.'

It was just before he had been summoned to the Houses of Parliament; before he had first travelled to Huntingdon. Pyke closed his eyes and tried to imagine the headless corpse he'd seen there. 'Did Johnny have a scar running down the entire length of one of his arms?'

The actor seemed too bewildered to speak.

'Well, did he or not?' Pyke reined in the urge to shake him.

'Yes, he did. I think it was his right arm. I remember seeing it when he took off his shirt to give a speech from *Hamlet*.'

Pyke contemplated this for a moment, reeling from the shock.

'Was Johnny about six feet tall, with broad shoulders and well-developed arm and leg muscles?'

The man nodded dumbly. 'And dark curly hair.'

So it had to be true. The headless corpse in Huntingdon belonged to Kate Sutton's lover.

Pyke steadied himself against the trough and tried to collect his thoughts. It still didn't make any sense. How was Johnny's murder linked to the troubles in Huntingdon? He thought about the decapitated corpse he had seen in the cellar of the watch-house and about the bloody demise of his own assistant, unable to see how the two deaths might be connected.

'Has something happened to him? Has something happened to Johnny?'

'You could say that.' Pyke looked at the people still streaming out of the building. 'Did you ever see him with a girl?' He gave a brief description of Kate.

'No, but he used to boast about fucking a girl who worked in one of the palaces.'

'And he didn't say anything to you about some letters that might have come into his possession?'

The actor shook his head forlornly. 'We weren't never close. Johnny was always too full of himself for the rest of us.'

Pyke waited for a moment. 'Is there anything else you can tell me about the man who attacked you? Anything at all that might help me find him.'

The young actor closed his eyes and opened them again. 'What he did to me.' He pointed to the burn marks on his chest and winced. 'It was the longest cigar I've ever seen in my life.' There were tears in his eyes. Pyke left him next to the pig trough to reminisce about his unpleasant experiences.

'A plot by Cumberland to seize the throne from the young princess, eh?' Godfrey removed his spectacles and rubbed his eyes. He was stretched out on the sofa in the front room of his Camden Town apartment, a blanket covering his legs. 'I seem to remember a rumour to that effect circulating five or six years ago, though Cumberland always denied it.'

'Weren't there claims he had paid one of the princess's servants to slip something into her bread and milk?'

'Indeed,' Godfrey said, with a frown. 'But you say this "play" had Cumberland in league with Conroy?'

'That's right.'

'Ah, you see, as far as I know, those two men have always despised one another. The duke of Cumberland might covet the throne but Conroy's long-term interests depend on *preserving* the princess's health. I just can't see what he'd gain by switching to another horse halfway through the race.'

Pyke scratched his chin. 'Of course, Cumberland is soon to appear before a select committee chaired by the radical, Joseph Hume, accused of using his position as Imperial Grand Master of the Orange Order to ferment opposition to the King.'

It was a well-known secret that the duke held his older brother in low regard and considered his heir, a sixteen-year-old girl, unfit for the task of defending the ascendancy and the British Empire from foreign aggressors. Whether he would sanction a *coup d'état* against his brother and young niece and risk certain death if he failed was another matter. But as the grand master of more than three hundred thousand Orangemen, many of them belonging to the armed forces, the cantankerous duke was certainly *capable* of launching such an action.

'Surely even the Prince of Blood wouldn't be stupid enough to try and seize the throne from the King or the princess.' Godfrey sipped his claret. 'To say there'd be an outcry would be an understatement. Working folk wouldn't wear it. It would bring the country to the brink of revolution.'

Pyke agreed. It was a horrible proposition. 'But let's just say there was something in the letters that encouraged Cumberland's prospects ...'

'What kind of thing?'

'I don't know. Some kind of damaging revelation about the King or the princess.'

Godfrey sat up on the sofa and rearranged the blanket. 'In which case Cumberland would want to find the letters every bit as much as Conroy. If, that is, he's learned of their existence.'

Pyke got up from the armchair and wandered across to the window. He had grown up in this apartment and still found its musty smell vaguely reassuring. 'Did you have any luck examining that cravat pin?'

Godfrey shook his head but told Pyke that he'd invited an expert in military affairs over for lunch the next day and would pick his brains then.

'Because I was thinking about the two men who came to your shop. You reckoned one of them said something about "H" not being pleased. What if you missed the first bit? What if he'd actually said, "*HRH* won't be pleased"?' You see what I mean? Perhaps they were sent there by Cumberland.'

'His Royal Highness,' Godfrey said, reaching for his wineglass.

'It's just an idea,' Pyke said, shrugging.

Godfrey looked up at him. 'You have an idea what might be in those letters, don't you?'

Pyke smiled, as he always did when his uncle displayed his quickness of thought. 'If I told you the play I saw was Johnny's creation, would it shed light on my suspicions?'

'You're saying that Johnny read something in the letters and decided to dramatise the material in his play?'

'Perhaps.' He thought again about Peel and the fact that the Tory leader despised the duke as much as everyone else. But there was also the small matter of Peel's visit to Huntingdon in person to inspect the headless corpse. Did he know or suspect it belonged to Johnny?

'But that still doesn't explain how or why Cumberland and Conroy are now on the same side.'

'No, it doesn't.' Pyke hesitated, to gather together his thoughts. 'But if Johnny did read the letters and dramatise their contents, it might explain why someone wanted to kill him.'

'And let the play continue for almost a month?'

'Perhaps the one who was looking for him, the glass-eyed man, didn't wait around to watch the show.' Pyke paused, and added, 'And the fact it was shut down by the police suggests the involvement of some important figures. That kind of order would have come directly from Scotland Yard.'

Skin wrinkled at the corners of his uncle's eyes. 'Are you suggesting what I think you're suggesting?'

Pyke shrugged. 'I just don't think we can rule anything out. If I'm right, whatever was written in those letters has the potential to blow the current arrangements right out of the water.'

Godfrey took a gulp of air. 'Even so, decapitating someone is a bit much, isn't it?'

'Not if whoever ordered it wanted Johnny dead and gone for ever. After all, it's not easy identifying a man without a head.'

'You managed.'

Pyke shrugged. 'The man who killed Johnny and Kate Sutton's parents won't stop there, if he hasn't already found the letters.'

Colour drained from his uncle's cheeks. 'It doesn't augur well for Kate's safety, does it?'

'Not just Kate. I'd say you might be in the firing line. Me, as well.' Pyke thought about the threat the glass-eyed man had made against Emily.

'But those men only roughed me up. They didn't try and kill me.'

'Who knows what might have happened if I hadn't shown up when I did.'

'I know, dear boy. I know I'm in your debt.'

'That's not why I mentioned it,' Pyke said, with a sigh. 'I just think we both need to take extra precautions. Freddie Sutton wasn't a threat to anyone and yet someone slit his throat as though he were no better than a tubercular pig.'

'Quite.'

Pyke stood up and squeezed his hand. 'Will you be all right?'

'Me? I've never been better,' Godfrey said, gloomily. 'In case you wanted to have a little chat with him, I know Conroy lunches every Friday, without fail, at the Travellers' Club. But be careful with him, my boy. If you push him too far he's liable to explode.'

'And that's supposed to put me off?'

Godfrey acknowledged Pyke's remark with a tilt of his head and a glint in his eye. 'By the way, those handbills detailing Rockingham's cruel practices are currently heading for Newmarket, even as we speak.'

Pyke couldn't help but smile. 'You wrote them yourself?'

'In my best Marquis de Sade prose.'

'He's not going to like it, is he?'

'You mean, when one of them gets posted through the door of the president of the Jockey Club?'

It was a moment of light relief but outside, when Pyke hailed a hackney coachman and asked the driver to take him back to Hambledon, he was still thinking about the glass-eyed man and the nonchalant way he had drawn his blade across the throat of the priest.

Emily was playing with Felix on the floor of the nursery when Pyke got home, and for a while he watched from the threshold; Emily had such an easy manner with the boy, Pyke thought with pride, and anyone could see that he adored her. When Pyke coughed, to draw attention to himself, Felix looked up and raced across to greet him. 'Mummy was just tickling my feet,' he said, as though the crime were a serious one.

'Really?' Pyke said, winking at Emily. 'And do you think we should tickle Mummy's feet?'

That made Felix squeal with delight and he raced back across the room to where Emily was sitting. 'We're going to tickle your feet,' he boasted, 'and it's going to *hurt*.' Pyke joined them, bending over to give Emily a kiss. 'Why are you kissing her?' Felix wanted to know.

'If you like, I'll kiss you, too,' Pyke said, trying to grab his son.

Felix, though, was too quick for him. 'Kissing's for girls,' he said authoritatively. 'Girls and old people.' Chasing after Felix on his hands and knees, Pyke caught up with him just as he was about to disappear under his bed and scooped him up into his arms, showering his head with kisses. Eventually Felix managed to wriggle free and demonstrably wiped both cheeks. 'That was *disgusting*,' he added firmly.

When Pyke next looked up, Milly was standing in the doorway, clutching her blanket.

'Do you want to join us, Milly?' Sitting up, Pyke held out his hand.

For a moment it looked as if she might take him up on his offer but her fortitude seemed to desert her at the last minute and she scurried back into her room.

When Pyke poked his head around her door, he saw that she had climbed back into bed. Stepping into the room, he told her that she didn't need to be afraid, but she scuttled over to the far side of the bed and pulled the blankets over her head. Tentatively Pyke sat down on the edge of the bed and waited for a few moments. Finally Milly's head emerged from under the sheet and she stared at him, perhaps trying to work out whether he posed a threat to her or not.

'Do you like it here, Milly?' He hesitated and looked around at the room. 'Do you like your new room?'

After what seemed like an eternity, she gave him a very brief nod.

'Do you want to stay?'

Again, another nod, this one more emphatic than the last.

'You do? Because everyone here seems to think you're unhappy and that I should take you back to your other home.' He paused for a short while. 'Are you unhappy here?'

This time she shook her head.

'Can you talk, Milly? Because I want you to tell me what you saw that night . . .'

She stared down at the blanket, her head not moving.

'Did you see the man who hurt your mama and papa?'

Milly looked up at him, a tear rolling down one of her cheeks. Pyke opened up his arms and the girl shuffled nervously across the thin bed. He gave her an awkward hug and told her that she didn't have to say anything if she didn't want to. She began to sob harder and before Pyke knew it her entire body was shaking in his arms, her arms clutching hold of him as though her life depended on it.

Later, Royce opened a bottle of claret and poured Pyke and Emily a glass each in the living room.

'Did you think about what we talked about at the hospital?' he asked, as he sat on the sofa next to her.

'And what was that?'

'About maybe spending more time here at Hambledon, until I've had the chance to determine what threat the man I told you about poses.'

'I'm not going to be made a prisoner in my own home.'

'And I'm just suggesting for a week or so.'

Emily put the wineglass down on the side table and turned to him. 'I can't do it. Not now. Not right at the moment.'

'Why not?'

'Because there are things that I've committed to; things I want to do, things I *need* to do.'

'Such as?'

'Just things.' Emily shook her head angrily.

'Things you can't tell me about?'

'It's not that I *can't* tell you,' she said, sounding pained.

'Then what is it?'

'Don't use that tone with me,' Emily retorted, quickly. 'It's not as though you tell me everything you do, whether that's fighting alongside the navvies or sniffing around an old *acquaintance*.'

'That's nothing by comparison.'

'Nothing? An old lover suddenly becomes our closest neighbour and I'm meant to dismiss it as *nothing*?'

'This is about your safety, your *life*. You think I'm just going to stand by and watch someone harm you?'

'And I can't just give up what I'm doing.'

'This man killed a priest for no other reason than he was in the wrong place at the wrong time. Think what he might be capable of, if he put his mind to it.'

'All right,' Emily said, finally giving a little ground. 'Just give me a couple more days to tie up some loose ends.'

'And then you'll stop for a while?'

'For a while.' She reached for her glass and took another sip of claret.

'But you won't tell me what it is you're working on?'

Emily sighed. 'Don't put a pistol to my head. I'll tell you in my own time.'

A brief silence hung between them. 'I'd like you to pass on a message to Jackman. Tell him I want to meet.'

'What do you want with him?' There was a sharpness in Emily's tone that hadn't been there before.

'Can you arrange it or not?'

'Not until I know why you want to see him.'

'For God's sake, Emily, the man saved my life in Huntingdon,' Pyke said, angrily. 'Did he tell you that? Someone was about to pull the trigger on me. He intervened. I think I have a right to see him and express my gratitude.'

From Emily's expression, it was clear that Jackman hadn't told her and some of her resolve left her. 'I'm sorry. I didn't know.'

'So you'll arrange a meeting?'

She bit her lip and nodded.

For the rest of the night they barely said another word to each other, and when it came time to go to bed, they gravitated towards their separate bedrooms without having to articulate their need to be alone. As he lay in his bed, Pyke listened to the branches of the trees swaying in the wind and thought about what to do. It was no longer a question of being nice or accommodating. If he couldn't guarantee Emily's safety, either in public or, for that matter, at Hambledon, then he would have to find another place for them to live, if only temporarily. At least until he'd tracked down the glass-eyed man, which was now his top priority.

NINETEEN

The sky was low and grey and reminded him of why he detested this time of year, the prospect of a long, cold winter ahead, months of damp coats, coal fires, sodden earth and seasonal chills. Pyke was waiting at the bottom of Park Lane with Green Park on one side of him and Hyde Park on the other. The location meant he had little protection from the squally wind, and as the leaves fell from almost denuded trees and glistened underfoot, a carpet of wet slime as smelly as it was treacherous, he was put in mind of funerals. This was the time of year when his own father had been killed, the victim of a crowd stampede in the vicinity of Newgate prison, a herd of frightened, angry people pushed into a space that couldn't accommodate them as they waited for the execution of two men found guilty of killing a botanist. Even now the smell of wet leaves conjured memories of that moment when his father's calloused hand had slipped from his own and he had stumbled and been swallowed up by the terrified mob, a clutched fist disappearing into an ocean of contorted faces. Some thirty years later, he might see a glimpse of his father's dark, weather-beaten face in a dream or, fleetingly, in a crowd, but it was never enough to sustain a picture of him in his head. Often Pyke wondered how his life might have been different, if his father hadn't lost his footing and fallen to his death under the boots and shoes of people as poor as him.

Ned Villums shuffled into view, a black, woollen muffler around his neck and a greatcoat pulled tightly around his waist. 'Come on, let's walk,' he muttered as he came up alongside Pyke. He was carrying a newspaper under his arm. *The Times* or the *Morning Chronicle*.

'Any news about the leak at your bank?'

Pyke was about to say the leak couldn't have been at his end but stopped himself at the last minute. Why? Perhaps Villums was correct. Perhaps someone at the bank *had* passed information on to the Tory leader. 'The matter's in hand,' was all he said.

'Good.' Villums headed into Hyde Park and Pyke followed him.

'Any news on the man I asked you about?'

They had walked twenty or thirty yards into the park when Villums turned to face him. 'His name's Jimmy Trotter.'

'What can you tell me about him?'

'He's a nasty one, that's for certain.'

'Oh?'

'You name it, he's done it. Theft with violence, larceny, embezzlement, burglary, assault, housebreaking, pickpocketing.'

'Murder?'

'You tell me.'

Pyke pointed to the newspaper. 'Did you read about the priest who was killed in St Paul's?'

Villums' face hardened. 'That was Trotter?'

Pyke told him what had happened, including the threat Trotter had made against Emily.

'Your business with him is your business, but if you want my advice I'd get my family as far away from him as possible.'

'You know where I can find him?'

Villums started to walk, his hands dug deep into the pocket of his coat. 'I heard he was working for a man called Field in the East End. Embezzling money from shopkeepers and small businessmen.' He paused to clear his throat. 'Actually there's a story about that you might want to hear. Or not, as the case may be.'

'What story?'

'A cabinetmaker in Bow wouldn't pay, so Field sent Trotter to *persuade* him. Trotter saw the man's wife was pregnant and when the cull refused to pay, he tied him up and went for the wife with a red-hot poker. According to my source, Trotter knocked her down and shoved the poker right up inside her, if you know what I mean, with this cully looking on, helpless. It killed the baby straight away and, after a long, painful illness, the wife, too. The cabinetmaker disappeared shortly afterwards, as well. After that no one in the East End ever refused to pay Field again.'

For a moment neither of them said anything. The gusting wind rustled the tops of the trees. In the distance, they could hear the sound of horses' hoofs and carriage wheels clattering past Apsley House at Hyde Park Corner.

'Does your source have an address?'

Villums nodded. 'A former crimping house on the river, just along from Cowgate. After the war, it was turned into a con-valescence home for soldiers wounded in action but the funds ran out a few years ago and now it's been overrun by petty thieves and the likes of Jimmy Trotter.'

'And Field?'

'He owns a slaughterhouse near Smithfield.' Villums' expression clouded over. 'But I wouldn't go there if I were you. Not if Field was the last man alive.' He looked up at the army of jackdaws perched in the treetops. 'Listen, Pyke, I'm well aware you don't need my advice and I've seen with my own eyes that you can take care of yourself . . .'

'But?'

'We both know you haven't been out there for a while. All I'm saying is take care with Field. If you're going to tackle him, make sure you're unfailingly polite and careful about what you say.'

They walked back to Hyde Park Corner and 'Rotten Row', where, despite the foul conditions, men and women dressed in the finest clothes, attended to by liveried servants, rode up and down on magnificent groomed horses, as they had always done, past the Duke of Wellington's Apsley House.

'A few years ago, I wouldn't have dared to show my face at a place like this one. I'm sure you were the same.'

Pyke shrugged. But it was true that, until recently, he'd had little need to visit the West End.

'I used to think folk riding horses like those ones owned the city and everything in it. But you know what I think now?'

'That it actually belongs to people like you and me.'

'It's what I've always liked about you,' Villums said, beaming. 'You always seem to know exactly what other people are thinking.'

After surveying the front page of *The Times* for houses to rent in the vicinity of the park, Pyke spent the rest of the morning sizing up the potential options. The one he liked best was, unsurprisingly, the most expensive, an enormous terraced property on Berkeley Square that rented for just under a thousand pounds a year and which contained within its walls the most extravagantly ornate marble staircase and domed ceiling he had ever seen. The agent who showed him the house, number forty-four on the west side of the square, explained that it was one of the finest eighteenth-century residences in the city, adding that the inside had been planned and designed by the renowned architect William Kent and that its 'baroque theatricality' perfectly matched the scale of the building. Pyke thought it looked a little like a Roman bordello but liked the fact that a house that looked quite normal from the outside contained so many architectural wonders within. For a start, the white marble staircase extended up through the full height of the building, almost up to the domed roof, which put him in mind of St Paul's. There were also the marble columns on the first-floor mezzanine and the great chamber room with its panelled walls and hand-carved Italianate ceiling.

The agent informed him that the house was available immediately and, if he paid a deposit of a hundred pounds, he could move in right away. The remaining balance would be due within a month. The house was already furnished, too, which meant less expense for him. His plan was to take it and stay there just for a month. In the light of his financial problems, Pyke couldn't justify spending a thousand pounds on rent, but if he managed to resolve matters and settle his dispute with Blackwood, and if they liked the house and the new location, then what was to stop it becoming a more permanent move? Pyke knew that Emily would take one look at it and dismiss it as too grand and indeed too large for their needs, but if she could see its advantages – its proximity to the city and to Hyde Park – she might be talked around. He told the agent he would have to think about it but in his own mind he had already decided to take it.

Even as he made this decision, Pyke knew that he wouldn't be able to keep Emily and Felix locked up in the new house and that if someone really wanted to find them, they would find them: at Hambledon or a new domicile. More to the point, Emily would not be talked out of doing her work for ever. In the end, it would be easy for someone, someone like Trotter, to find and hurt her. It crossed his mind only afterwards that he'd used the present uncertainties to justify a move that he had wanted to make for a while. Still, he lingered for a while in Berkeley Square, looking up at the first-floor windows of number forty-four and trying to imagine the three of them, and possibly the little girl, Milly, setting up a new home within its walls. As Ned Villums had said, old barriers were beginning to crumble. Why shouldn't a man like him live in such a residence?

Pyke hadn't been inside the Spotted Dog on King Street in Holborn for a number of years, and walking into the taproom was like stepping back into his former life. Then it had been a meeting place for gamblers and petty thieves and, as one of the most feared Bow Street Runners in the capital, his presence had sent even the flashest of men scuttling for their boltholes. This time his entrance merited no more than a ripple of interest, and he made his way to the table at the back of the dark, smoky room where Julian Jackman was sipping from a pot of ale. The floor was covered with hay and a thick coating of butcher's sawdust, and the gas lamps fixed to the walls produced a greasy, reddish flame that smelt almost as bad as the drying clothes of the men and women huddled around the blazing fire. For a while after he had quit as a Runner, he had missed the sensation of being feared in such establishments – it meant that people generally left him alone – but more recently he had warmed to the anonymity that his new role offered him and, anyway, he rarely had reason to visit low taverns any more.

It was the first time Pyke had seen Jackman since he had saved his life in a field outside Huntingdon. They shook hands, but not warmly – mutual suspicion still informed their dealings. Jackman looked older and more worn than Pyke remembered. His skin was pale and mottled and his red-rimmed eyes were supported by large black bags. When the potboy came, Jackman asked for another Perkins' ale, Pyke ordering the same.

'How long have you been back in the city?' Pyke asked, even though he knew the answer already.

Jackman told him a week or two. Nodding, Pyke asked him about the situation in Huntingdon when he'd left.

'Three of the navvies drowned in the Ouse. Another five are injured so badly they can't walk and may never be able to work again.'

The pot-boy returned with their drinks. Pyke took a sip of ale and wiped the foam from his top lip with his tongue. 'And what happened to the rest of the navvies?'

'Someone authorised the use of troops to round them up and shut down the camp. A few men are still being held in the town's gaol, most have been released and told never to set foot in the county again.'

Pyke considered telling Jackman about his own encounter with the dragoons but relented at the last minute, still not sure whether he could trust the man or not.

'You think you know who it was?' he asked instead.

'I have an idea.' Jackman looked up from his ale pot, one side of his face lit up by the greasy flame of the gas lamp. 'You?'

'You know a landowner called Rockingham?'

Jackman's curt nod gave little else away. 'What about him?'

'He's affiliated to the thirty-first regiment barracked near Huntingdon. So, too, was the magistrate you shot, Septimus Yellowplush, and an associate of Rockingham's here in London called Jake Bolter. Is that name familiar to you?'

'Bolter?' Jackman scratched his chin and shook his head. 'Can't say it is.' Taking a sip of ale, he added, 'You think Rockingham planned the whole thing?'

'He's been campaigning against the railway crossing his land since the enterprise was first mooted.' Pyke waited for a moment and said, 'Now Morris is dead, it looks like his wish might be granted. No one on the committee seems very keen on the prospect of pushing on beyond Cambridge.'

'Yes, I heard about that. Suicide, I read.'

His elbows on the table, Pyke leaned forward and whispered, 'What if I told you I thought Morris was killed?'

'Well, was he?'

'Perhaps.' Pyke took another slug of ale. 'I think so.'

'Any proof?'

Pyke thought about his suspicion about Bellows and the dealings between Bolter and Rockingham. 'Not yet.' He wiped his mouth and added, without altering his tone, 'How about the name Jimmy Trotter?'

Jackman stared at him blankly. 'What's he supposed to have done?'

Briefly Pyke told him about Trotter's role in inciting the navvies to violence but decided not to mention anything about the headless corpse and a possible link to letters stolen from Sir John Conroy.

'Do you know where one might find this Jimmy Trotter?'

'Not yet.'

'Because when you do, I'd be interested in paying him a visit.'

'You'll have to get in line.'

That drew a thin smile. 'You're not a bad sort, for a capitalist.'

'Tell me something, Jackman. What is it that you're planning?'

'I'm not sure what you mean.'

'It's just that you don't strike me as the kind of man who's going to do nothing.'

The radical's eyelids twitched. 'The Grand National Consolidated Trades Union is planning another march through the capital. They've been gathering together signatures for a petition in support of the navvies for the past week.'

'I take it from your tone that you don't think much of their plans.'

Jackman shrugged. 'Something happens, people's first thought is to plan a march. It might look impressive on the day, thousands of folk filing through the streets, but what's changed at the end of the day when it's over and everyone goes home?'

'So you're planning a more lasting action?'

The radical stared down at the wooden table. 'I'm presuming you've heard of Wat Tyler.'

'He was hung in Bartholomew's Field for his part in the Peasants' Revolt.'

'Tyler had the whole of the city within his grasp but he chose to negotiate with the King and his ministers. At first, they agreed to his demands: his army disbanded and went home. Then Tyler and his ringleaders were arrested, tried and put to death.'

'It's an interesting story,' Pyke said, staring at the radical, trying to determine why he'd told it.

'We've decided to call ourselves the Wat Tyler Brigade.'

'Then let's hope for your sake that you don't end up like your namesake.'

'It's important to learn from history, from other people's mistakes.'

'Such as?'

'Don't negotiate, for a start.'

'That's a tough position to take. Politics is all about compromise.'

Jackman leaned forward across the table and whispered, 'Did you learn that from Peel?'

'Why do you say that?' Pyke asked, the skin tightening across his face.

'I heard you were close to the Tory leader,' the radical said dismissively, as though the matter weren't important.

'From?' Pyke turned the options over in his mind. Emily? She had no idea about their current arrangement and, anyway, she would never betray his confidence. Or would she?

Jackman tapped the end of his nose. 'That would be telling, now, wouldn't it?'

'If you knew me better, you'd know I'm not one for playing games. If you've got something to say, say it.'

'What if I were to tell you there's a gentleman, here in London, who's determined to wipe us out?'

'I'd want to know more.' Pyke waited for a moment. 'I'd also want to know what you're busy planning.'

'Who said we're planning something?' Jackman's eyes glistened. 'Did Emily tell you that?'

Pyke finished his ale and put the pot down on the table. 'I've told you I'm not one for playing games but let me give you a little warning, something to take to heart.'

Jackman's eyes rose lazily to meet Pyke's stare. 'Oh?'

'I know you saved my life and I owe you for that, but if Emily is hurt in any way because of her involvement in your affairs, I'll come down on you so hard you'll think what happened in Huntingdon was a gentle scolding.'

It was a chilly evening, with just a hint of coal dust in the raw air, but under starry skies, the promenade of the pleasure gardens at Vauxhall was already beginning to fill up with strollers. Under gas lamps and strings of lanterns symmetrically arranged in the bare branches of trees, the gardens looked immaculate, though in recent years the clientele had fallen with the entrance fee and now you were just as likely to see milliners and shop girls mixing with the elegantly attired ladies who paraded up and down the promenade in their silk dresses.

Most had escorts and wore their hair piled up in curls under wide-brimmed straw bonnets trimmed with different colours of silk ribbon.

Pyke saw Marguerite Morris strolling towards him from a distance, as though she had all the time in the world. It was hard not to notice the admiring and jealous glances of other people, for even in her mourning clothes she turned heads in a way that few women would be capable of. An elaborately darted black silk dress was drawn tightly around her waist to reveal her hourglass figure and cut low around the neck to show off her flesh.

Marguerite seemed oblivious to the attention and greeted Pyke with a flicker of her eyelashes.

Pyke had requested to meet her here, rather than at her house or the bank, because he hadn't wanted to risk a meeting in private, but almost immediately he wondered about the wisdom of this decision: this was a place where lovers came to flirt and cavort away from the eyes of their parents and guardians.

'Eddy's will was read yesterday. His lawyer confirmed what I already knew. He left it all to me.' As they walked, Marguerite threaded her arm through his, as though it were the most natural thing in the world to do.

'You don't seem very excited about it.' As they walked, Pyke thought about his conversation with Jackman and the radical's offhand reference to someone who wanted to wipe out the Wat Tyler Brigade. Who had he been referring to, and why had he told Pyke about it? Was it some kind of warning?

'Eddy wasn't as wealthy as some might have imagined. He had money tied up in stocks and shares, mostly in the Grand Northern, and as you know he bought Cranborne Park ...' Up close her breath smelled of stale wine.

'Not something to be sniffed at.'

'He owned it outright. But his lawyer told me that Eddy had recently requested the deeds to the estate and when I looked for them in his safe, I couldn't find them.'

Pyke nodded, as though he appreciated the dilemma. 'And without the deeds, the ownership of the estate can't be transferred into your name.'

Marguerite's body stiffened. 'Don't play games with me, Pyke. He gave the deeds to you, as security for the personal loan you told me you made to him.'

'So you believe me now?'

Pyke walked ahead and, having gathered up her skirt, she hurried to keep up with him. 'How much did Eddy borrow?'

'Ten thousand.'

She absorbed this information without comment or apparent response. 'Then why don't you produce the loan papers, together with the deeds, and lodge your claim against Eddy's estate?'

'You sound angry at this prospect.'

'Why shouldn't I be? Bankers always have a way of clawing back their money.'

This time, he stopped to look at her. 'But it still doesn't explain where the money went, does it?'

'You mean, the money you *claimed* you lent him?'

'Your husband walked out of my bank with ten thousand pounds of my money. I intend to get it back.'

Out of the blue, Marguerite broke into a throaty laugh and said, 'God, you haven't changed much, have you, Pyke. You were always so serious, especially when money was being discussed.'

'Back in those days it was harder for some of us to earn our bread than others,' he said, walking ahead. In the distance, he could the drum of a military band.

Marguerite hurried after him. 'And you were always a self-righteous prig too,' she said, a little out of breath.

Above them, the night sky was momentarily illuminated by a volley of fireworks. They paused for a moment, to look up at the spectacle, sparks of light fanning out across the sky in a giant spider's web. 'Look, I'll make you a deal,' she added, in the same flinty tone. 'If you can unearth the deeds to Cranborne Park, I'll give you Eddy's shares in the Grand Northern.' She laughed bitterly. 'Right now, they're hardly worth the paper they're written on.'

'How many shares are we talking about?'

'I don't know. Five thousand, maybe.'

Pyke did a quick calculation. At face value these shares were worth fifty thousand pounds. Marguerite was quite right to say their actual valuation was far lower, but even so they could be sold on the stock exchange for perhaps five thousand, still a vast amount of money. He was immediately suspicious. 'And why would you make me such a generous offer?'

'I need the deeds. Eddy gave them to you as collateral for a loan you made him. If you give them back to me, I'm prepared to make it worth your while. That's how business is done.'

'But at current value, the shares still don't cover the cost of the loan.'

Marguerite turned to him and smiled. 'So find the money you loaned my husband and you can keep that, as well.'

'And where would I look for it?' Pyke caught her eyes and felt a sudden jolt in his stomach. 'Under your pillow?'

But Marguerite had walked ahead of him without answering and the moment was lost. Pyke followed her, as they headed off the beaten track. 'Do you know when the next meeting of the Grand Northern committee is?'

She looked at him, laughing bitterly. 'You mean when they can all pick over poor Eddy's carcass?'

'And decide what will happen to the railway.'

'Next week, I think. But you can find out for yourself easily enough.' Marguerite shrugged, as though the matter weren't important.

They walked for a while in silence. 'There was a man at your ball with a mastiff. Jake Bolter. He said you gave him permission to bring the dog with him.'

'So?' Marguerite continued to walk, but a note of caution had crept into her voice.

'So I was curious to know how you first became acquainted with someone of his character.'

'I take it the two of you didn't see eye to eye.'

'You could say that.' Pyke waited for a moment. 'I don't tend to think too warmly of people involved in the procurement and selling of children for profit.'

This time she stopped to face him. Her expression was a mixture of bewilderment and anger. 'That's a terrible thing to accuse him of. I've found him uncouth, of course, but quite reasonable.'

'So you do know him, then?'

She looked over his shoulder. 'From time to time, I donate a little bit of money to the orphans' school in Tooting where he works. The man's never been anything less than courteous to me. Unlike others I could mention.'

'The man who owns the school, Bartholomew Prosser, procures children from the workhouses in the city, earns a fee from the workhouse managers, and then loans them to the sweaters in the East End, who put the children to work in their hovels for sixteen hours a day and pay them slave wages.' He paused. 'Your good friend Bolter helps to transport the children from the school to the sweat hovels.'

They walked for another hundred yards in silence, into an area of the gardens that was deserted and shrouded in darkness. 'What's it like?' Marguerite asked eventually. 'To always be right? To always know what to do and make the choices. It must be hard being so perfect.'

They were now facing one another and he could feel the heat coming off her face. 'Is that what you think? That I don't have to live every day with the consequences of bad choices I've made?'

'Give me an example.'

'My bank lent the sweater I've just described the money to start up his business.'

That mollified her a little. When Marguerite next looked up at him, her eyes had moistened and she even managed a smile. 'And was letting me go all those years ago one of those bad choices, too?'

Pyke was momentarily lost for words.

'Or marrying the wrong woman?'

In the darkness he could see her breath vaporise in the chilly night air. 'Who said I married the wrong woman?' But he could feel his heart beating a little quicker.

'Don't you ever wonder what would have happened if you'd come with me to France?'

Pyke swallowed some cold air and tried to avoid meeting her stare. 'You know, I watched you climb aboard that stagecoach from the other side of the street. I hid behind a flower stall.'

'You were there?' Her voice was suddenly softer, warmer. 'I looked up and down the street for you, willing you to appear.'

'But you still left without me.'

'And you chose not to join me,' she said, stiffly. 'I didn't have a choice. I *had* to leave.'

She had owed money to someone, he remembered, and faced the prospect of a few years in a debtor's prison.

'We always have choices, Maggie. It's just that the things we have to choose between aren't always pleasant.'

This time her laugh was without any warmth. 'You always did know how to hide behind false principles.'

Pyke chose not to respond and a fragile silence settled between them.

'Do you remember how it used to be?' Marguerite said eventually, while fingering the stitching on her skirt.

'Fifteen years is a long time.'

'Nearly sixteen.' Marguerite hitched up her skirt and turned to leave. 'And what pains me the most is thinking about the good life we could have had together.' But before he had the opportunity to respond, she had started to walk away, leaving him in the park alone.

When Pyke returned to Blackwood's bank, Sir Henry Bellows was waiting for him in a carriage parked opposite the Royal Exchange on Cornhill. At first Pyke thought about ignoring him, but one of his officers made it clear that the chief magistrate wanted to talk to him so finally Pyke relented. But rather than climbing into the carriage, Pyke peered in through the open window. Bellows sat forward, the light from a gas lamp illuminating his high forehead.

'What do you know about a man called Septimus Yellowplush?' Bellows wanted to know.

The question took Pyke by surprise. He hadn't imagined that the chief magistrate had connections with Huntingdon. 'Why is Yellowplush any of your business?'

'His body was dug up the other day in a field outside the town.' Bellows's voice was as dry as a tinderbox. 'He had been shot.'

'It would seem that Huntingdon's a dangerous place at the moment. Just ask the navvies who died there.'

'An off-duty soldier was also shot and killed while pursuing a suspect.'

'Then the question you should be asking is what an off-duty soldier was doing trying to keep the peace.'

Bellows leaned forwards and whispered, 'There are a dozen witnesses who saw you playing cards with Yellowplush on the night before he was shot in a coaching inn on the High Street.'

'I thought your jurisdiction ended at Temple Bar.'

'So you don't deny arguing with Yellowplush?'

'I asked him how much his integrity as a judge had cost. I might ask you the same question.'

Bellows looked at him, almost amused. 'You've no idea what you're dealing with here, do you?'

'So enlighten me.'

'Two fine men died that night in Huntingdon. As a man of the law, I intend to see that justice is served.'

'And will the navvies get the same kind of justice?'

The skin wrinkled at the corners of the chief magistrate's eyes. 'Go back to your family and stay out of this.' He paused for a few moments, his Adam's apple bobbing in his throat. 'And if you had any sense, you would persuade your wife to do the same.'

Pyke put his head through the carriage window. The inside smelt mildewed and sour. 'What did you just say, Bellows?'

'You heard me the first time. I'm not going to repeat myself.'

'Then clear something up for me. Did you just threaten my wife?'

'Threaten is an ugly word. Let's just say I've simply given you a friendly warning.'

'And if I don't choose to take it?' Pyke hesitated. 'And if my wife chooses not to take it?'

Bellows looked at him and shrugged. 'Then you'll only have yourselves to blame, won't you?'

As Pyke watched the carriage disappear along the street, he couldn't get rid of the sour taste their exchange had left.

TWENTY

A fine mist had drifted up the Thames by the time Pyke reached the creaking old wharf at Cowgate, a mist that just obscured the tops of the ships' masts as they bobbed up and down in the choppy waters of the river. It was late, maybe as late as midnight, and the wharf was deserted. Early morning was the time to see warehousemen carrying crates of sugar, rum, rubber, tea and coffee to the stores, and gangs of coal-whippers unloading the colliers lined up along the river. Pyke looked over towards the Southwark bank, the giant brewery just about visible through the dense forest of rigging, cables and masts, though it, too, was silent. What never changed, he thought, was the smell. The river was at low tide and when this happened, the raw sewage that flowed into the river from the cess trenches that criss-crossed the city gathered on exposed banks to form mountains of slime; slime that produced gas bubbles whose stench was bad enough to make your teeth rattle.

Pyke found the former crimping house easily enough. In fact, he had once tracked down a man who had returned from transportation to one of its rooms and remembered its inside a little. During the Napoleonic wars, the building had been used to hold 'pressed' seamen before they were transported to vessels, and afterwards it had briefly been used as a place where sailors wounded in combat could convalesce. But money made available by the Admiralty had long since dried up, and in recent years the building had become home to every kind of docker, mudlark and scavenger that depended upon the river to earn their living. Downstairs, there was a long, narrow passageway that led to a communal kitchen, if he remembered correctly, and upstairs was a rabbit warren of interconnecting rooms and passageways. He would have to be lucky to surprise Trotter, if he was there, and even if he was, the chances were that

Trotter would hear him coming and escape to somewhere else in the building.

There was another possibility, of course, one he didn't like to think about, and to ward it off he had brought with him two fully loaded flintlock pistols and a knife that he had strapped to his left ankle. Even then, he felt somehow underprepared, as though the weapons at his disposal were a poor match when pitted against the ferocity and cruelty of the man he was attempting to capture. Villums's warning was still ringing in his ears when he pushed open the front door.

The smell was a familiar one: damp, stale food and human sweat. At the end of the long passageway, he stepped into the kitchen, both pistols hidden under his black cutaway coat. Four men were sitting on makeshift furniture around a fire that burned warmly in the grate; all looked up at him but none with very much interest. Their clothes were dirty and torn and their faces smudged with soot. Checking behind him, Pyke walked a little farther into the dilapidated room and cleared his throat. 'I'm looking for Jimmy Trotter,' he said, in barely more than a whisper. If Trotter was somewhere in the building, Pyke didn't want to alert him.

No one looked across at him. Rather, the four continued to stare gloomily into the fire, minding their own business.

'I said I'm looking for Jimmy Trotter. I was told he sometimes puts his head down here.' This time, he pulled back his coat and let the four men see his pistols. He put some metal into his voice, too.

'That blackguard ain't been here in months,' one of them muttered.

'Do you know where he's gone?'

The man shrugged. 'Didn't ask and don't care. But it's good riddance as far as I'm concerned. Man was nothing but trouble.'

'How about the rest of you? Anyone know where I can find him?' Pyke waited for a moment. 'There's a reward in it.'

'How much?' one of them asked.

'Do you know anything or not?' Pyke rested his fingers on the wooden butt of one of his pistols.

But the man shook his head; the others did likewise. One told him that Trotter had boasted about coming into some money and said he wasn't likely to be back.

'Did he have any friends or acquaintances when he was here?'

A man with fat cheeks and vermilion lips looked at him, frowning. 'A cully like that doesn't make friends.'

'Which room did he use when he stayed here?' Perhaps Trotter had left something that might be of use.

'Top floor, along the passageway, last door on the right.'

Feeling the tension drain from him, he thanked them for their time and turned to leave the room. One of them shouted after him, 'What about that reward?' Pyke ignored him. But the man with fat cheeks and greasy lips shuffled after him and said, 'Mostly we don't go up there. It's meant to be kept for men who fought in the war but the real reason is none of us much care for the smell. Ripe flesh and camphor don't make for a pleasant odour.' He was carrying a lantern and offered it to Pyke, who rummaged in his pocket for a few coins. The man accepted them gratefully and shuffled along the passageway back to the kitchen.

But there was nothing of interest in the room that had been described to him and Pyke was just about to make his way back along the passageway when he noticed a light in the room opposite.

He knocked on the door and pushed it open. The room was tidy and warm, a fire blazing in the grate. Sitting in front of it was a grey-haired gentleman in a rocking chair. A blanket warmed his legs. He introduced himself as Midshipman Salt and proceeded to complain about the 'thieves' and 'vagabonds' that had taken over what had once been a respectable convalescence home. Since men like him who had not been *badly* injured in the war did not merit a place at Chelsea, he explained bitterly, this was the only place left to them. He spoke about the war as though it had happened the previous year rather than more than twenty years earlier. Pyke found himself feeling sorry for him.

He asked the old man whether he'd known Jimmy Trotter, who had once used the room opposite him. Salt shook his head, muttering that Trotter was a 'bad egg' who liked to hurt people out of a misplaced sense of enjoyment. He added that he was happy Trotter had gone and said, no, he didn't know where he had gone *to* and, quite frankly, didn't care. 'If someone had gouged out his eyes with a spoon,' he said, reflecting on the matter, 'it would have been too good a death.' But when Pyke asked him why he felt so strongly about the man, Salt wouldn't answer him.

Pyke looked around the well-ordered room. There were framed

prints of ships on the wall. That was when he had the idea. 'What about a man called Jake Bolter? Never goes anywhere without his mastiff, Copper.'

The older man's face reddened, his hands starting to shake. He tried to recover his composure but Pyke had seen the reaction and the ex-sailor knew that he had seen it.

'Bolter had a room here?' Pyke tried to keep his excitement in check. This was what he'd been looking for, something that tied Trotter to Bolter and Rockingham.

The old man stared down at his blanket. 'For a long while, Jake lived in the room across the hall.'

'And then Trotter moved in too?'

'I thought we were friends.' The midshipman's eyes filled with water. 'For years, we'd sit here in this very room and talk about the old days.'

'And Trotter's arrival disrupted all that?'

The man nodded sullenly. 'Jake's an impressionable chap, easily gulled. Jimmy Trotter got him involved in something rotten and after that he stopped coming to see me. To my mind, he couldn't face me out of the shame.'

'But you don't know what it was?'

'No.'

Pyke digested this information. 'Did they both move out about the same time?'

The midshipman stared forlornly into the fire. 'About three months ago, I'd say.'

They talked in halting sentences for a few minutes more but Salt had no additional information about Trotter or Bolter and didn't know where they might have gone to. Pyke made his excuses to leave and Salt muttered something under his breath, refusing to meet his stare.

It was hard not to feel sorry for the old man. He had faithfully served his country and had been rewarded with a drab, windowless room in a convalescence home that had long since been overrun by thieves. Still, there was also something pitiful about someone who'd spent the last twenty years of his life reliving former glories and, in the end, Pyke had nothing more to say to him, no words of reassurance that might lift his despondency. He left quickly without saying goodbye.

It was a ten-minute walk through the deserted wharves and jetties back to London Bridge and after just a few paces Pyke realised he was being followed. It was just a sense at first, an intuitive feeling heightened by his awareness that the man he was trying to find posed a very serious threat to his personal safety. It was as though his footsteps along the slippery, creaking wharf were somehow echoing fifty or a hundred yards behind him. To prepare himself, Pyke took one of the pistols in his hand and coiled his finger around the trigger. He kept on walking, though, and even picked up his pace a little, to see whether his pursuer would follow. Whoever it was, and Pyke had no idea whether Trotter had seen him enter the former crimping house or not, displayed an adeptness for courting shadows. Whenever he glanced behind him, his pursuer would somehow disappear from view. But when he continued on his way, the faint thud of someone else's footsteps filled the eerie silence, and if he stopped suddenly, the footsteps behind stopped, too. He had hoped that whoever was behind him would get too close to him and afford him the chance of an ambush, but his pursuer took care to maintain a discreet distance between them. Pyke took a quick note of what lay around him: on one side was the river itself, extending off into the darkness; on the other side were a collection of warehouses, some used and some derelict. If he could duck into one of the warehouses, and wait for whoever was following him to do likewise, he might stand a better chance of apprehending them. His armpits were moist with sweat. In the distance, he could see the vague outline of the new London Bridge, the old one, nearer, and now dilapidated, like a relic of a bygone era, crumbling into the river. Ahead, he saw an alleyway running alongside one of the warehouses and ducked into it. He waited; the only noise he could hear was the thumping of his heart. The footsteps came to a halt. Pyke raised the barrel of the pistol and waited. Nothing moved; the air was utterly still.

Peering out from his hiding place, Pyke tried to determine where his pursuer was, and how close. But the wharf was deserted; nothing stirred. He was about to give up when he saw a cloaked figure disappear into a doorway about fifty yards behind him and he set off in pursuit, pistol in one hand. He followed the figure into the warehouse and waited – listening – trying to decide whether to take the staircase or push ahead into the building. He heard footsteps somewhere above him and decided to climb the stairs. At the top Pyke followed a passageway as far it took him, passed through a doorway and entered a storage room, with wooden crates stacked in rows, three or four on top of each other. He saw the figure disappear through another door on the far side of the room and set off after him. For a moment, he thought about firing the pistol but he didn't have a clear shot. The door led to another flight of stairs and at the top, having sprinted the length of a dark, narrow corridor, Pyke found himself on the flat roof of the old building. Momentarily breathless, he stopped to assess the situation, and realised that the cloaked figure had nowhere else to go. He aimed the pistol and shouted, 'Stop right there. Don't take another step or I'll shoot you.' He kept the pistol raised and walked quickly across the roof to where the man had backed away, almost to the edge of the building. The figure was slight in stature and wore a black cloak over his head to conceal his identity. 'Who are you?' Pyke called out, as he came closer. Still breathless from the pursuit, he was about fifteen or twenty yards away when the figure pulled off the cloak and he found himself staring at the apologetic face of his own wife.

'What are you ...?' But Pyke couldn't bring himself to finish the sentence. He was too confused, his bewilderment quickly turning to anger. 'I could have shot you. I could have *killed* you, Emily.'

Emily bowed her head. She was breathing heavily too. 'I know. I'm sorry. I didn't mean for you to see me.'

'Is that supposed to make it acceptable?'

'I said I was sorry.'

Pyke put the pistol back in his belt, his anger abating a little. 'So why were you following me?'

'I had some business in the city this evening. It finished earlier than I'd expected. So I went to your office, to see whether you were still there. I thought we could ride home together. When I got there you were just leaving. I should have called out but you seemed so serious. I was curious. You didn't hail a cab, so I guessed you weren't about to go back to Hambledon. On the spot, I decided to follow you. It's stupid, I know, but I thought you might be meeting her.'

'Her?'

'Marguerite.'

Pyke stared at her, dumbfounded. 'Is this what we've been reduced to? Is that how little we trust each other?'

'I'm sorry,' she whispered.

'You shouldn't be here, Emily. This is a dangerous part of the world at night. Do you have any idea what the jackals here would do to a woman of your looks and standing, if they came upon you?' Pyke shook his head.

'I can take care of myself well enough,' Emily muttered.

'And if you came across someone like Jimmy Trotter?'

She screwed up her face. 'Who's he?'

'The blackguard who killed the canon in St Paul's. The man who threatened you,' Pyke said, still shaking from the thought of what might have happened, the fact that he'd considered firing a shot. 'That's what I was doing tonight. Trying to track him down.'

'There will always be threats. You can't deal with them all.'

'Why will there always be threats, Emily?' Pyke took a step towards her. 'Isn't it time we started being honest with each other?'

'What I do is upsetting to some people.'

'And what exactly do you do?'

'I'm a socialist, Pyke. An Owenite. A radical. I don't believe the current system can be reformed. I think we need to tear it down and start again.'

'The men of the French Revolution tried that already and look where it got them. Their own heads on poles.'

Emily shook her head. 'This isn't the time and place for a political argument. This should be about us. You and me, Pyke. Why we're standing on a roof in the middle of the city at past midnight.'

'Why you took it upon yourself to follow me,' he reminded her.

'What? And you've been entirely open and honest with me?'

Pyke held her stare. 'I had a visit tonight from Sir Henry Bellows, chief magistrate at Bow Street. He told me I had no idea what I was dealing with. He warned me to stay at home and not get involved in whatever I'm supposed to be involved with. He also advised you to do the same. That's two threats made against you in as many days. How can I keep you safe if you won't tell me what you're doing?'

'It's not that I won't. I *can't*. I promised.' Emily offered him a pained look.

'Promised who? Jackman?'

'I can't say. I'm sorry.'

'I'm your husband, Emily. You're my wife. We're not leaving this place until you tell me.'

'I want to tell you. And I will. I just need a few more days.' Her tone was pleading now.

'To do what?'

'I want us to be a family again, Pyke. A proper family. But I need a few more days.'

'And if I say no?'

'We're both keeping secrets here. Don't try and colonise the high moral ground.'

'What secrets am I keeping?'

Emily took his hand and placed it on her heart. 'Promise me you haven't been to see Marguerite since Morris's funeral.'

Pyke faltered slightly but it was enough to sink him. He saw the disappointment in Emily's eyes.

The following morning, when Pyke arrived at the bank, Townsend was waiting for him outside his office. One of the porters had already lit a fire, so the room was warm, but when he looked out of the window to see whether the ravens had returned, the sill and roof were bare. Pyke turned to face Townsend, who was standing awkwardly by one of the chairs, waiting to be asked to sit. Pyke did so with a flourish of his arm and asked whether his former colleague had unearthed anything significant either about his partner, William Blackwood, or Jake Bolter. Townsend said that he'd followed Blackwood for a couple of days and hadn't turned anything up.

'And Bolter?'

Townsend explained that when not occupied at Prosser's asylum, Bolter had been accompanying an elderly gentleman around town. When Pyke asked where they had been and what they had done, Townsend shrugged and said they'd been to the old man's club, to his bank, to some fairly 'low' taverns, and that was about it. Pyke told him to stick with it.

A little later, still thinking about the missing loan papers, he had told one of his clerks to round up everyone who worked at the bank and took the unprecedented step of closing the doors while he addressed them all in the main hall. He made sure William

Blackwood was present too. Having checked and rechecked all the possibilities regarding the theft of the documents from the vault, and repeatedly questioned the watchmen, who continued to insist they hadn't seen anyone in the building on the night of the theft, he had come to the conclusion that it had to have been perpetrated by an insider, an employee, someone who worked at the bank, and while Blackwood remained his chief suspect, he couldn't rule out the possibility that someone else was involved. To gain entry to the vault, four keys were needed; three were locked up in a cabinet in the banking hall, and hence could have been accessed by anyone, but only Pyke and William Blackwood had a copy of the other key, which meant either that Blackwood was involved or the perpetrator had used the key that someone, most likely the old gypsy, had stolen from him.

In his address to the bank's staff, he explained that there had been a serious breach of security and that no one was beyond suspicion. He said that some important documents had gone missing from the vault and until they had been found or returned everyone's pay would be docked by five shillings a week. He explained that this wasn't a punishment but rather a collective inducement to compel those who were harbouring information to come forward with it.

'Someone has stolen what belongs to me,' Pyke said, staring out at their glaring faces. No one wanted their pay to be docked. 'I want the papers returned to me. And I'll do whatever it takes to make sure this happens. I'll make your lives miserable if I have to. I'll hound each and every one of you until someone tells me something. Someone in this room knows what happened. And I'll find you. Believe me, I'll find you, and when I do I won't be merciful.'

Afterwards Pyke waited until the hall had cleared before tackling his partner on the stairs.

Until now he hadn't really thought what he might do if he couldn't find either the loan documents or the missing ten thousand pounds, but as his partner's resolve to address the matter through the law strengthened, he would have to take action. And there was no way he'd spend a single night in prison or pay a single penny of what he allegedly owed the bank from his own savings.

'That was quite a speech,' Blackwood said, apparently without a hint of mockery.

249

'No one steals from me and gets away with it.' Pyke kept his stare hard and firm. 'You, of all people, should know that.'

Blackwood bowed his head, revealing a shining pate. 'I had a visit from Mr Groat this morning. It appears an entire row of houses on Granby Street that he uses as a factory was burned down last night. A painted message claimed Captain Paine was responsible.' He must have seen Pyke's expression because he added, 'No one was hurt. It seems all of the occupants had been forewarned. But he doesn't have insurance and, in the light of your rather obtuse decision to call in what we loaned him last week, he fell on his knees and begged for more time to meet his debts. I said I'd ask you.'

'In what way was my decision obtuse?'

'You approved the loans in the first place.' Blackwood sighed. 'He's been a good customer. I think, in the light of this abominable attack, we should give him the time he's asking for.'

'You do, do you?'

'Unlike some, he hasn't missed a single payment.'

'Tell him if he doesn't pay back what he owes by the end of the week, I'll pursue the matter in the courts.'

'But it's Thursday today.' Blackwood seemed appalled.

'Yes, so it is.' Pyke waited, and added, 'And for the time being I'm still in charge of this bank.'

Blackwood licked his lips, his hand trembling a little. 'On that matter, you should know that the lawyer Herries intends to issue a warrant for your arrest early next week, if suitable evidence corroborating the loan you made to Morris isn't recovered.'

Pyke clenched his jaw and reined in an urge to rip his partner's head clean off his shoulders. There was no way that William Blackwood would dare to speak to him in such a manner unless he had a serious backer. Stepping into the gap between them, he watched Blackwood flinch, but rather than strike him, Pyke tapped him gently on the left cheek and whispered, 'Then I still have a few days.'

On the north side of Pall Mall the Travellers' Club was housed in a grand building clad with dazzling stucco that resembled an Italian palazzo. There were two major-domos dressed in liveried uniform standing on guard, but Pyke managed to slip past them among a party of three well-fed older men. Inside, the lofty ceilings, intricate cornicing, walnut-panelled walls and marble floors testified to the wealth and standing of its members. If the Wat Tyler Brigade wanted to wipe out the Establishment in a stroke, Pyke mused, this was the place to target. Forget the Houses of Parliament or the King's Palace. In the space of a few minutes he'd spotted Lord Auckland, the governor-general of India, and Palmerston, who was Foreign Secretary. It was the kind of place where the small matter of running the country was conducted between courses and in the smoking room over a couple of Cuban cigars.

Pyke found Sir John Conroy sitting alone at a table that looked out on to Pall Mall. The table had been laid for two and he was expecting someone to join him because when Pyke came up behind him, the royal comptroller leapt to his feet and looked expectantly into his face. His disappointment was replaced by suspicion. Recognising Pyke from the Bow Street courtroom, Conroy returned to his chair and folded his arms, waiting for Pyke to leave him alone. He cut a tall, handsome figure in his dark blue frock-coat worn over a frilly white shirt and cravat, with his grey hair, smooth complexion and strong jaw, but his swashbuckling charm was in short supply. He warned Pyke to leave or he would call the major-domos.

'I wouldn't do that, if I were you,' Pyke said, making himself comfortable in the chair opposite him.

'And why's that?' Conroy tried to appear composed, but his eyes darted back and forth across the room.

'Because then I wouldn't be able to tell you about some letters that have come into my possession and that I'm considering taking to the Duke of Cumberland.'

It had been a calculated gamble but almost at once Pyke knew he'd scored a direct hit. Conroy tried, too late, to feign indifference, but a momentary widening of his eyes and a slight puckering of his lip had told Pyke all he needed to know. 'I don't know what you're talking about,' he said, smoothing the ends of his silver moustache.

'No? Then you won't mind if I take what I've got to Cumberland, then.'

That drew a pained smile. 'You don't have to do that, sir. Perhaps we should talk about the matter like gentlemen.'

'Gentlemen who beat up a defenceless old man in his shop and nearly give him a heart attack?'

Conroy frowned, seemingly puzzled by Pyke's remark. 'I'm sorry, sir, but I don't know what you're talking about.'

'You didn't send two well-dressed coves to my uncle's shop to forcibly retrieve your property?'

'No, I didn't.' Conroy ran his fingers through his silver hair. 'Why should I want something from your uncle?'

'Because Kate Sutton was, or rather is, the source of his information regarding the piece he wrote about you.'

A look of recognition and panic flashed across Conroy's face. 'Ah. I see.'

'What do you see?' Pyke thought about his uncle's description of Conroy as a hothead and wondered whether the comptroller's temper would get the better of him on this occasion.

'Someone believed that that wretched creature had passed what she'd stolen from me on to your uncle for safe-keeping and paid him a visit.' But Pyke could see he was far from happy with this idea.

'So you're not denying that Kate Sutton stole some letters from you or that you've been hunting her down, or rather you've employed others to do this job for you?'

'I'm not admitting anything of the sort.'

'But Kate Sutton did steal some letters from you.' Pyke watched him from across the table. 'I know this because, as I said, they've come into my possession.'

The anger returned. 'So she *did* give them to your uncle?'

'The question is whether I should return them to you or sell them to Cumberland.'

'Now why on earth would you want to do something like the latter?' Conroy said, his composure returning.

'Because I'm certain he'd be interested to learn about their content and, of course, willing to pay a significant sum of money ...'

Conroy interrupted, as Pyke hoped he would. 'If it's a question of money, perhaps you and I can come to an accommodation.' It was as good as an admission that the letters contained potentially explosive revelations.

Pyke sat forward, his elbows resting on the linen tablecloth. It was time to turn the screw. 'It's very simple. I want you to own up to what you've done. To me, if not the law. I want you to tell me about your part in the murder and decapitation of a fourth-rate actor called Johnny who, as I'm you sure you know, was Kate Sutton's betrothed. I also want to know how and why his body came to be dumped in a river outside Huntingdon, just as I want you to tell about the nature of your association with Jimmy Trotter, Jake Bolter, Sir Henry Bellows and Sir Horsley Rockingham. Additionally, I'd like you to own up to your culpability in the deaths of Freddie Sutton and his wife in their Spitalfields home, and give me your word, for what little it's worth, that if Kate Sutton is, by some miracle, still alive, she won't be harmed by one of your ruffians.'

For a moment Conroy looked as if he had been run over by a fast-moving mail coach.

'I want the truth, Conroy. That's all. Either I get it from you or I take what I have to the duke.'

'I could have you thrown out of here for talking to me in such a manner.' A little of the comptroller's composure had returned.

'Except you won't, will you? Because we both know I'm holding all the good cards.'

'You're pretty sure of yourself, aren't you?'

'With Cumberland waiting in the wings, I can afford to be. I don't think you can.'

'And how do I know you have what you claim?'

'You don't. That's the beauty of this arrangement.'

'Then I'm hardly likely to take a risk and try to meet some of your rather puzzling demands.'

Pyke leaned across the table and whispered, 'In which case I'll take it upon myself to further ruin your pathetic, sleazy little life.' He paused to lick his lips. 'And unlike my uncle, I'll finish the job.'

The blood started to rise in Conroy's neck and very soon his entire face had turned bright scarlet. 'You might dress like a gentleman, sir,' he spluttered, 'but your presence in an establishment such as this one puts me in mind of the barbarians massing at the gates of Rome.'

'Except I'm now well and truly inside the gates and sitting comfortably at the top table.' Pyke offered Conroy a patronising smile. He knew he was close to his aim of pushing him over the edge.

'And yet I can smell the gutter on you from here.'

'Are you sure that wouldn't be your dubious morals?' Pyke folded his arms and relaxed. 'Tell me. What was it actually like, fucking the Duchess of Kent up the arse? Did she scream?' He made sure he spoke in a loud enough voice so that those sitting at nearby tables heard him.

Pyke watched with interest as Conroy struggled to control his fury, embarrassment and hatred.

Standing up, Pyke was halfway across the dining room when Conroy caught up with him. The comptroller's face was flushed and blotchy. He tried to grab Pyke's sleeve but Pyke was waiting for him. Spinning around, he landed a clean blow on Conroy's chin and heard the comptroller grunt as he fell backwards on to a table where two elderly military gentlemen were quietly dining. Trying to hold on to something, Conroy grabbed the linen tablecloth, and as he toppled on to the floor, he pulled the cloth off the table and two bowls of soup landed on top of him. The hot liquid stung his scalp and cheeks and caused him to scream from the pain.

Pyke took a napkin from another table and wiped his hands before discarding it on the floor.

He had reached the marble-floored entrance hall before he was confronted by two burly major-domos, sweating in their liveried outfits, their faces grim with determination as they blocked his path. Pyke took a deep breath and readied himself. He would fight his way out of the building, if need be.

In the end, however, such action wasn't necessary. He heard Gore's voice before he saw him, and when he turned to face him, Gore had already come between him and the major-domos, assuring them that he would take care of the situation. Pyke saw him slip a few coins into their hands. That took some of the sting out of their desire to teach Pyke a lesson.

'Perhaps you should attend to the disturbance in the dining room,' Gore told them, 'rather than bothering my good friend here.'

'But ...' one of them started, before realising that he was talking back to a man of Gore's standing.

'Very good, sir.'

Pyke allowed Gore to lead him into the smoking room, where red leather armchairs supported well-fed old men smoking cigars and sleeping off their lunches. 'I don't think we've seen a proper to-do in this establishment since it opened.' Gore broke into a laugh. He seemed delighted by what had happened. 'I was just entering the dining room when you stuck it to the other fellow. It was as if you'd hit him with a bag of hammers. By the way, who was he?'

A turbid haze filled the room, drifting slowly upwards until it hovered just below the ceiling, while beneath their feet, a thick-pile carpet muffled their steps. No one looked up at them as they repaired to the corner of the room and a couple of empty armchairs.

'Sir John Conroy.'

Gore's avuncular face broke into a smile. 'Ah. The gentleman who caused all that trouble for your uncle. But I thought that business had been resolved?'

'I thought so, too.'

'I take it the matter is settled now,' Gore said, still enjoying himself.

'In a manner.'

'And that you didn't object to my intervening to calm the situation down.'

'On the contrary,' Pyke said, bowing his head. 'It seems I'm indebted to you once again.'

As Gore put on his spectacles, Pyke thought about this intervention and wondered again about the man's motives and whether he was to be trusted or not.

'Actually,' Gore started, 'I was hoping to run into you sooner rather than later, so this is very fortuitous.' His expression assumed a serious air. 'For a start, I was wondering whether you'd made any progress on the delicate matter we discussed at Morris's funeral.'

'You mean, finding his killer?'

Nodding, Gore reached into his pocket and fished out two expensive-looking cigars. He offered one to Pyke, who declined, and then, reaching for the candle, he added, 'Exactly.'

'I've nothing new to report, if that's what you mean.' Pyke didn't yet trust Gore enough to tell him what he really suspected had happened.

'But I don't doubt you're taking the challenge seriously. As today's little fracas has proven, I can see you're quite a tenacious chap, once you get the sniff of something.' Gore tapped some ash into a silver ashtray.

'I do what I can.'

'You're too modest, Pyke. I can see for myself what a success you've made of the bank.' Gore blew out some smoke and said, 'Actually that was the other thing I wanted to talk to you about.'

'Blackwood's?'

'That's right,' Gore said, nodding. 'I have no idea how you're going to react, but I have an offer to make you.'

'What kind of an offer?'

'A very lucrative one,' Gore said, smiling. 'Look, I'm sure you don't need me to tell you that Gore's is the largest private bank in the city. However, at present, we don't have representation in the East End, where, I'm told by my advisers, significant money is to be made.'

Pyke allowed himself a smile. 'I didn't think an institution as venerable as Gore's would want to chase after the slop trade.'

'All institutions need to change with the times. But of course you're quite right to suggest that any explicit involvement on our part in what you rather delightfully call the "slop" trade may indeed upset some of our more sensitive customers.'

'So what are you suggesting?'

'Straight to the point, eh? I like you, Pyke. I like you a lot. You're just the kind of man I could do business with.'

Pyke waited but didn't say anything. He still couldn't work out what he thought of the banker, whether he liked him or not.

'I'm offering to buy a third share of Blackwood's.' Gore paused for a moment, to check Pyke's reaction. 'In effect, my bank would underwrite a massive expansion of loan capital to a fledgling business in the east of the city. Of course, you would remain in overall charge of the bank. In addition to the increased profits we'd all share, the current partners at Blackwood's could expect to receive remuneration of, let's say, sixty thousand pounds for the stake that's being relinquished.'

Pyke studied Gore's face, its features partially obscured by the smoky haze. 'And how would this remuneration be divided between my partner and me?'

'That would be up to you to determine,' Gore said, a little puzzled by the question.

'You miss my point. At present, I own a two-thirds stake in Blackwood's and my partner owns the other third.' He didn't

256

mention the five per cent stake that he'd given to Nash from his share. In light of the contract they'd drawn up prior to his death, Nash's stake would automatically revert to him. 'I'm asking how you'd envisage the shares in this new venture being allocated.'

'Ah, I understand.' Gore's expression became serious. 'Well, Gore's would claim a third stake: after that, it would be up to you and your partner to work out how to allocate things between yourselves.'

'So you wouldn't object if I insisted on retaining a fifty-one per cent stake in the bank?'

'Object? Not in the slightest, old chap,' Gore said, easily. 'In fact, I'd insist on it. I'd be investing in your expertise as much as the bricks and mortar of your bank. If you remained at the helm, I could rest assured that my investment was being soundly looked after.'

Pyke did a quick calculation. He could sell off fifteen per cent of the bank, retain overall control and earn twenty thousand pounds in the process. In the short term at least, the money would be very useful.

'Sixty thousand for a third share of the bank? It's a generous offer.'

Gore chuckled lightly. 'Remember we would receive a third of the profits. I'm not running a charity.'

'Of course.'

'Well, what do you think?' Gore asked.

'Before I do anything, I'd need to discuss the offer with my partner,' Pyke said, wondering what Blackwood might say about it.

Gore nodded pleasantly. 'I quite understand.'

But did Pyke completely trust Gore and did he want him as a business partner?

It had been easier, he thought, when people came at him with pistols and brickbats rather than handshakes and contracts. As a Bow Street Runner, he had trusted no one and used maximum force in every situation: he knew where he stood when someone pulled a knife on him. But the world of commerce was not nearly as clear cut. For a start, it wasn't possible to work independently of others. Doing business necessarily involved delegating responsibilities, taking a chance and trusting those around you. As such it left him feeling constantly exposed.

'At least think about my offer, Pyke,' Gore said. 'I think we could do great things together, given the chance.'

Pyke thought about replying but managed to maintain his silence.

TWENTY-ONE

It was raining by the time Pyke emerged from the bank the following afternoon. He passed through the alley and looked up and down Cornhill for his carriage, stepping back from the kerb and cursing a passing omnibus that splashed the bottom part of his trousers with a brownish slush of mud and horse dung. He was searching once more for his carriage when he heard someone behind him call out his name. Fitzroy Tilling was standing by the door of the New York Coffee House. Peel's long-time private secretary wore a black frock-coat over a pale grey waistcoat, a white necktie and matching pale grey trousers. It had been a few years since Pyke had last seen him, and while his coal-black hair had thinned a little, he retained the same air of brooding intensity that Pyke remembered, the product of piercing bug-like eyes and a protruding forehead. Pyke had always liked Tilling and, in contrast to Peel, he had always found him to be open, fair minded and well read.

They shook hands and took a table in the damp, crowded coffee house. The smell of wet clothes and foul breath filled the room, and the windows had steamed up so that it was impossible to see the alley. Tilling ordered two mugs of coffee.

'To what do I owe this honour?' Pyke asked. 'Am I to be taken away to the Tower and pressed?'

'I'd heard you'd moved up in the world but I'm glad to see you haven't lost your irrepressible sense of humour.'

'Just as I'm glad to see you haven't *yet* wearied of serving a selfish and capricious master.'

'That kind of talk might really earn you a session on the press,' Tilling said, with a chuckle. 'But you're correct to assume I'm here at the behest of Sir Robert.'

'I can quite understand a man like Peel not wanting to dirty his hands but it means yours must be filthy by comparison.'

That drew a sharp stare. 'You seem to think the worst of Peel when he has nothing but kind words about you.'

'I can imagine.'

'He was under no obligation to inform you of what I'm about to tell you. My visit is a product of *his* desire to assist you.'

'Forgive me if I don't fall on my knees and kiss your feet. I've had his help before and I almost ended up with my neck in a noose.'

'If you'd prefer, I can always leave ...'

Pyke patted him on the arm. 'I was only joking. I'm pleased to see you, of course.'

'I can see that in your eyes.' Tilling wiped his forehead and smiled.

'So what have you come to tell me?'

'It's come to our attention there's soon to be a very significant crackdown against the radicals in London. Particularly, we're told, those belonging to an organisation called the Wat Tyler Brigade.'

'And Peel wanted me to know this?'

Tilling nodded once. His forehead was beaded with sweat. He wiped it again with a handkerchief. The serving girl returned with their coffees and Tilling paid her.

'Do you mind telling me why?'

'Why do you think?' Tilling said, quickly. 'I'm told your wife has close links with the aforementioned group.'

'Peel sent me on a wild-goose chase to try and prove Julian Jackman is none other than Captain Paine.' Pyke picked up his coffee and warmed his hands. 'I take it you know who Jackman is.'

'Why do you imagine it was a wild-goose chase?'

Pyke shrugged. 'If Jackman was as much of a threat as Peel made out, why's your master now passing me information that will help him to evade capture?'

'Because he didn't want your wife caught up in the middle of something nasty,' Tilling said, his irritation showing for the first time.

'Who says it's going to get nasty?'

Tilling buried his head in his mug of coffee.

'Let me put it another way. Who's in charge of the crackdown?'

This time Tilling looked directly at him, his stare dark and intense.

'If I tell you, I want your assurance it will go no farther. Is that understood?'

Pyke nodded.

'Bow Street.'

'You mean Bellows?' Pyke felt his heart beat a little quicker.

'If you like.'

Pyke turned this revelation over in his mind. 'You're saying Peel has no interest in the matter, one way or the other?'

Tilling looked uncomfortable for the first time. 'He has no affinity for the radicals and no love for the chief magistrate, if that's what you mean.'

'Then what does he want?' When Tilling didn't answer him, Pyke added, 'If I said the name Abraham Gore, how would you respond?'

For a moment Pyke thought he saw the faintest of smiles on Tilling's face but then it was gone. 'I'd say, Abraham who?'

'And if I asked you why the hell Peel made the journey to Huntingdon to inspect the headless corpse for himself, and why he didn't tell me about it, what would you say?'

Tilling's face hardened. 'I don't understand, Pyke. What exactly are you accusing Peel of having done?'

That night, when Pyke's carriage drew up outside Hambledon, he saw they had a visitor. Judging by the enormous four-wheeled brougham that sat in the driveway, all lacquered and shiny, attended to by liveried footmen, five as far as Pyke could tell, their visitor was an important one. It was only later, as the brougham was leaving, that he noticed the royal crest. Running up the steps to the portico to evade the storm, he handed Jennings his coat at the door and made his way through the vast mausoleum of a house to the drawing room, his heels clipping against the wooden floors and echoing through the full height of the building. From the end of one of the passageways, he heard the soothing sound of the piano and recognised Emily's distinctive playing style, at once aggressive and melodious. When Pyke finally stepped into the warm, well-lit room, Emily looked up at him, startled, from behind the piano and stopped playing. Meanwhile the King's brother, Ernest, Duke of Cumberland, who had been warming himself in front of the roaring log fire, strode across the room to greet him.

The duke was a few inches taller than Pyke and unlike either of his older brothers, podgy William or porter-guzzling, elephantine George, he carried almost no excess fat. In his tailored military-style tailcoat, broad at the shoulders and narrow at the waist, he cut a commanding figure, and despite the battle scars on his face, he wore his age well. His full brow, Gallic nose, white hair and preened moustache made him seem distinguished, even perhaps noble, rather than the overbearing, reactionary bully and bigot that he was, in reality.

'Excellent to see you again, Pyke,' Cumberland said, pumping his hand, as though they were old friends. Apart from their very brief encounter in Westminster's New Palace Yard, the last time Pyke had seen the duke had been in the witness box at his own trial six years earlier when Pyke had humiliated him in front of the packed courtroom.

Pyke waited until Cumberland's smile had faded and asked him what he wanted, though in actuality he already knew. Earlier his uncle had confirmed that the tiny coat of arms on the head of the cravat pin retrieved from one of the men who had tried to attack him in his shop belonged to the 15th Hussars, the duke's own regiment.

Ignoring the question, the duke reminded Pyke and Emily that he'd been a good friend of Emily's 'dear, departed father' and proceeded to tell them about his 'wonderful' memories both of the house and the 'indomitable' Lord Edmonton. Pyke listened with gritted teeth and briefly entertained the notion of telling him about the time he'd pushed a pillow against Edmonton's face and held it there until the garrulous aristocrat had passed away.

'Tradition,' the duke continued extravagantly, 'the passing on of a family's home and ancestry from one generation to the next, is the bedrock of our nation.' He paused, perhaps looking for the framed portraits that had once hung on the wall but which Pyke had used for firewood.

'Yes, with the current pace of reform,' Pyke said, 'we're in danger of losing touch with our past.'

The duke observed him cautiously. 'Indeed, I couldn't have put it better myself.'

'I was thinking only the other day that the ancient practice of hanging, drawing and quartering for those found guilty of treason should be revived.'

Cumberland looked anxiously at Emily and asked whether he might have a quick word with her husband alone. Emily made her excuses, wished him a safe trip back to the city and shot Pyke a quizzical stare as she left. When they were alone, the duke put down the sherry glass he'd been give by Jennings and twisted the ends of his moustache.

'By way of response to your remark, sir,' he started, his voice tighter and colder, 'I agree that all acts of treason should be punished by the full weight of the law. If, that is, treason can be proved.'

'So, in your thinking, when does plotting against the King, or indeed the princess, become a legitimate act?'

'I don't know what you're talking about.'

'Well, if we were to take your situation as an example. Let's just say, for the sake of argument, that the future of the Protestant ascendancy in these islands and the British Empire throughout the world could only be ensured by the succession to the throne of a firm, capable and above all experienced ruler, might it not be acceptable to *make* this prospect a reality?'

Cumberland regarded him sceptically. 'One cannot select kings and queens. Only God has that right.'

'And yet what if one discovered that someone else's claims to the throne weren't as strong as most believed?'

'If that could ever be proven, it would change the situation considerably.'

This time Pyke stared directly at him. 'Do you think the young princess's claims on the throne are weak?'

'She is my older brother's child. Therefore her claim is a legitimate one.'

'Of course,' Pyke said, racking his brains for additional ways to draw the duke out of himself.

'But perhaps that is a question I should ask you.'

'What?'

'Whether or not the young princess's claims on the throne are weak.'

'Why ask me?'

Cumberland allowed himself a thin smile. 'Perhaps I should be a little more bold. I think it would be fair to suggest that, until now, we haven't enjoyed the most cordial of relations. But I don't want to dwell on the past ...'

'How big of you,' Pyke interrupted.

The duke shot him a fierce scowl. 'It might also be true that you have held me in contempt and that, in the past at least, this feeling has been reciprocated on my part. But, and it's an important but, we are both men of the world, are we not, and we don't have to accept this state of affairs as preordained. You strike me as a practical sort of a chap, one not weighed down too greatly by wearisome morals, and as such I thought we might be able to come to an accommodation based on the laws of the marketplace. That is to say, you have something I might want and would be prepared to pay more than the going rate to secure.'

'I'm not sure what you're referring to.' Pyke waited for a moment and stepped a little closer to the duke. 'But I did want to tell you about the thuggish actions of two men who needlessly attacked a defenceless old man, my uncle no less, in his place of business, almost giving him a heart seizure.'

Cumberland licked his lips but said nothing.

'One of these men wore a tiepin bearing the coat of arms of the Fifteenth Hussars. Your old regiment, I believe.'

The duke could have denied all knowledge of it but wanted to remain in Pyke's favour. In the end, he reddened and stammered, 'A most unfortunate business, that was. It should never have happened.'

'But it did, didn't it?'

'I heard your uncle was recovering admirably. You'll pass on my best wishes to him, I hope.'

'For what they're worth.'

For a moment, Cumberland appeared on the verge of apoplexy, being addressed in this manner by a commoner, but he managed to contain his outrage. 'As I said, you're a flexible fellow. And I could guarantee to top any offer that you might be made.'

Pyke walked round the piano in the direction of the door and yawned. 'I'm afraid you'll have to excuse me, sir. I've had a long day and I'm dead on my feet.'

The duke met him halfway across the room. 'In a few days

I have to return to my beloved wife and child in Berlin. Until then I can be reached at my house on Kew Green.'

'And if I decide not to contact you?'

'Then you'll lose out on the chance to greatly add to your already considerable wealth.'

'Perhaps I will, but then again perhaps I won't.' Pyke yawned again, this time not holding his hand up to his mouth.

Cumberland tried to hide his revulsion, not very well. 'You have a couple of days. Use them wisely.'

Emily was waiting for him in her bedroom. She'd changed into her nightdress and was sitting up on the bed. Her hair was parted in the centre and had been swept back off her face; her pale skin glistened in the candlelight and there was a hint of a smile on her lips.

'What did that old baggage want?'

Pyke went across to the window and watched as the duke's carriage disappeared up the drive. It was a long story and he didn't feel like going into it. The less Emily knew, the safer it would be for her.

'Aren't you going to tell me?' she said, an edge to her tone.

He turned around. 'As you've been so forthcoming about what Jackman and the Wat Tyler Brigade have been planning?'

Her body stiffened with barely repressed anger. 'Why does it always come back to that?'

'I had it confirmed today that a senior judicial figure is about to lead a crackdown against the Wat Tyler Brigade. I was told it could get nasty.'

'By whom?'

'It would seem they've frightened some very influential people. You don't do that by twiddling your thumbs.'

Emily let out a long, heavy sigh. 'I said I'd tell you about everything in a couple of days.'

'And what if by then it's too late?'

'Too late for what?'

This time Pyke didn't know how to answer her question. They sat on the bed, each contemplating the other's silence.

'Do you remember the first time we kissed?' Emily asked, eventually, at the same time brushing her hair.

'It was in the cloakroom at the Theatre Royal during a performance of *The Barber of Seville*.'

The skin wrinkled slightly at the edges of her eyes. 'At first that's what I thought but I'm not sure we actually kissed on that night. I know I wanted to ...'

'You were wearing a pale pink crêpe dress with thin gauze sleeves.' Pyke smiled. 'I wanted to throw you down on the carpet and take you there and then.'

'Take me where?' Nervously she fiddled with her hair.

'Don't make me answer.' His smile broadened. 'We kissed outside a tavern, if you remember. We'd just escaped from an angry mob.'

'But that wasn't a proper kiss, was it? It was the relief more than anything.'

'It felt proper to me at the time.' His smile suddenly evaporated.

'I'm not saying it didn't.' But her expression seemed pained. 'But I remember the time we kissed in your uncle's apartment more clearly.'

'Was that the night you told me you wouldn't marry me?'

Emily shrugged. 'I waited for hours. I didn't know where you were or what you'd been doing.'

'You didn't tell me you were going to be there,' he said, indignantly.

Emily's eyes settled on him. 'That's exactly my point. We've always kept things from each other, played games. *Both* of us. I want it all to stop.'

'The other day I saw a house for us in the West End.' He tried to assess her reaction but her face remained opaque. 'I put down a deposit. If you don't like it, we don't have to take it.'

'Whereabouts in the West End?'

'Berkeley Square.'

Emily whistled. 'That's quite an address.'

'What you said the other night about wanting to be a proper family. I want that, too. This could be our chance to start again. I've never liked this old pile and the house in Islington is too cramped for all of us.'

'Dare I ask how much or how big it is?'

Pyke tried to seem indifferent. 'It's modest, but large enough to accommodate our needs.' Briefly he thought about the grandiose entrance hall, which extended up through the full height of the building and was topped by a pale blue dome that resembled Wren's creation. 'Will you at least come and see it?'

'Do I have a choice? I mean, you've already paid a deposit.'

'It can be a new start for us. All of us. You, me, Felix . . .'

'And the girl?'

Pyke shrugged. 'Will you come and see it tomorrow? We'll all go together, Felix, too.' He leaned across and kissed her on the cheek. 'Afterwards, he can go for a walk in Hyde Park.'

'All right.' Smiling, Emily returned the kiss, this time on the mouth. 'I thought you'd like to know I'm expecting our child.'

Pyke looked at her, his mouth open. 'You mean we're going to have a baby?' His voice shook with excitement.

Emily nodded, trembling. 'The physician came to see me today. He confirmed it. But I've suspected it for a while.'

'That's wonderful.' He embraced her with a hug. 'I can't believe it. After all these years. It's really true?'

'I know it's time for me to slow down for a while . . .' But there was a discomfort in her tone.

'Then why do you sound so unsure?' Pyke pulled away and looked at her. 'Come to think of it, why did you put yourself at such risk the other night?'

'We both need to change, Pyke.' Her voice turned harder. 'Both of us, Pyke. That means you, as well as me.'

'I know. And we can. God, I can't believe it. We're really going to have another child.'

Pyke got up, barely able to contain himself. But when he tried to pull Emily up on to her feet she resisted. Smiling, he asked her what the matter was. From beneath the sheets, she told him she was tired. Pyke sensed there was something else on her mind, but when he tried to find out what it was he was rebuffed.

'We'll talk tomorrow and over the weekend,' Emily reassured him.

'You'll come and see the house?'

Emily feigned a pout. 'It doesn't look as if I have a choice, does it?'

For a while afterwards, Pyke held her in his arms, thinking that even if she hated it, he'd keep her there, if necessary by force, until any threat against her had blown over. Especially now she was expecting his child.

They had travelled from Hambledon – the three of them. The girl, Milly, had been sick in the night and was resting in bed. She still hadn't uttered a word. If anything, the storm had worsened overnight: the easterly winds had picked up and the rain fell from an overcast sky like spears. It was only as they reached the city that the rain began to ease and the winds lighten, but when Pyke instructed the driver to pull over on Cornhill and told Emily and Felix he had to pick up something from the bank, he still had to run across the street to avoid getting soaked.

Five minutes later, he was crossing the road to rejoin Emily and Felix when he saw a carriage parked behind them. Through the open window the cadaverous face of Sir Horsley Rockingham was just about visible. Closer inspection confirmed this. Diverting his path, Pyke approached the stationary vehicle with caution. As he neared the window, he heard a dog barking and saw that Rockingham was accompanied by Jake Bolter. Pyke came alongside the carriage and peered inside. Rockingham and Bolter both smiled. Pyke was no longer concerned about the rain, which had petered out into a drizzle.

'Have you been following me?'

Rockingham sat forward, his pale face slick with perspiration. 'Not so pleasant, is it, eh, boy? When the shoe's on the other foot.'

Pyke glanced over at Bolter who was patting his mastiff on the head. 'Is that some kind of threat?'

'You reckon you can slander me in my own neighbourhood and actually get away with it?'

Pyke met his stare. 'I don't know what you're talking about.' But it struck him that he didn't even know what Godfrey had written on the handbills he'd dispatched up to Huntingdon and Newmarket.

'Still, the embarrassment is inconsequential compared to what I've got planned for you and your family, boy.'

Pyke held his stare. 'Did you just threaten my family?'

Rockingham receded a little but remained unapologetic. 'No more than you did to me.'

'You come anywhere near my wife or my son and I'll beat you to death with my bare hands.'

'See?' Bolter said, to Rockingham. 'You've rattled him. I told you.'

Rockingham just smirked.

Ignoring him, Pyke turned to Bolter. 'I know you once roomed at a former crimping house near Cowgate with Jimmy Trotter. Trotter was spotted leaving the scene where an old woman was raped and murdered in Huntingdon: the incident that started the violence in the town. Trotter also killed and beheaded an actor called Johnny and dumped his body in a river outside Huntingdon. I believe you were involved,' he said, turning his attention back to Rockingham, 'and acting under this man's instruction. I also believe you planned the murder of Edward James Morris between you, with the ultimate aim of curtailing the progress of the Grand Northern Railway across your land.'

Pyke didn't know what kind of a reaction he might provoke. At best, he expected mild indifference and resolute silence. He certainly didn't expect the older man to turn to Bolter and give him a hard stare. That was it. Afterwards, Bolter banged on the roof of the carriage and the driver took up the reins. The carriage rolled forward and, as it did so, he saw the two men exchange heated words: words that made him wonder about the veracity of the scenario he'd just painted.

Thankfully, when he returned to his own carriage, Emily didn't ask him who he'd been talking to. He felt himself relax.

The rain had now stopped falling and the pavements had begun to fill up. From the cocoon of their carriage, they were protected from the filth and din of the street, but while, for Pyke, it represented a humdrum scene, the vast, stinking city going about its everyday business, to the uninitiated, like Felix, who had never seen so many people of every class and hue, let alone giant advertising boards, omnibuses creaking under the weight of their passengers, hurdy-gurdy men, organ-grinders with their pet monkeys and buildings so tall and imposing they cast the entire street into shadow, there was almost too much to take in. He sat there in awed silence, his face pressed up against the glass, devouring the sheer spectacle of it. Pyke pointed to a giant board advertising a show that featured giraffes and a dancing bear, and Felix rolled his eyes in fear and amazement. These were creatures that until now had come alive only in the pages of books. He wanted to go and see the animal show until another board proclaimed the wonders of a ten-foot man, and then Felix wanted to see that show instead. Promising to take him on another occasion, Pyke noticed a board advertising Groat's 'All-New Retail Emporium' on the Strand, and wondered whether this had closed its doors. He thought, too, about his own action regarding one of the overseers and compared it with what had been achieved by Captain Paine – and without any loss of life. Groat wouldn't trade again, Pyke mused, but there were plenty of men like him, just as there were bankers like Gore, and indeed himself, queuing up to lend them money. He wanted to say something to Emily but didn't want to acknowledge that she had been right. The moment slipped by, unnoticed by her or Felix. Squeezing her hand, he thought about the house and whether she would hate it as much as he feared she might.

They had rattled along Cheapside and, passing St Paul's on their left, crossed over on to Newgate Street. Pyke put his arm around Felix's shoulder and wiped the steam from the glass so they could see more clearly. This was the part of the city he had grown up in and he wanted to point out some of its landmarks. But as they clattered past the buckling, squalid buildings and grubby alleyways, he couldn't think of anything that might interest his son. They passed the place where he had once tended to a dying man, his belly carved open by a hunting knife, while on the other side of the street, in the Black Boar, through a morass of drinkers, he had shot dead a man wanted for killing his own wife. Farther along the street was the ancient prison where he had once been held, awaiting the noose, and from where he'd escaped with Emily's help, and a few hundred yards along Giltspur Street was the ginnery he'd once owned, where his former mistress had been killed in her sleep. It was near there, too, that as a boy barely older than Felix he had watched helplessly as his own father had been trampled to death under the feet of a terrified mob. These were his landmarks, Pyke mused, and he wanted to share them with his son: he wanted to point to the spot where his father had fallen and say, 'This is where my childhood ended, at the age of eight.' But he held his tongue and thought instead about the very different life Felix now led, one where his every need was catered for and his every whim indulged. What kind of man would *his* son grow up to be?

Just past the junction, their carriage came to a halt and Pyke pulled down the glass and poked his head through the window. Ahead, the street was blocked by a procession of long-horned Spanish cattle heading in the direction of Smithfield. Two young drove-boys, aided by a couple of sheepdogs, were trying to herd the beasts on to one side of the broad thoroughfare, so that traffic could pass on the other side, but their attempts to push and prod the frightened cattle seemed to have the opposite effect, because a breakaway group had split from the main herd and had fanned out across the entire road.

'Where are the moo-cows going?' Felix asked.

'I don't know. To the slaughterhouse, I suppose,' Pyke said, not really thinking about his answer.

'What's a slaughterhouse?'

'It's a place where cows go before they go to heaven,' Emily interrupted, giving him a sharp stare.

'Oh.' Felix continued to look at the cattle.

'When they arrive, they're knifed and flayed with a sharp cleaver. Their skins and hides are cut from their bodies and put to one side for the tanners and then the fleshy parts of their bodies, the rump, the loin, the legs and the hindquarters, are sliced up into chunks and finally the rest of the beast, the glands, bones, brains, bladder and hoofs, is scooped up and thrown into a big vat of boiling water.'

Emily stared at him aghast. '*Pyke.*' The sharpness of her tone frightened Felix, whose face had turned white. She would blame him if the boy started to weep, Pyke thought, angry at himself that he'd broken the harmony of the moment, even before they'd reached the new house.

Opening the door, he climbed down from the carriage and shouted at the drovers to do their job.

Someone moved behind him, on top of the carriage, but Pyke presumed it was the driver. Out of the corner of his eye, he saw a metallic glint as the double-barrelled pistol swung towards him.

The first blast whistled past his head with a sudden whoosh of air, a giant sucking noise, the spent ball-shot peppering the cobble-stones. The second blast came even closer, part of the shot ripping his frock-coat at the shoulder. If the masked man had aimed a little lower, Pyke thought grimly, he would now be dead.

Falling to the ground, he looked up at the roof; his would-be assassin had disappeared. Pyke was still on the ground when the vehicle started to roll forward. He realised that the masked man was at the helm, urging the horses to go faster.

Panic tore through Pyke's stomach. He was on his feet in a matter of seconds and took off after the speeding carriage.

It had started to rain again, the darkening skies suddenly opening, and ahead of him the vehicle appeared as indistinct as the figures in a Turner painting. He tried to run harder. But now the procession of Spanish cattle had come to his rescue. The carriage had been forced to slow down, almost to a standstill, allowing Pyke the chance to close some ground. It was still moving too quickly for Emily and Felix to jump, though, and doing so into a herd of terrified long-horned cattle was all but suicidal. Now only a hundred yards away, Pyke could see that the masked man was attempting to steer a path directly through the stampeding animals. If *he* had been the target, Pyke thought to himself as he ran, then why didn't the gunman abandon the vehicle and make his escape on foot? It would surely be easier to lose himself in the rabbit warren of alleyways and courts that criss-crossed the neighbourhood.

Ahead, some of the cattle broke away from the herd and swarmed around the stricken carriage, one of the horses rearing up on its hind legs and nearly toppling it in the process. His arms pumping like pistons on a steam engine, Pyke narrowed the gap to less than fifty yards and started to push his way through the scattered herd, ignoring the fact that one sudden turn of the head could impale him on a set of horns and kill him in a few seconds. The masked man had seen that Pyke was closing and lashed the backs of the two horses with the whip, spurring them on, in spite of the obstacles they faced. The carriage had almost cleared the herd and Pyke knew that if he didn't make up the ground now, his chances of catching it up were slim. On an empty street, a well-oiled carriage pulled by a couple of powerful mares would be out of his range in a matter of seconds. He could not let this happen. Ignoring a sharp pain in his abdomen and realising too late that one of the cattle's horns had sliced his stomach, he made a last, desperate lunge for the rear axle of the carriage, just as it cleared the last of the cows and bolted forward, just out of his reach.

Pyke saw Emily and Felix through the rear window of the vehicle as he fell to the ground.

PART III

*

The Quality of Rage

TWENTY-TWO

Amid gusts of wind that nearly picked them up off their feet and rain that lashed the deserted farmyard, turning the already sodden ground into a filthy sponge of mud and faeces, Pyke climbed down from the carriage and waited for Townsend. The November air smelled of wet leaves and a sulphurous fug produced by gases that bubbled up through the mud. With Townsend's help, Pyke pulled Sir Horsley Rockingham out of the carriage and together they dragged him, trussed and gagged, by his arms and dumped him next to a feeding trough. They had set upon Rockingham as he conducted one of his post-dinner tours of his stables and transported him, by carriage, to a farmyard less than a mile from the edge of his estate. The farmer's acquiescence had already been bought. It was dark, with no moonlight to guide them, the sky thick with brooding clouds. The yard was quiet apart from some giant hogs that squealed and snorted in a nearby sty. To Pyke, the hogs resembled grotesque wild creatures rather than farm-reared animals.

Bending over the wizened landowner, Pyke removed his gag and waited for a few moments. Rockingham looked up at him, bewildered, as though he had no idea what had happened. His eyes were empty, the colour of dishwater, and a strand of saliva hung from his unshaven chin.

'I'm only going to ask this question once,' Pyke said, kneeling over the older man. 'What have you done with my wife and child?'

Rockingham stared at him, uncomprehending.

'I said, where are my wife and child?' Pyke wiped the raindrops from his face and eyes. His greatcoat was already sodden.

'Your wife and child?' Rockingham repeated, as though the words made no sense to him.

Pyke hauled him up by the neck, as though he were a rag doll, and forced his head down into the gruel-like liquid in the trough.

276

Counting to five, he pulled his head up and held it just above the slime, while he spat, 'If I have to, old man, I'll search every building on your estate and I'll turn your nice Queen Anne mansion upside down, too.'

The hog's gruel seemed to have brought Rockingham around because his eyes suddenly looked more focused, as though he understood what was happening to him and indeed who Pyke was. He strained his wrists, which had been bound behind his back by bailing wire, but couldn't free them. The scum from the trough dripped from his face. 'I don't know a thing about your wife and child,' he whispered, trying to catch his breath.

'So why did you threaten them?' Pyke said, close enough to the landowner's face to lick it.

At the time Pyke interpreted Rockingham's silence as an admission of culpability, but later he couldn't help but think that his glazed face held little more than an expression of bewilderment. Even in his damp clothes, he could feel himself sweat. He could smell himself, too. Thrusting the older man's acorn-like head under the viscous water, he held it there for a little longer.

Rockingham was sick as soon as his head cleared the slime, a string of bile traced with blood hanging from his lips. Lumps of the gruel-like water hung from his mouth and cheeks.

From behind, Pyke heard Townsend mutter, 'He won't be able to take much more of this.'

But Pyke continued to hold Rockingham's head over the trough. 'Tell me how you know Jake Bolter.'

'What's Bolter got to do with anything?'

'Just answer the question.'

'He used to serve in the Thirty-first. I hold occasional dinners and a ball in my home for the regiment.'

'And did you meet Jimmy Trotter through him?'

'Trotter?'

'The man with a glass eye.'

'I don't know such a man.' He tried to clear his throat.

Pyke dunked Rockingham's head into the hog's gruel once again but this time, when he pulled it clear of the liquid, the old man's entire body began to spasm and a froth of blood and saliva started to seep from his mouth. Pyke dropped him on to the ground and tried to revive him, at first with a hard slap to the face and then with a few pumps on his chest. His body stopped convulsing and he must have died shortly afterwards because there was silence. In the yard, the only noises were the grunting and squealing of the hogs and the pitter-patter of rain. Pyke stood up and drew the sleeve of his coat over his mouth, staring down at Rockingham's limp form. Another wave of anger and self-hatred washed over him.

'*What?*' Pyke said, turning around to look at Townsend, who hadn't spoken a word. 'He must have had a heart seizure. There was nothing I could have done.'

Townsend stood there, his arms folded. His clothes were soaking and rain dripped from his chin.

Pyke bent down and quickly stripped the old man naked. Then he scooped the body up in his arms and carried it across to the sty. The landowner couldn't have weighed more than six stone, but it still took a monumental effort to lift him up over the chest-high fence and drop him into the sty. At first the reluctant beasts didn't know what to do with the body. A few of them prodded the naked corpse with their snouts and jostled with one another to get the best vantage point. It wasn't until one of them tasted a trace of blood on the old man's mouth that the feeding frenzy began in earnest, but when it did it was a truly sickening sight. In ankle-deep filth, Rockingham's arms and then his legs disappeared under a melee of trotters, and soon all that could be heard was a few quiet grunts as the creatures ripped into the old man's flesh and crunched his bones. Before too long there was nothing left.

'Tell the farmer we're done and meet me in the carriage.' Pyke stared up into the dark skies at the rain. 'I want to be back in London by daybreak.' The driver would have to be paid off, as well.

The odour of death had seeped into his fingers, clothes, skin and hair until it was all Pyke could taste, all he could smell. He had shot and, doubtless, killed the dragoon outside Huntingdon, but he hadn't tasted death in such a visceral way for a long time and had forgotten the unpleasantness of the feeling: knowing he had taken everything the old man had, and everything he would ever have. Pyke had killed him, plain and simple, and whether he deserved to die was beside the point. He could save the self-justifications and regret for later. An image of his son wouldn't leave his mind, and Pyke felt a gnawing emptiness building within him. It felt as if he were standing on the edge of a cliff, about to hurl himself to his own death. More than anything else he craved the reassurance of laudanum.

'Do you still think he was responsible?' Townsend asked, quietly. They had been travelling through the storm for almost two hours, and if anything the rain had intensified. The inside of the carriage smelled of mouldy hay and drying clothes.

Pyke gave him an empty look. 'You heard him. He didn't seem to know anything about it.'

Townsend put his legs up on the seat opposite. 'Tell me again why you thought it might have been him.' He tried to adjust his position, wincing as though in pain.

'Rockingham had been following me on the day of the kidnapping. He would've seen Emily and Felix in the carriage. He had the opportunity and the motive . . .'

'Motive?'

Pyke sighed. 'I was getting close to exposing his involvement in the deaths of an actor called Johnny, whose headless corpse was found in a river bordering Rockingham's land, an old crone who was raped and beaten to death just outside a navvy encampment, again in Huntingdon, and possibly also Edward James Morris.'

'And these deaths directly benefited the old man?'

'Certainly the last two did. More than anything, he didn't want this railway being built across his land. In different ways, both deaths retarded its progress.'

'Cold comfort for him now.' Townsend stared out of the window as the rain beat ceaselessly against the roof. 'And you had hard evidence linking him with all these murders?'

Pyke shook his head. He didn't know for certain that Morris *hadn't* killed himself and had no hard evidence, just a gut feeling that Morris wouldn't have taken his own life and a suspicion that Bolter had somehow been involved. Regarding the other two murders he tried to explain his suspicions concerning Jimmy Trotter – that the glass-eyed man had been trying to find the actor and had been spotted near the scene of the old crone's killing and that both corpses had been peppered with the same burn marks, possibly from a cigar. He also explained the connections between Trotter and Bolter – both had once lodged in the same guest house – and Bolter and Rockingham. Bolter, Pyke added, had been the old man's escort during a recent trip to the capital and, as the old man had admitted, they had met at social occasions hosted by Rockingham for personnel and former personnel of the 31st Regiment. Pyke also pointed out that the magistrate who had initially stirred up the trouble in Huntingdon about the time of the first two deaths had once belonged to this regiment too. He didn't tell Townsend that he had shot and killed a soldier while trying to escape the violence in Huntingdon but made a mental note to check on this. Maybe Emily and Felix had been abducted as punishment for that?

'But there's something about what you've just told me that's bothering you, isn't there?'

Pyke nodded, surprised by the acuteness of Townsend's insight. 'Someone *wanted* me to see Jake Bolter with Rockingham.' Briefly Pyke described the anonymous letter he had received, alerting him to Rockingham's arrival in the city. He thought, too, about the odd expression on the older man's face when Pyke had accused him of conspiring against the railway, and wondered whether it could really be true that Rockingham had never met or even known about Jimmy Trotter.

'Why would someone have sent you that note?'

'I don't know. As I said, perhaps they *wanted* me to see Bolter and Rockingham together. Perhaps they wanted me to suspect the old man.'

'Why?'

'If I had to guess, I'd say to divert suspicion from themselves.'

'You have anyone in mind?'

Pyke considered this for a moment. 'A couple of people.'

'You want to talk about it?'

Pyke shook his head. 'Not yet.' He didn't quite feel ready. But he closed his eyes and thought about it.

As the carriage rocked gently backwards and forwards, the names of his suspects slithered in and out of his mind, each vying for his attention.

When Pyke next opened his eyes, a few hours must have passed because the first signs of daylight were visible across the flat, barren landscape. His first thoughts were of Emily and Felix: where they might be or whether they were still alive. Emily, who'd just told him she was pregnant. He felt queasy, scared. Perhaps there would be news waiting for him in London.

'Who's done this to me?' he asked, not really expecting a response.

'The list of people bearing a grudge against you could be a long one,' Townsend replied. He looked pale and tired and each time he moved, he winced a little, as though trying to hide some kind of ailment.

Pyke thought about his own predicament. Given what had happened, he had to at least entertain the possibility that he, not Emily or Felix, had been the target of a failed assassination attempt, but this didn't explain why the masked man, who'd fired two shots at him, had driven off with his wife and son. Or why he'd heard nothing in the subsequent twenty-four hours.

'You think this could be someone trying to settle an old score?'

'You've made plenty of enemies.'

Pyke rubbed his eyes and stared out of the window. 'Then why hasn't there been a ransom demand?'

'Maybe there will be one waiting for you when you get home.'

Pyke nodded, slightly reassured by this hope. At least then, he would know that Emily and Felix were alive.

'On his third birthday I took my son to Bartholomew's Fair. I thought he'd like the noise and the colour. Maybe the animal exhibits, too. In the end, we spent most of our time by a stall where newborn babies were being sold. He didn't ask me about it once, not at the time and not on the way home, but later he had the most terrible nightmares, woke up the entire house with his screams.' Pyke paused, not sure why he'd remembered this or decided to tell Townsend about it.

Was it a happy memory of their time together or an example of his failings?

'Maybe what happened had nothing to do with you,' Townsend said, a while later. 'What if your wife was kidnapped because of something *she'd* done? You said she'd been involved with the radicals ...'

Pyke nodded. He had thought about this already, of course. He had considered Tilling's warning of an imminent crackdown and Bellows's suggestion that he keep a tighter rein on Emily. But would the chief magistrate really have targeted her in such an apparently random way?

'I don't know,' Pyke said, shaking his head. 'Perhaps you're right. Perhaps I'm missing something. But would Emily really have been their main target? And if she was, why not just kill her? Why go to the bother of hijacking a carriage with our son inside too?'

Townsend didn't have an answer. 'When we get back to the city, what d'you want me to do?'

'For a start, you can take up residence in my office at the bank. I want you there in case a ransom demand is delivered. I'm afraid if I go anywhere near the bank's premises, I'll be arrested.' When Townsend looked up at him, intrigued, Pyke added, 'I know. It's a long story.' It was Monday morning, and a warrant for his arrest might already have been issued. 'I'd also like you to keep an eye on William Blackwood. Every evening this week, I'll expect you at my new house, number forty-four Berkeley Square, at six o'clock sharp for a report. Of course, if there's a ransom note, I'll want to hear about it immediately. No one else knows about that address. I'd like it to remain that way.'

Townsend winced, as though in pain, and tried to get comfortable. 'What will you do?'

'I'm going to find Jake Bolter and Jimmy Trotter.'

'And when you find them?'

'I'll cross that bridge when I come to it.' Pyke looked out of the smeared window at the orange sun that had just appeared over an allotment site.

As they neared the city, Pyke's sense of foreboding grew. What if Emily and Felix were already dead?

TWENTY-THREE

Pyke found Harold Field attending to a young lamb in the pit of his underground slaughterhouse. He wore a clean, white apron and was surrounded by five or six younger meat cutters. Gripping the terrified creature with one arm, its feet scraping against the cobblestones, he held the knife with his other hand and slit the lamb's throat with a single draw of the blade. With another seven or eight strokes, Field had flayed and dissected the limp creature, his white apron now stained with the lamb's blood and entrails. In a nearby pen, the other lambs mewed and bleated, the ground beneath their feet thick with dried blood and fat. Field wiped his hands on his apron and said something to the gathered meat cutters. Then the circle around him broke up, and Field made his way up to the top of the stairs where Pyke was standing.

'Would you believe it? They call themselves butchers but some of 'em don't even know how to flay a lamb.' His hands were still caked in blood. 'I take it you want to talk to me?'

Pyke hadn't seen Field before – he knew of his reputation, as most people did who lived or worked around Smithfield – and was surprised to find that he was such a neat and fussy dresser. Underneath the apron, he wore a fashionable black frock-coat and a blue silk cravat, tied in an immaculate bow. His hair had a reddish tinge but it had been neatly trimmed and his beard and whiskers glistened with pomade.

'I was told that Jimmy Trotter does some work for you.'

'Is that right?' Field smiled easily, a mask for the violence that lurked within him. 'And who told you that?'

'Ned Villums.'

This time Field regarded him with renewed caution. 'So you're a friend of that old rogue.'

'My name's Pyke.' He waited and saw Field's pupils dilate slightly.

'I'm a banker now but I used to be a Bow Street Runner. And I once owned a ginnery around the corner from here on Giltspur Street.'

'Lizzie's place. I remember you now.' Field's smile was confined to the corners of his mouth. 'You had some trouble with the law, if I recall.'

'A long time ago now.'

'People around here have long memories.' Field shrugged. 'You once had quite a reputation.'

'Coming from you, I'll take that as a compliment.'

Field regarded him suspiciously. 'So what's your business with Jimmy?'

'I'd prefer to keep that to myself.'

'And you think I'm just going to hand him to you on a plate?' He seemed amused by this notion.

'From time to time, you may have need of a banker whose discretion you can rely on.'

Field's eyes narrowed. 'Is that how you know Ned?'

'I've known Ned from even before his tenure at the Old Cock.'

'I remember now. You were something of a villain even as a Bow Street Runner.' Field wiped his hands on his apron. 'But I'm afraid I can't help you. Jimmy doesn't work for me any more.'

'What happened? Did someone make him a better offer?'

For the first time, Pyke saw real menace in Field's eyes. 'Don't try and mock me. You've seen my handiwork with a knife.'

Pyke thought about responding but remembered Villums's warning. 'So you don't know where I could find him?'

Field's smile returned, perhaps because he sensed he had unsettled Pyke. 'Jimmy always was a bit of a wanderer.' He paused, then added, 'But I do remember how he liked his cigars. He always bought them from a shop on Oxford Street. You could try asking for him there.'

Pyke realised this was all he was likely get from the man and thanked him for his help. As he turned to leave, Field stepped forward and laid a hand on his arm. 'What did you say the name of your bank was?'

'Blackwood's. You can find us above Sweeting's Alley in the City.'

'I might just take you up on your offer one of these days.' Field was smiling. 'And if you do see Jimmy, remember to give him my best wishes. I'm guessing he'll need them if that look on your face is anything to go by.'

Outside on the same street as Field's slaughterhouse was a fat-boiler, tripe-scraper, glue-renderer and a small tannery. The air stank of offal, drying hides and mephitic fumes. Looking back into the slaughterhouse, Pyke wondered how many human beings had been murdered within its walls.

Earlier in the day he had looked for Jake Bolter at Prosser's asylum in Tooting but had been told by one of the staff that neither Bolter nor 'Mr Prosser' had been seen there for a few days. Back at the crimping house, he had learned nothing new about Bolter or Trotter. Earlier still, Pyke had interrupted the journey back from Huntingdon by insisting that they stop at Hambledon, but no ransom demand had been delivered. Only Jo had been told what had happened and, if she heard *anything* at all, she'd been instructed to contact Townsend, day or night, at the bank. Nor had a ransom demand been left for Pyke at Blackwood's. He had remained in the carriage while Townsend made his enquiries there.

Overnight the storm had passed and the temperatures had plummeted, a cool wind from the north replacing the easterly gales. The air was cold and dry and the sky a crisp blue. It took him half an hour to walk from Smithfield along High Holborn to the start of Oxford Street, and there he sat on the pavement and ate a meat pie bought from a stall, his fingers dripping with hot gravy. As he licked the gravy from his fingers, he could see his own breath. Once he'd finished the pie, he fumbled around in his pocket for the bottle of laudanum, unscrewed the top and drank almost half of it. The syrupy tincture, mixed with port rather than gin, made him shudder, and for a moment Pyke thought he might bring up the pie.

He visited three tobacconists at the eastern end of Oxford Street, none of whom recognised Jimmy Trotter from his description. Having picked up the cigar stub he'd been given by the navvy, Red, from the Hall, Pyke showed it to the three men, but none of them was able to identify the brand or shed light on where it might have been purchased.

Oxford Street was a tumult of noise and motion: pedestrians five or six deep on the flagstone pavement streaming in and out of the bazaars and shops. Silversmiths, shoe- and bootmakers, fruiterers whose windows displayed exotic fare like pineapples and figs, spirit booths selling hot gin and Jamaica rum by the quart, and large emporia selling everything from the finest silks to Staffordshire bone china. Here the idle rich, waited upon by their liveried servants, rubbed shoulders with ragged hawkers whose kerbside stalls were piled up with old boots, broken umbrellas, stolen handkerchiefs and strips of ribbon.

Usually Pyke would have taken the bustle in his stride but the laudanum and a lack of sleep made everything seem strange and disjointed. People's faces drifted in and out of focus, their smiles turning into grimaces and vice versa. Pyke liked the anonymity that the city afforded him but, all of a sudden, he felt exposed and perhaps threatened by the faces that passed him by. No one knew. No one understood. He wanted to stop the next man he saw and shake him by the collar. 'My wife and child have been kidnapped,' he wanted to say, even though he knew how ridiculous it made him sound. Why should anyone else but him care?

At the junction with Regent Street, the shops became grander and the pavements wider still. A crowd had built up and it took Pyke a few moments to realise that everyone was looking at a procession of three giraffes, with their Nubian attendants, heading along Regent Street in the direction of the new zoological gardens in the park. Pausing to watch these strangely graceful creatures, he thought how excited Felix would have been, if he'd been there, and felt another wave of anguished sadness wash over him.

When the procession had passed, Pyke crossed the road just in front of a brightly painted carriage and, startled from his thoughts, he looked at the window and saw Emily, her face pressed up against the glass.

Running behind the carriage, waving his arms and shouting, Pyke caught up with it at the next junction, the driver and footman both looking at him as if he were an escaped Bedlamite.

'That's my wife in there,' he said, panting, his lungs ready to burst.

But it wasn't Emily, of course. Nor did the delicate, effete woman in the carriage look anything like her, apart from having the same colour hair.

Pyke sat down on the kerb and tried to catch his breath. Perhaps the laudanum had affected his vision. He was joined briefly by a young girl in a flimsy white dress. She shot him a wan smile and held up a bunch of wilting cress. 'Ha'penny for some watercresses,' she croaked. Her arms were skeletal and uncovered, her dress offering no protection from the elements. He got up and bought her a meat pie from a nearby stall, but when he came back she had gone.

Darkness had begun to gnaw at the edges of the sky and the lamplighters were out on Oxford Street, moving from lamp to lamp with their ladders and tools. Pyke had nearly walked the entire length of the street. He was cold and his feet ached. There was one final tobacconist hemmed in between a grocer's and a barber's shop. He pushed open the door and heard a bell ring. The tobacconist wore wire-rimmed spectacles and a blue-and-white-striped apron. Pyke showed the man what little remained of the stub and asked whether he could identify the brand.

The tobacconist pushed his spectacles back up his nose. 'Not the exact brand but it looks like a well-rolled cigar. Something we might stock.'

His assistant, a pretty young woman with blonde braids, hovered to one side of the counter.

'I'm looking for the man who purchased it. His name's Jimmy Trotter.' Pyke gave them a description.

The tobacconist shook his head and said he didn't recognise the name or the description, but out of the corner of his eye Pyke saw the young assistant flinch. It was all he needed.

It was another half-hour before the tobacconist pulled down the wooden shutters and locked up the shop. Wearing a shawl now, the young assistant bade him farewell and set off along Oxford Street. Pyke caught up with her at the corner of Duke Street. At first she didn't seem to recognise him but when he mentioned Trotter's name her face fell and her lips began to quiver. Pyke told her not to be scared, he just wanted some information, and if she told him what he needed to know, he would buy her a hot roast beef dinner and as much beer as she wanted. That seemed to do it, and she led him around the corner to a pub called the Three Geese.

'He's been a regular in the shop for a year. Always gives me these looks and tries to touch me when Mr Bent ain't looking. He always buys the same thing, too: a box of Fuentes cigars, from the

West Indies. Expensive, they are. He calls 'em his Prometheus sticks.'

She was a slight, willowy girl with fine blond ehair and a freckled face, but she had already finished one mug of beer and ordered another.

'Do you know where he lives?'

'Not where he *lives*,' she said, licking foam from her top lip.

'Then where I can find him?'

'Last month, Mr Bent made me deliver the cigars to him in person. I didn't want to but he told me 'less I did, I'd lose my job. He said Mr Trotter was one of his very best customers. I didn't tell him about the looks and the groping. And he said he'd pay me sixpence for it.'

'Where did you deliver them to?'

'That was the thing. When I left them for him, he weren't there. But as soon as I stepped out of the pub, I felt something touch me and he was there, leering at me. I could tell he was in the gun, his eyes were crossed and I could smell the rum on his breath, but I could see he meant business. I'd say he's a mean one. He tried to grab my wrist and pull me into the alley but I was too quick for him and then a gentl'man happened to walk past and I latched on to him.'

'You did well,' Pyke said, waving at the pot-boy to bring her another beer.

She gave him a toothy smile but he could see she was still shaken by the incident.

'So you were told to deliver the cigars to a public house?' When she nodded, Pyke added, 'Do you remember which one?'

She screwed up her face and tried to think. 'I'd say it was on Tooley Street, across the river in Bermondsey.'

Silently, Pyke kicked himself. 'The Jolly Sailor.' He should have thought about it without the girl's prompt.

'You know it?' She looked at him, surprised. 'It don't seem like the kind of place a gentl'man would go.'

But he didn't want to make the long journey down to Bermondsey that night and, having met Townsend at the house in Berkeley Square and been told there were no new developments, he couldn't face its silence and emptiness and caught a hackney carriage from a stand on the south side of the square all the way to his uncle's apartment in Camden.

Pyke had already told Godfrey the bad news about Emily and Felix in a note. His uncle ushered him into the parlour and put a glass of claret in his hand. 'I haven't heard a thing, either,' Godfrey said, when Pyke told him there had been no word of them and no ransom letter. 'We need to be careful, though, dear boy,' he went on, peering through the curtains at the street. 'I had a visit earlier from two very unfriendly peelers. They showed me a warrant for your arrest. I read it. It alleged you embezzled ten thousand pounds from your own bank.'

So Blackwood had come good on his promise, Pyke noted with grim satisfaction. Again he wondered who was pulling his partner's strings.

Briefly Pyke explained what had happened while Godfrey listened, his lips rouged with claret. 'And you think this might be related to what's happened to Emily and Felix?' he asked, when Pyke had finished.

'Your guess is as good as mine.'

'But you suspect who might have stolen the documents and set you up?'

'Apart from Blackwood, there isn't anyone else.'

'Then that's where you start.'

Pyke explained he was paying Townsend to keep an eye on his partner but that his own priorities lay elsewhere.

'Of course they do, dear boy, of course they do. And if there's anything I can do to help, you know you just have to ask.' Godfrey offered him a pained expression and shook his head. 'A terrible, *terrible* business. I've been so worried. Emily, and that darling child of yours.'

Pyke felt another wave of tiredness engulf him. He had hardly slept at all since the abduction. 'Townsend made an interesting comment. That Emily may have been targeted for something she'd done, rather than to hurt me.'

'But to involve a young child as well,' Godfrey said, shaking his head.

'I know, I know ...' Pyke thought about her reluctance to tell him what she had been involved in. Looking up, he noticed that a peculiar expression had taken over Godfrey's face. 'What is it?'

'I heard some bad news today. A couple of the lads who help deliver the *Scourge* came to tell me.'

'About?'

'Apparently the Standard of Liberty beer shop on Brick Lane was raided earlier this morning and closed down. Everyone they could find was bundled into one of those secure carriages and taken away. There were similar raids on the Albion coffee house in Shoreditch, the Spotted Cow on Old Kent Road and the Barley Mow on Upper Thames Street.'

Frowning, Pyke turned this new information over in his head and thought about something Tilling had told him. 'Was Jackman's brigade the main target?'

Godfrey's Adam's apple bobbed up and down while he finished what was in his glass. 'From what I understand.'

'Sir Henry Bellows was planning a crackdown against the radicals. I was told it might get nasty.'

'You mean the windbag magistrate who wanted to lock me up and throw away the key?'

Pyke nodded and asked Godfrey whether he'd had any joy chasing up information regarding the properties Bellows was alleged to have bought in Somers Town.

'Not just yet, dear boy. But I have my feelers out there. Something will turn up. It always does.'

Pyke thought again about Bellows and his connections both to Huntingdon, where he seemed to know everything that had happened, and to Sir John Conroy, and wondered whether he had had anything to do with the kidnapping. The answer seemed to lie in front of him but just beyond his comprehension.

'What is it, dear boy?'

'Do you mind if I stay here tonight? I just can't ...' Suddenly he felt overwhelmed by tiredness.

His uncle held up the palms of his hands. 'No need to explain. You know this has always been your home, too.'

They sat in silence for a few minutes, both occupied with their own thoughts. 'It's obtuse, dear boy, obtuse,' Godfrey said, breaking the silence. 'I do what I do because I no longer care. I like to rattle people's cages. I can see the corruptness of government as well as anyone else but I don't give a rat's arse about the poor. Not really. Not like Emily. She wants to really change things and she thinks it's still possible. A true believer. Always the most dangerous kind.'

'Dangerous in what sense?'

Godfrey wiped away a strand of dribble that had escaped from his mouth. 'I don't mean to further alarm you, my boy ...'

'But?'

'How can I put this?' He sat up in his chair, drumming the arms with his fingers. 'I just don't think you should underestimate the seriousness of the wider situation we're facing here. There's a small, dirty war going on out there and I suspect Emily might be caught right in the middle of it.'

It had been more than three days since the kidnapping and still no one had heard or knew a thing about it. If it had, indeed, been a kidnapping.

The following morning, more from a sense of desperation than realistic hope, Pyke found himself waiting for Gore at the head office of his bank on Leadenhall Street.

As befitted the public face of London's largest private bank, Gore's banking hall was a cathedral to commerce and the power of money, a place that sought to display the wealth of its owner and customers. In architectural terms, the building was bettered in the Square Mile only by the head offices of the East India Company. The neoclassical façade, clad in brilliant white stucco, resembled an Italian palazzo, and inside, the ornate ceilings, the decorative pilasters and the giant silk damasks that hung on the walls, together with a glass chandelier that wouldn't have looked out of place in the Palace of Versailles, gave the impression of imperial majesty. In the hall itself, queues of well-fed customers were serviced by as many as twenty cashiers, and the whole room had an air of quiet efficiency and money that, at one time, Pyke might have found intoxicating.

He arrived alone and was escorted up the marble staircase to the top floor, where he was told to wait. In fact, he'd barely had the chance to get comfortable in the armchair before Abraham Gore himself burst through one of the doors and strode over to greet him, concern etched on his face. 'What is it, old friend?' he asked, as he led Pyke towards his private office. 'Have you discovered something about Morris's death?'

Pyke had expected Gore to occupy a large, palatial office more akin to something one might find at a gentleman's club than a bank, and was therefore surprised to find himself in a room barely larger than his own, with just a medium-sized mahogany desk, two chairs, a half-empty bookshelf and a bureau as furniture. Gore invited Pyke to sit down on the other chair and said, 'If you don't mind me saying so, my friend, you look terrible. Is something the matter?'

Somehow he found the utilitarian modesty of Gore's office reassuring.

Pyke took a deep breath and told Gore about the abduction. Gore's jaw dropped as he did so, the colour draining from his ruddy cheeks. He listened patiently to Pyke's brief precis of what had happened and wiped his forehead with a pocket handkerchief while muttering, 'My God,' and then, 'A monstrous business.' When Pyke had finished, he got up, walked around the desk and tried to embrace Pyke, a gesture that turned into a rather awkward fumble. Still, his intentions seemed genuine enough, and as far as Pyke had been able to tell the news had been as shocking to him as it was unexpected. Either that or Gore was a better actor than Pyke imagined.

'You must be beside yourself with worry,' Gore began, still shaking his head. 'It's truly monstrous. Who would do such a thing? And to involve your delightful boy, as well. If there's anything I can do, anything at all . . .'

'I'm afraid that's why I'm here.' Pyke looked at Gore across the desk. 'I might be clutching at straws but I'm worried my wife might have been targeted in a more general clampdown on radical activities here in the capital. I was hoping you might be able to call upon your various connections to determine whether this was the case or not.'

'Your wife?' Gore asked, sounding surprised. 'Why on earth would she have been the target?'

'You heard her last week at Morris's house. She's long been an ardent campaigner for political reform.'

'Indeed, indeed,' Gore said, rubbing his chin. 'But do you really think a politician or a judge would really sanction such an action? Your lad was involved, after all. I mean to say, would someone with their hands on the reins of power sink to such depths? I can't think that your wife, delightful as she is, poses such a significant threat to the powers that be.'

'Perhaps not, but in the week preceding the abduction I received two vague threats directed towards Emily.'

'Threats from whom?'

'A savage called Jimmy Trotter and Sir Henry Bellows.'

'Bellows?' Gore appeared upset by this news. 'What's that blithering idiot got to do with any of this?'

Pyke explained that Bellows was orchestrating this clampdown on radical activity in the city and that a number of arrests had been made over the past couple of days.

'Arrests, but not a kidnapping, not abducting a woman and a young child in broad daylight ...'

'Will you at least see what you can find out for me? Who knows? You might be quite right. Bellows might have had nothing at all to do with the abduction. But I'd like to hear this confirmed by one of your contacts. I'm not accusing him of anything just yet but he's never liked me and my recent encounters with him have all been acrimonious.'

'Of course, I'll do whatever I can. I'll get to work on it immediately. I'm just glad you felt you could confide in me.'

Pyke nodded his gratitude. 'It goes without saying that the fewer people who hear about the kidnapping the better. I don't suddenly want to be inundated with false ransom demands.'

'Quite, quite,' Gore said, sitting forward in his chair, his face lined with concern. 'In the light of this awful news, perhaps we should think about postponing our little piece of business ...'

'Why?' Pyke said, more sharply than he had intended. 'Are you suddenly having second thoughts?'

That seemed to wound Gore. 'Not at all, my friend. Quite the opposite, in fact. I'm chomping at the bit to get going with it.'

'Then we should proceed as planned. After all, business is business.'

'Admirable sentiments,' Gore said, seriously. 'Even more so in the light of your ... *difficulties.*' He paused for a moment. 'And rest assured, I will do everything I can to help you. Everything in my power. I'm certain this dreadful business will work out in the end. Even though I have no faith to speak of, at times like this I can see why people turn to the Church. I wish I could offer you more than I've been able to.'

*

When the hack-chaise dropped him at the steps of Hambledon, he was met by Jo, the only servant Pyke had told about the kidnapping. Jo said that no ransom demand had been delivered to the hall and no new information had come to light She added that some of the servants were starting to question the story they'd been told – that Emily and Felix were visiting an old friend of hers on the south coast. Why hadn't she told any of them about this trip? Royce had apparently been asking. Pyke dismissed these concerns with a shake of the hand. 'So what,' he said, bounding up the steps two at a time. He asked how Milly was. Jo explained that she was eating properly and looked quite well but that she still hadn't spoken a word or ventured out of her room.

Pyke found Milly sitting on her bed, humming to herself. Laid out in front of her were a series of pencil drawings; one of a horse, one of a tree, one of a flower and one of a dog.

When she saw him, Milly tried to gather up and hide the drawings but he managed to retrieve the one of the flower from the bed before she could crumple it up. 'This is very good, Milly,' Pyke said, looking at the drawing from different angles. Clearly the girl had a talent for draughtsmanship.

Blushing a little, she relinquished the other drawings from her grip and Pyke took them in his hands and admired them in passing. He told her the drawing of the flower was his favourite and without hesitation Milly thrust it into his hand.

'You mean I can keep it?'

She nodded.

'Really? Are you quite sure you want to part with it?'

Smiling now, she nodded again.

'Then I'll tell you what I'll do. I'll put it in a frame and hang it over there on that wall. Would you like that?'

This time her nod of the head was less forthright.

'I want to help you, Milly. I really do.' He reached out to touch her gently on the cheek but she shrank from him, her blue eyes widening with fear. 'But to help you, I need to know what happened that night when I found you under the table. Do you understand what I'm asking?'

She stared at him without blinking.

'Please, Milly. I know it's hard for you. I can't imagine how difficult it must have been, having to see what you saw ...'

Milly retreated farther up the bed until her back was pressed against the frame. She had started to shake a little too.

Sighing, Pyke glanced down at the drawings on the bed and noticed that the dog was a mastiff. He picked it up and studied it more carefully. In the drawing, the beast had a sturdy, muscular frame, a fawn coat and a black face.

'Have you ever seen a dog like this one before?' When she refused to answer him, Pyke added, 'Please, Milly. This is very important. Did you see a dog like this one on the night your mama and papa were . . .?'

Milly turned towards the wall and started to hum.

'Milly, please . . .'

But she wouldn't turn around and look at him.

That afternoon Pyke journeyed back into the city in his own carriage and arrived at the house on Berkeley Square just after five. For an hour, he wandered listlessly around the empty building, wondering quite what he had seen in it to begin with: the whole place had the feel of a mausoleum. Just after six, he met Townsend at the front door and saw at once from his expression that he had no news about Emily. The previous day, Townsend had seemed a little intimidated by the house so Pyke suggested they take a stroll around the square instead.

'I talked with one of the watchmen at the bank,' Townsend explained. 'I hadn't seen him before. He told me he'd been ill with a fever. He hadn't even heard about the burglary, the fact that some papers had gone missing from the vault, but he was on duty that night. I asked him if he'd seen anything. He looked at me and said, "Not if you don't count Jem Nash." Apparently, Nash was there in the building between about two and two thirty in the morning.'

Walking ahead, Pyke contemplated this for a moment. Perhaps Nash had allowed himself to get mixed up in something untoward and had been killed for it? Perhaps he had stolen the documents for someone else, to clear his debt, and then been killed?

Turning to Townsend, who was lagging slightly behind, he said, 'I'd still like you to keep a close eye on Blackwood and continue to maintain a presence at the bank.'

Townsend nodded.

'That was very fine work with the watchman by the way,' Pyke said, noticing that Townsend was grimacing slightly and that he limped when he walked.

Pyke wanted to invite him into the house and talk about the old days, but somehow it didn't seem appropriate. Their lives had moved on and an unbridgeable gap had opened up between them. He handed Townsend an envelope stuffed with money. Townsend took it and was gone.

TWENTY-FOUR

The last time he had visited the Jolly Sailor in Bermondsey he had seen three dogs fight a bull and had taken a billiard cue to the head of Jake Bolter. But when he entered the taproom later that night, no one took any notice of him, at least not until he had asked the landlord where he could find Jake Bolter or Jimmy Trotter. It was late, after midnight, but the tavern was thronging with drinkers.

'I can see from your reaction you know who I'm talking about,' he added, tipping the Jamaica rum he'd been served down his throat in a single movement.

The rough spirit burned the sides of his throat and forced him to shudder slightly. Someone chuckled next to him. Pyke let him see the two pistols in his belt – the landlord, too – and the chuckling stopped. The rum, mixed with some laudanum he'd taken earlier, put him at ease.

Looking around the dirty, low-ceilinged room, he decided the Jolly Sailor didn't live up to its name. It was the kind of place where petty thieves congregated with sailors on shore leave to drink themselves into a stupor and gamble what little money they had on rats, dogs, bulls, bears, cockerels and perhaps even human beings. The place stank of unwashed bodies, gin vapours and stale tobacco. Along the zinc-topped counter stood a motley collection of bedraggled men wearing soiled smock-frocks, shooting jackets and blue-flannelled sailor's shirts. He could feel the heat of their stares burning into his face.

'I asked a question.' He waited, and folded his arms. 'I was told Trotter once had his cigars delivered here.'

Pyke sensed the man's presence behind him but when he turned around, he found himself staring at someone's chest. He had to look upward to see the man's face, and this almost caused him to crick his neck.

'You've had your drink.' The man glowered. 'Now you can leave.' His arms, like small oak trees, rippled with veins.

'Someone here knows where I can find Trotter and I'm prepared to pay for this information.' Pyke raised his voice so that the entire room could hear him. After that, you could have heard a mouse scamper across the floor.

'But are you prepared to fight for it?' someone asked him, from farther along the counter. A ripple of approval spread throughout the room. The prospect of spilled blood never failed to arouse appetites.

'Fight who?'

'Fight me, if you like.' This time a man stepped out from the line of drinkers to reveal himself to be a nine-stone specimen with a collapsed chest and a set of elaborately coiled whiskers.

'And if I beat you, you'll tell me where I can find Trotter?'

'Aye, I'm sure it can be arranged,' the man said, glancing surreptitiously at the landlord, who gave him a curt nod.

'And if you beat me?'

'Then everyone here gets to see a gentl'man suffer. That's always the best show in town.' He grinned, pointing at the pistols. ''Course, you'll have to leave your pops behind the counter.'

'If I agree, what's to stop someone going to warn Trotter so that when I turn up at his lodgings he's long gone?'

'You won't find anyone here who likes that cur.' The man twisted the ends of his moustache. 'Ask folk if you don't believe me.'

A little later, stripped down to the waist, Pyke was led into the same yard where the mastiff, Copper, had torn apart the stricken bull. Someone had opened the door of the pen and Pyke was jostled into the makeshift arena, crowds building around the wooden fence, red-faced men and women gesticulating and arguing with each other, a few coins changing hands. The remains of the bull had been cleared away, Pyke was pleased to see, but the enormous pool of blood had left a dark stain on the hard ground. Looking around him, he tried to see his puny opponent in the crowd of faces leering and shouting at him. A few left-right combinations would shut them up. He may have put on weight around the midriff but he still knew how to throw, and take, a punch.

Some cheers went up inside the taproom and soon eager faces turned to greet his opponent. A path was cleared and the gate swung open. Pyke should have seen it coming. He had walked straight into it.

Above the heads of the gathered crowd, Pyke saw the man who had first accosted him in the taproom, and when the seven-foot giant stepped into the pen his bare torso was glistening with oil.

The cheers and jeers around him reached a climax and Pyke realised he was trapped. He could plead a mismatch but the giant would still do his best and take him apart. He could try to make a run for it but the hostile crowd was seven or eight deep all the way around the fence and they would kick him to death before they let him leave. No, his only choice was to stay and fight, but when he looked across at his opponent limbering up, he wondered whether suicide might be a better option. If only he hadn't agreed to give up his pistols.

Pyke measured himself against his opponent and realised that the top of his head didn't quite reach the man's chin. More gas lamps were lit, flooding the arena with additional light.

Before he could take further action, the fight had started and his opponent tried to bear down on him, throwing punches like a windmill. With some ease, Pyke ducked under his opening barrage, staying light on his toes and keeping his breathing regular. The giant grunted with anger and turned on him, this time not bothering to throw a punch but rather pushing him against the fence and head-butting him in the face. The bridge of his nose exploded, blood and cartilage spraying from both nostrils. His opponent stepped back and grinned, this time acknowledging the applause of the crowd, his torso barely damp with perspiration. Swallowing his own blood, Pyke seized upon his opponent's temporary loss of concentration and landed a left and a right blow, both under the short ribs, to deprive the big man of air. The punches surprised more than hurt his opponent and, responding with an embarrassed fury, he swung wildly and missed, Pyke ducking inside the blows and landed two more punches, this time to the kidneys. A few cheers of support greeted his left-right combination, further infuriating the giant, who shoved Pyke back into the fence and tried to grab him in a headlock. Pyke stamped on his toe with the heel of his boot, causing his opponent to grunt with pain for the first time, but he didn't move back quickly enough and the giant caught him with a straight punch just under the eye. It was like being hit with a sledgehammer. The next thing Pyke knew, he was on his hands and knees: a gash had opened up under his eye and he could taste blood and saliva in his mouth. Staggering to his feet, Pyke cleared his throat, blinked twice and tried to focus, but the gash under his eye had swollen up so much he could barely see out of it. He certainly didn't see the blow that caught him on the temple and sent him crashing to the floor again. His opponent stood over him and told him to stay on the ground. All around him was a blur of screaming and motion.

Pyke remained on his hands and knees a little longer this time, to try to clear his head. Pain from the last blow was strangely welcome, though. It helped to focus his mind. He stood up quickly and raised his guard. The giant rushed at him but Pyke stepped inside his reach and landed another left-right combination in the kidneys, blows that winded the giant a little. That enraged the big man and caused him to lose his composure. He came at Pyke throwing wild punches, but they were easy to evade. Sensing an opportunity, Pyke ducked under one blow, reached down and grabbed his opponent's scrotum. With all his strength, Pyke jerked the sack upwards and felt the skin tear. At first the giant didn't seem to know what had happened, nor did any of the baying crowd, who looked on with stunned bewilderment. The man blinked twice, his jaw slackening and his eyes widening, before a low, piercing scream tumbled from his mouth. Pyke looked down and saw he was still holding part of the man's scrotum. He opened his fingers and let the thin strip of skin fall silently to the ground. The giant stumbled around the ring screaming, throwing wild punches into thin air, blood gushing from his wound. Seizing his chance, Pyke landed three telling left-right combinations under the short ribs and to the kidneys and followed them up with another series of blows to the body. The crowd had fallen silent. The only sounds were the hissing of the gas lamps and the ragged panting of the wounded man. Pausing to gather himself for the 'kill', Pyke wiped blood from his mouth with his bare arm, took aim and landed a kick directly into his opponent's groin. There were a few gasps from the crowd. The giant went down easily after that and he didn't get up. Blinking, Pyke looked around him at the sea of hostile faces. No one had wanted him to win and no one had bet any money on this outcome. The slain giant reminded Pyke of the stricken bull.

In the taproom Pyke retrieved his pistols and shirt from the landlord. He couldn't see out of one eye and his head throbbed with pain, but apart from that he felt all right. He was alive. That was the most important thing.

The man with the coiled whiskers slapped him on the back. 'That was quite a performance.' But he was wary of Pyke now. There was fear in his voice.

'The address.'

'A half mile farther along this street, opposite the turn for Porter's Field, there's a brothel run by an old dowdy called Bennett. Trotter's taken a room there.'

'There's another man called Bolter. He sometimes fights a mastiff, Copper, here. You know him?'

'Aye, I seen him.'

'But you don't know where I can find him?'

The man shrugged apologetically.

Pyke tucked the pistols into his belt and turned to leave.

'Why don't you stay for a drink?' the whiskered man called out. 'Well, be careful, then. Trotter's not a fella you want to turn your back on.'

But Pyke made it only a few steps out of the tavern before the effects of the fight, together with the alcohol and laudanum, caught up with him. He felt dizzy and nauseous, in no condition to take on someone as dangerous as Trotter. If the giant had come at him with fists like anvils, Trotter would be armed with pistols and knives. He found a scrub of land set back from the street with a ragged hawthorn bush in the middle of it. He lay down behind the bush, out of sight of the street, and within a few moments he had passed out.

A dog's bark woke Pyke just before dawn. He sat upright and looked around him, trying to gather his bearings and remember where he was. The throbbing in his head had subsided to a dull ache but the bruise under his eye had swollen up still further, making it all but impossible for him to see out of it, and the inside of his mouth tasted as if a cat had defecated into it during the night. Standing up, he checked to make sure he still had his purse and the two pistols and gently touched the bruise under his eye. Through the rows of houses and derelict cottages he could just about see the river, dappled by the early morning sunlight. He stretched and let out a brief yawn. He didn't feel *good* but he felt better than he had done when he had left the tavern. Tooley Street was deserted and it took him only ten minutes to walk to the brothel, a tenement building that had long since fallen into disrepair. His watch told him it was half-past five. It wasn't likely there'd be anyone up at such an early hour, but if Trotter was there, and asleep, it would be a good time to surprise him.

It took him a few minutes of continuing banging on the door to raise the harridan who ran the brothel. Grumbling, she unbolted the door from the inside and peered around the edge of it. Pyke dug the barrel of his pistol into her cheek and whispered, 'I just want Jimmy Trotter. Tell me where I can find his room and I'll let you get back to bed. It'll be like I was never even here. Nod your head once if you understand.'

She nodded.

'Is he here?'

'I don't know,' she croaked. 'But he owes me a week's rent. You can tell him that if you see him.'

Pyke pushed her back into the gloomy hallway and closed the door behind him. It smelled of fried fish and mould.

'Which room?' With the hand not holding the pistol, Pyke dug into his pocket and produced a half-crown.

That settled the matter. She snatched the coin from his hand and muttered, 'Up the stairs to the back of the building. Last door on your right.' Slamming the door behind her, she disappeared into her apartment. After that everything went quiet. He heard a mouse or a rat scurry across the floorboards above him and somewhere on the street a cockerel had begun to crow.

As quietly as he could, Pyke started to mount the rickety staircase, two steps at a time, his pistol still in his hand. A certain amount of creaking could not be avoided. At the top of the stairs he paused, to give his eyes time to adjust to the darkness, and surveyed the long, narrow passageway. It wasn't fried fish he'd smelt earlier, he realised. It was the stink of stale sex. Halfway along the passageway

Pyke hesitated again, this time because he heard voices in one of the rooms. A prostitute and her mark, he hoped. Startled by his presence, a tiny field mouse bolted from its hiding place and fled past him in the direction of the stairs. He edged farther along the passageway and waited, listening for any sounds. There were none. At the end of the passageway he stopped, checked to see his pistol was cocked and took a couple of breaths. The only sound he could hear was the beating of his own heart.

He kicked the door open with the heel of his boot and stepped into the tiny room. Jimmy Trotter, naked apart from a pair of underpants and his work boots, was urinating into a bucket. Bleary eyed, he looked up, startled at first, and then smiling. His beard and whiskers were more ragged and overgrown than Pyke remembered. He could have shot him then but he needed Trotter to answer some questions and perhaps Trotter sensed his indecision. Pyke raised the pistol to his face and said, 'Move slowly and quietly back into the room and keep your hands where I see them.'

Trotter finished his piss, tapping his flaccid penis to get rid of the last drops.

'Do you know where I can find my wife and child?' Up close, Trotter had a pungent, feral scent, but his body was lean and hard.

'Best place I've ever lived,' he said, casually. 'If I'm hard in the morning, I just go next door and get the biter to French-kiss me.' His grin revealed gums that were black and bloody and his naked flesh was gnarled, like old leather.

'I asked you a question. If you don't answer, I'll blow a hole in your face the size of a grapefruit.'

'I don't know anything about your piece ...' He licked his lips and raised his one good eye to meet Pyke's stare. 'Except I've heard she's a screamer and she likes it hard and rough.' Wiggling his hips to simulate the sex act, Trotter grinned more broadly. 'I heard she likes to fuck horses, too.'

'You move another muscle in your body and you're dead.' Pyke kept the pistol trained at Trotter's head and thought about the unspeakable things Trotter had done to the old woman at the navvy camp in Huntingdon. 'Tell me why you made a threat against her in St Paul's.'

'That upset you, eh?'

'More than pulling the trigger and decorating the wall behind you with pieces of your skull.' Pyke poked the end of the pistol harder into his cheek. 'Who told you about my wife? And what were you doing following me?' He had other questions, about the old woman in Huntingdon, the actor Johnny and Freddie Sutton and his wife, but he would start here.

When he moved, Trotter was as quick as a whip. In a single movement he picked up the metal bucket and hurled it as Pyke at the same time as diving for something next to his mattress.

Pyke aimed and squeezed the trigger. The blast was deafening in such a confined space and the ball-shot tore into Trotter's flesh, shattering his ribs and peppering his heart. The contents of the bucket, Trotter's urine, stung his eyes and mouth.

Trotter fell on to the mattress, a pool of blood spreading beneath him. Turning him over, Pyke stood above him, whispering, 'Where can I find my wife and child? Try doing one good thing before you die.' He could smell Trotter's urine on his face and clothes.

A blast of fetid air escaped from Trotter's mouth and blood pooled around his chest. He was trying to whisper something. Pyke came closer. 'What was that?'

'I hope the bitch and brat die.' His head lolled backwards and the spasms stopped. Blood continued to leak from the wound but Jimmy Trotter was dead.

Pyke gave the room a quick search but apart from a knife that he kept next to his mattress there was nothing of interest. Downstairs he found the madam, Mrs Bennett, and paid her five pounds to arrange to have the body thrown into the river. He asked her about Bolter and the dog and whether they had ever visited Trotter, but she shook her head and said she'd never seen them.

Pyke had shot a man but didn't feel a thing: neither vindication nor relief, despite the unforgivable crimes that Trotter had committed. Still, as he walked back along Tooley Street in the direction of the river, he thought about what Trotter had said and experienced a sudden flutter in his heart. *I hope they die.* It suggested to him that Emily and Felix were both still alive.

At half-past midday he met Godfrey's lawyer, Geoffrey Quince, a King's bencher no less, on the other side of Bow Street from the magistrates' court. He had bought a new set of clothes and had washed himself in a tub of icy water in the kitchen of number forty-four but he could still smell his own sweat. Quince didn't seem to notice or care and didn't comment on the bruise under Pyke's eye or his broken nose. Either he was completely unobservant, Pyke decided, or very diplomatic.

'Did you see Bellows, then?' Pyke asked, once they had found a seat in the nearby Brown Bear tavern.

Quince nodded. He placed his stovepipe hat on his lap and adjusted his pale grey cravat. 'But the man you described, Julian Jackman, wasn't being held in any of the cells or the felons' room.' He glanced disparagingly around the smoky room. 'To be honest, there wasn't anyone down there who didn't look like they belonged.'

'And how was Bellows when you demanded to be allowed to inspect the cells?'

Quince shrugged. 'He didn't seem concerned one way or the other.'

Silently Pyke cursed his luck. He'd hoped that finding Jackman might shed some light on what had happened to Emily, and now he didn't know where else to look for the radical.

'Did he admit to playing a role in the raiding of various haunts frequented by the radicals in the East End?'

Quince paused to consider this. 'I think he might have smiled a little when I put the question to him but he chose not to answer it.'

'Smiled? As if he was amused?'

'I don't know. Perhaps it wasn't a smile. Look, Pyke, I did what you wanted me to do and your friend wasn't there. Perhaps Bellows had some idea why I was there but then again perhaps he didn't.'

'And he didn't come across as nervous, as if he was trying to hide something?'

'I don't understand.' Quince stared down his long nose at Pyke. 'What would the chief magistrate be trying to hide?'

That afternoon, while he waited for Townsend to see whether there had been any further news delivered to the bank or Hambledon, he paid Barnaby Hodges a visit at his gaming house in Regent's Quadrant. He was a squirrelly, ferret-faced man with sharp features and a mop of raven-black hair, and he agreed to talk to Pyke only when Jem Nash's name was mentioned. Pyke also let it be known that he was an associate of Villums. That helped to open doors as well.

'I'm presuming Villums explained that your boy owed my establishment just over seven thousand pounds when he was killed.'

'Don't get excited,' Pyke said, staring at Hodges across his desk. 'I'm not here to settle his debt.'

Hodges wrapped his spindly fingers around a glass of whisky and brought it up to his lips. 'I heard you'd made him a minor partner in the bank. I talked to my lawyer. We would be within our rights to claim our debt against his share of your profits.'

'If you want to try, be my guest.'

Hodges drank some more of the whisky. 'Ned Villums warned me about you. Said I should be especially careful in your company.'

'I just want to know whether you or anyone sent by you had any contact with Jem Nash on the night he was killed.'

Hodges sat back in his chair and looked around his small office. 'Like I told Ned, I sent one of my best men to chivvy Nash along a bit. He disappeared around the time that Nash was murdered.'

'And you haven't seen or heard from him since?' Pyke regarded him sceptically.

'That's right.'

Abruptly Pyke stood up and pulled down his frock-coat. 'I won't take up any more of your time.'

'If you hear something from my lawyer,' Hodges called out after him, 'try not to take it personally.'

But when six rolled around Townsend brought him no further news. Jo had passed word from Hambledon that no ransom letter had been delivered there. Nor had there been any word from Gore.

It had been more than four days since the abduction and Pyke was still no closer to finding Emily and Felix.

For an hour or so after Townsend had left, he wandered up and down the staircase of the enormous house, both to keep warm and to try to think of anything he might have missed. The Ionic columns of the first-floor mezzanine and the cut-glass chandelier that hung from the roof seemed to mock his pretensions, and the architectural flourishes, which he had initially found so entrancing, now seemed to be no more than bloated monuments to his vanity. As his footsteps echoed right the way up into the dome he tried to reassure himself with the thought that he had only paid a deposit and hadn't committed himself for the whole year.

In the grand chamber room – that was what the agent had called it, anyway – Pyke built a fire using the last of the kindling wood and tried to warm his hands, but the flames were weak and the wood quickly burned down. To replenish the fire, he ripped down the velvet curtains so carefully installed by the upholsterer, tore them into strips and fed them to the fire. Gleefully he sat cross-legged in front of the blaze and inspected his work. But the curtains didn't last long. Before long he had broken up the Hepplewhite table and chairs and loaded them on to the burgeoning fire, and soon after that there was nothing left in the room to burn. As he stared into the flames, Pyke retrieved the bottle of laudanum from his pocket, removed the cork stopper and pressed it to his lips. He drank until the sickly clear tincture was gone.

It was dark and now he had burned the velvet curtains he could see outside to the square. The trees were bare and it had started to rain, little drops beating against the glass window. He stared into the darkness. Somewhere out there was Emily, pregnant with his child. And poor, frail little Felix. Settling himself by the fire again, he tried to get warm but the blaze had dwindled to nothing and he was soon shivering. Even the gin he drank on top of the laudanum failed to combat his shakes.

At ten, when he knew that sleep was beyond him, Pyke collected his greatcoat from the entrance hall and stepped out into the rain. The pavement in front of the house was wet and slippery from the fallen leaves. He walked briskly over to the other side of the square and then followed Berkeley Street to Piccadilly, where he crossed the road into Green Park. The park was deserted and the ground was marshy and sodden. In the dark sky, the yellow moon came and went behind clouds like a gargoyle. Pyke followed a track southwards towards Birdcage Walk, the outline of the new King's Palace just about visible in the distance. From Green Park, he crossed over into St James's Park and skirted around one end of the shallow lake. From there, he could see the army barracks, but when he finally reached Birdcage Walk there were no prostitutes or dolly mops idly patrolling the pavement in front of the barracks. The rain must have driven them indoors.

There was a solitary carriage parked about a hundred yards farther back along the walk, and when he looked around, he saw the door swing open and heard a voice through the rain. Later, Pyke would find out that Marguerite had been following him for much of the day and had shadowed him to Birdcage Walk from the house on Berkeley Square, but at the time he followed the voice as if in a trance. There was something familiar about it.

'Pyke.'

Someone was calling his name.

'*Pyke.*'

He walked around the two black mares, both tossing their heads and snorting, and nodded to the driver.

Slick with perspiration and illuminated by a gas lamp, Marguerite's face looked as though it had somehow drifted free from the rest of her body, the whiteness of her skin set against her black cloak and the dark furnishings of the carriage.

Pyke climbed up into the carriage and the door swung closed after him. His hands were still trembling. He felt a little feverish, despite the dampness of his clothes.

'What happened to you?' Gently she touched the gash under his eye and winced, out of empathy. 'My poor darling.'

They were sitting next to each other on the horsehair seat, the floor covered with wet straw.

She pulled him towards her and kissed him on the mouth. It was like opening the door on to another time. For many years after she had left for Paris, he had thought of her almost every day, wondering what she might be doing and whether she still thought about him. With the passage of time, these thoughts had faded and dwindled to almost nothing. Or had they? Because the moment their lips touched, Pyke wanted to kiss her again, only harder this time, as Marguerite threaded her fingers through his coarse hair and pulled him still closer, their tongues intertwined in a sticky embrace. Now, all these years later, Pyke could taste only her sadness, and he wanted more of it because it spoke to a feeling locked up inside him that he couldn't find any other way of touching. Pyke drew the curtains and grappled with the layers of her petticoats, too far gone to care about what he was doing or who he was with, but afterwards all he would remember was a blur of unfulfilled desire. Trousers around his ankles, he pulled up her petticoats and took her there in the carriage, the creaking vehicle rocking back and forth on that wet, deserted street as he finished in a series of jolting, painful spasms that made him feel simultaneously alive and yet one step from death.

TWENTY-FIVE

As the first shards of watery daylight leaked through the muslin curtains, Pyke was jolted from his sleep by a pungent smell that seemed as deeply familiar as his adolescent memories. He lay there for a while, the thought of what he had done flooding back to him along with the guilt. Next to him, the quiet murmurs of Marguerite's breathing reassured Pyke she was still asleep, but he hardly dared turn his head to make sure, in case he woke her up. Where were they? He looked around the unfamiliar room, guessing that they had returned to Cranborne Park. He blinked and opened his eyes. Yes, he remembered now. What they had done in the carriage and then again in the bedroom. Was it shame he felt most acutely or guilt? he wondered. And what was the difference? Taking care not to disturb her, he slid from underneath the sheet and realised he was naked. Various items of his clothing were strewn across the floor. He had just put on his trousers when Marguerite called out, 'You don't have to creep around on my behalf, you know, Pyke.' Her tone was warm and playful.

Perhaps there had been news about Emily and Felix. He had to make his excuses and go. Turning around, he saw she was sitting up in the bed, the sheet pulled up around her shoulders, to cover her nakedness. She smiled. 'I've often imagined what it would be like, waking up next to you again.'

He picked up his shirt from the floor and started to put it on. 'What happened last night shouldn't have happened, Maggie.'

'But it did, didn't it?'

Pyke couldn't bring himself to look at her.

'Do you regret it?'

'I'm married to someone else, Maggie. I love my wife.'

'Then why did you fuck me?' she said, her tone becoming harder. She coiled the sheet a little more tightly around her body.

'Because ...' He looked over at her and hesitated, not sure what to say. There were so many reasons he couldn't fathom them all. And he detested having to make excuses for something he'd done. Accept, learn and move on. That was usually the way he did things. He wondered what he might learn from this.

'Let's face it, Pyke. You fucked me because you wanted to,' she said, rearranging her hair. 'You always did try to over-complicate things.'

'And you're the same old Maggie Shaw. Nothing ever got to you, did it?'

'Is that what you thought?' She stopped fiddling with her hair, her face quizzical rather than angry.

'What I thought fifteen years ago doesn't really matter now, does it?'

'Maybe you should have looked a little more closely,' she said, with a small shake of the head.

'Would it have made a difference?'

'You tell me.' Marguerite waited until she was certain he was listening and added, without changing her tone, 'You know I was carrying our child when I left for Paris all those years ago.'

Her tone had been so matter-of-fact that it took him a few seconds to comprehend what she'd just told him. He hadn't known, of course. And yes, it might have made all the difference. He had to sit down on the end of the bed, his head suddenly alive with useless possibilities.

'I had it in Paris,' she said, without shifting position in the bed.

'A boy or a girl?' Finally he managed to look at her, not sure whether he wanted to hug or beat her with his fists.

'A boy.'

'Is he still ...'

'Alive?' Marguerite shook her head, her eyes empty and sad. 'He died just before his fifth birthday.'

'Why didn't you tell me?'

'I didn't know I was pregnant when I left London.'

'But why didn't you send me a note from Paris once he'd been born?'

'I didn't have an address.'

'But you knew where Godfrey lived. Where Godfrey still lives.' He heard himself getting angry.

Perhaps that's what she wanted, Pyke thought, trying to make sense of the opaque expression on her face.

'Would it have made a difference if you'd known?' This time her tone was gentler and more conciliatory.

'He was my son.' Briefly Pyke thought about the burial ceremony he'd witnessed, Marguerite and Bolter standing over the freshly dug grave. Had that been *him*? The grave had surely been too small. The boy, if he'd lived, would have been fifteen or sixteen years old. And Marguerite had just told him that he had died when he was five, the same age as Felix, some time in the twenties: 1826 or '27.

'He was *my* son, Pyke. You'd already chosen a different life.'

'And this was your way of punishing me for that decision? Keeping me from my own flesh and blood?'

'It wasn't about you. Don't you understand that? I didn't have time to think about what was right or wrong. In case you didn't know, raising a child in a foreign city on your own isn't an easy task.'

Pyke nodded, not wanting her to see he was as angry as he was. 'So what was his name?'

'James.'

'James.' He repeated the name. Saying it out loud didn't make him any more real.

'He was the most beautiful boy you've ever seen. White-blond hair and the bluest eyes.' She was crying now but Pyke didn't feel like trying to comfort her.

'How did he die?'

Marguerite sniffed and dried her eyes on the sheet. 'He caught a fever. He fought it like a little tiger but, in the end, the fever spread to his lungs.'

'Why tell me about it now? I mean, what fucking purpose has it served, telling me after all these years, apart from rubbing my nose in it?'

'I thought ...'

'You thought *what*?'

She stared at him, shocked by his anger. 'God, you're a cold, self-centred bastard. I thought last night meant something.'

'One fuck and everything is just as it was before. Is that it?' Pyke shook his head, already sorry he'd said it. 'I *have* a family, Maggie. I have a wife and I have a son.'

For a moment he wasn't sure whether she'd cry or scream. In the end, it was something between the two. 'Well, I fucking don't.'

'Is that what this is about? Punishing me because I have what you want?'

'Do you think I want you? Eddy may have been a molly but he was still twice the man you'll ever be ...'

'*What* did you say?'

Ignoring him, Marguerite said, 'After James died, Eddy picked me up out of the gutter and took care of me. I always felt safe with him, Pyke. That's something I never knew with you.'

'You said Edward was a molly?'

'What?' She laughed bitterly. 'Didn't you know? Pyke, the once famous detective, didn't know my husband was a mandrake?'

Pyke stood up and walked across to the window. She was right. All the signs had been there. He'd just missed them: her offhand references to a Platonic marriage, Morris's outburst on the night of his death when, apparently, he'd called himself a 'dirty monster'. Rationally Pyke knew it made sense but it didn't alleviate his shock.

'I never asked what he did or who he slept with. It didn't bother me at first. And I slept with other men.'

'And later?'

'Later it disgusted me.'

'What Morris did with other men?'

She shook her head. 'The *situation* disgusted me, what we'd allowed ourselves to become, a sham of a marriage.'

Could she have killed Morris? No, she had arrived home around the same time he had last been seen alive. Perhaps she had paid someone to do it for her. Or perhaps Morris killed himself. That was another possibility he'd have to consider.

'You should be glad he's dead, then.'

Marguerite sniffed and cleared her throat. 'Maybe you're right. I should be. But I still miss him.'

'Do you think he killed himself?'

She shrugged, the hardness returning to her face. 'Like I said before, I don't know. It's possible. Most of the time, Eddy put on a jovial face, but deep down I think he hated what he was.'

Pyke sat down again on the edge of the bed and touched her ankle. She flinched ever so slightly. 'So what happens now?'

'What do you mean, what happens now? You go back to your

nice family and live happily ever after. I get to keep this place.' Marguerite looked at him and smiled. 'I forgot to tell you. Someone sent me the deeds in the mail.'

That got his attention. 'Who?'

'It was an anonymous letter sent from somewhere in the city. There was no return-to-sender address.'

'Just like that?'

She stared at him and shook her head. 'Why does that upset you?'

'It doesn't *upset* me; it just follows that whoever sent you the deeds also stole the money I lent Eddy.'

'Maybe no one stole it. Maybe Eddy hid the money somewhere and it's waiting to be found.'

'The deeds and the loan papers were stolen from the vault at my bank. Now they just turn up on your doorstep.'

'I hope you're not accusing *me* of theft.'

'I'm not accusing you of anything.' Pyke let out a sigh. 'Listen. A while ago, you mentioned you wanted to sell Eddy's shares in the Grand Northern. I'll buy them off you at the market rate, plus an additional ten per cent.'

'Is that why you fucked me? To lay your hands on my late husband's shares?'

'It's a simple question,' Pyke said, ignoring the insult. 'Do you want to sell me his shares or not?'

Marguerite fiddled with her hair. 'I'm afraid I've promised them to someone else.'

'Who?' he said, quickly. Perhaps too quickly. 'Who have you promised them to?'

'That's none of your business.'

Pyke went to pick up his coat from the floor. 'There's a meeting early next week to decide the fate of Eddy's railway.'

'It isn't Eddy's railway and it never was. And as far as I'm concerned, I don't care if a single yard more of track is laid or not.'

'Eddy put the last years of his life into that enterprise. Are you going to let some chinless fools piss his legacy up the wall?'

'You'll excuse me if I don't see you to the door,' Marguerite said, without looking up at him.

*

Pyke hadn't told her about Emily and Felix and, as he walked along the driveway, he wondered why not. He hadn't wanted her pity, for a start. But was that all? The question that he kept returning to was this. Did Marguerite already know? Was it possible she had somehow been involved? She hadn't made any reference to his difficulties but there were elements of their conversation that bothered him, in addition to her revelations about their son and Morris. James, if indeed he had ever existed, had perished shortly before his fifth birthday. Felix's fifth birthday was fast approaching and now he was in grave danger, too. Marguerite had met Emily, as well. What if she had decided to drive a stagecoach through their lives, ruin things for them just as her life had been ruined? As soon as he'd had these thoughts, he dismissed them as ridiculous. Ultimately Marguerite was as selfish as he was but she wasn't a kidnapper, or worse, a murderess. She wouldn't deliberately harm anyone. He was relieved by this realisation, but as soon as he'd reassured himself of Marguerite's innocence, another thought struck him. She was somehow acquainted with Bolter. Bolter and his mutt had stood alongside her when she had buried someone – or something – in a field on the estate. He had to know who or what had been buried that day. He'd intended to walk the five miles back to Hambledon. Now he would just take a path that skirted the same field; and, hopefully, a shed where he would find a shovel *and* a pick . . .

It was a cold, blustery morning and the ground was almost frozen. Having found a shovel and a pickaxe, Pyke retraced his steps to the spot where he had seen Marguerite and Jake Bolter that day and paced around the sodden field, trying to determine the exact place where the hole had been dug. There was no makeshift headstone or cross, but right in the middle of the field the grass was shorter and dirtier, and Pyke started to dig there. It was back-breaking work and at times he needed the pickaxe to break the frozen ground. After an hour of digging, the hole came up to his chest and a further half-hour after that, the tip of his shovel struck something hard. It took fifteen minutes to clear enough earth away in order to see what he'd found. The coffin was made of solid wood but by Pyke's estimate it was only four feet in length. For a while, Pyke stood in the tiny annexe he had dug next to the coffin and thought about what he was about to do, how wrong it was to desecrate a grave.

Tentatively Pyke tied a handkerchief around his mouth and bent over, gripping the lid of the coffin with his fingers. He eased the lid upwards and, as he did so, a sulphurous whiff escaped from the coffin, its pungency almost inducing him to retch. Pulling the lid a little higher, he saw that the body was human rather than animal. A little boy. Pyke had to blink, to make sure his eyes weren't playing tricks; he looked again and saw what seemed to be the body of his own son. This had been his first impression, but when the shock had finally subsided he saw the little differences. This boy was taller and broader than Felix, for a start. His face was fuller and his blond hair was less wispy. Nonetheless the likeness was startling, and for a while Pyke stood there staring down into the coffin, both appalled and relieved at the same time. It had been more than a month since he had watched, with Felix, the informal burial, and the corpse had started to decompose. Taking care to replace the lid, Pyke pulled himself out of the hole and, from there, began to shovel the earth back into the grave.

Perspiring, his thoughts remained with the dead boy. Whose lad was it? From what Marguerite had told him, James, their son, had died ten years ago, and this boy had seemed only a few months older than Felix.

So who was he and why did he bear an uncanny resemblance to Felix? And why had Jake Bolter rather than Morris mourned in this very field alongside Marguerite?

It took Pyke almost two hours to walk back across the fields to Hambledon, and as he approached the old hall from the driveway, he looked up and saw someone scampering to meet him.

Jo was red faced and out of breath by the time she reached him and, not bothering to try to speak, she thrust an official-looking letter into his hand. 'This was discovered about half an hour ago by Royce. It wasn't delivered with the rest of the post.' Pyke had instructed Royce, who usually dealt with the mail, to pass all correspondence unopened to Jo, who would then open it to see whether it carried any news of Emily and Felix.

Jo was staring at the bruises on his face but was too polite, or well trained, to make a comment about them.

Hands shaking, Pyke took the letter and inspected it. There was a red wax seal on the back. Tearing the envelope open, he removed the note and briefly studied its contents.

'Well?' Jo asked, unable to contain herself. 'I was about to open it when I saw you coming up the driveway.'

Too stunned to speak, Pyke folded the letter up, put it in his pocket and started to walk towards the house.

'What does it say?' Jo said, persisting. When Pyke didn't answer her, she added, 'I don't know how they know but the whole house is talking about it. Royce, Jennings, Mary, everyone.'

Pyke turned to her, his face suddenly pink with anger. 'Fuck them. Fuck the lot of them. Fuck them. They're just worried about their jobs. Fuck them. They've always hated me, the lot of 'em.' He looked up at the old hall and thought about its funereal atmosphere, the creaking floors and draughty rooms. His hands were shaking uncontrollably and a solitary tear trickled down his cheek. If he had his way, he'd torch the building with all of them locked up inside.

'What's the matter, Pyke? Is it bad news?'

Jo had been with Emily for almost ten years and was the only one of the staff who addressed them in such a casual manner.

Still in shock, he turned to her. 'I'd say that Emily and Felix are alive.' His hands were shaking from the relief.

'Alive?'

He tapped the letter in his pocket. 'They've been ransomed.'

'Ransomed? For what?' She hitched up her skirt and followed Pyke up the drive. 'By whom?'

'Not a word of this to any of the servants. Let 'em gossip all they like,' Pyke said, walking briskly now.

Of all the people who might have had a reason to kidnap Emily and Felix, Ernest, Duke of Cumberland, had been somewhere near the bottom of Pyke's list. But the letter had been explicit. Pyke's presence was demanded at Smithfield at dawn on Sunday, where he would give up certain correspondences in exchange for the safe return of his wife and child. Cumberland. Pyke thought about his recent visit to the hall and his ingratiating, unctuous manner. That left him just over two days to find the duke, the letters and perhaps Emily and Felix, too.

TWENTY-SIX

The Duke of Cumberland's residence in Kew was a three-floor, red-brick Georgian mansion on the north side of the green, near the entrance to the botanical gardens. There was a shoulder-high wrought-iron fence running around the perimeter of the property but the gate was unlocked, and when Pyke presented himself at the front door, he was greeted by one of Cumberland's servants and invited into the hall. Pyke didn't have a plan beyond confronting the duke, by force if necessary, and wringing the truth out of him. Therefore he was taken aback when the servant informed him in a matter-of-fact voice that the duke had recently left for his family home on the Continent. The man explained that his master had caught an afternoon steamer from Deptford two days earlier and, if the sailing had been a smooth one, he would be docking in Hamburg some time later that evening. From there, the man added, it was a further two hundred miles across country to the duke's home in Berlin. He gave Pyke this information freely and seemed bemused when Pyke asked him whether Cumberland had left the house in the company of an attractive woman and a small child. No, the servant assured him, the duke had left the house alone. Trying to hide his frustration, Pyke asked when Cumberland was due to return to London. The servant shrugged and said that his master was not expected back at the house until the New Year. Pyke didn't say anything else to the man but wondered how the duke planned to oversee the exchange of Conroy's letters for Emily and Felix from the Continent. If the letters had been important enough to kidnap Emily and Felix, why had Cumberland opted to travel to Berlin rather than remain in London for a few extra days?

Pyke was perturbed by this turn of events but didn't believe the servant was lying. In the drawing room and billiards room, maids were covering the furniture with sheets, as though preparing for the duke's lengthy absence. Fired up by his frustration, Pyke briefly thought about forcing his way into the rest of the house to check for signs of Emily and Felix, but he knew that if he did the servant would call for help, and instinct told him that he wouldn't find anything.

What if Cumberland had told his servants he was leaving for the Continent but, in fact, was holed up somewhere in London waiting for the letters?

But when Pyke enquired after Cumberland at his apartments in St James's Palace, he was told exactly the same thing: the duke had left two days earlier for Berlin and wasn't expected back in England until the New Year. There, too, the housemaids appeared to be preparing the rooms for a lengthy hiatus, and while Pyke felt like ramming the barrel of his pistol down the footman's throat, he knew it wouldn't achieve anything. The man didn't appear to be covering up for the duke or, indeed, seem to know anything about Emily and Felix and their possible whereabouts.

Pyke had reached another dead end and, as he trudged despondently back to his carriage, he turned over what he had found out in his mind, trying to figure out whether he had missed something important.

Perhaps Cumberland had entrusted someone else with the task of bringing Emily and Felix to Smithfield at dawn on Sunday. In which case Emily and Felix were being held somewhere in the capital and Cumberland's apparent return to Berlin was some kind of diversionary tactic. A visit to the Admiralty in St James's confirmed what Pyke already knew: that the journey from Dover to Calais and on to Berlin via Brussels and Cologne would take a minimum of three days. When Pyke had first heard that Cumberland had fled to the Continent, he had briefly considered pursuing him, but if he did so, he would miss the rendezvous at Smithfield on Sunday. Quickly he ruled out this option. He could always make the long journey to Berlin if, or when, nothing came of his encounter at Smithfield.

It was four in the afternoon on Thursday and the autumnal light was already fading. It hadn't snowed but the temperature was hovering just above or below freezing, and men wearing warm coats and stovepipe hats hurried out of buildings to their waiting carriages. The once gleaming Portland stone of the Admiralty building had new turned a dirty, yellow colour, and farther along Whitehall the grand buildings of state – the Houses of Parliament, Downing Street, the King's Palace and the new clubs of Pall Mall, where politicians and their peers socialised with their own – stood impervious against the shrill winds gusting off the river. But Pyke wasn't concerned by the sudden cold snap. With his hands in his pockets, he wandered along Whitehall, turning over what he had learnt and wondering whether Cumberland really had kidnapped his wife and child. Certainly if he believed, as he seemed to, that Pyke had come into possession of Conroy's letters, he had a sufficient motive, and the letter delivered to Hambledon undoubtedly bore the duke's private seal, which would have been impossible to forge and which therefore confirmed the duke's culpability.

In his recent visit to Hambledon, Cumberland had told Pyke that he was about to leave for the Continent. But why had he decided to make this journey if the prospect of laying his hands on Conroy's letters loomed on his immediate horizon? And another more worrying question niggled at Pyke's mind. Why had it taken Cumberland a full five days since the abduction to issue the ransom demand? Why hadn't he delivered it the morning after the kidnapping?

With these questions foremost in his thoughts, Pyke crossed the city in a hackney carriage and asked the driver to wait while he got out on the New Road just past Euston Square. It was nearly dark and the air was bitingly cold. This was where Peel had said Sir Henry Bellows had bought a number of properties in the past year. Digging his hands into the pockets of his greatcoat, he crossed the road, narrowly avoiding an omnibus weighed down with passengers, inside and out, and started to walk towards a deserted construction site a few hundred yards farther along the thoroughfare. Pyke had read about the arch that was under construction. The Grand Doric portico was being built to mark the terminus of the London-to-Birmingham railway. *Gore's railway*. Pyke felt a sudden queasiness in his stomach. Was it a coincidence that Bellows had bought land and properties in the vicinity of the London terminus of the Birmingham railway? For that matter, could he take Peel's word at face value? Was it true that Bellows had made these investments in the first place, and if so why had Peel wanted Pyke to know about them? Was there, as Gore had seemed to suggest, some kind of bad blood between him and the Tory leader?

Number forty-four Berkeley Square was like an ice house when Pyke unlocked the door, but he had to wait only a few minutes before a hackney carriage dropped Townsend off. Pyke suggested they walk briskly around the square to keep warm, rather than trying to get comfortable in the house. Townsend agreed, but after just a few paces he seemed a little breathless. Pyke asked him whether he was all right. 'I'm just coming down with a chill,' Townsend assured him.

As they walked Pyke said, 'Have you put that personal advertisement in *The Times* yet?'

'This has been running all week.' Townsend took out a copy of the newspaper and directed Pyke's attention to a box about halfway up the front page on the left-hand side. It read: '*Wanted: rare and valuable gold watches from the last century for collectors. Top prices paid. Bentley's Jewellers, thirty-seven, the Strand.*'

Pyke handed it back to Townsend. 'Any responses?'

'None that would interest you. At least not yet.'

Pyke nodded. It would have to do for now. 'I want you to gather twenty men, or as many as you can round up at short notice, and have them assemble in the Old Red Lion near Smithfield on Saturday night.'

'What kind of men?'

'The kind who know how to fire a rifle and won't ask too many questions, so long as the price is right.'

'And how right will the price be?' Townsend stopped and turned to face Pyke.

'Ten pounds a man,' Pyke said, without thinking about it. 'But I need men who've fired a rifle before. Ex-soldiers, if possible. And I need you to keep them sober for me.'

Townsend whistled. 'Ten pounds ought to do it.' He blew into his hands and said, 'There was someone looking for you earlier. A young fellow, William something. I didn't catch his surname. He said he had news about a man called Jackman.'

Pyke's throat tightened. 'Did he say where I could find him?'

'He told me to tell you he'd be drinking at the Queen's Head in Battle Bridge until about nine.'

*

It was a miserable night: very dark, very cold and very muddy, and a blanket of fog had fallen on the capital. Even the occasional gas lamp did little to illuminate the street and make it easy to see where they were going. They left the road and cut through some carpet-beating grounds and vegetable patches left derelict by the building work, as Pyke followed William Hancock down a steep, treacherous path into the giant man-made ravine created by the railway construction work. As Hancock explained, when it was completed, a vast, stationary steam engine would pull the trains up the steep hill from the railway's terminus at Euston Square to join up with the railway line at Camden Town. In fact, Hancock had said little to him in the pub: only that he had been instructed to show Pyke something. He wouldn't say what it was and he seemed nervous, on edge. Now, half an hour later, Pyke wondered about the wisdom of following a man he'd never met before into the bowels of a deserted construction site. Their descent was slow-going, not helped by the ankle-deep mud and the dense wall of fog that made it hard to see more than a few yards in front. After perhaps fifteen minutes of painstaking progress, on their hands and backsides at times, the ground levelled out and he guessed they must have reached the floor of the construction site. He looked back up the slope but couldn't see a thing. The fog was at its thickest at the very bottom of the ravine, a swirling, freezing blanket of white that made it hard for Pyke to see his own hands, let alone follow Hancock. They stayed close to each other and Hancock skilfully negotiated a path through piles of brick rubble and lengths of iron rails. Finally they came to a halt by a tall stack of wooden sleepers, Hancock turning to him and whispering, 'Jackman told me to find you, if something happened to him.' In the fog and the darkness, Pyke couldn't properly see his expression but his voice sounded feathery and nervous.

'And has something happened?' Pyke looked around and saw an earth mound and a half-built brick wall.

'You could say that.' Hancock laughed bitterly and pointed at something behind Pyke. 'If and when it clears ...'

Pyke spun around but couldn't see anything for a few moments, just a blanket of dense fog. He was expecting the worst, though, his heart thumping, his mouth parched of moisture. Still, in spite of his preparedness, he had to blink twice when the fog did finally clear. His legs buckled and bile tickled his throat. For there in front of him, rising above them in the night sky, was a makeshift crucifix, and affixed to it, with nails that had been hammered through his hands and ankles, was the figure of Julian Jackman. The fog rolled back across the ravine floor, temporarily obscuring the wooden cross, but when it next cleared, Pyke had positioned himself almost directly under the crucifix and stared up at Jackman's contorted face. Pyke couldn't tell how recently the radical had died but his blood, which had dripped on to the cross, had now dried. If they'd bound Jackman's hands and ankles to the crucifix with rope and hammered the nails in while he'd still been alive, Pyke could only imagine the terrible pain the radical must have suffered. Certainly his face was almost unrecognisable: his hair matted to his face with sweat and his eyes, as large as walnuts, almost bulging out of their sockets. The man's neck was corded with veins, too. In the end, Pyke had to look away, and it was only then he saw the plaque, nailed clumsily to the foot of the cross. Crouching down, he had a closer look. The words *'Swinish multitude: know thy place and stay there'* had been scratched on to a piece of wood and underneath had been added *'Captain Paine, RIP'*.

'What's that?' Hancock asked, bending down next to him.

For a few moments, Pyke was too nonplussed to speak. The dawning realisation of what Jackman's corpse meant and who, doubtless, had ordered the crucifixion struck him with the force of a cannonball. There could be no other explanation. The killing was a warning to the navvies. *Know thy place.* Later William Hancock would confirm what Pyke had already surmised: that Jackman and the Wat Tyler Brigade had been agitating amongst the navvies on the Birmingham railway. But in those first seconds it was instinct which led Pyke's thoughts in a particular direction. The bloodied corpse was a warning. To whom? The navvies. And from whom? The only possible answer was the owners of the Birmingham railway. The men who would stand to lose most if Jackman's agitation mutated into strikes and other actions. And who was the chairman and largest shareholder of the Birmingham railway? All roads came back to Gore. Rage, humiliation and consternation assaulted Pyke in equal measure. Gore wasn't the potential ally he had imagined. Over and over, Pyke kept returning to the same question. How could he have been so stupid and so blind? The events in

Huntingdon had just been a distraction. The real fight had been over unionising the navvies working on the Birmingham railway. Gore's railway. Gore, who had overseen a bloody campaign of retribution and punishment while simultaneously presenting himself to Pyke as a fair-minded, kindly soul. A champion of English liberty and a defender of the right to free speech. It was all a sham. And Pyke had believed him. It was this which galled him the most.

'Whoever killed him believed that Jackman was Captain Paine.' Pyke stood up and waited for Hancock to do likewise. When Hancock offered no response, he added, 'Who found him?'

'A couple of the navvies came to our safe house earlier today and told us about it.'

Pyke nodded. 'I'm guessing this was left here during the day.'

'For everyone to look at,' Hancock, said trying to hold back his tears. 'Apparently one of the navvies demanded that someone take it down and he was beaten by the ganger with a truncheon.'

Hundreds of navvies would have seen it. Gore would have wanted it that way. This was meant to be a warning, after all.

'What were you trying to do here?'

'Who, me?'

'The Wat Tyler Brigade.'

Hancock stared down at his boots. 'Next week, Jackman was going to tell the world that more 'n three-quarters of the navvies working on the Birmingham railway had sworn their oaths and they were going to call a strike demanding more money and better working conditions. Once that news had broken, Jackman was going to announce that the navvies working on the Great Western, the Grand Northern and the Brighton and Greenwich lines had joined the strike as well: one big union joining the navvy men together up and down the whole country.'

'And that's what you've all been working to do, these past few months? Gather signatures and give the navvies reassurance, moral support . . .' Pyke already knew that Jackman and his crew had been agitating among the navvies but, even so, he was taken aback by the scale of their plans: what they had been able to do and how close they had come to achieving their ambitions.

'And money,' Hancock said, quickly, looking down at the mud, perhaps realising he'd said too much.

'That's where my wife, Emily, came in, I presume.' He paused, and added, 'With her money.'

Hancock shuffled awkwardly from leg to leg. 'It's been an expensive business, sir, travelling the length of the country. We also promised the navvy men money to keep 'em in food and ale while they striked.'

'Lucky for you my wife has deep pockets.'

But Hancock shook his head, apparently angered by this insinuation. 'No, sir, that weren't it at all. Not at all.'

'Then how was it?'

'We weren't taking money from her pocket like you just said. She wanted to give it, sir.'

Pyke shook his head, irritated. He didn't want to be having this conversation with a stranger.

'You still don't understand, sir. All of this was her idea. *All of it.* She weren't just a little rich girl giving us her money.' There were tears in his eyes now.

Pyke's legs buckled. The shock was palpable. But Hancock hadn't finished, not by a long chalk. He dug his hands into his pockets and said, in the same frightened tone, 'You see, she's Captain Paine, sir. She has been from the very beginning. Not Jackman or no one else. It's always been Mrs Emily.' Hancock had finished his speech but he couldn't bring himself to look at Pyke.

For a few moments Pyke wandered around in the shadow of the crucifix in a daze, the news he had been given too overwhelming to take in. *Emily was Captain Paine.* Still the idea refused to sink in. Was it possible? He took a few gulps of cold air and tried to focus his mind.

'The arson attack on the Granby Street terraces?' Pyke racked his brains for other snippets of information.

Hancock nodded. 'That was Mrs Emily. Some of us helped clear out the houses, though.'

'And the fire at the warehouse near Birmingham?'

'That was us, too.'

'Emily picked up a bruise,' Pyke started, still too dazed to think clearly.

'We were ambushed by a couple of watchmen and had to fight our way out of the warehouse.'

Not knowing whether to feel angry or proud, Pyke looked at the half-naked figure of Jackman, hanging from the crucifix. No, he felt *stupid.* That was it. He felt stupid and betrayed. How could he not have noticed? And how could she not have told him? Didn't she trust him enough? But as the sheer shock of Hancock's hammer blows started to wear off, Pyke found himself thinking about other, even less palatable possibilities. If Jackman had been nailed to two planks of wood for his part in this business, what might lie in store for Emily, especially since, if Hancock was to be believed, she had orchestrated the whole thing? That possibility made him feel sick, and he tried to reassure himself, perversely, with the thought that Cumberland had arranged her kidnapping and she would be safe in his protection for as long as he believed that Pyke had Conroy's letters. The fact that the duke had snatched her, rather than someone else, might be what kept her alive, he thought, savouring the irony. His pregnant wife. And Felix. He couldn't forget about his frail little son.

'So what will happen now?' Pyke asked, staring up at Jackman's hollow, bloated face.

Hancock looked at him and shrugged. 'I'd like it if you could help me take this thing down and bury Jackman's body.'

'I meant with the plans to get the navvies to swear their oaths and call a strike?'

'Word of this will have spread as far as Birmingham by first thing in the morning. Do you really think anyone will want to strike now?'

Pyke put his hands around the foot of the crucifix to see how deeply the stake had been driven into the ground. 'In which case Jackman will have lost his life for nothing.'

'Not for nothing, sir. He died a hero, a martyr, and by the time we're finished, folk up and down the coun'ry will know his name and his sacrifice.'

'And Emily?' Pyke's mouth was still dry and his head dizzy. 'You have any news about her?'

Hancock stopped trying to loosen the crucifix and looked over at Pyke. 'She told us she was giving it all up for you and your son. Because it's what you wanted.' His tone was cold and accusatory. 'These last few weeks had taken it out of her. She said that once the strike was announced, she was going to withdraw from her role: spend more time with you.'

'That might have been her intention, but she was abducted five days ago, together with our son.'

Later, after they had taken Jackman down from the cross and buried him, using a pick and spade Hancock had brought with him, Pyke followed the radical back up the side of the ravine, but one question, more than any other, dominated his thoughts.

Did Gore know that Emily was Captain Paine?

It was a ten-minute walk from the top of the Hampstead Road to Godfrey's apartment in Camden Town, and once there Pyke proceeded to tell his uncle everything he had found out.

When he had finished, Godfrey poured them both a glass of claret and asked him how or whether this new revelation affected the search for Emily and Felix. Pyke told him about the ransom demand he'd received from the Duke of Cumberland and said that the safest place for Emily and Felix right now was in the duke's care.

'But Gore now knows that she's been abducted,' Godfrey said. 'Perhaps he'll be looking for her, too.'

Pyke conceded the point and again kicked himself for having taken Gore into his confidence.

'I heard back from this fellow I'd asked to look into Bellows's recent activities in the property market.'

'And?'

'It seems the chief magistrate started to buy up derelict buildings along the New Road at the beginning of last year. He now owns ten or so properties, all within spitting distance of Euston Square.' There was a spark in Godfrey's eye. He'd already reached the same conclusion as Pyke.

'The terminus of the Birmingham railway.'

'Exactly, dear boy. But if you remember, at the time, the plan was for the railway to terminate just around the corner from here, not down the hill in Euston. The buildings nearest to the proposed station were snapped up by developers. The plan was to turn them into a railway hotel and boarding houses.'

'Then in June or July, an Act of Parliament comes along authorising the extension of the railway line to Euston.'

'July,' Godfrey said. 'And the company pushed hard for it. They had to go back to Parliament because the extension is going to cost another four hundred thousand pounds. They're building this monstrous contraption just down the road from here that will pull the trains up the hill from Euston. I'm told the company reckoned a terminus there would be more convenient than one in Camden.'

'And in the meantime, let me guess. The price of property along the New Road in Somers Town has soared, and Bellows has made himself a small fortune.'

'I think it's fair to assume that Bellows was forewarned about plans to move the terminus to Euston.'

Pyke nodded, his fists clenched into balls. 'One presumes by Abraham Gore.' He thought about Gore's intervention in Godfrey's libel trial and the violent words he had exchanged with Bellows at the coroner's meeting. These, Pyke supposed now, had merely been cynical ploys to win Pyke's friendship and favour and to distract his attention from what was really happening. All of which threw fresh light on to Morris's death and, in turn, cast suspicion back on to Gore. Had he conspired, after all, to murder his 'oldest, dearest' friend? The thought was almost too monstrous to imagine. If Pyke hadn't seen Jackman's body nailed to the crucifix, he might not have believed it possible. But who knew what a man like Gore was capable of?

'Gore and Bellows,' Pyke said, gritting his teeth. More than anything else he wanted to confront the banker and beat the truth out of him, but a more subtle strategy was required.

'Gore, Bellows *and* Conroy,' Godfrey corrected him. 'Don't forget the egregious comptroller.'

Pyke took a sip of wine and felt the excitement building in his stomach. Godfrey was quite right. The three of them *were* tied up together. Everything was starting to make more sense.

TWENTY-SEVEN

It was after one o'clock in the morning by the time Pyke made it up to Hampstead Heath and hammered on the front door of Fitzroy Tilling's home. The worst of the fog had cleared but in front of the stout, red-brick property, mist-covered allotments and denuded apple trees shivered in the freezing temperatures. It took a number of thumps to arouse Sir Robert Peel's private secretary, and when he finally opened the door, wearing a gown and carrying a lantern, and saw it was Pyke, he wearily shook his head, muttering, 'I might've guessed it would be you.' Rubbing his eyes, he invited Pyke into the front room. As he did so, a ginger cat bolted past their ankles into the warm house. 'I see things haven't changed much,' Pyke commented, as he settled into one of the uncomfortable horsehair chairs and watched as Tilling poured them both a glass of brandy, the cat coiled around his leg. It didn't take much to revive the fire and, with a little brandy inside him, Pyke quickly felt sensation returning to his fingers and toes.

'God, you look like shit, Pyke,' Tilling said, peering at him from the other side of the hearth. He was, by no means, a good-looking man, with his receding hairline and bug-like eyes, but his olive skin and ink-black hair glowed in the flickering light produced by the candle and fire.

'You mean the bruise?' Pyke rubbed his cheek and smiled. 'I got into a tussle with a bareknuckle fighter and lived to tell the tale.'

'Should have seen the other man, eh?'

'I ripped off his scrotum.' Pyke hesitated and shrugged. 'I don't imagine he'll be adding his progeny to the human race.'

Tilling took a sip of brandy, not reacting to the story. 'Why don't you tell me what brings you to my house at half-past one in the morning?' With a nimble leap, the marmalade cat jumped up into Tilling's lap.

'I need to talk to Peel.'

Tilling waited for the cat to settle down in his lap. 'Peel's convalescing at Drayton Manor. He caught a fever and isn't planning to return to London for at least another week or two.'

'You'll forgive me if I don't pass on my condolences.'

Tilling regarded him carefully. 'I take it you have a particular gripe with Peel?'

'A gripe. Hmm.' Pyke considered this for a moment. 'You could say that. Do you remember the radical, Julian Jackman? Peel certainly knows him.'

Tilling didn't answer but rather waited for Pyke to continue, stroking the purring cat.

'I found Jackman about two hours ago nailed to a cross on the construction site of the Birmingham railway near Camden.'

If the news was a surprise to Tilling, he didn't show it. 'And that's what you woke me up to tell me?'

'Is that all you're prepared to say? A man was *crucified*. Six-inch nails were driven through his ankles and hands. He died the most horrible death imaginable.'

Tilling nodded, acknowledging Pyke's outrage and anger. 'Perhaps you should tell me how you think any of this relates to Peel.'

'About a month ago, he called me to his office at Westminster and persuaded me, you might even say blackmailed me, to perform a dirty little task for him. He wanted me to prove or disprove that Jackman was Captain Paine.'

Tilling's expression remained inscrutable.

'At the time he tried to make out that he was simply helping out a friend, Edward James Morris. Morris was about to begin work on the next section of the Grand Northern Railway and Peel made it appear that the venture was beset by problems mostly caused by the radicals; radicals, that is, like Jackman, who, according to Peel, were stirring up dissent among the navvies.' Pyke paused for a moment, to gather his thoughts. 'Then there was the matter of the headless body which had turned up a few miles from the navvy camp in Huntingdon. I heard later that Peel had already been to Huntingdon himself. He asked me to investigate that death, too.'

Tilling was apparently absorbed in stroking the cat but looked up at the last moment, a frown on his face. 'I'm not sure what it is Peel has supposed to have done here. I mean, surely you don't suspect him of any involvement in the unfortunate death of this Jackman figure?'

'Involvement. That's a fine word, isn't it? No, I don't think Peel had any *direct* involvement in the matter but his hands aren't clean either.'

'Perhaps you should explain yourself.'

'I don't believe Peel ever cared one little bit either about the problems facing the Grand Northern Railway or the threat posed by the radicals.'

'Is that so?'

'It's my guess Peel suspected Abraham Gore was involved in the struggle against the radicals in London *and* Cambridgeshire and sent me off into the lion's den hoping I might turn up something he could use against him.'

Tilling shoved the purring cat off his lap and sat forward, his eyes fixed on Pyke. 'You know, there are some who believe that Gore effectively controls this current Liberal government from behind the scenes, but without ever having to show his hand or answer to the electorate.'

'Is that an admission that your master tried to use me to do his dirty work?' Pyke had used the term 'master' deliberately, to cause offence, the insult registering in Tilling's stare.

'If Peel suspected Gore of wrongdoing, why shouldn't he try and gather evidence against him?'

'*Gathering evidence* implies Peel sanctioned some kind of official investigation in which his full intentions were disclosed. What actually happened was he dispatched me to Huntingdon without an inkling of what or who I was dealing with.'

Tilling's face reddened a little and Pyke knew he'd scored a hit. 'He made certain you were adequately compensated for your troubles. I heard that Morris gave you a plum contract, one you couldn't fail to make money from.'

'And that's supposed to make everything all right? Some gold coins in return for my silence and acquiescence?'

'I don't imagine Peel ever thought you would be either silent *or* acquiescent.'

'But ruthless, maybe. I expect he hoped I might be ruthless. Do what other men might not have the stomach to do. Put a pistol against Gore's head and pull the trigger ...'

'I can safely say Sir Robert would definitely not sanction such a drastic course of action.'

'Who said I needed his sanction?'

Tilling took a sip of brandy and put the glass down in front of the fire. 'Then why are you here?'

'Perhaps without realising it, Peel opened up a whole Pandora's box when he sent me to Huntingdon. I want him to face up to his responsibilities.'

A vague smile creased the corners of Tilling's mouth. '*You're* telling the leader of the Tory party that he has to face up to *his* responsibilities?'

'Everything is going to get a whole lot worse here in London and elsewhere before it gets better. I want Peel here to help clean up the mess.'

'And what mess are you referring to?'

'The mess that'll happen when I finally make a move against Gore and Sir Henry Bellows.'

'What's Sir Henry got to do with any of this?'

'Like Gore, Bellows might claim to hate the radicals but *this*, as you put it, is about money, plain and simple. Jackman's plans to unionise the navvies threatened the progress of Gore's railway. And as the competition, Morris's Grand Northern threatened to severely limit the sums of money Gore might earn from his venture. So he planned something that would effectively take care of both problems. To do this, he required Bellows's assistance. I'm guessing the crackdown against Jackman and the rest of the Wat Tyler Brigade was Gore's idea but Bellows orchestrated it: that's how Jackman's carcass came to be hanging from a makeshift cross. A nice, cosy arrangement. Gore gets what he wants and Bellows is amply rewarded for his efforts.' Briefly Pyke told Tilling about the properties Bellows had purchased in Somers Town eighteen months earlier, *before* it was announced that the new terminus for the Birmingham railway would be Euston rather than Camden Town, and the fortune he stood to make when he sold them.

Tilling shook his head, clearly agitated now. 'Whatever might or might not have happened, Peel simply won't tolerate some kind of vigilante action.'

'He should have thought of that before he sent me off on a wild-goose chase after Jackman and Captain Paine.'

Tilling tried to wave the point away. 'As you said, Captain Paine is nothing, a minor nuisance ...'

Pyke interrupted. 'Except I found out tonight my wife is none other than Captain Paine and five days ago she was kidnapped together with my child.'

For a long while after that, Fitzroy Tilling said nothing, but the stunned expression on his face told Pyke everything he needed to know.

'And you think Gore might have arranged it?' Tilling asked, still trying to come to terms with the shock.

Pyke looked at Tilling and shrugged. He didn't plan to tell him about Cumberland. He wanted to keep the pressure on Peel and his private secretary.

'There hasn't been a ransom demand yet?'

'No.'

'Then how do you know they were kidnapped?'

'I don't. Perhaps it's the optimist in me. I prefer to think they've been kidnapped rather than butchered like Jackman.' Pyke swallowed the rest of his brandy and rose to his feet. 'But maybe you can understand now why I want to do things my way.'

'Pyke ... I don't know what to say apart from I'm sorry.' All the wind had been taken from his sails.

'Send word to Peel.'

'And if he decides to stay in Drayton Manor?'

Pyke allowed himself a smile. 'Oh, he'll return as quickly as his carriage'll permit it. Don't you worry about that.'

Tilling stood up and followed him out into the hall. 'Will you promise me to look after yourself?'

'What? Peel cares about my safety now?'

'I'm not speaking for Sir Robert now.' He went to pat Pyke gently on the shoulder. 'Look after yourself and be very careful. Underneath his charming façade, Abraham Gore is the nastiest, most ruthless man I have ever come across.'

'By a degree, perhaps, but if you scratch the surface you'll find that men like Gore and Peel have more in common than you think. Both are happy to employ abstract principles in order to conceal the whiff of moral depravity.'

'If all politics was really like that, Pyke, we would have been buried as a human race long ago.'

Pyke looked up at Tilling's face and smiled. 'You know something, Fitzroy? It's a real shame you've devoted your life to cleaning up other people's messes. You're a much better and more intelligent man than the people you work for.'

Tilling looked around him at the candle-blackened walls. 'More intelligent maybe, but not nearly as rich.' And when Pyke had reached the bottom of the steps that led down to the street, he called out, 'Do you still want to know how Peel knew about you and Ned Villums?'

Pyke spun around and felt the skin tighten across his face.

'Your assistant, Nash.'

'Nash told you?'

Tilling nodded. 'Peel needed something he could hold over your head.'

'Do you know anything about his death?'

'It was as much a surprise to us as I hope it was to you.'

'And what's that supposed to mean?'

'For a while Peel reckoned you might have found out about his conversations with me and taken appropriate action.'

'Cut off someone's head?'

Tilling reached down to pat the ginger cat on its head. 'Well, you're not exactly the squeamish type.'

From the point at which the new railway disappeared under the Hampstead Road, Pyke gazed down at the man-made excavation cut deep into the earth beneath him and the intricate system of ropes and pulleys by which the workers hauled earth out of the ravine. A brick wall, fifty feet in height, had been built to support each side of the embankment and along each wall was a complex lattice of scaffolding and wooden planks for the barrows to move along. Farther down the hill, he could see the hazy outlines of Somers Town and New Road, where Bellows had bought up disused properties that would now be converted into railway hotels, boarding houses and cab stands at great profit. For a moment he watched as a crew of navvies hauled buckets of earth up out of the ravine using the pulley system. Red had been right, Pyke thought. It was grim, back-breaking toil and the navvies did it without complaint or pause for breath.

A mammoth stationary engine house was starting to take shape on the east side of the ravine. This would house the monstrous contraption that Godfrey had told him about: the engine that would draw the trains up the steep incline from Euston. At present, however, its embryonic structure, a steam room and two half-built chimneys, teetered precariously on the bank and looked as though it might topple over into the ravine. Pyke continued to watch the comings and goings for a few minutes and, though it was hard not be impressed by the sheer scale of the project, he could think only about Jackman's crucified body as he had seen it the previous night.

Pyke found Abraham Gore where his private secretary said he would be – talking to the engineer and surveyor. When Gore saw him, he waved, as if greeting an old friend. Breaking off his conversation, he came over to where Pyke was standing and shook both his hands.

'I've been trying to reach you at your bank,' Gore said, his expression suddenly grave. 'I'm afraid I've drawn a blank on the very serious matter we discussed at my office yesterday. But I'm still hopeful my contacts will be able to wheedle some information out of that idiot Bellows.'

Pyke kept his expression composed. 'I'm sure you're doing all you can and it goes without saying your help is much appreciated.'

Gore nodded his gratitude. 'So what brings you here today?' He glanced down at the scene in front of them with evident satisfaction.

'If possible,' Pyke started, trying to keep his tone matter-of-fact, 'I'd like to revise the terms of our business agreement.'

'Oh?' Lines of concern instantly creased Gore's forehead. This wasn't what he'd been expecting.

'You were willing to pay sixty thousand for a third stake in Blackwood's bank.'

'That's right.'

'So would you be prepared to pay one hundred thousand for my entire two-thirds stake?'

Gore's unease was suddenly palpable. He hadn't expected this and for a while he was silent. 'You want to sell me your entire stake in the bank?'

'That's what I said.' Pyke checked himself, aware that his tone had perhaps been a little sharp.

'Do you mind if I ask you why?'

'After what's happened to my wife and child,' Pyke said carefully, 'my heart is no longer in it.'

Gore nodded, as though he understood. 'But you surely don't equate the two? This dreadful business regarding your family, on the one hand, and your running of the bank, on the other.'

'To be perfectly honest, I don't know what to think any more.'

'I can well understand how you must be worried half to death at the moment and, believe me, no one wants to help you more than I do. But have you really thought about this? That's to say, is it what you really want? You see, Pyke, I'd rather hoped we might work together. My reasons are selfish, I know, but as the years pass and my age catches up with me, I've started to look for suitable candidates to take over from me at Gore's and I have to say no one has really excited me. I rather thought you were different.'

'You had considered *me* as a candidate to take over from you at Gore's when you retire?' Pyke tried to feign both amazement and enthusiasm. He didn't know whether he'd done a good job or not.

'I thought you were a man cut from the same cloth as me,' Gore replied, sounding injured and self-righteous.

'But not any more?' Pyke asked, fighting the urge to reach into Gore's mouth and rip out his tongue.

'Do you really think that when I was your age, I would have sold out my interest in Gore's?'

'Then we're perhaps not as alike as you imagined we were.'

Gore studied him for a moment, his eyes narrowed to slits. 'I'd say you're a rather complex man, Pyke. Relentlessly self-interested and oddly principled. Until now, I'd been hoping your better self might win the day.'

'And that would be?'

'Misguided principles have led many a good man to ruin.'

This time Pyke let a little of his anger show. 'And is the love of one's family such a principle?' He thought about Jackman, nailed to the crucifix, and the others who'd been killed, too.

'A man's place is in the public realm. That's where his reputation and fortune are earned. And lost.'

'So you're intimating that my decision to want to sell my share in Blackwood's is misguided?'

Gore turned from him and gazed out across the construction site. 'In its own way, it's rather beautiful, isn't it? Mark my words.

It won't be long before our poets are writing about scenes like this rather than mountains and lakes.'

Pyke laughed bitterly. 'I don't think human exploitation will ever be celebrated as an aesthetic achievement.' The words were out of his mouth before he could stop himself. He waited to see how Gore would react.

'I look down there and I see admittedly coarse specimens who are, nevertheless, being assimilated into the workforce. Is that such an evil? A year ago, many of these men would have qualified for poor relief. Now they've learned to sell their labour at the marketplace and they're earning a fair wage dictated by the forces of supply and demand. And in the process, they're helping to build something that will change everyone's lives for ever.'

Pyke allowed himself a quiet sigh. He would have to be more careful. His slip had unnecessarily alerted Gore's suspicions. 'I'm sure you're right. But I didn't come here today to debate the undoubted merits of your railway.'

'No, you came to try and sell me your entire stake in Blackwood's.' Gore studied his expression.

'If you wanted a third, then why not extend your stake to two-thirds? The bank's a very profitable enterprise.'

'I don't doubt it.'

'So what's the problem?'

'The problem?' Gore looked at him. 'Who said there was a problem?'

'You don't seem to be particularly keen on the revised terms I'm offering you.'

'Perhaps you're right,' Gore murmured, scratching his chin. 'Can I be blunt with you, Pyke?'

'By all means.'

'A man of your mettle doesn't simply walk away when things get difficult and his problems mount up.'

'Is that what you think I'm doing?'

Gore eyed him cautiously. 'It looks very much like that.'

'What's happened in the last few weeks has made me reassess my priorities. Let's just say your initial offer came at an opportune moment.'

'Then it's to be my fault the world of commerce loses one of its brightest stars?'

337

A brief silence lingered between them. Pyke tried not to think about how Gore had used and betrayed him and how ruthlessly he had exploited his perceived friendship with Morris. 'So does that mean we have an agreement?' Pyke tried to inject a degree of hope into his voice.

'I think you're a fool but yes, we have an agreement.' They shook hands but there was suddenly no warmth in Gore's actions. Briefly Pyke wondered whether Gore already suspected that he knew about his complicity in Jackman's death.

If so, it meant Pyke would have to tread very carefully. It wasn't just a question of getting his hands on Gore's money. That was simply a means to an end.

'Now it's just a matter of agreeing a schedule for the exchange of contracts,' Pyke said, trying to appear calm, when all he wanted to do was squeeze Gore's neck with his hands.

'I see no reason for delaying the matter.'

'Nor I.' Pyke even managed a smile. 'In fact, I'd be happy to proceed as quickly as possible.'

'What if I were to instruct my lawyers to draw up the contracts today? You could join me at my office later this afternoon and sign them then.'

'In principle, it sounds perfectly acceptable,' Pyke said, working out a way to turn the situation further to his advantage. 'The only problem is whether you could arrange for the money to be transferred into my bank account by then.'

That seemed to throw Gore off his stride, as it was meant to.

'Of course,' Pyke added quickly, 'if you opened an account for me at Gore's and credited my balance to the tune of a hundred thousand pounds, I could sign the necessary paperwork this afternoon.'

The suspicion seemed to return to Gore's eyes. 'It's a slightly odd request but one that could be accommodated.'

'So we have a deal?' Pyke held out his hand again.

This time Gore took a little longer to shake it. The sun was directly in his eyes and he held up his hand to shield them from its glare. 'I'm disappointed not to have you as my business partner,' he said, gravely, 'but it goes without saying I'll continue to work round the clock to try and get to the bottom of this despicable business involving your wife and child. Who knows? Perhaps I'll have more news for you when you come to my office this afternoon. Shall we say four? That should give my lawyers plenty of time to draw up the necessary contracts.'

But Gore wasn't quite finished with Pyke. Turning to him, he indicated the construction site and added, 'They look like tiny ants, don't they? Do you imagine for one second that if a terrible accident was to befall one of them, if someone was to drop dead right in front of our eyes, I would lose any sleep over it?' Blinking, he continued to gaze out at the landscape before them. 'A sense of perspective is sometimes needed, don't you think?'

Pyke watched Gore as he strolled back to rejoin the two surveyors and wondered whether he knew more about Emily's and Felix's abduction than he was letting on. Could he trust anything at all the man said or did? And had Gore already implicitly grasped the changed nature of their association?

At least Pyke knew why Gore wanted to buy a stake in his bank. The committee of the Grand Northern Railway was due to meet early in the following week to appoint a new chairman and discuss future plans for the troubled venture. As Blackwood's was one of the railway's major creditors, a nominated figure from the bank would be allowed to sit on the committee and, as Morris had suggested at the outset, would be given three votes on any substantial issues. In a potentially tight contest, these votes could make all the difference.

But according to Gore's initial terms, Pyke could have retained a fifty-one per cent stake in Blackwood's and therefore taken this position for himself. The question remained therefore: what did Gore know that he didn't?

Perhaps William Blackwood himself would have some answers.

An hour or so later, Pyke found Blackwood sitting at the writing table in his office, stacking papers into neat piles. It was an orderly room with papered walls and varnished, grained oak furniture, a black marble fireplace and a clock ticking on the mantelpiece. Blackwood looked up at Pyke, his expression betraying surprise and fear. Nervously, he went to arrange a stray hair on his balding pate. Pyke closed the door and sat down. He waited for Blackwood to look at him and said, 'You needn't be afraid. I haven't come to harm you. I just want to talk about our recent *difficulties*.'

Blackwood glanced over at the door. 'You do know if the police find you, they'll arrest you on sight.'

'Very soon, I'll be the least of your worries.'

'In what sense?'

'I want to know whether you took the loan papers from the vault.' Pyke hesitated. 'It's a simple question and I'd like a straight-forward answer.'

'Of course I didn't. To be honest, I thought you'd made the whole thing up, just to defraud the bank of the money.' The indignation on Blackwood's face appeared genuine.

'William, William.' Pyke sighed. 'Where did it all go wrong? For a few years we were a good team.' He looked around the room. It was odd to think that this would be his last time in the building.

When Blackwood didn't speak, Pyke tapped his fingers on the polished surface of the writing table. 'And that's why you brought in this lawyer, Herries?'

Blackwood nodded.

'And no one prompted you to do it, had a quiet word in your ear, a few firm words of encouragement?'

Pyke studied Blackwood's expression carefully; in the end it was a slight twitch of the eyelid which gave his partner away. The indignation was gone, too. He was trying to give the impression he didn't know what Pyke was talking about, but his denial struck a hollow note.

Pyke pulled his chair a little closer to the table and said, 'I've agreed to sell my share of the bank to an interested party. It's something I thought you had a right to know.'

Blackwood licked his lips and mopped his forehead with a handkerchief. 'Do I get to find out who I'm to be sold to?'

'I think you already know the answer to that question.'

'How on earth would I know?'

'Initially Abraham Gore just wanted a third share of the bank. I proposed to retain a fifty-one per cent stake, which in effect would've meant selling Gore fifteen per cent of my stock and forcing you to relinquish, let's say, eighteen per cent of your holdings. But you see, even if you voted with Gore, this would only have given him forty-eight or forty-nine per cent of the bank. I'd still retain overall control. What I can't work out is why he only wanted a third of the bank and why, when I offered to sell him my entire share, he didn't leap at the chance with both hands. Do you understand my predicament?'

Blackwood fidgeted in his chair, not answering for a while. 'Are you suggesting I've somehow been conspiring with this man behind your back?'

'I've paid a man to follow you, William. You were seen having lunch with Gore a few days ago.' Townsend had confirmed this when Pyke had last spoken to him.

Blackwood started to say something but Pyke stood up and held up his hand. 'You miss my point. I'm not interested in listening to your explanations. But you *will* hear from me soon enough and, when that time comes, you'll wish you'd made a different decision when Gore first approached you.'

'I didn't take those papers from the vault,' Blackwood said, almost pleadingly.

'That's not the question I asked.'

'I don't know anything about Abraham Gore. I had lunch with him. That was all. You have to believe me.'

Pyke left the room without turning around or saying another word. It would be the last time he ever saw William Blackwood.

Pyke found Milly curled up on the bed, staring at the wall. He had just returned to Hambledon from the city and his afternoon appointment with Gore; the contracts had all been signed and Pyke was no longer the majority partner in Blackwood's bank. He wasn't sure whether this was something to be celebrated or mourned.

On his way up to Milly's room, Jo had told him that, even by her standards, Milly had gone into a decline and hadn't taken any food or water in more than a day. Pyke shut the door behind him, opened the curtains and waited for the girl to turn around and face him. He sat down on the edge of the bed. 'I've been told you're refusing to eat or drink anything. Is that right, Milly?'

Her small, quick eyes glowed in the half-light but still she refused to look at him, let alone speak.

'Can I tell you a story, Milly? Would that be all right?'

This time she looked at him and gave him a curt nod of her head.

'I never knew my mother and my father died when I was about the same age as you. I was there when he died too. There was this vast sea of faces and he lost his footing and was crushed under people's feet. I remember that feeling, when the crowd dispersed, and I found his body. It wasn't moving. I knew he was dead. I don't know if I cried or not but I do remember holding my breath, closing my eyes and counting to ten, then twenty, thirty, forty, fifty even. Somehow I thought if I held my breath long enough or counted hard enough it would bring him back. Of course it never did but later, when I went to live with my uncle and I couldn't sleep, I'd lie there and count the different things I'd seen or done since he died and somehow that helped me. It made me see that, whether I liked it or not, things moved on. Life moved on. I still thought about him, and about the day he died, but I thought about others things, as well. And I learned how to take care of myself.' Pyke waited for a moment and then added, gently, 'That's the most important lesson a boy or a girl can learn. If I helped you at first, would you like to learn how to take care of yourself, Milly?'

She was staring at him but managed a slight nod.

'Would you like to come with me on a trip to the seaside, Milly? Would you like to see the English Channel?'

Again she nodded, this time a little more vigorously. She may even have smiled, too.

'Now shut your eyes, hold your breath and count to ten.'

Milly did as she was told and Pyke counted with her, 'One, two, three ...', her face reddening as she did so. 'Six, seven, eight, nine, *ten*.' Her eyes opened and she gasped for breath.

Before she'd had time to think, Pyke asked, 'What did you see?'

'Dog.' The word tumbled out of her mouth before she could stop it. For a moment they looked at each other, trying to come to terms with what had just happened. Her voice had sounded like a tiny croak.

'What kind of a dog, Milly?'

She looked away and pursed her lips.

'A big dog, Milly? Was it a big dog with a light brown coat and a black face? The dog you drew in the picture?' He had tried to conceal his excitement but hadn't done a good enough job because she looked at him, startled, and then folded her arms.

'Was there a dog in the room the night your parents were killed, Milly?'

When Milly didn't answer him, Pyke grabbed her shoulder and

jerked her towards him, harder than he perhaps should have, hard enough to make her gasp. But something inside him had snapped and he couldn't stop himself from shaking her and demanding to know about the dog, until her sobs became screams and it wasn't until Pyke put his arms around her, whispered that everything would be all right and stroked her matted hair, that her wails started to ebb.

'It was a big brown dog with a black face and it saw me hiding under the table but even though it growled and sniffed, it didn't give me away. The gemmen never even saw me.' Milly spoke in halting sentences between the sobs.

He hugged her tiny, trembling body and whispered that everything would be all right.

'I heard 'em shout, Ma and Pa, but there weren't nuffin' I could do. I tried to help but my legs and arms wouldn't move. I sat under that table while it happened, listening to their screams, but I couldn't move. I couldn't even open my mouth ...' She began to wail again, this time pausing only for breath. Pyke held her tightly and tried to mop her sweat-stained brow. 'Let it out, let it all out,' he whispered, as her wailing intensified. He heard footsteps outside the door.

Finally, when the sobs had started to subside, Pyke called out, 'Royce, would you step into the room.'

Annoyed that Pyke had heard him, and knew it was him, the elderly butler shuffled into the nursery holding a lantern and muttered, 'I heard the girl crying and wondered if I might be of assistance.'

'That's good of you, Royce. Actually there is something you could do.'

'Yes, sir?'

'Tell Jennings to prepare the carriage. I'll need to be at the Swan with Two Necks tomorrow morning at six.'

'At six, sir? In the *morning*?' Royce frowned and shook his head. 'Jennings will be asleep by now. I'm not sure it's possible ...'

'Then wake the lazy codger up and tell him to have the carriage waiting for me at half-past four or I'll come and find him and pummel him to a pulp.'

For a moment Royce stared at him open mouthed, unable to hide his shock that he'd been spoken to in this manner, but then his training and a lifetime of subordination took over, the outrage in his eyes glazed over and his composure returned. 'Very good, sir. Will there be anything else, sir?'

'Yes, wake and dress Milly here and make sure she's ready to leave at four thirty on the dot.' Pyke looked at the girl, who was clinging to him and sniffing. 'We're going to try and find your sister Kate. Do you remember Kate?'

'Kate?' Milly's eyes widened and her expression seemed to lift. He had given her hope and he hated himself for it.

'It's a long journey, Milly, and you'll need to be strong for it. If Royce here brings you some food, will you eat it?'

Even before Milly had nodded, Pyke called the butler back into the room and told him to bring her some dinner. This time Royce didn't offer any protest.

TWENTY-EIGHT

There were two coaches departing for Ramsgate the following morning, the faster mail coach at six o'clock and the other, run by a different company, half an hour later at six thirty. Pyke had hoped to secure two inside seats on the six o'clock coach but was told by a bored clerk that the mail coach was already full. Not content with this answer, Pyke went looking for the stand where the mail coach was due to depart from and saw only at the very last moment that Sir John Conroy was waiting to catch the same coach. Pulling Milly, who was staring in wonderment at the horses and giant painted carriages, behind a group of passengers waiting to board another coach, he stole another glance, to make sure his eyes hadn't deceived him, and cursed. If, as seemed most likely, Conroy was returning to Ramsgate to rejoin the royal party, his task had suddenly become much more difficult. Pyke needed to talk with one of the princess's ladies-in-waiting, Helen Milner-Gibson, the name he had been given by Freddie Sutton before his death, without threat of running into the comptroller. Above all, Pyke didn't want Conroy to know he'd visited the south coast.

The six o'clock mail coach departed on time. Pyke watched it leave the yard, Sir John Conroy sitting next to the window reading a newspaper. But the half-six coach that they had been forced to take didn't leave until nearer seven, after Pyke had taken the driver and young groom to one side and offered them an inducement of ten pounds if they managed to beat the mail-coach to Ramsgate.

'Beat the mail coach?' The driver had stared at Pyke, as though he were a madman. 'They've got eight horses to our six and a faster carriage.'

'But they're carrying more passengers and more luggage,' Pyke had said. 'And if you get me to Ramsgate before the mail coach, I'll give you fifty pounds, not ten.'

That swung it. The coach pulled out of the yard just a few minutes later, without a couple of the passengers who had been dawdling in the waiting area.

Not including the two of them, there were five passengers inside the coach sitting opposite each other and another four riding on the roof, together with the luggage. To his immense relief, no one seemed to want to talk inside the coach – it was too early and too cold – and very soon they had all settled into their thoughts, Milly staring in wonder out of the window, making the occasional remark, but on the whole too preoccupied to want to speak. They crossed the Thames using London Bridge and clattered along the Old Kent Road at an amble, there being too much traffic and too many people to go any quicker, but once they had passed through Deptford and climbed up the steep hill into Blackheath, the driver and groom chivvied the horses from a canter to a gallop, so that even those inside the carriage had to keep hold of their hats.

The journey as far as Rochester took a little over four hours and as their carriage pulled into the inn and was surrounded by a swarm of vendors, ostlers and pot-boys, the mail coach was just departing. The driver and groom hurried the feeding and watering of the horses and chivvied the passengers back into, and on top of, the coach and they were on their way within twenty minutes. Out on the open road, they quickly urged the horses into a gallop and very soon all that could be heard inside the carriage was the clattering of the wheels and the clanking of the brass-and-steel harness. About an hour into the journey one of the passengers, a middle-aged woman, professed to feeling unwell and asked the driver to stop for a while, but her request was turned down. Rather the carriage continued along the newly macadamised road at a very brisk pace, and by the time they reached the town of Sittingbourne, the mail coach hadn't yet left the inn's yard. While the grooms attended to the horses, Pyke took the opportunity to loosen one of the fastenings on the harness. At one point he had to duck under the window that Conroy was looking out of but he didn't think the comptroller had seen him. This time they had to change horses, and when they finally pulled out of the yard, they were still half an hour behind the mail coach. Milly sat by the window, still rapt at the sight and sound of open fields, and from time to time she would ask questions about things that he knew nothing about: why cows slept standing up, what made the rain, the difference between wheat and barley. It was odd, to hear her talk with such confidence, and Pyke wondered what might happen to her if they couldn't find Kate, her sister.

By the time they had pulled into Canterbury, a little after two o'clock in the afternoon, the town dominated by the soaring Norman cathedral, the mail coach was nowhere to be seen, and while the rest of the passengers stretched their legs and took their lunch, as well as some brandy and water, Pyke asked the driver and groom where the rival coach might be, whether it had already started back on the road. Shaking his head, the driver assured him that the mail coach stopped at a different inn and, after he had harried the passengers back into and on to the carriage, they had soon left the old cathedral town behind them. For the final leg of the journey, Pyke had insisted on swapping places with the groom and, having convinced Milly that she would be all right without him inside the carriage, he had taken his seat next to the driver. As the horses pounded the road, straining in their harnesses to go faster, the open land passing by them on either side as a blur, the driver cracking his whip to further encourage them, it was hard not to feel exhilaration at the mixture of speed and fresh air. Behind him Pyke could hear those travelling up on the roof chatting nervously about the prospect of the carriage overturning or coming off the road.

Half an hour after they had left Canterbury, he spotted the mail coach on the road ahead of them and, having pointed it out to the driver, he borrowed the whip and cracked it over the backs of the already straining horses. The coach ahead of them was both newer and faster, especially as it was pulled by eight horses rather than six, but it was carrying at least four more passengers in addition to the sacks of mail, and as such they were able to make up a little ground. But at some point the driver of the mail coach realised that they were closing, the gap no more than a few hundred yards, and urged his own horses to go faster, and soon the final leg of the journey had turned into a full-blown race, one that the passengers riding outside the carriage embraced without question, egging the driver and horses on. Over the next mile or so they closed the gap to less than a hundred yards, close enough to see the faces of those travelling on top of the mail coach, but after that the gap between them remained constant and Pyke realised that if they were going to catch or pass the mail coach they would have to lose some weight. Without saying anything to the driver, he clambered back to where the four passengers were sitting and the luggage was stowed and asked for their help. The plan, he whispered so the driver wouldn't hear him, was to discard the luggage, piece by piece, off the back of the coach. He paid them a half-crown each and said they could keep their own cases. Then he rejoined the driver at the front of the coach. The gradual loss of weight helped a little and though their horses were beginning to tire, they closed the gap still further, until the mail coach was perhaps only ten or twenty yards ahead of them. At this point, Pyke relieved the driver of the reins and urged the six horses to go faster, looking ahead of them for a suitable place to try to pass the mail coach. It came in the form of a long, wide, straight section of the road. Taking his chance, he steered the coach out on to the other side of the road and lashed the horses' backs with the whip, shouting and urging them on. Above the rattle of the harness and the sound of hoofs and wheels clattering in unison across the ground, the cheers of support from the other passengers and the bray of the driver's horn took them alongside the mail coach just as the road ahead of them fell away sharply to the right. At the last moment, Pyke (who had pulled his cloak up around his neck to try to conceal his identity) saw a hay wagon moving slowly towards them in the other direction. They had pulled ahead of the mail coach by a nose and rather than trying to slow down Pyke cracked the whip even harder and went for the fast-closing gap, moving across the mail coach's line. This drew enraged shouts from the driver of the mail coach but Pyke held his line and continued to race for the gap and then, within the space of a few seconds, it was over. Afterwards, Pyke wasn't exactly sure what had happened, whether their wheels might have touched or whether the mail coach had struck something in the road and one of the wheels had come loose, but the result was the same: the mail coach skidded off the road, careening into a field and finally toppling over and overturning, the harness snapping loose and freeing the eight horses, which cantered on for a few hundred yards, eventually coming to a halt in the middle of the field. The driver of their coach wanted to stop to make sure no one was hurt but Pyke assured him the best thing they could do was make it to Ramsgate as quickly as possible and send another carriage out to pick up the passengers. It would give the mail coach's driver time to cool down, too. Despite the fifty pounds he would earn, the driver appeared anxious about the repercussions and insisted that Pyke return to his berth inside the carriage.

Pyke willingly agreed and spent the final hour of the journey chatting with Milly. By the time they had started the slow, tortuous descent into the small port of Ramsgate, the afternoon light was starting to fade and it was almost dark when the weary horses trudged into the coaching yard. Pyke settled his debt with the driver and led Milly to an inn across the road, before any of the passengers realised their cases had been thrown from the roof of the carriage.

Despite the pleasant setting between two chalk cliffs, Ramsgate was a dismal little town and Pyke was glad to be staying only for a night. Having left Milly in their room and assuring her he would return within an hour, he hailed a coachman from a stand in front of the inn and instructed the driver to take him to the Albion hotel. It was a clear, chilly evening and away from the smog of the city the air smelled fresh and the sky was filled with seagulls circling above the returning fishing boats. At the front desk, Pyke asked the hotel's porters to pass a message to Helen Milner-Gibson and returned to the carriage. He had to wait only a few minutes before the bonneted figure of the princess's lady-in-waiting emerged from the hotel.

'Am I to believe you have word from my family, sir?' she asked, peering into the carriage. This was the message Pyke had told the porter to pass to her.

'Please, it's such a chilly evening, why don't you step in here out of the wind.' He smiled disarmingly and moved across to the far side of the carriage.

Reluctantly she hitched up her skirt and did as he'd suggested, but left the door ajar in case she needed to make a quick exit. She was an attractive woman with a pale, angular face dotted with freckles, doe-like eyes, dark brown hair gathered up in a comb and long, wispy eyelashes. Without having to ask, he could tell she came from a wealthy family: it was the way in which she carried herself, as though the world owed her something, rather than the other way around.

'Please, sir, you said you had news from my family. Is it good news or bad news?' She removed her straw bonnet and looked at him pleadingly.

Pyke waited for a moment, staring out of the window at the masts bobbing up and down in the harbour. 'I'm told you're an acquaintance of Kate Sutton.'

Before she could scramble to safety, he had grabbed hold of her wrist and reached across to shut the door. The driver had already been instructed, and indeed paid, to ignore what happened in the back of his cab, and took up the reins, the carriage rolling slowly forward.

'I just want to know whether Kate is still alive or not,' Pyke said, quietly, once the cab was moving.

Helen looked at him, her expression revealing antipathy and fear.

'I'm here to help but I can only do this if you're honest with me. I'm sure I don't need to underline the seriousness of the situation but, even so, you might not realise just how much danger you're in as a friend of Kate's. Her disappearance has left behind a trail of bodies, including her betrothed as well as her mother and father.'

This revelation brought a gasp of astonishment. For a short while, she couldn't even bring herself to look at him.

'I'm not going to harm you, Helen. I just want to know whether Kate is still alive and if so where I can find her.'

She stared down at the straw on the floor of the cab. 'I don't know what you're talking about, sir.'

Pyke nodded calmly. He'd expected to meet some resistance. 'How long have you been the princess's lady-in-waiting?'

'I'm not her lady-in-waiting. I'm her lady of the bedchamber.'

Pyke bowed his head, acknowledging the mistake. 'How long have you been her lady of the bedchamber?'

'About a year.'

'And were you first appointed to this post by the duchess's comptroller, Sir John Conroy?'

A brief tilt of her head confirmed this.

'So how would you describe your dealings with Sir John? Do you find him to be a trustworthy employer?'

Gingerly she shook her head. They had travelled along the seafront and had come to a halt at the end of a track. Outside, the chalk cliff rose up from the sea like a vertical wall and the wind buffeted the side of the carriage.

'In what way is he untrustworthy?' When she didn't answer, Pyke let out a heavy sigh and added, 'Look, Helen, I can't help either you or Kate unless you tell me something I don't already know.'

This time she turned to face him, her eyes blazing with indignation. 'Why should I tell *you* anything?'

'Because I can help you. At the very least, I can keep you both alive.'

'And who are you?' she asked, suddenly curious.

'My name's Pyke. Before he was killed, Freddie Sutton asked me to try and find his daughter.'

'Kate's father?' This seemed to change things and Helen stared out of the window, biting her lip.

'If it helps, I think Sir John Conroy is a morally repugnant coward. But that's just my opinion.'

She smiled at his apparent boldness before the frown returned to her expression. 'Do you want to know something? The princess still believes I was planted by Conroy to spy on her.'

'And were you?'

'At first he wanted me to.' She chuckled bitterly. 'But he wanted me to do a lot of things for him.'

Pyke's nod suggested he already knew about Conroy's sleazy reputation. 'I take it the princess isn't exactly enamoured at her mother's comptroller.'

'That would be a gross understatement, sir. She hates him. Yes, hate would not be too strong a word.'

'And this feeling is mutual?'

'I should say so.' Helen waited for a moment, to reflect on her answer. 'But if he's to be her private secretary when she becomes queen, I'd say he needs her more than she needs him.'

Pyke allowed a short silence to settle between them. Finally he turned to face her and said, 'I don't mean to alarm you, Helen, but I have another reason for wanting to find the letters that I believe Kate stole from Conroy. My wife and child have been kidnapped and, in order to secure their safe return, I need to produce the letters *this* Sunday morning. I want you to understand that I'll do anything to make this happen. *Anything.* Now, if that means dragging you up those steps over there to the top of the cliff and holding you over the edge until you tell me what you know, I'll do it without batting an eyelid. Now nod your head once if you understand my predicament.'

Dumbstruck, she nodded her head.

'Good,' he said, with a smile. 'Now why don't you take me to see Kate or tell me what happened to her?'

Helen stared at him with her large, liquid eyes and nervously licked her lips. 'But I promised ...'

'So Kate's still alive?'

Helen gave Pyke a forlorn nod. 'But I swear, she'll kill me, and maybe even shoot herself, if she thinks you're there to harm her.'

'What if I brought along her little sister?'

That drew another gasp of surprise. 'You mean, you have Milly *here*?'

The girl before Pyke, wielding a pistol, in a sodden dress with pale, dirty skin, blue lips and dark, greasy hair, was more like a feral creature than the dutiful daughter Freddie Sutton had described.

But her resistance crumbled as soon as she saw Milly and her pistol slipped from her fingers as her sister ran towards her, Kate gathering her up in her arms. Their combined sobs lasted for more than a minute. Pyke and Helen stepped back across the threshold of the disused labourer's cottage to give them a little privacy. They had walked for a mile or two across the top of the windswept cliff, Pyke carrying a tired Milly for some of the way on his shoulders. Now at the abandoned cottage, little more than a pile of stones and some branches with an old canvas tarpaulin as a roof, Pyke and Helen waited outside, staring up at the starry sky.

After about ten minutes, Kate appeared in the doorway and waved him and Helen back into the cottage. In place of her scowl, she now bore a smile and thanked him for what he'd done for Milly. Her cheeks were stained with tears. Milly stood at her side trembling but trying to hold herself together. Pyke supposed Milly had told Kate about their parents and could only wonder at the bewilderment and sadness she must now be feeling.

'Milly tells me you took her into your home and treated her like she was your own daughter, Mr Pyke. For that, I'll always be grateful.'

'Did she tell you how I first came upon her?' Pyke looked first at Milly and then at her sister.

Kate bit her lip and nodded, tears filling her eyes. 'What were you doing there in the first place?'

'My uncle's Godfrey Bond. He asked me to try and find you.'

Her expression darkened. 'No disrespect, Mr Pyke, but I wish I'd never laid eyes on that man.'

'None taken. And just Pyke will do.' He coughed. 'In my uncle's defence, he only gave you what you and Johnny wanted.'

Pyke's mention of Johnny brought further discomfort to her face. 'Have you seen or heard from him?'

The way Pyke shook his head told her what she needed to know. She gasped, tears flowing down her cheeks now. 'My God, what have I done? Ma and Pa and now Johnny …'

'You shouldn't have to answer for Johnny. He saw a way of making some money and grabbed it with both hands.'

'And my ma and pa?'

Pyke glanced over at Helen. 'You did what you thought you had to.'

'No, I did what I did because I was a greedy little bitch.' Kate's laugh was devoid of humour. 'It's been funny. I've lived here, with Helen's help, for three weeks now, and you know something? I haven't missed the fine bedding and fancy foods in the slightest. I can see the stars at night through the holes in the roof and I've even grown used to the cold. I used to think that having money would be the greatest thing in the world. Now Ma and Pa are dead and so is Johnny and I don't give a damn whether I ever see a gold coin again in my lifetime.' She reached down and gave Milly a hug.

'Perhaps you'd like to tell me what happened, Kate. How you came to be caught up in this mess …'

'Have you a few days to spare?'

'I'd just like the truth.' Pyke dug his hands into the pockets of his greatcoat. 'You owe me that much.'

Kate nodded solemnly. 'I can't offer you anything to eat or drink but maybe you'd like to take a seat.' She motioned at the pile of hay.

Pyke told her he was happy to stand.

The tale that Kate Sutton told him was a depressingly familiar one in which none of the players, including herself and even Godfrey, came out looking good.

Pyke had already been told the first part of it by his uncle but listened quietly while she described her unwitting discovery of Conroy's sexual liaison with the duchess and the pressure brought to bear on her by Johnny, when she mentioned it to him, to try to trade her revelation for money.

It wasn't difficult for Pyke to see why a struggling actor and a lowly kitchen hand might have been suitably tempted by Godfrey's initial payment to take further risks, but he found her insistence that it was Johnny, rather than her, who had pushed the issue harder to swallow. But then Kate's story took an unexpected twist, one that partly explained the show Pyke had seen at the penny gaff in Lambeth, and left him wondering why the royal comptroller hadn't yet been dismissed from his position and arrested for high treason.

It had started earlier in the summer while the royal party had been living at 'home' in Kensington Palace. One of Kate's tasks had been to deliver the princess's lunch to her at midday and one day, early in July, a Monday or a Tuesday, she had witnessed something she wasn't meant to, something she could not explain. Unbeknown to him, Kate had seen Sir John Conroy surreptitiously emptying a few drops of clear liquid from a bottle into the princess's lunch. After this incident a pattern had developed. She would carry the princess's food on a tray from the kitchen as far as the stairs, whereupon Conroy would intercept her and insist upon taking it up to the princess herself. This had lasted for at least a couple of weeks.

Pyke could only imagine how the notion that the comptroller was trying to poison the princess might have terrified the kitchen hand, especially as the princess's health did start to deteriorate rapidly throughout the rest of the summer and at the start of the autumn. Motivated by a fear that Victoria might perish, and that she would be blamed for holding something back, Kate told her only friend in the palace what she'd seen. Helen Milner-Gibson initially treated Kate's story with scepticism but took steps to warn the princess's governess, the formidable Baroness Lehzen, who in turn made certain that Conroy never got his hands on her charge's food again. But the princess's illness, thought to be a bilious fever, had worsened throughout the autumn, to the point where their week-long stay in Ramsgate became a two-month sojourn, with the young princess too weak to travel back to London.

Despite her lowly status, Kate had travelled with the royal party to the south coast at Lehzen's insistence, in order to work in the hotel's kitchen and oversee the preparation of the princess's food.

But Kate had also told her betrothed, Johnny Evans, about what she had seen and, apparently, the scent of fresh scandal and the possibility of using the information to make more money had sent the struggling actor into a frenzy. Pursuing his own agenda, he'd set to work trying to dig up some background information and had been told about a rumour, circulating a few years earlier, that the Duke of Cumberland had once tried to murder the young princess by introducing arsenic into her bread and milk. Unaware of the fact that Cumberland and Conroy despised each other, Johnny had concocted a scenario in which both men were conspiring to kill the princess. This had formed the basis of the show he'd put together and which Pyke had seen performed at the penny gaff. But Johnny still needed some hard evidence if he was going to sell this new story to Godfrey, and tried to pester Kate into snooping around Conroy's private quarters. By her account, Kate had refused to do so, but before the royal party left for Ramsgate Johnny had badgered her to such an extent that she ended up providing him with enough information that he could plan his own raid on the empty palace.

According to her, Kate had played no further part in Johnny's successful burglary of Conroy's private quarters and she didn't find out, until later, that he had taken a cracksman called Hayes along with him and that the two of them had found a way of breaking into Conroy's safe. The first she knew that something was amiss was Conroy's fury when he'd discovered his safe had been burgled, and his belief that the burglary had been assisted by someone from within the palace. During their stay at Ramsgate, he had begun a witch-hunt, trying to find out who'd helped the thieves break into the palace in the first place. About the same time, Johnny had shown up at the Albion hotel, apparently flush with his own success. The problem was that he couldn't read and therefore left the letters he'd stolen from Conroy's safe with Kate for her to peruse. But Johnny hadn't been able to keep quiet about the burglary and word had quickly got back to Conroy that a certain 'gentleman' staying at an inn on the seafront had been boasting about his exploits. It was also reported that this same man had been seen in the company of one of the royal party. Once this rumour had begun to spread around the hotel, Kate fled, taking with her the letters, first to try to find Johnny and when she couldn't find him, seeking refuge in an abandoned cottage she had previously noticed on her clifftop walks. Only Helen Milner-Gibson had been told of her whereabouts and she had been sworn to the strictest secrecy. Kate had sought sanctuary in the cottage, where she had spent the time reading and re-reading the letters while trying to determine what to do, and how to extricate herself from the mess she had, partly, landed herself in.

'You hoped it might all go away if you hid out here for long enough?' Pyke asked, gently.

Kate gave him a desperate nod.

'But it hasn't gone away, has it? If anything it's got worse.' Pyke pulled his coat more tightly around his body and asked, 'Do you think they found Johnny here in Ramsgate or followed him back to London?'

'I don't know. I never saw him again.'

'And he had no idea what had actually been written in the letters?'

That drew a jaundiced laugh. 'Johnny liked to think of himself as an actor but he couldn't read or write.' Pyke told her about the show he'd seen at the penny gaff and she shook her head, adding, 'Doesn't mean he actually wrote anything down: he probably just told folk what to say or do.' Then, remembering something she'd meant to say earlier, she continued, 'Of course, not knowing what he'd stumbled on didn't stop him from passing word to the Duke of Cumberland, accusing him of trying to kill Victoria and saying that he had physical evidence – letters – to support his claim. Johnny told about me this, the last time we spoke here in Ramsgate. Apparently he'd demanded a thousand pounds from the duke in return for his silence.'

This got Pyke's attention. His pulse quickened and his mouth dried up. 'So what you're saying is that Johnny's disappearance, and his death, might have been the work of Cumberland *or* Conroy?'

Kate shrugged and said she had no idea. She didn't even know whether he'd made it back to London, as he'd told her he was planning to.

Worried, Pyke turned this new information over in his mind. Up until then, he had assumed that Johnny's murder and beheading had been carried out on Conroy's behalf by Jimmy Trotter and the body dumped in the river near Huntingdon. But what if this wasn't the case? What if Trotter had, indeed, committed this dastardly act, but on Cumberland's orders? Cumberland, who'd subsequently orchestrated the kidnapping of Pyke's pregnant wife and son . . .

At least Pyke now knew how Cumberland had first been alerted to the existence of the letters.

Another even more unpalatable thought crossed his mind. Indeed, it was something that had been bothering him ever since he had first received the ransom demand and then discovered that Cumberland had left for the Continent. What if the kidnapping had not, in fact, been planned and overseen by the duke? What if someone else had perpetrated it and tried to pass it off as Cumberland's work in order to shield themselves from Pyke's vengeance? Pyke had told Conroy about the duke's interest in the letters. What if the comptroller had orchestrated the abduction and somehow managed to procure Cumberland's seal in order to shift blame on to the duke? That might also explain why it had taken a full five days for the ransom note to reach Hambledon. Conroy had been waiting for the duke to leave the country; otherwise Pyke would have found a way of talking to him and would have found out that the duke had had nothing to do with the kidnapping. This was only conjecture, of course, but it made a certain amount of sense. And it raised the spectre of other, even more disturbing possibilities. For wasn't Conroy an associate of Sir Henry Bellows and wasn't Bellows in charge of a crackdown against leading London radicals, of which Emily was most definitely one?

'What was it in the letters Johnny stole that's whipped everyone up into a frenzy?'

Kate sat up, pulled two crumpled letters from under her bodice and handed them to Pyke. When he'd finished reading them, he looked at her and whistled but didn't hand them back. Briefly he wondered whether Kate realised just how explosive the revelations would be if they were ever made public.

The first letter was written by the princess's mother, Victoria, Duchess of Kent, to Conroy. It was dated the twenty-ninth of August 1818. In the letter, she rhapsodised about Conroy's visit to the Saxe-Coburg home she shared with her husband, Edward, the Duke of York, and her 'ardent' hopes that Conroy would be appointed as her husband's private equerry. In florid language, the duchess had recounted some of the more intimate details of Conroy's visit, happily remembering details of their 'passionate' exchanges and making explicit references to Edward's 'inadequacies' and the fact they hadn't 'enjoyed proper marital relations' for four or five years. But the second letter was the real fox in the henhouse. This one was much briefer and was seemingly written in response to something Conroy had written. It simply said, 'In answer to your question, my darling, I can only say yes, she is yours. But I'm sure I don't need to impress on you the importance of never, ever speaking again of this matter so long as we both may live.' The second letter was dated the twenty-sixth of May 1819.

Pyke looked at Helen and Kate and said, 'And the princess was born on the twenty-fifth of May?'

'The twenty-fourth,' Helen said, in a tone that suggested she'd read the letters, too, and *knew*.

'Even if it's not definitive proof,' Pyke said, 'a man like Cumberland would seize hold of this and never let it go. He's like a dog with a bone that way.'

Cumberland, who was next in line to the throne; Cumberland, who had kidnapped Emily and Felix ...

'It isn't ever going to go away, is it?' Kate asked, staring glumly at her little sister. Milly gave her a supportive hug.

'Not unless you allow me to do something with this.' He held up the second letter and briefly wondered why Conroy hadn't destroyed it; perhaps he'd kept it to use for his own purpose at some future point.

'Make it public?' Kate seemed aghast and Helen stepped in and said, '*Never*. I'll not allow the princess to be hurt.'

Pyke gave them both a hard stare. 'Listen, I want Cumberland to be our next king even less than you do, but in order to be able to make this problem go away, I'm going to need two things. The letters ...'

'And?' Helen and Kate said at the same time.

'An audience with the princess.' Among other things, he needed to ask her about royal seals.

'You're planning to tell her about this?' Helen said, appalled.

Pyke shook his head. 'But I need to see her, for her own good, if nothing else.'

'Conroy won't sanction it.'

'Allow me to worry about the comptroller,' he said, wondering whether the replacement carriage had yet returned to Ramsgate with the stranded passengers.

'Lehzen would never allow it, either. She's very, *very* protective of the princess.'

'I'm not planning to ask her permission.'

'You mean you're just going to barge into the princess's room?'

He looked at the lady of the bedchamber and smiled. 'That's where you're going to help me.'

TWENTY-NINE

In the darkness Pyke moved carefully around the dressing table, taking care not to disturb the yellow chintz curtains, and approached the four-poster bed where the princess lay under a Marseilles quilt. A sharp intake of breath was quickly followed by her sudden move bolt upright. 'Who's there?' a small, timid voice asked. 'Is that you, Lehzen?' The sixteen-year-old princess was sitting up in the bed, her pinched cheeks and pointy chin just about visible in the gloom.

'Don't be alarmed and above all don't shout for help. My name's Pyke. I come as a friend. I have information about Sir John Conroy I know you'll want to hear.' He spoke quietly but firmly and stood at the end of the bed, not daring or wanting to get any closer to her.

There was a long pause, neither of them moving at all, and Pyke prepared himself for a scream or a cry for help.

It didn't come.

'Rest assured, sir, that if you come any closer or attempt to hurt or even touch me in any way I will scream as loudly as I can and within seconds there will sufficient bodies in this room to restrain you. Is that quite clear?'

'Yes.'

'Please continue.' Pyke could hear the tension in her voice but she didn't sound panicked.

'Do you remember a female servant called Kate Sutton who worked in the kitchen at Kensington Palace and came with you here to Ramsgate?'

The princess sat forward in her bed. 'Yes, I do. I was sorry to hear that she left her post. She was a sweet thing.'

A moment's silence passed between them. 'Do you know why she left?'

She laughed gently. 'I'm afraid I'm never told about such matters.'

'She was put in fear for her life because she saw something in the kitchen,' Pyke whispered, taking a step closer to the bed.

'Come closer, sir. I can't hear you properly.' Victoria pointed to a chair. 'Sit down and tell me about the young girl.'

'She saw Sir John Conroy introducing something into your food.' He paused for a moment, to allow the information to be absorbed, and then sat down on the chair. 'A small dose of arsenic perhaps.' Up close, he saw that the skin was hanging off her cheekbones and her head was almost entirely bald, just a few wisps remaining at the back and the sides.

'You're suggesting Conroy has been trying to poison me?' There was incredulity in her voice.

'Fortunately for you, Kate informed your lady of the bedchamber, Helen Milner-Gibson, who in turn told Lehzen. For the last few months, I'm told, Lehzen has overseen the preparation and delivery of all your meals.'

This seemed to intrigue her. 'I've been wondering why Lehzen has shown such an interest in what I eat.' She paused for a moment, to digest this news. 'You say Helen M-G is a friend? I always thought she'd been chosen for the post by Conroy to spy on me.' The princess laughed and became self-conscious, trying to arrange her few remaining locks of hair. 'It was falling out due to my illness. Lehzen cut the rest of it off but she assures me it'll grow back.'

Pyke watched her for a while and decided that she reminded him of Felix; they were both frail, both prone to illness and both isolated from the world. 'Perhaps whatever Conroy put in your food contributed to your illness.'

'Dr Clark said I'd contracted some kind of fever.'

'And was Dr Clark brought here to look after you by Conroy?'

The princess was silent while she considered what he'd told her. 'Just before I got sick,' she said, eventually, 'I had a visit from my beloved uncle, Leopold, and his darling wife, Louise. I asked how I should go about preparing to be queen. He told me to beware of wolves in sheep's clothing.'

'And you think he was referring to Conroy?'

'Perhaps.' She shrugged. 'Uncle Leopold didn't mention anyone in particular. But I do know Conroy dislikes me. He thinks I'm sickly, spoiled, girlish, prone to whims and flights of fancy, frivolous and intellectually younger than my years.' She spoke as if she were quoting him.

'Should I assume that the antipathy is mutual?'

That drew a slight giggle. 'Perhaps, but I'm afraid my mother adores him and in case you haven't noticed I'm a minor.' She paused for a moment to rearrange her pillows. 'But he also needs me. I should add that he calls me those things merely to press my mother's case for a regency, even if the King lives until I come of age.'

'I don't think Conroy wanted to kill you. I'm guessing he wanted to weaken you in order to tighten his control over your affairs.' Pyke hesitated. 'Tell me this: did Conroy try and seize upon your illness for his own ends?'

Victoria considered this for a moment. 'A few weeks ago, when the fever was at its worst, he tried to put a quill in my shaking hand and persuade me to sign a document appointing him as my private secretary when I become queen.'

If you become queen, Pyke thought grimly, as he considered the letter hidden in his pocket.

'Lehzen chased Conroy out of the room. She hates him even more than I do.' This memory seemed to cheer her up.

'And where does your mother stand in all this?'

'My mother claims to have my best interests at heart. It's why I'm locked up like a common prisoner at Kensington Palace and not permitted to play any part in court life. Apparently it's for my own good. I'm to be protected from the loose morals of my uncle's court: *the vice of Windsor versus the virtue of Kensington.*' She laughed bitterly. 'In fact, my mother yearns for the prestige and wealth a regency would give her and she's utterly under Conroy's influence, even to the ...'

The young princess froze. Footsteps approached the door and someone turned the handle. Pyke had no choice but to hide under the bed. He did so quickly and quietly but still didn't know whether he'd been heard. 'My dear? Are you awake?' The voice was a female one, with a faintly Germanic accent. 'I thought I heard voices,' Baroness Lehzen whispered to someone else. Pyke could see her ankles silhouetted against the light from the other room and briefly wondered whether she was talking to the comptroller. If either of them decided to look under the bed, he would be finished. Who would believe he hadn't tried to defile the impressionable princess? People had hung for far less.

But then Lehzen crept back out of the room and gently closed the door behind her. Pyke slid out from under the bed, stood up and straightened his frock-coat. The princess giggled a little and whispered, 'That was a close shave.' And when Pyke didn't respond, she added, in the same breathy tone, 'You wouldn't believe how dull my life is, Mr Pyke. I'm a girl and I want to do some of the things that girls of my age are meant to do. Go to balls, dance, listen to music, meet brilliant people.' This time she looked directly at him. 'It's like a prison with golden bars.'

Suddenly nervous, Pyke looked across at the closed door. 'Can I offer you a word of advice before I go?'

She nodded meekly but seemed upset that he was about to leave her.

'Make what I've told you yours and Lehzen's secret. Helen knows, too, and you should remember what she's done for you. In addition, you should insist that the kitchen girl, Kate, is reinstated, if, that is, she wants her old job back.'

'And if Conroy objects?'

'I don't think Conroy will be a problem. He'll be as meek as a lamb when I've finished with him.'

That precipitated a sharp intake of breath. 'You won't hurt him, will you?'

'Try to be strong and resolute, but don't let Conroy know that you know anything. His own belief in your ignorance will be your strength. You mightn't have the power at the moment to deal with him or your mother but when you become queen, that's the time to take action. Until then, just remember this: keep your friends close but your enemies closer.'

'Do you have to go?' she asked, with a pout.

'I do have a question I'd like to put to you, if you don't mind.'
'Oh?'

'Might it be possible for someone with, let's say, the right connections to steal your royal seal and thereby pass off a letter they'd written as one of yours?'

The young princess sat up in her bed, intrigued now. 'I always keep my seal close at hand but I suppose it's always possible that someone could steal it. Why do you ask?'

Pyke removed the ransom note he'd received apparently from the duke. He hadn't wanted to involve the princess in the unsavoury business of the abduction but it suddenly struck him that she might recognise the handwriting.

Victoria took the note and, to help her read it, Pyke took out a box of matches and struck one against the wooden floor. It flared into light and he held it up to the note as the princess studied it.

'Well?'

The match had died, once again returning the room to near-darkness.

'Your wife and child are being held for a ransom?' The horror in her voice was unmistakable.

'Do you know whether the handwriting is Conroy's?'

'No, it's not his.'

Pyke exhaled, not sure whether he was relieved or disappointed.

'But I think I might recognise it.' The princess was frowning. 'I can't think how or where from, though.'

'His private secretary, perhaps?'

'No, that wouldn't be it. His writing is much harder to read.'

'Please. It's very important ...'

'I can see that, sir. I just can't recall ...' She closed her eyes and tried to will an answer from her mind.

Pyke wondered whether a sudden, hard slap to her face might jog her memory, but she would probably scream. He checked his watch. The sun would be rising soon and he needed to wake Milly and Kate and get them all to the mail coach before it left for the capital at six.

'But you think it might be someone in Conroy's employ?'

'Possibly.' The princess looked up at him sorrowfully. 'I'm sorry I haven't been of more help.'

Pyke assured her that she had been a great help and prepared himself to depart. As he did so, the princess said, 'But you really think Conroy might have been the one who's kidnapped your wife and child?' She almost seemed to shudder at the possibility.

'I don't know. It's possible.'

'And this letter that's referred to in the ransom note? If you don't mind me asking, what is it?'

'I can't tell you,' Pyke said, bluntly.

'Of course you can tell me.'

'I'm sorry.' Pyke bowed his head. 'But did you notice the seal at the bottom of the note?' Lighting a second match, he let her have another look at it.

She studied it carefully, her frown deepening. 'That would seem to be my uncle's seal.'

'Would it be possible for someone else to have sent the letter?'

'You mean, for someone to have stolen my uncle's seal?'

Pyke nodded.

The princess thought about it for a few moments and shrugged. 'One tends to keep one's seal well guarded for obvious reasons. But it wouldn't be impossible for a servant, let's say, to purloin it.' She sat up further in the bed. 'You suspect Conroy, don't you?'

'I suspect everyone until they prove themselves innocent.'

'Even me?'

Laughing, Pyke turned towards the door.

But the princess called him back. 'You've made a powerful impression on me, Mr Pyke. I feel much better knowing what I now know, and I'm very grateful for the news you brought me. I'm also appalled by the prospect that Conroy might have had something to do with the letter you showed me and I'm desperately sorry for your predicament.' She looked across at him, a pained expression on her face.

'But?'

'But whether I like it or not, Conroy is an integral part of this household and any misdeed that he may or may not have committed will necessarily tarnish the reputation of Kensington itself. That would have very serious repercussions. What I'm labouring to say is that while I despise Conroy perhaps more than any person alive, if something were to happen to him, if some terrible calamity were to befall him, I might decide you're not as well meaning as I think you are. Is that understood?'

Their eyes met. Pyke smiled to himself. His initial impression had been wrong. Felix would have to do a lot of growing up before he was anything like this formidable person.

Then making an exaggerated bow, Pyke knelt down in front of her and bowed his head. 'Your majesty.' That made her squeal with delight and once again she was a sixteen-year-old girl.

Pyke travelled back to London with Kate and Milly Sutton and put them up in a hotel in Leicester Square until the matter with Conroy was resolved. From there, he took a hackney cab back to his Islington town house, where he rested for a while, washed and changed his clothes. It was almost midnight by the time he met Townsend in the taproom of the Old Red Lion. The three-mile walk from Islington had woken him up but Pyke felt anything but relaxed. He looked around the crowded room at the costermongers dressed in long shooting jackets and the petty thieves in their dirty smock-frocks. The tiled floor was damp with butcher's sawdust and the air was laced with the scent of sweat, cheap tobacco and gin.

'I could only round up eleven men at such short notice,' Townsend explained, 'but the rifles weren't a problem. I managed to lay my hands on half a dozen Baker's rifles, with enough ammunition to start a small war.'

'Just eleven?' It wouldn't be enough. But to properly seal off the whole field, he would have needed a hundred men.

'You're not going to be happy with the ones you've got, either.'

'Why?'

'Follow me.'

Townsend was right. They were a motley bunch, a ragbag mixture of ex-soldiers, retired Bow Street Runners and petty criminals. More worryingly, from his point of view, they were halfway to being drunk. Pyke could see it in their glassy, bloodshot stares and smell it on their breath. Having cleared it first with the landlord, he ordered them outside into the yard at the back of the building. It was a cold night and the men quickly started to grumble.

'Do you want the ten pounds I'm offering to pay you?'

They looked at one another, perplexed, and then at him. A few of them mumbled their assent.

'Then strip.'

Their bewildered looks hardened into recalcitrant stares; a few of them shook their heads.

The landlord appeared carrying two metal pails full of water and behind him were two potboys, each with a single pail. They left the pails in the yard and disappeared back into the building.

'I said strip.'

Some of the men realised he was being serious and grudgingly started to remove their boots and socks. A few stood there, their arms folded, not moving, and one man in particular, a brutish fellow with a prison-cropped head and a scar running down one side of his face, muttered, 'I ain't taking my clothes off for no one.' The others stopped what they were doing to see how Pyke would respond.

'Then you can leave now.' Pyke met his stare. 'You're no longer wanted.'

Arms still folded, he sniffed and looked around him. Perhaps he felt safe among his fellow mercenaries. 'I gave up another job to be here. I still expect to be paid.' He had a knife in his belt, Pyke noted, wondering how quickly he would be able to retrieve it.

'Strip or leave.'

The man's calloused fingers brushed against the handle of the knife. He took another step forward. 'I ain't going nowhere till I've been paid.'

Murmurs of approval buoyed the man, who doubtless believed the tide of opinion was turning in his favour.

'The rest of you, strip.'

Some continued to do as they had been told but others seemed to take heart from the man's refusal and stopped removing their clothing.

'This is your final warning: strip now or leave.' Pyke kept his voice hard and firm.

'No.'

In one fluent action, Pyke removed his pistol and shot the man in the middle of his chest, watching, without sentiment, as he fell to the ground, clutching his wound.

'Anyone else?' Pyke wiped saliva from his mouth with the sleeve of his coat and glanced across at Townsend, whose expression was unreadable.

The remaining ten had removed their clothes by the time Pyke had counted to thirty. Taking one bucket at a time, he threw the icy water over their naked, shivering bodies. 'I need you all sober. Is that understood?' Water dripping from their whiskers, they nodded their assent, hardly daring to look down at the pool of blood spreading out beneath the dead man. 'Now dry off, put your clothes back on and meet me at the coffee house across the street.

I'll buy everyone dinner and explain why I've gathered you together and what I want you to do.'

After they had rubbed themselves down and started to put on their clothes, Pyke checked his fob-watch. It was almost one o'clock, which meant he had less than five hours to turn them into a viable force.

As they shuffled out of the yard, he turned to Townsend, who was doubled up next to the wall, coughing up phlegm and blood.

'Are you all right?'

'Am I all right?' Townsend laughed bitterly and pulled down his shirt. There was a large, black tumour bulging out of his neck.

Pyke had to look away. 'My God. I'm so sorry. I didn't know ...'

'That's because you never asked.' Townsend pulled down his collar to cover the growth. 'I went to see a physician last week. He told me there was nothing he could do. He also reckoned I'd be dead by the end of the year.'

'You didn't say anything ...'

'And you didn't notice how thin I am, how pale I look?'

Pyke stared down at his boots, not knowing what else to say.

Townsend kicked the dead body in front of him and looked up at Pyke. 'I've never been able to work you out. You despise poor folk almost as much as rich ones. You seem to think you can take on the world on your own terms and do it without help from anyone else.'

'I need *your* help.'

'But deep down, you despise me, too. Because I remind you of who you were and where you came from.'

Pyke stared at him, momentarily lost for words. 'Where's all this come from?' he managed finally.

'I'm no longer frightened of you, Pyke.' Townsend rubbed the lump on his neck. 'I'm not afraid of anything any more.'

'Even dying?'

That drew a jaundiced laugh. 'Right now dying is the best thing that could happen to me.' Whatever had brought on this outburst soon dissipated and he added, in an almost pleasant tone, 'I talked to Bentley at the jeweller's shop yesterday. He thinks you might've got a bite.'

'A diamond-encrusted solid gold pocket watch, more than a hundred years old, with a *champlevé* face?'

'The seller's bringing it to him next week. Tuesday or Wednesday.'

'Find out which one it is. And get an exact time,' Pyke said. 'I want to be there to meet him.'

THIRTY

The field at Smithfield, almost five acres in size, was deserted as Pyke surveyed it from his vantage point on the roof of a tenement building. It was four in the morning and the first glimpses of dawn wouldn't come for at least another hour, perhaps two now that winter was upon them. On Mondays and Fridays, when the main livestock market took place, the field would, by now, have started to fill with sheep and cattle herded from their grazing pastures by drove-boys and their dogs, but because it was Sunday, the whole place was still eerily quiet, and briefly Pyke wondered whether Cumberland or indeed Conroy had wanted it to be this way. From a tactical point of view, there were many, many things about the location which concerned Pyke. For a start, its sheer size meant that it was all but impossible to seal it off and police its dark corners, just as it was hard to determine which street or alley the kidnapper or kidnappers would approach the field from and use to try to escape. A force of a hundred might have been adequate for this task, not ten sullen, ill-disciplined mercenaries. A man could instantly lose himself in the warren of alleys and courts surrounding Smith-field. And there was little chance of successfully pursuing someone on foot through its narrow windy lanes.

Alone up on the roof, Pyke thought about Emily and Felix and sought, in vain, to convince himself that he'd made every effort to ensure their safety. Earlier he had taken some laudanum to settle his stomach but the drug had had little noticeable impact. It still felt as if he was swallowing shards of glass. Climbing back into the garret at the top of the building, he tried to ignore the stink of ripe animal flesh that filled the room – the cellar had once been used as a slaughterhouse – and checked his fob-watch. The hands had hardly moved since he had last looked. Back at the window, Pyke saw what looked like an old man scavenging for scraps in the middle of the field, but within a few moments two of his men had appeared from the shadows, rifles slung over their shoulders, and dragged him from the field.

Afterwards, everything went quiet again. There was nothing left for him to do but wait.

An hour later, he left the building by the front door and stepped out into the field, staring up at the dark, starless sky. There were no sounds at all, not even the barking of a dog or the crowing of an early-rising cockerel. Soon the first glimpses of light would be visible to the east and then it would all happen, Pyke thought, trying to keep his nerves under control. The ransom demand had simply said '*Sunday. Smithfield at dawn*'. It was freezing, and Pyke pulled his greatcoat around him and dug his hands into his pockets. Sleet had started to fall and Pyke moved around quickly to keep warm, having a final word with each of the men before returning to his original position in the middle of the field. Though it was surrounded on all sides by buildings, no candles were burning in any of the windows and even the old hospital, on the north side of the field, looked to be deserted. On another day, Pyke might have appreciated the stark beauty and solitude of the scene, but his thoughts were elsewhere. Were Emily and Felix close at hand? And who would actually oversee the planned exchange, the letters in return for Emily and Felix? A dog barked and he jumped, startled by the sudden noise. He checked to see that both pistols were in his belt and ready to fire. A cockerel began to crow and Pyke surveyed the field, gulping down cold air. It was almost time.

Just before six, the sleet turned to snow: not just a light flurry but thick, heavy flakes that fell relentlessly from a grey sky and made it hard for Pyke to see more than a few yards in front of him. He was standing in the middle of the field and couldn't see any of the buildings that surrounded him, nor any of the men he'd positioned at various places around the field's perimeter. The settling snow, which had turned the field into a blanket of brilliant white, had also muffled any noise, and when the chimes of St Paul's struck in the distance, it sounded as if Wren's cathedral were miles away, rather than a few hundred yards. Feeling isolated and exposed, Pyke tried to quell a mounting feeling that he had already lost control of the situation. To calm himself down, he tried to think about what it would feel like to be reunited with Emily and Felix: to hold them in his arms. They would be close by now.

In the end he saw the carriage before he heard it, the clip-clopping of hoofs and the rattling of iron-shod wheels muffled by the snow. The carriage had emerged from a small street on the north side of the square, in the shadows of the hospital, one that Pyke hadn't put a man on. Long Lane, perhaps. Or Cloth Lane, an even smaller street just to the south. It was pulled by two horses and it came to a halt in front of the hospital gates. Pyke didn't stop to think about it. He ran towards it, his arms pumping up and down like pistons, and saw the cloaked driver jump from his station and land awkwardly on the hard ground. He saw the man dart into a nearby alleyway and wondered whether one of his men would chase after, and apprehend, him. No one apart from him was to approach the carriage. That had been the instruction he'd given to the men. Anyone who did was to be shot dead on sight. And under no circumstances were any shots to be fired in the direction of the carriage. Pyke didn't want a stray bullet killing Emily or Felix. The field was still quiet as he neared the carriage. The two black horses tossed their heads up in the air and whinnied. Removing one of the pistols from his belt, Pyke circumnavigated the horses and approached the door. He peered through the mud-smeared glass and that was when he saw her. Alive. His heart leapt. Emily had been tied up and gagged and was wriggling to free herself. There was no sign of Felix. Ripping the door open, he pulled the gag from Emily's mouth and took her in his arms. For a moment, he clutched her and sobbed, their mouths meeting in a messy embrace, a surge of desire rising up in him. She tried to say something but the words tumbled too quickly out of her mouth and he took her face in his hands, kissed her lips and told her to slow down. He pulled out his knife and began to cut the bindings around her wrist.

'Felix,' he started. 'Where's Felix?'

'I don't know. I don't know. They came and took him from me yesterday. I tried to stop them but they tied me up. They were too strong.'

'Who came to take him?' Pyke had cut the bindings around Emily's ankles and now helped her to her feet.

The snow had stopped falling and the entire field was quiet.

'I don't know.' The panic in her voice was unmistakable. 'They wore masks. We were locked in a cellar, not too far from here. But they came and took him away and now I don't know where he is.' Tears were streaming down her cheeks. They embraced again, Pyke taking her in his arms and whispering, 'I love you so much,' and then adding, in the same breath, 'You didn't see their faces?'

Emily pulled away from him and shook her head. There were heavy bags under her eyes and slight bruising around her mouth where the gag had been tied, but otherwise she appeared unharmed.

'I'm sorry, Pyke. I'm sorry for everything. I'm sorry for keeping things from you. I want to tell you the truth.'

'You're Captain Paine. I know.'

Silently she mouthed the word 'how'?

That was when he heard a dog's bark. Close by. Pyke looked up and saw the tawny mastiff, Copper, standing no less than ten yards away, his black head cocked inquisitively to one side.

The first crack of the rifle came shortly afterwards and it took him a few moments to work out that it had come from one of the upper windows in the main hospital building in front of them.

Panicked, Pyke looked around and tried to make sense of what had just happened, Emily, toppling backwards, hands raised to her neck, blood pumping from a wound. She fell and he dived on top of her, instinctively, and far too late to save her from the bullet that had torn a hole in her neck and ripped through her jugular. Another shot was fired, this one whistling harmlessly past them, but the damage had already been done. As hard as he tried, there was nothing he could do to halt the flow of blood gushing from the wound. She looked at him, her eyes swollen with fear, and then tried to speak but the words wouldn't come and then her eyes glazed over and her body went limp. Emily died in his arms, blood still pouring freely from where the bullet had hit her.

The first two rifle shots had taken the men he'd hired by surprise but they quickly retaliated, four or five of them firing shots at the upper-floor windows where the assassin had positioned himself; windowpanes shattering as their bullets punctured one side of the building.

Pyke didn't know how long he sat there, covered – *soaking* – in his wife's blood. A few minutes, perhaps. Maybe as much an hour. He held her blood-drenched head and kissed her still-warm lips. He held her and he wouldn't let go. As he retched and sobbed, giant flakes of snow fell around them, a patch of crimson in an otherwise endless sea of white. Finally he looked up and saw the mastiff, Copper, stooped next to him, licking her blood as if it were a puddle of water.

Captain Paine, RIP.

Without thinking about it, Pyke hurled himself at the dog, going for its throat, but the giant mastiff was too quick for him and sunk its powerful jaws into his wrist and didn't let go until it had touched bone. Screaming, he tried to wrap his other arm around the dog's neck and use his weight to twist the snarling creature on to its back, its tawny fur now also smeared with Emily's blood. Too late, Pyke remembered that Copper was a fighting beast, trained to attack when scenting blood, and though both his arms were now coiled around the animal's throat and its front legs were dangling in the air, the mastiff was still stronger than him, its jaws locked on to his wrist. In the end Pyke had to poke the creature in its eye, to stop it from tearing off his hand, and when its jaws snapped open, he pulled it up off its feet and started to squeeze, the dog snarling at first and then whimpering, but exhaustion did for them both and eventually they came to rest on the hard, frozen ground, Pyke's efforts to strangle the dog becoming, through tiredness, a muted embrace, and very soon the only noise he could hear was the breathy pants of the living dog.

Then he was surrounded by his marksmen. They looked at him, then at Emily and the dog, not knowing what to say. Townsend was there, too, attempting to take charge of the situation. The police would be there soon, he kept saying. Rising to his feet, Pyke told half the group to take Emily's body and the carriage to his uncle's basement shop in St Paul's Yard and wait for him there. The others would come with him: they still had to find the assassin.

Having made a leash from one of the horse's reins, Pyke coiled it around the dog's neck and held on to the other end. Copper tugged hard on his new leash and Pyke allowed the eager mastiff to lead him through the hospital's wrought-iron gates and up some stone steps into the main building. The entrance hall was a frenzy of activity; clearly the volley of rifle shots had sent the porters, nurses and patients into a panic, and some were trying to evacuate the building using a rear entrance. In the mayhem, no one even seemed to notice a man and a dog, both smeared in blood, running across the hall, the dog leading the way to the main staircase, taking the steps two at a time, perhaps following his master's scent.

Holding on to the lead, Pyke followed Copper up a further flight of stairs and along a long, narrow passageway as far as a closed door, where the mastiff hesitated and sniffed, its tail wagging from side to side. It let out an excited bark, and from the other side Pyke heard Jake Bolter say, 'Is that you, Copper?' When the door swung open, Copper pushed ahead of him but Pyke had his pistol ready and swung it around to face Bolter, who'd been shot in the shoulder and stomach and sat propped up against a wall in a small, bare room that reminded Pyke of a prison cell. Pieces of smashed glass lay all around the wounded man. Copper bounded across to greet his master, while Pyke kept the pistol trained on him and kicked the rifle Bolter had used to shoot Emily out of the ex-soldier's reach.

'Who sent you here to kill my wife?'

Bolter had lost a lot of blood and could barely summon enough strength to pat the dog on its head. 'I was meant to get the pair of you, then collect any letters you'd brought with you. I hadn't counted on there being other folk with rifles. You outfoxed me there.' He tried to smile.

'Who gave you the orders?'

'A soldier never gives up the name of his superior officer.'

Pyke stood over him and rammed the pistol into his face. 'My wife was pregnant when you killed her.'

That seemed to cause Bolter a little distress. 'I didn't have nothing against her but I wouldn't have shed any tears over you.'

'Just like you didn't have anything in particular against Johnny Evans and Freddie Sutton?'

'You care about those cullies?'

'So you don't deny killing them?'

'I did the Suttons but Johnny was Trotter's work. Reckoned cutting off the head would spook the folk in Huntingdon as much as the threat of the navvies.' For a moment he shut his eyes and Pyke thought he might have passed away.

But a lick from the mastiff brought him around, and when Bolter next looked up at him, Pyke had trained the pistol on the dog. 'Tell me who gave you your orders or I'll kill your dog.'

'You wouldn't hurt a poor, dumb animal, would you, sir?'

Pyke took aim and fired. The shot tore through one of the dog's legs and the beast flopped to the floor, yelping.

Bolter looked at him, uncomprehending. 'You shot my Copper,' he whispered, the life ebbing from him.

'If you don't tell me who sent you here to kill my wife, I'll aim the next one at his head.'

On the floor, the terrified mutt whimpered and yelped.

'Well?' Pyke removed the other pistol from his belt, raised the barrel and coiled his finger around the trigger.

'Please don't kill my Copper,' Bolter whispered.

Pyke knelt over him. 'Tell me who sent you.'

Bolter slumped forward and murmured, 'Gore.'

'And my son. Where's my child?'

'Your child?'

'Has Gore got my son?'

Bolter took his last breath and died, Copper's attempts to crawl towards his master and bring him back to life coming to nothing. The mastiff tried in vain to haul itself up on to its three good legs but it didn't have enough strength. Like its master, it had lost too much blood. Pyke went to try to pick the dog up but it was too heavy for him to carry on his own. He found a trolley in the passageway and with Townsend's help, he managed to haul the shivering beast up on to it. Pushing the trolley back along the passageway towards the staircase, Pyke reached down and patted Copper on the head. The dog whimpered by way of response.

It took them a half-hour to find a surgeon and another ten minutes for Pyke and two of the men to carry the dying animal from the trolley and down two flights of stairs as far as the operating room. When the man realised what he was being asked to do, he put down his scalpel, removed his gown and said he wouldn't demean his profession by operating on a dog. Pyke offered him fifty pounds if the mastiff survived and the surgeon hurriedly ushered them out of the room to begin his work.

It rained on the morning of Emily's funeral. It rained the day before and it rained the following day, too. The northerly wind that had brought snow with it was replaced by a brisk westerly breeze that warmed things up but swept in wave after wave of thick, dark clouds. The water dripped from branches and gathered in stagnant pools; it turned the already sodden ground into a boggy mush and it drained into rivers and canals until their banks were on the verge of bursting. But still it continued to fall, relentlessly, from skies as black as gunmetal, and though it eased a little when Pyke and three of the servants carried Emily's coffin from the hall on their shoulders, when it came to lowering it down into the freshly dug grave, the skies opened once again and soaked the small congregation of servants.

Pyke hadn't announced the funeral in any of the newspapers, nor invited any of the radicals to attend it. He was determined that she would be buried not as Captain Paine but simply as Emily. He didn't want her death to be turned into a political event.

Some, like Jo, who had known Emily for many years, wept inconsolably; others stared down into the grave, keeping their thoughts to themselves. Pyke stood on his own, at the front of the group, with Godfrey just behind him, lost in his grief, hardly noticing the rainwater as it dripped down his cheeks and neck. He could still taste her in his mouth; he could still smell her on his clothes; his skin was still stained with her blood. There was no formal service and no vicar presided over the short ceremony. No one gave a eulogy or said a few words. To the sound of Jo's sobs, Pyke stared at nothing, thought nothing and felt nothing. In the end, the rain drove everyone back to the hall, where the gloom masked a general air of anxiety, none of the servants knowing what would happen to the hall or their posts. Pyke remained at Emily's graveside, thinking about his wife and the child that had died in her womb. Thinking it was his fault. That was the worst part. Thinking, *knowing* he could have done more.

'You'll catch a terrible chill out here, m'boy. Won't you come inside with me and dry off, have a whisky?'

Pyke turned to his uncle and said, 'I need to find my son.'

'Of course.' Godfrey nodded. 'Is there anything at all I can do?'

'I want you to go and visit a man called Fitzroy Tilling. I'll give you the address. Tell him I need an audience with Peel and the prime minister, Viscount Melbourne, the day after tomorrow. Make it clear that if I don't get what I've asked for, I'll make public information that will threaten the orderly succession of Princess Victoria to the throne and raise the spectre of a Cumberland monarchy. Oh, and insist that Sir John Conroy is forced to attend the meeting, as well.'

Godfrey stared at him, seemingly not knowing what to say or even where to start. 'You have the letters?'

'One day I'll tell you the whole story.'

His uncle nodded. It would have to be enough for the moment. Wet and dejected, he turned and began to trudge back towards the hall.

THIRTY-ONE

The venue chosen for the hastily arranged meeting was Lansdowne House, as coincidence would have it a Palladian mansion on the south side of Berkeley Square, just a few doors from the house that Pyke had rented. The third Marquess of Lansdowne was the Lord President of the Council in Melbourne's cabinet, and Pyke had heard that the marquess sometimes hosted cabinet meetings in his stately home. Pyke viewed the arrivals from his window, and it was only when Peel and Conroy had been deposited at the front steps by their respective carriages that he made the short journey across the square and presented himself at the door. He was ushered into the entrance hall, an elegant room with a marble floor, a carved ceiling and columns leading to the stairs. Having left his coat with the butler, who he then followed into the drawing room, he was announced to Melbourne, Peel and Conroy, who sat in grim-faced silence. Fitzroy Tilling hovered unobtrusively by the door.

'What in God's name is this all about, Pyke ...' Peel stood up to confront him, his eyes blazing with indignation.

Viscount Melbourne had a high forehead partly covered with curly greying hair that extended seamlessly down his long, angular face into bushy sideburns, a beak-like nose and a cleft chin. His demeanour seemed dour and melancholic, as though he wanted neither to be there in the room nor, indeed, to be prime minister, and contrasted with Peel's brusque energy.

Conroy sat to one side and said nothing. His face didn't move when he saw Pyke, nor did his expression give anything away.

'Gentlemen,' Pyke said, ignoring Peel's question and choosing to stand rather than sit down in the armchair they had prepared for him, 'I know you're busy and I won't keep you any longer than I have to.'

But they had all come. That was the most important thing. It showed they took his threat seriously.

Pyke took out both letters and held them up. Still Conroy's expression remained opaque. 'These are copies of letters written by the Duchess of Kent to Sir John Conroy.' With a theatrical flourish he pointed at the comptroller. 'I'll read these, if I may.' Pausing to clear his throat, Pyke presented the evidence that damned Conroy and, by association, the young princess.

After he had finished both letters and returned them to his pocket, Pyke looked up. Peel and the prime minister had gone very still. The two politicians exchanged a nervous look.

'So?' Conroy smoothed back his silver hair and coiled the end of his moustache. 'It doesn't prove anything. There's not one scrap of hard evidence that says I'm the girl's father.'

'You don't deny the letter was written by the duchess, then?'

The comptroller stared at the mantelpiece, not dignifying Pyke with a response.

Pyke glanced over at Tilling. 'Two days ago my wife was assassinated by a man called Jake Bolter at Smithfield.' He saw the shock register on Tilling's face. 'One of the assassin's aims was to secure the safe return of the letters I just read out to you. The other was to kill my wife and me.'

The ransom demand Pyke had received apparently from the Duke of Cumberland had in fact been sent by Sir John Conroy, doubtless with the blessing of both Bellows and Gore. Conroy had waited for Cumberland to depart for Berlin before finally dispatching the note so that Pyke would have no way of finding out from the duke himself whether he really had kidnapped Emily or Felix. As someone with many contacts in royal circles, he had clearly been able to procure Cumberland's seal, and by implicating the duke, Conroy had saved himself from Pyke's wrath in the immediate aftermath of the kidnapping. If all had gone to plan, Conroy would have got his letters back and Pyke would now be dead. Unfortunately for the comptroller neither of these things had come to pass.

The prime minister's frown deepened. 'Why in God's name would anyone want to kill your wife?'

'Because, Prime Minister, she was the radical figure otherwise known as Captain Paine, and her money was being used to try and unionise the navvies working to build the Birmingham railway.'

Peel swapped a brief glance with Tilling. It told Pyke that he had already been told about this development. But Melbourne seemed utterly flummoxed and said, 'I'm sorry, sir, but you've lost me. How is any of this related to the letters you just read out?'

Pyke apologised for the confusion and said it would maybe be best if he explained everything in full. Melbourne nodded in agreement. Pyke walked over to the fireplace and tried to clear his mind. He still didn't have the complete picture and he had to be careful about what he said about Peel's involvement, how much he wanted to implicate the Tory leader. But he knew enough to be able to guess the rest. He waited until he had their full attention before he started.

'About ten months ago, Abraham Gore, the chairman of the Birmingham railway, first came upon rumours that radicals planned to try and persuade the navvies employed to build his railway, and also the Grand Northern, to take their union oaths. Fearing that this would absolutely retard the progress of his railway, Gore decided to act and, in doing so, pursue measures that would both thwart the radicals' plans and damage the prospects of the Grand Northern. But Gore had to tread very carefully. As someone who was well respected in the business world and a close friend of Edward James Morris, the chairman of the Grand Northern, he needed to shield himself from all repercussions that might arise from his actions. In other words, what he needed was someone to blame if things blew up in his face: someone who was violently opposed to the progress of the Grand Northern for his own reasons. This man was Sir Horsley Rockingham, a Huntingdon landowner who'd campaigned against the Grand Northern from the moment he had first heard that it would pass across his land. From the outset, it had been Gore's intention to set up Rockingham to take the blame, if and when his action against the navvies in Huntingdon threatened to unravel out of control. To do this, Gore needed a go-between; someone he could rely on to cajole and prod Rockingham in the "right" direction. He selected someone by the name of Jake Bolter, an ex-soldier who had once served in the same regiment that Rockingham was affiliated to and who had been willing to trade his loyalty to his regiment for large sums of money. In the meantime, Bolter requisitioned the help of a ruffian called Jimmy Trotter, someone he'd met in his former lodging house and a man with even fewer moral scruples than himself.'

Pyke didn't tell them about his own association with Abraham Gore and Gore's attempts to implicate Rockingham in *his* eyes. The anonymous letter alerting him to the landowner's presence in the capital was part of this strategy. That and having Bolter meet Rockingham and show him around. Pyke thought about Gore's unswerving insistence that Morris would never have taken his own life and his suggestion that Bolter may have had something to do with Morris's death, and wondered what he should make of these claims in the light of what he'd discovered about Gore.

'About the same time, the letters I've just read to you were stolen from Conroy's safe and the comptroller here went to see his good friend, Sir Henry Bellows, in a state of what I can only assume was blind panic. You've seen for yourselves the significance of what was taken. I'm sure Conroy was quick to impress this point upon Bellows. And I'm guessing he asked the chief magistrate to assign his best men to the task of recovering the letters. But Bellows would have known right away that he couldn't assign any of his own officers to this task. The work was too dirty and he needed to use people who couldn't be traced back to him. So he turned to his *good* friend Abraham Gore. I know for a fact that Gore and Bellows had already liaised about ways of stamping out radical activity, and the chief magistrate was about to spearhead a crackdown against Julian Jackman and the Wat Tyler Brigade here in London. Gore had already "bought" the chief magistrate's favour by alerting him to plans to move the terminus of the Birmingham railway from Camden to Euston before anyone knew of it, thereby allowing Bellows to buy up properties in the area at a fraction of what they'd eventually be worth.'

Pyke paused for a moment and thought about the performance that Gore had put on for him at the coroner's inquest. All to throw suspicion elsewhere and maintain Pyke's trust, at least until Gore gained control of Blackwood's bank. It was impressive in its own way.

'So Gore employed Jake Bolter and by association Jimmy Trotter to hunt for the stolen letters and told them what he heard from Bellows and hence the comptroller here. That the chief suspect was a kitchen hand who'd worked at Kensington Palace called Kate

Sutton and her betrothed, Johnny Evans. Bolter and Trotter found Johnny easily enough and exhaustive interrogation – Trotter burnt Johnny's flesh with the end of a lighted cigar – revealed that Johnny had given the letters to Kate for safe keeping. But rightly fearing for her life, Kate went into hiding, and Bolter and Trotter were both unable to find where she had gone. Bolter even interrogated her parents in their Spitalfields home, to no avail. When he realised they couldn't tell him what he wanted to know, he slit their throats and let them bleed to death.' Pyke glanced up at the prime minister, who visibly winced at this particular detail.

'Perhaps Johnny died as a result of the torture, perhaps they killed him because he was no longer of any use to them. I don't know. But needing to dispose of his body, they stumbled on the idea of taking it with them to Huntingdon and dumping it there. After all, who would think of looking for a penniless London actor in the middle of the countryside? But just to make sure, they hacked off the man's head and then, rather than bury the headless corpse in a field, they decided to throw it into a river near Huntingdon. Their aim was to further frighten and unsettle the men and women of the town. Remember, they also wanted these same men to violently defend their home against the navvies if and when the navvies could be provoked into attacking it. They did this very successfully. The navvies were routed in the ensuing violence and, in the process, the radicals were driven out of the town and the progress of the Grand Northern Railway arrested. More recently, it should be added, Gore has been using his influence to make sure that the Grand Northern terminates at Cambridge, thereby affording his own railway line a monopoly on all traffic between London and the industrial heartlands of the Midlands and the North. At its most basic, this whole thing was devised by Abraham Gore to break his railway's closest competitor and destroy all attempts to unionise the railway's workforce. A few days ago I saw the radical leader, Julian Jackman. He had been crucified, as a warning to others. My wife, who was also Captain Paine, was shot dead in Smithfield and died in my arms.'

For a while after Pyke had finished telling his story, the room was very quiet. No one was sure how to proceed. As befitted his rank, it was the prime minister who spoke first, sitting forward in his armchair, his hands pressed together. 'I assume you have proof of these very grave accusations.' He would know Abraham Gore very well, Pyke thought, and would perhaps be a little frightened of him, and frightened of any scandal involving a long-time supporter of the Liberals and someone who'd donated large sums of money to the party's coffers.

'Proof?' Pyke wetted his lips.

'Proof that my very good friend, Abraham Gore, was involved in these matters as you have described them.' His eyes were cold and blue.

'No.'

'No?' Melbourne frowned. 'If the law cannot assist your case then I'm afraid you have no case.'

'I'm not intending to plead my case before a court of law.'

'That's because there's no case to answer.' Melbourne clapped his hands together triumphantly. 'My God, I should have you taken off to the Tower just for making such an impertinent accusation.'

'In which case, the letters I read out earlier would be in Cumberland's hands even before the cell door was bolted.' Pyke stared at him. 'In case of my death, my lawyer has been instructed to make the content of the letters public.'

Melbourne studied Pyke's expression, trying to assess the threat he posed. It took Peel's intervention to move the matter forward. 'I'm afraid I can't advise you what to do, Prime Minister, but I'd just like to say that it would be highly dangerous to underestimate this man's resolve or indeed his ruthlessness.'

'You know this man?' Melbourne seemed appalled at this fact.

Peel bowed his head. 'I'm afraid we've had dealings in the past.'

'A man of principle such as yourself.' Melbourne shook his head. 'You disappoint me, Sir Robert. You disappoint me greatly.'

Despite the fact that they led different parties, neither man wanted to entertain the prospect of Cumberland seizing the throne.

Finally Melbourne's morose stare returned wearily to Pyke. 'What is it you want, sir?'

Pyke took out another letter, this time from a different pocket, and held it up. 'This is a hastily scribed letter from Sir Henry Bellows to Gore that bears next Monday's date. I want you to convince the comptroller here that it's in his best interests to deliver it to Gore in person. Convince Conroy that if he does this, and gives Gore an inkling that something is amiss, his future will be no bleaker than it is already. Convince him that this represents his only chance to hold on to what he's already pilfered from the state and avoid punishment for his role in the murders of Johnny Evans and Kate Sutton's parents. Convince him that if he refuses or tries to tip Gore a wink he'll be drummed out of his role at Kensington Palace quicker than you can say Jack Robinson.'

Finally Conroy could contain himself no longer. He sprang up from his chair and screeched, 'This is absolutely unacceptable. I will not be dictated to in these terms.'

But Melbourne ordered him to sit down and not interrupt them again. As Conroy did as he was told, dejected and beaten, Melbourne looked at the letter Pyke was holding and asked what it said.

'Sir Henry wants Gore to know that, fearing my retaliation, he's gone into hiding, and asks Gore to meet him at the address of a property he owns in Somers Town.'

'And has the letter, in fact, been penned by Sir Henry Bellows?' Melbourne asked, confused.

'It's the chief magistrate's handwriting. I helped him with the content.'

The penny finally dropped. 'You mean you ... *forced* him to write it?'

In fact, Pyke had hijacked the chief magistrate's brougham as it left his home in Holland Park earlier that morning and had already taken him to the aforementioned house in Somers Town.

'And you expect me to sit back and do nothing while you propagate this deception against one of my oldest and dearest friends?'

'A friend who's put his advancement and material betterment above any loyalty to you or your party, who's killed or had people killed on his orders, who'll stop at nothing to get what he wants.'

Pyke noticed that Peel had gone very quiet, perhaps fearing that he was about to expose his role in the affair: the fact that he, Peel, had first sent Pyke to Huntingdon in the hope he might dig up something which, in turn, could be used against Abraham Gore. That was why Pyke had wanted the Tory leader to be present at the meeting. He hadn't planned to say anything about Peel's role in the whole business but he wanted the Tory leader to *know* that he'd held his tongue.

This time he wanted Peel in his debt.

'I have to say, Prime Minister, I've conducted my own investigation into Pyke's claims and I feel there's some validity to them,' Peel said, unexpectedly coming to Pyke's rescue.

It was unexpected until Pyke remembered that Peel had wanted to drive a wedge between Gore and Melbourne from the outset.

'You think he's telling the truth? My God ...' Melbourne complexion had turned a ghastly white.

'And what if I refuse to do what this *guttersnipe* is asking me to do?' Conroy said, unable to hold his silence.

Pyke turned his gaze on the comptroller. 'Then I'll pass word to the princess that you sought to weaken her by introducing poison into her food, thereby strengthening your hand in negotiations to become her private secretary. I know you tried to get her to sign a document to this effect only a few weeks ago when she lay on her sickbed with a fever of your making.'

Melbourne slumped back in his armchair, seemingly unable to take on board these further allegations.

To a stunned Conroy, Pyke added, 'Baroness Lehzen suspects you already. You'll have noticed how she won't let you anywhere near the princess's food.'

The comptroller evidently didn't know how to respond, especially in front of two such powerful figures. He licked his parched lips but didn't say anything.

Pyke turned back to Melbourne and said, 'This arrangement suits everyone's best interests. Conroy holds on to his job, the equilibrium is maintained, and you escape from being tainted by the whiff of scandal. Above all, Cumberland is kept in the dark about his claims on the throne. That's what we all want, after all, isn't it? Princess Victoria as our next queen.' He put the letter Bellows had written on the table next to the prime minister, adding, 'Remember, it's to be delivered on Monday. No earlier than Monday.' And then, apparently as an afterthought, Pyke said, 'Oh, and when I take action against the Grand Northern next week, when I do what I plan to do, I want your government and indeed His Majesty's opposition to do precisely nothing. As Abraham Gore might say, I want you to place your faith in the efficacy of the market.' He allowed himself a smile. 'Thank you all for coming and I'll bid you good day.'

Pyke strode calmly out of the room. A slightly flushed Tilling caught up with him in the entrance hall. 'I'm so sorry about your wife. I had no idea ...'

'I know.'

Tilling shifted awkwardly from foot to foot. 'What are you planning to do?'

'I can't tell you.'

'You do know you can't hold the government to ransom.'

Pyke collected his greatcoat from the butler and nodded his thanks. 'I've played my hand: what they decide to do is up to them.' He paused for a moment and added, 'And Peel knows I could have exposed his own complicity in this whole sorry business in front of Melbourne. If he flies off in a rage at me, remind him of that.'

'Pyke ...' Tilling shouted after him as he stepped out on to Berkeley Square.

Pyke turned around, squinting in the sunlight.

'Just remember, nothing you do will bring your wife back.'

Much later Pyke would find out from one of the committee members still loyal to Morris and his vision for the railway that on the same day he had met with Peel and the prime minister, a heavily guarded meeting of the committee and proprietors of the Grand Northern Railway at their head offices in the Square Mile had also met. By all accounts it was a fractious, heated meeting with frank opinions exchanged by all parties. In the first motion, Chauncey Bledisloe was narrowly elected as chairman of the company and in the second it was agreed, by just three votes, that the construction work would terminate at Cambridge. It was also agreed that every effort would be made to ensure that the railway line to Cambridge was completed as quickly as possible. The three votes cast by William Blackwood, representing the interests of Blackwood's bank, proved to be decisive. Gore, who was not present at the meeting and who, according to close friends, had been taken ill, had retreated to his suite of rooms at the Richmond Hotel. Apparently Gore was said to be 'delighted' at the outcome of the Grand Northern's meeting. It meant that he'd finally achieved his long-held objective: a monopoly for *his* railway on all passenger and freight traffic between the capital and points north. Pyke was also told that Gore had employed as many as fifty men to guard the hotel and, for a while at least, he became a self-imposed prisoner there. But his triumph had also come at a hidden cost. As the new majority shareholder in Black-wood's bank, which had invested heavily in the Grand Northern, Gore now needed this venture to be moderately successful. Not perhaps as successful as the Birmingham railway, *his* railway, was and would be, but certainly Gore didn't want the Grand Northern to fail.

If it failed, Blackwood's would suffer and, in turn, he would suffer, too.

It was this Pyke was counting on, and this he would exploit to his own advantage.

The following morning, Pyke rode northwards from Hambledon Hall on a young grey horse and reached Huntingdon by nightfall. It took him all the next day and most of the following one to find what, or rather who, he had been looking for. Red, Billygoat and the other navvies he'd encountered in Huntingdon were drinking in an inn on the road between Peterborough and Ely. As Red explained later that night, after the violent clashes in the town they had been expelled from the parish and told never to return, otherwise they would be charged with conspiracy to riot, criminal damage and disturbing the peace. Red also said they had not managed to find any work in the last month and were down to their last few pennies.

'Perhaps I can help you there,' Pyke said, when he had stood them all a round of drinks. They were sitting around an oak table at the back of the room.

'You mean to say you're offering us work?' Red said, removing his white felt hat and scratching his matted ginger hair.

'Of a sort.'

Red leaned forward, his elbows resting on the table. 'I'm listening.'

Quickly Pyke whispered to Red what he wanted them to do. When he'd finished, the navvy whistled and shook his head. 'That's a serious business. What makes you think we're the men to help you?'

'The same man who orchestrated the rape and murder of Mary and planned for the townsmen in Huntingdon to drive your men into that river, and to their deaths, has greatly profited from the situation.'

Red eyed him carefully. 'So what you're proposing to do would hit him hard?'

'If it was done right, it could ruin him. And many others like him.' He didn't want to go into the details and Red didn't look as if he wanted to hear them.

'You're asking us to break the law.'

'And I'm prepared to pay you handsomely for doing so.'

'What do you mean by handsome?' Red said, his gappy teeth showing behind his lips.

'Fifty guineas a man.' With the money he'd made from the deal with Gore, Pyke could easily afford it. Not that Red knew it, but he'd be willing to pay up to ten times that figure.

'Fifty guineas?' Red hardly seemed to know what to do. It would take them two or three years to earn that kind of sum.

'I'd need more than the nine of you, though,' Pyke said, matter-of-factly. 'At short notice, how many others do you think you could get?'

Red scratched the stubble on his chin and shrugged. 'I reckon we could gather up, say, twenty more bodies by the end of tomorrow.'

'As many as you can get.'

Red seemed surprised. 'And you'll pay 'em all fifty guineas? A man like you must have mighty deep pockets, if you don't mind me sayin' so.'

'How I spend my money is my business,' Pyke said, brusquely. 'I'll need you all down at my home near Enfield by Sunday night. I'll arrange transportation. Two wagons ought to do it. The drivers will know where to go. Just have your men ready and waiting at the Stag in Peterborough by two on Sunday afternoon. Weather permitting, the journey shouldn't take longer than five hours.'

'You're assuming we've already agreed to help you.'

Pyke held his gaze. 'Are you saying you won't?'

Red looked at the others. 'There'll be repercussions. We'll be hunted down, won't we?'

'What if I could guarantee that no one will ever hold you responsible?'

'An act like you're planning? They'll chase you and anyone involved to the ends of the earth.'

'But as I just said, what if I could guarantee that this wouldn't happen?'

Red stared at him. 'And how could you do that?'

'I'm a resourceful man.' Pyke shrugged. 'But I'm also a man of my word and as a man of my word, if I say there will be no repercussions, I'd expect you to believe me.'

Red put the white felt cap back on his head. 'Reckon you've got all the answers, don't you?'

'In this instance, yes.' Pyke saw something in his eyes and added, 'But you're still not convinced?'

'You're right. I'm torn.'

'Between?'

'I'd like to see this gen'leman get what's coming to him, that's for certain.'

'But?'

Red took a slurp of his beer. 'We like to *build* things,' he said, simply. 'It's what we do.'

Pyke nodded. 'Someone I knew who died recently also liked to build things. You've never seen anyone with more energy, more passion. He had a vision. He wanted to build a railway that ran from London all the way to York, a cheap, quick form of transportation that would change people's lives for ever and would last for a hundred years.' He waited for a few moments and looked into Red's piercing green eyes. 'His dream died with him. That railway isn't going to be built. Greed and self-interest on the part of shareholders and committee members have won the day. You might think what I propose to do is nihilistic ...'

Red was frowning. 'Nihilistic?'

'Pointless, barbaric even.'

'And you don't?'

Pyke thought about Emily and felt his anger return. 'Sometimes all we've got left is the impulse to destroy.'

Red thought about this. 'You talk about greed and self-interest like they're wrong but you're offering to pay us an enormous amount of money.'

'So?'

'So maybe there's a virtue in greed, after all.'

Pyke looked at him and smiled. 'You could be a philosopher yet.'

'Does the job pay well?' Red asked, playfully.

Pyke shrugged. 'Fifty guineas for a morning's work isn't a bad start.'

THIRTY-TWO

At dawn on the following Monday morning, the first of a multitude of explosions could be heard in the vicinity of the town of Bishop's Stortford in Hertfordshire. It was a loud blast that woke up many of the town's residents and was quickly followed by further explosions detonated at intervals of approximately five hundred yards along the railway line. Similar blasts were heard in the vicinity of Hertford, Ware, Hoddesdon, Broxbourne, Waltham Cross, Edmonton, Ponders End, Angel Road, Tottenham Hale, Lea Bridge and Stratford. Initially, once the acrid plumes of black smoke had cleared, those who chose to investigate the blasts reached the same conclusion: that some kind of terrible accident had befallen the fledgling railway and that stores of black powder used by the navvies to blast their way through rocky impediments had spontaneously combusted. But it was only later, when the subcontractors responsible for overseeing the work at different points along the line inspected the terrible damage, that it dawned on people that the railway had been victim to a series of co-ordinated attacks: carefully planned explosions that had decimated much or all of the track already laid and created blast craters as deep as six feet along every part of the line.

At first light that same morning, thirty-six men, each one responsible for a mile of the thirty-six miles of track already completed or under construction, had moved along the railway line from Bishop's Stortford in the north to Stratford in the south, lighting and setting off pre-prepared, carefully positioned charges along the way. In order to prepare for this, Pyke had broken into a storage warehouse belonging to a contractor working for the Birmingham railway – hoped Gore would later appreciate the irony – and loaded up his carriage with more than a ton of black powder. Having transported this material back to Hambledon, he had then set about assembling a hundred or so explosive devices. To do this, he had poured equal measures of the powder into already prepared parchment tubes and, employing a design associated with a Cornishman, William Bickford, had made a safety fuse for each tube by carefully wrapping strands of jute around a core of powder and coating it with varnish. To detonate the powder all the navvies had to do was light the end of the fuse and move on to the next device.

Under Red's command, it had taken the crew of navvies less than fifteen minutes to set off a total of one hundred and thirty-seven explosive devices: the sheer extent of the devastation caused would not become apparent until later. No lives were lost and none of the navvies was injured while trying to set off the parchment tubes. Bickford's fuse had been an unqualified success.

On that morning, aided by Townsend, Pyke had ridden between the warehouses and storage barns utilised by the various sub-contactors charged with the task of building different sections of the railway line and set light to them with rags doused in lamp oil. In all, they razed four large warehouses and eighteen smaller barns to the ground during the course of the morning.

At the same time in London, the crew of boys Godfrey employed to distribute his weekly unstamped newspaper, the *Scourge*, passed out more than ten thousand printed handbills announcing that Captain Paine had just declared war on the tyrants and devil-capitalists of the ruling class and stating that the action taken against the Grand Northern Railway, in retaliation for the deaths of three navvies in Huntingdon earlier in the autumn, would be just the start of a vicious campaign waged by the working poor up and down the country in support of a more equitable distribution of wealth. Pyke, who had overseen the contents of the handbill, signed off with the line: 'The whole commercial system needs to be smashed and nothing short of revolution will produce a corrective'. Pyke had found it scribbled in one of Emily's diaries.

Once the initial shock had subsided, representatives from Grand Northern ventured out to inspect the damage and discovered it to be even worse than they had feared. Whole sections of the completed or half-completed track lay in ruins, the iron rails torn apart and bent jagged by the blast and the wooden sleepers utterly obliterated; blast craters deep and wide enough to accommodate ten men punctuated the entire line at regular intervals of a few hundred yards; and in many cases the various embankments and cuttings, which had taken months if not years to forge, had been damaged beyond recognition. Surveyors and engineers who inspected the devastation informally told the subcontractors and representatives from the railway that the cost of repairing and replacing the damaged track might exceed half a million pounds.

On that Monday Pyke waited, at the address he'd designated in Somers Town, for Abraham Gore, who would have been expecting to meet Sir Henry Bellows, but the banker and railwayman didn't show up, nor was any explanation offered as to why he had turned down his friend's plea for help. Later, Pyke heard a rumour that he was too ill to travel. Undeterred, Pyke passed word to the prime minister that Gore was to be delivered, without further delay, to Hambledon.

In terms of the railway, it didn't take long for the bickering to start. The suppliers, many of whom hadn't been paid for what they had sent to the subcontractors, demanded what was owed to them because they too were being hounded by those who provided the raw materials. The subcontractors, who had lost everything in the fires Pyke had started, then demanded money owed to them by the Grand Northern, and the railway company, in turn, went cap in hand to the proprietors for additional funds – because its own reserves had been depleted by the expense of having to buy land for building on at extortionate prices. News of the devastation quickly reached the City and the scale of the damage was reported in all the newspapers. All condemned it as a 'terrorist outrage' and called for the perpetrators, particularly the mysterious figure known as Captain Paine, to be hunted down and then hung, drawn and quartered. The immediate effect was a cataclysmic fall in the Grand Northern's share price. For the previous few weeks, buoyed by rumours that a new chairman would focus resources on completing a section of the line by the end of the following year, the share price had risen from a low of eleven pounds to almost thirty-seven pounds on the morning of the attacks. By the next day the price has slumped to less than ten pounds, and by the end of the week, amidst growing rancour, trading in Grand Northern's shares was suspended when the price fell to nothing. Investors who had been tempted by the lure of rising share prices and quick profits saw the value of their holdings decimated. Overnight people's life savings were destroyed. Certainly these same people were in no mood, or indeed no position, to pay a penny to the company when, more out of desperation than judicious thinking, it put out a call to proprietors for the next instalment of capital. By law the proprietors were obliged to cough up what the company demanded. None of them did, of course, and the entire system ground to a standstill. The spectre of mass bankruptcy began to hover over people's heads.

Just when it looked as if the situation couldn't get any more serious, Pyke moved to intensify the crisis. In his last days at Blackwood's bank, he had borrowed a large sum of money on short notice from a bill-broking friend who, under Pyke's instructions and in the wake of the financial crisis that was threatening to engulf the entire City, recalled the loan. With too little held in reserve to meet this debt, William Blackwood had no choice but to call in the money Blackwood's had loaned the Grand Northern – all one hundred thousand pounds – to cover what it owed. He had to give a significant period of notice, of course, but since everyone knew that the Grand Northern was in no position to pay back the loan and had no funds to begin the enormous task of repairing the damage, those who had deposited their hard-earned savings with Blackwood's started to demand their money back. Overnight panic among its customers spread, and by the middle of the week there were queues stretching down the stairs from the main banking hall into Sweeting's Alley and along Cornhill as far as Bishopsgate. The bank's already depleted reserves could not meet this demand and despite the large sums of his own money that Gore ploughed into it to plug the hole, Blackwood's was forced to close its doors to note-holders and depositors: the crisis had gained its first casualty. Later on, it was reported that the bank's chairman, William Blackwood, had slit his wrists with a razor and bled to death in his own home.

As the situation started to unravel further, calls for the government to intervene and bail out the Grand Northern – or at the very least make available funds so that it could pay off some of its creditors and start the clean-up work – intensified. Newspaper editors demanded that Melbourne's cabinet take immediate action to restore confidence in the battered financial system and prop up the ailing railway company. Investors who had lost their life-savings when the Grand Northern's shares were rendered worthless marched on

Whitehall demanding recompense. Everyone, it seemed, expected the government to step in and announce a series of measures that would alleviate the problem, but it did nothing. And when the government did nothing, pressure was brought to bear on the opposition to take a stance but the Tory leader, Robert Peel, was apparently unwell and convalescing at his country home.

During this time, despite the near-continuous delegations that were sent to Pyke's new home in Berkeley Square, and the Hambledon estate, begging that he at least discuss the situation with representatives sent by Melbourne and Peel, Pyke turned them away with a simple message. They knew what he wanted; if he didn't get what he wanted, the threat of a Cumberland monarchy remained.

During this time, Pyke dozed fitfully at night and sleep-walked through the day drugged on laudanum. If he shut his eyes, she was there; if he saw faces moving towards him in a crowd, she was among them; if he walked into a room, it was as though she'd just left, a trace of her perfume lingering in the air. At night, she would come to him in his dreams, begging him to find Felix and telling him not to give up on himself. Pyke found there was something reassuring about those dreams until Emily's face transformed into a grinning demon and all he could hear were the same words repeated over and over: *when will it all be enough?* He would wake up, his body drenched with sweat, disoriented until he remembered where he was and what had happened, and then a feeling of shame, guilt and loss would wash over him until he could lie there no more. On such occasions, he would reach for his laudanum and kill the time until dawn walking the dark corridors of the old hall, thinking about what he might have done, what might have saved Emily's life. He would pause only in Felix's room, and he might pick up his son's blanket, bring it to his nose and inhale the scent, trying to keep alive, if only in his own mind, the hope that Felix wasn't dead; that something good might yet come from the hole he had dug himself.

Bentley's jewellers was a tall, narrow shop on the south side of the Strand, a little before Temple Bar, in between a bookseller and a stationer's. Inside was a cornucopia of silver and gold bracelets, pins, necklaces, rings and timepieces of every size, make and denomination. Townsend had already explained to the owner, Jeremy

Bentley, what was going to happen – and he'd already been well paid for his services – so that when the bell rang at the front of the shop, just before closing time, indicating that their visitor had arrived, Pyke retreated to the back room and waited, while Bentley introduced himself and invited the new arrival to join him in the parlour, where the light was better and they wouldn't be interrupted. Bentley stepped to one side and allowed the customer to enter the back room first; Pyke was waiting for him and after a few moments, Jem Nash knew he was trapped. It was written all over his face: the shock, the thought of escape, the fear and finally the resignation.

Pyke shoved Nash down into a chair. For some reason, his assistant looked older, as though the difficulties of the previous month had aged him beyond recognition. His once sparkling eyes were lifeless; his skin was grey and his hair seemed suddenly thinner. Bentley had left them alone, as he'd been instructed to do, and for a while, the only noise in the building was the sound of the ticking clocks. Pyke held out his hand and said, 'The watch, if you please.' He added, almost as an afterthought, 'The watch you stole from Morris when you killed him.'

Nash tried to laugh but it was flat and hollow and his eyes betrayed him. 'I don't know what you mean ...'

'*The watch*,' Pyke shouted, so loudly it made Nash jump.

Nash fumbled in his pocket and pulled out the timepiece, handing it to Pyke but not meeting his gaze. Pyke took it and inspected the diamond-encrusted case.

'It's fitting, in a way, that your greed was your undoing, don't you think?' When Nash didn't answer, Pyke said, 'What did you hope to get for the watch? A few hundred at most?' He waited and added, 'It's not much, is it? If you consider what you're going to lose as a result.'

'Pyke, I know what you must be thinking ...'

Pyke punched Nash in the face, splitting open his cheek and sending him spinning to the floor. 'Don't presume to know anything about me, you miserable little shit.' He ordered Nash to get up, and when he did, Pyke pushed him down on to the chair. Nash clutched his bruised cheek and started to cry. It took every ounce of Pyke's self-control not to beat him further.

'There's a price to pay for what you've done, Nash,' Pyke said, 'and this is your chance to atone.' He waited for a moment. 'Had

Morris found out you were blackmailing him? And what did you have over him? A love letter he'd written to one of your friends perhaps?'

'He was a sentimental old man. What he wrote didn't leave too much room for the imagination. A jury wouldn't have needed much else to put him up on the gallows.'

Pyke gritted his teeth. He wanted hit Nash again but managed to restrain himself. 'And you find it amusing?'

'To be honest, I find it a little pathetic.'

'That he had feelings for another human being and took the time to express them in words?'

Chastened, Nash gripped the edge of his chair.

'I take it you'd had your eyes on Morris for a while,' Pyke said, 'but then you lost seven thousand on one of Barnaby Hodges' tables and suddenly you needed some money quickly.'

'If I didn't pay him, Hodges would have killed me. Even if I'd run away, he would have paid someone to track me down.'

'Did you know Morris would come to *me* for the money you were blackmailing him for?'

'No.' Nash shook his head vigorously as if to underline the point.

'So what did you think when you found out that Morris was borrowing it from the bank?'

'At first, I didn't think about it. I mean, it didn't matter to me where the money came from. Morris could afford it, and he didn't know I had anything to do with the blackmail. If he borrowed it from the bank, then he'd have to pay it back, wouldn't he?'

'But then you saw this chance of fucking me and you grabbed it with both your grubby little hands.'

'No! *God*. It was never about you.' He sounded angry for the first time.

'Not about me?'

'Hodges sent one of his doormen to my lodgings. A brute called Miller. He was the one who'd beaten me before. This time I was ready for him. I didn't intend to kill him until he took out a piece of lead pipe and told me he was going to smash my brains into a pulp. I had a knife on me and I used it. He bled all over the floor. I'd never seen so much blood. And I panicked. I didn't know what to do with the body. There was no way I could carry it down the stairs, into the yard and somehow dispose of it. Someone would have seen me and, anyway, if Hodges ever found out I'd stabbed one of his men, he wouldn't have left me alone. Not ever.'

'That's when you came upon the idea of faking your own murder.' Pyke could see it now. It made a certain amount of sense.

'I'd read about the headless corpse in Huntingdon like everyone else. I thought if I dressed Miller in my clothes and managed to hack off his head, everyone would mistake him for me and assume I'd been killed by the Huntingdon madman. That way, I'd solve the problem of what to do with the body in my lodgings. I'd still get the money from Morris and I'd get to keep it, too. Hodges would think I was dead. It was the only way out of the hole I'd dug myself.'

'And when your body was stolen before the inquest, people would just blame the resurrectionists.'

Nash nursed his bruised cheek and nodded.

'So why did you have to steal the loan documents from the vault? That's when it became personal. Did you do it just to spite me? Because I'd humiliated you in front of the cashiers?'

'Not at all,' he said, shaking his head. 'But once I'd made the decision, you were always going to be my problem.'

'Me?'

'You told me you were going to Huntingdon. I guessed your visit there must have had something to do with the headless corpse.'

'So?'

'If my body was found in a similar state, I knew for a fact you wouldn't accept the coincidence. That's why I had to make it *seem* personal. I didn't *want* to drag you into it but I didn't have a choice.' Nash managed a faint smile. 'I don't know if you've noticed, but you tend to believe people are out to get you. If you believed what happened was part of a plot against *you*, you wouldn't see my death purely as a coincidence. You'd see it as a concerted attempt to harm you ...'

Pyke considered what he'd been just told and weighed it up in the light of his own discoveries.

'So you paid the gypsy woman to harass me in front of the bank and steal the safe key from my chain.'

Nash bowed his head and nodded.

'There were two keys: the key to the safe and another one. I want that other one back.'

'I don't know where it is,' Nash muttered, still staring at the floor. 'I think the old woman kept it or threw it away.'

Pyke felt a surge of anger rip through his body. The knife was in his hand and he jabbed the tip of the blade into Nash's chin.

Hands trembling, Nash produced a different key from his pocket. 'Please, *take it*. I've been living in lodgings in Fulham. Most of my share of the money is still there, hidden under the floorboards.'

Pyke took a sharp breath. He wasn't irritated by Nash's efforts to try to ingratiate himself or even by his callow efforts at self-justification but by the realisation that he'd once seen, or thought he'd seen, a little of himself in his young assistant. Could he have been that blind? To have imagined he shared anything with this petulant liar?

'I said earlier it was time for you to answer for what you've done.'

'And I have. I've told you the truth. And you can have the money back. All of it. I'll make sure you get the whole ten thousand, too.' Nash described where the lodgings were and let out a brief sob.

'I'm not interested in the money.'

He looked up at Pyke, this time with a frown. 'What?'

'I said I'm not interested in the money. I'm not even interested in the fact that you betrayed my association with Ned Villums to Peel and Fitzroy Tilling.'

That made Nash's eyes bulge. 'What *do* you want, then?' He seemed bewildered.

'I want to know why you killed Morris.'

Nash fell silent and his legs stopped twitching.

'You've got the watch. I know you killed him. I just want you to own up to your mistakes.' Pyke made out he was about to strike Nash again and the young man cowered, his hands raised to protect himself.

'I didn't *mean to*,' he said, on the verge of tears again. 'Or I didn't plan to.'

'Then why do it?'

'It was late. Most of the guests had left already. Morris was drunk. Drunker than I've ever seen him before and irate as well.'

'Is it any wonder?' Pyke said, interrupting. 'You'd just blackmailed him out of ten thousand pounds.'

'But Morris didn't know it was me, did he?'

Pyke nodded for him to continue.

'He cornered me in the supper room. He wanted someone to confide in. He knew I knew about the ten thousand. He told me someone was blackmailing him. He didn't say what it was about and I didn't ask. But he also told me he knew who it was. He said he'd hired someone to follow the money. I thought we'd been careful but he knew; he gave me my friend's name. The right address, as well. He'd only just heard about it that night. He told me he was going to take action in the morning. I panicked. At first I just wanted to shut him up. I grabbed the nearest thing I could find – a table weight – and hit him with it. I must have hit him harder than I'd first thought. He went down and stopped moving. I didn't stop to see whether I'd killed him or not. I fled through one of the doors at the back of the building.'

Pyke studied his expression, trying to detect obvious signs that he'd been lying, but there weren't any. Nash was good. He deserved credit for that, at least. 'But someone saw you, didn't they? Someone saw what you'd done; someone saw you standing there over Morris's body. Tell me. Was it Gore and Bolter or just Bolter on his own? No, Gore would have had to have been there.'

Nash stared at him, aghast. 'How did you know?'

'Gore liked Morris. Even though they were rivals and despite the fact that he had no compunction about killing insignificant people, *poor* people, Gore had never wanted to actually kill Morris. Of course, he could have called the police there and then and handed you to them on a plate. But Gore saw an opportunity, didn't he? He recognised you. He realised you worked for me. He had Bolter hide the body. Then he sat you down and proceeded to get everything he wanted out of you. I'm guessing he approved of your plan to steal the loan papers from the vault: anything to weaken my grip on the bank. But he must have asked for something else; he must have wanted something else. That's when I thought about your five per cent stake in the bank. In the case of your death, your shares were meant to come back to me. I assumed you were dead. I assumed the five per cent stake would revert to my ownership. Gore made an offer for a third share of the bank and told me he'd be happy if I retained a fifty-one per cent controlling interest in it. In reality he had your five per cent in his pocket as well. I wouldn't have known this at the time but you'd already agreed to sell him your shares, hadn't you? And together with William's holdings, it would have given Gore a controlling interest in the bank and allowed him to steal it from under my nose.' Pyke looked around him and shrugged. 'All Bolter had to do was stay behind, with or without the caretaker's knowledge, and make Morris's death look like a suicide. If Morris's death had been proven to be murder, the spotlight might have fallen on Gore's sharp business practices. No, suicide was the best verdict all around. The best for you; the best for Gore. But I just have one more question that I need you to answer.' Pyke knelt down on the carpet and whispered in Nash's ear, 'Why did you send the deeds to Morris's estate to his widow?'

'Because Gore asked me to.'

'Just like that?'

Nash shrugged. 'The papers didn't mean anything to me.'

Pyke thought about it for a moment. What did it prove? On its own, nothing. But it did raise another, altogether more disturbing prospect. What if Gore was involved with Marguerite?

'What's going to happen to me?' Nash looked around for a possible escape route but there was nowhere for him to go.

Pyke pointed down at the Turkey carpet. 'There's a wheelbarrow waiting outside and a skiff moored by the Arundel stairs. I'm going to wrap you up in the carpet, haul you outside to the barrow and wheel you down to the skiff. Of course by then you'll be dead and none of this will matter.'

Nash started to smile. 'That's a joke, right?'

Removing his knife, Pyke shook his head. 'You should know by now I never joke when it comes to killing someone.'

'You can't help me?' Nash's pleading expression made Pyke hate him even more. 'Not even for old time's sake? *Please* ...' He tried to leap up from his chair and push past Pyke but didn't make it up off his feet.

It took him less than five minutes to cart the large barrow down the narrow lane to the waiting skiff and another few minutes to lift the carpet, which he'd tied up with rope and weighed down with stones, into the boat. The chilly night air smelled of rotten fish and raw sewage. Leaving the barrow at the top of the stairs, Pyke used the sculls to push himself away from the bank and began to row, each stroke taking him farther towards the middle of the river and giving him a clearer view of the lattice of wharfs and warehouses that lined the bank. Despite its stench, Pyke had always loved the dirty brown Thames. He had always loved walking along the cramped, muddy lanes that led down to the river and suddenly coming on it and being assailed by its vastness, the flotsam and jetsam of humanity, water and sky merging into one, the buildings made to look insignificant in its wake. But on this occasion, Pyke wasn't thinking about the grubby majesty of the river or how small and quiet the city looked from such a vantage point. Rather he steered the skiff out into the part of the river where the tide was strongest, picked up one end of the carpet, lifted it over the edge of the boat and pushed from the other end. Weighed down by the stones, it sank without a trace, just a few bubbles rippling the surface, and then everything went quiet. Pyke started to row back towards the bank, thinking only about Felix and whether he had already met a similar fate.

'My dear boy, you look terrible.' Godfrey gave him an awkward hug. 'Aren't they feeding you properly?' They were standing in the entrance hall at Hambledon, the hack-chaise that his uncle had arrived in disappearing along the driveway. Royce appeared and took Godfrey's coat. Pyke told him to bring a bottle of claret to the drawing room and led his uncle past the old chapel, which he had converted into a billiards room, explaining that Royce hadn't spoken a word to him since he'd dismissed all but four of the servants a few days earlier.

'I hope you didn't get rid of the cook. As I said, you could do with being fed a little.'

'The cook, Royce, Jennings to drive the carriage, and Jo.' Pyke pushed open the door and looked at the piano, for a moment expecting Emily to be there playing, her face fixed in concentration and her body moving to the rhythm of the piece. Godfrey followed him into the room and they both gravitated towards the fire burning in the grate.

'Dare I even ask? Is there any news?'

Pyke shook his head.

There were a hundred men combing the streets of the city looking for any sign of his son – and he'd put up a reward of ten thousand pounds – but no one had seen or heard a thing.

'Royce thinks I've acted callously towards people, some of whom worked here for more than twenty years.'

Godfrey stared down at the fire. 'Well, the old place certainly seems a lot quieter.' Realising what he'd said, he added, quickly, 'I didn't mean ... I'm so sorry, dear boy. I just meant...'

Pyke waved away the apology. 'I'm sure he thinks I've pissed on everything he holds dear.'

'Perhaps you'll regret the hastiness of your actions later, once this is finished and Felix is returned to you, and you'll reconsider ...' Pyke gave his uncle a hard stare and he reddened and stammered, 'Then again, perhaps you won't.'

'Sometimes I think about taking a torch to this whole building and watching it go up in flames.'

Godfrey shuffled awkwardly in front of the fire. 'I've come from the city. The situation is still dire ...'

'And you think it's my fault?'

'I didn't say that, dear boy ...'

'But?'

'Some people have lost everything. Their life savings. Ordinary people with wives and families.'

'I just want my son. Gore knows where he is, what's happened to him. When they give me Gore, I'll let them do what they want.'

'But they can't hold out for much longer. Melbourne's being crucified in the press for not doing anything to help.'

'And if Cumberland gets the tiniest sniff that his claim to the throne might be a legitimate one, things will get much, much worse.'

Godfrey turned to face him, his expression almost pleading. 'And would anarchy on the streets and the whiff of revolution in the air be enough?'

'Enough in what sense?'

'Would it be enough to compensate you for what you've lost?' Godfrey patted him gently on the shoulder. 'You're grieving, my dear boy, and that's understandable. You've suffered a terrible, *terrible* loss. But is it right or fair that you make everyone else suffer with you?'

'Is that what you think I'm doing?'

'The handbills you asked me to distribute,' Godfrey said, shaking his head. 'This isn't about continuing Emily's legacy. She might have dreamed about bringing down this government but her ambitions always exceeded mere punishment and retribution. For her, it was about trying to build a fairer, more humane world. I look at what you're doing now and it's hard not to think this is about vengeance, pure and simple.'

'If the prime minister wants to step in and save the day for all those who've lost their fortunes, he knows what he needs to do first.'

'But he's not going to do it,' Godfrey said, exasperated. 'Don't you see that, dear boy? Gore's one of them. They won't give him up to a commoner like you. It's just not in their nature.'

'Then their nature will have to change.'

Royce appeared, carrying a bottle of claret and two glasses on a silver tray. There was a letter on the tray, too, and when Pyke asked why Royce hadn't brought it to him before, Royce told him that the staff, such as they were, were so overworked that little things, inevitably, would be overlooked. Pyke took the tray, handed it to Godfrey and slapped the butler in the face. 'The next time you don't bring me a letter the moment it's delivered, I'll kill you.'

Godfrey didn't say a word. He handed Pyke the letter, put the tray down on top of the piano and poured two large glasses of wine.

Pyke took the envelope, inspected it and then tore it open. Briefly he read the note, his expression giving nothing away.

'Well?' Godfrey asked, his lips moist with claret. 'Is it good news?'

'Not if you're Abraham Gore.'

That got his uncle's attention.

'Gore has given himself up to Melbourne. The note says he'll be delivered here, to me, tomorrow morning.'

'So you've won, my boy? You've done it. You've got what you wanted.' Godfrey sounded almost jovial.

'I know what I want,' Pyke said, staring out of the window, 'and I know it can never happen.' He turned back to his uncle. 'That's the hardest thing to come to terms with.'

THIRTY-THREE

Pyke walked the final half-mile up the drive towards the elegant Palladian house because he didn't want to give Marguerite the chance to prepare for his arrival. In spite of Gore's assurances, his stomach was knotted and he was so tired from the exertions of the previous week that he almost had to crawl on his hand and knees the final few yards to the front steps.

He found Felix sitting on Marguerite's lap on a sofa in the drawing room. She was reading him a story. For a moment he watched from the threshold. If he hadn't known otherwise, the scene could have been one of domestic bliss. A log fire burned in the grate and his son seemed enthralled by the story she was reading for him. With his rosy cheeks and sparkling eyes, Felix appeared to be in good health, and while she read, Marguerite stroked his hair with obvious affection. She wore a simple dress and her long blonde curls tumbled down around her glowing face, radiating a contentedness Pyke hadn't seen in her before.

It was Felix who noticed him standing in the doorway first and he bolted off her lap before she could stop him. 'Daddy, Daddy,' he screamed excitedly, as Pyke gathered him up into his arms and gave him a hug. His skin smelled of soap and his breath of chocolate. 'I've missed you so much,' he whispered in the boy's ear.

'Mrs Maggie promised that you and Mummy would come back and get me soon,' Felix said, once Pyke had put him down.

'And has Mrs Maggie treated you well?' he asked, glaring at her out of the corner of his eye.

'We've been walking every day and I've learned all these new words and we've been reading this story ...'

Pyke bent over and ruffled the boy's hair. 'Perhaps you could leave us alone for a few minutes.'

Felix looked up at Pyke, sighed and then glanced over at Marguerite. 'If I have to.'

When they were alone, Pyke remained where he was; not trusting himself to get any closer to her.

'I was told you were dead. I can't believe it. I'm so happy you're alive,' she cried, approaching and trying to embrace him, her face flushed with a look of relief that Pyke didn't find altogether convincing.

'Is that so?' He pushed her away.

'I was told you'd be killed ...'

'By whom?'

She again tried to embrace him but he pushed her away once more. For a short while they looked at one another, not speaking.

'He's a beautiful boy,' she said, after a few moments, adjusting her petticoats and sitting down.

Pyke looked into her face. 'What are you doing, Maggie?'

'I live here.'

'With my son?'

She was staring at the fire, one side of her face lit up by the flames. 'Gore told me you were dead. Emily, too. He offered me Felix. Either I took him, Gore said, or he would spend the rest of his childhood in Prosser's asylum.'

'Yes, he told me about your cosy arrangement. He gave you my son and the deeds to this place and by way of exchange you gave Gore Morris's shares in the Grand Northern Railway.' Pyke could feel the heat on his skin, his anger not yet tempered by relief.

'You make it sound so grubby.' But she still refused to look up at him.

'An *apparently* orphaned child for five thousand shares: how exactly does it sound to you?'

Maggie's face became thoughtful, her eyes staring into space. 'He looks so much like James. You know he's the age James was when he died. But they're such different personalities. James was rambunctious. Felix is far more circumspect, or perhaps cautious would be a better word, but he's got such a sharp mind.'

'And the other boy? The one you buried in the garden. Was he different again?'

She raised her eyes to meet his. 'James said the two of you had spied on me from the edge of the field that day.'

'James?'

'Did I really say James?' She laughed, as though the matter were inconsequential. 'I meant Felix, of course.'

Pyke shook his head. 'You need help, Maggie.'

That seemed to draw her out of herself. '*I* need help? Is it wrong to want to give a destitute child a loving home?'

'A child who I'd guess looks just like your dead son, plucked from the workhouse by Jake Bolter?' There had been a resemblance to Felix, too.

'*Our* son, Pyke. Remember he was your child, too.'

Pyke watched her carefully and said, 'You took him away from me. I never even knew he existed. As far as I'm concerned, Maggie, I've only ever had one son.'

A moment's silence passed between them. She looked away, frowning. 'How did you know the boy looked like James?'

When Pyke didn't say anything, she thought about it and stumbled on the answer herself. 'Oh God, you didn't desecrate his grave, did you?' Not trying to hide her disgust.

'Emily and Felix had just been kidnapped. For a while, I thought you might have been responsible.'

'*Me*? I didn't even know they'd been taken from you. I was just told you'd died in some terrible accident. You and Emily.'

'And you didn't think to investigate what Gore told you?' Pyke shook his head. 'You didn't make enquiries about the funeral?'

'I tried, but Gore told me I should concentrate on taking care of your son. He said that was what you would have wanted.'

'And you lapped it up like a kitten in front of a fresh saucer of milk.'

Insulted, Marguerite sprang to her feet and stepped towards him. 'Is that what you really think of me? Is that how little you know me?'

'I don't know you in the slightest. But I never really did, even when we were both younger.'

Her indignation cooled. 'You have to believe me, Pyke. I didn't know *any* of this. I didn't know Emily and Felix had been taken from you.' She hesitated, colour rising in her neck. 'Your wife must be beside herself with worry ...'

Pyke held up his hand. 'I'm not going to play along with your little games.'

'What games?'

'Emily's dead. But you knew that. You knew she'd been shot and killed by one of Gore's assassins.'

Her gasp of astonishment may have sounded convincing to some but he wasn't taken in by it. 'But Gore had already warned you I was alive, hadn't he? Warned you I'd come here looking for my son and told you Emily was dead.'

Marguerite stared down at her feet. The tips of her ears had turned crimson.

'You knew but you didn't leave. Why?'

When she looked at him, her eyes were cool and clear. 'Because I didn't want to steal your son from you.'

That, finally, broke him. 'I've been in that house for fucking days now, sick with worry, not knowing whether my son was dead or alive, and all the while he was here with you, and you knew this and still did nothing ...' Saliva flew from his mouth and he had to suppress an urge to punch her face.

'No, that's not true.' She stood and tried to grab his arm, his shoulder, anything she could hold on to.

He threw her to the ground. 'I don't ever want to see you again. If you ever try to contact us, me or my son, I'll make sure it's the last thing you ever do.'

Sobbing on the floor, she screamed, 'It's not finished for me. That's why I insisted Eddy buy this house. So I could be near to you.'

'Goodbye, Maggie.'

Felix appeared at the door and looked at them. He had been roused by their raised voices and was alarmed.

'Come on, Felix, we're going.' Perhaps too hard, he tried to grab his son's wrist.

Felix pulled his hand away and ran towards Marguerite, who gathered him up into her arms.

Pyke saw the wild look in her eyes and stepped towards her. 'Put him down and we'll talk. Please, Maggie. Don't do anything stupid.'

'Like fall in love with you?'

He took another step towards them. Felix tried to wriggle free but her grip around his waist tightened. 'That was a lifetime ago, Maggie. We married other people, our lives have moved on ...'

'*You* might have moved on ...'

'Maggie. Give me my son.'

'Our son *died.*' She retreated from him, towards the fire, her arms wrapped firmly around Felix, who was struggling to free himself.

'Can't you see, Maggie? You're hurting him. You're hurting the boy.' Pyke took another step towards her.

'That's *enough*. Stay where you are, Pyke.'

'Maggie, please. Think about Felix. Put him down and we can talk ...'

'I can't be tricked that easily,' she said, backing away, another step closer to the fire.

'It's not a trick. Put him down and we can talk. There's nowhere left for you to go, Maggie.'

Much later, Pyke would dwell on the moment when Marguerite had turned to the fire and wonder whether she had really thought about trying to harm his son. In the end, it didn't matter because she turned back towards him and let Felix go, her cheeks stained with her tears. Felix rushed into his arms and Pyke gathered him up and walked out of the room without looking at, or saying another word to Marguerite, who had crumpled to the floor and was sobbing uncontrollably.

That was the last time he saw her.

As Pyke led Felix down the stone steps at the front of the house, holding his hand, he said, 'I'll never, ever let anyone take you or try and hurt you again.'

'Mrs Maggie didn't actually hurt me,' Felix said, matter-of-factly.

They walked on a little way in silence; 'You know you've always wanted a dog,' Pyke said, after a few hundred yards.

Felix looked up at him and nodded. 'Mummy said she'd ask you.'

Pyke nodded, thinking about what Felix had just said. The boy didn't know and he couldn't bring himself to tell him. At least not yet. There was only so much the lad could take in a day.

'Well, I might have found us a dog.'

'A dog. We've got a dog.' He trotted happily ahead. 'What's his name?'

'Copper.'

'Copper,' Felix said, excitedly. 'What kind of a dog is he?'

'A mastiff. But you have to be very careful around him. He's been very ill. And he only has three good legs.' Pyke took Felix's hand and, together, they started across the fields towards Hambledon.

Using the narrow staircase next to the old housekeeper's room, Pyke descended into the cellar and, with only a lantern to guide him, followed the passageway as far as it would take him; at its end, just beyond the wine vault that he had steadily depleted in the six years since he'd been living at the hall, he unbolted a door and carefully negotiated his way down another flight of stairs, right into the belly of the building. Until a year ago, he had never been down there and didn't even know it existed. He had stumbled upon it by accident, while looking for a casket belonging to Emily's mother; in a rare lucid moment, just before her death, she'd told Emily about its existence, but neither Pyke nor Emily had been able to locate it. It was eerily quiet. This silence was reinforced by Pyke's insistence that the four remaining servants take a week's paid holiday and leave him alone in the old hall; but it didn't really matter because down here no one would hear a man scream. It felt odd, knowing that it was just Felix, Copper and him in the building: Felix, who was asleep in his room, and Copper, who was stretched out by the fire in the drawing room. Just the three of them, if he didn't count Sir Henry Bellows and Abraham Gore. Pyke followed a dark, winding corridor as far as it would take him and paused by the spot where he had left two pails of water and a tall stack of bricks earlier in the day. Unbolting another door, he pulled it open, the rusty hinges groaning as he did so. Putting the lantern down on the stone floor, he stepped into the room and saw the two of them, Gore and Bellows, tied up and gagged, on the other side of the wall that he had started to build and which already came up to his waist. Staring over the wall at the two men was like looking at hogs in a pen. The light had disturbed Gore and he squinted at Pyke, tugged at the bindings around his wrists and tried to speak through his gag. Bellows, who had been there almost a week, was slumped, unmoving, in the corner. The spartan room stank of the chief magistrate's faeces, so much so that Pyke had nearly retched when he'd gone down there earlier in the day. Now, though, he had been expecting the stench and it didn't affect him in the same way. It took him a while to climb through the narrow gap between the top of the wall and the ceiling and once he was inside the room, he removed Gore's gag and prodded Bellows with his boot to see whether he was still alive. Returning to the other side of the wall, he started to mix some cement with water on a mason's board. After a moment he heard Gore croak, 'For God's sake, man, can't you see he's dying? He needs food and water now.'

Pyke peered over the wall. Gore's chubby face glowed in the half-light. 'You want *me* to show *him* compassion?'

Gore peered up at him, seemingly confused. '*Yes.*'

'The same compassion you showed Mary, the old woman in Huntingdon that you had Trotter rape and murder, or the navvies who died in that river, or Freddie Sutton and his wife or Johnny Evans or Julian Jackman, who you had crucified, or my own Emily, who you had slaughtered just because her political views offended you.'

'Views are one thing. Actions are quite another. I couldn't just allow her to do as she was doing.' Gore waited for a moment, to gather his breath. '*She* understood we were fighting a war. Every man and woman to the death. She fell on the battlefield so that good men like you and me might escape the ignominy of having our heads cut off and stuck on to poles.'

In that moment, Pyke hated Gore as much as it was possible to hate any man, but rather than act on it immediately, he picked up the mason's board and carefully spread a layer of mortar on top of the bricks. 'Don't ever think you can speak for me.' If he shut his eyes, he could see Emily smiling at him. He felt another wave of grief swell up inside him.

'You were entirely comfortable with her political beliefs and allegiances?'

'I respected her right to express them,' Pyke said, placing a brick on to the layer of mortar. He could even taste his animosity towards Gore at the back of his throat.

'But they never brought you into conflict?'

'I loved my wife. And now she's dead.' He took another brick and placed it next to the one he had just laid. With each brick, the wall became a little higher. It was slow, painstaking work.

Pyke had added another three rows to the wall when Gore spoke again. Now Pyke couldn't see him over the wall. 'When I was young, I used to read about figures like Jack Sheppard and Dick Turpin. I used to scour the pages of the old Newgate calendars. They were *my* heroes. I loved their bravery, their wit, their boldness. When I was older, I learned that Sheppard was nothing but a housebreaker and Turpin a common horse thief. The rest of it, the derring-do, noble deeds and courage in the face of adversity, was just a fiction. I remember feeling cheated at first but it taught me a valuable lesson too. The idea that a solitary man can bring an order as civilised and magnificent as ours to its knees is a nonsense.'

'Then why go after my wife? I'm guessing you knew she was Captain Paine, and not Jackman.'

'Really?' The surprise in Gore's voice sounded genuine. 'No, I didn't know it, but Sir Henry here always took that whole thing more seriously than I did. I wasn't worried about a few sporadic arson attacks. But it's true to say your wife's money, coupled with the Wat Tyler Brigade's ruthlessness, concerned me greatly. Do you imagine I wanted my workers swearing oaths to a union and striking to demand higher wages? That would have hit me in the pocket and the bad publicity a strike might have generated would've sent our share price plummeting.'

'You turn my stomach, Gore. That you could do what you did just to further line your own pocket.' Pyke felt his bitterness and grief engulf him.

'I couldn't let everything I'd worked for slip away. You, of all people, should be able to understand that.'

'The old woman you paid Trotter to beat and kill in Huntingdon. I saw her body. I'll carry an image of it to my grave. She was nearly seventy and he beat her and tortured her and raped her, and for what? To try and provoke the navvies into a fight so you could cut them down.'

Pyke pasted another layer of mortar on top of the bricks: the gap between the ceiling and the top of the wall was now just a few feet. He wanted it to be finished; he could hardly bear to be in the same physical space as Gore.

'What are you doing, Pyke? C'mon, man, we can still thrash out some sort of deal here, can't we? I still have money. If you'll stop building that damned wall for a moment and we can talk like gentlemen ...' Gore's disembodied voice echoed around the chamber. 'If not for me, do it for Sir Henry here. He's in a terrible state. No man should have to go through what he's had to go through.'

'I liked you, Gore. I know you *wanted* me to like you. That was the whole point of the deception. But I did genuinely like you. And look where it's got us.' Pyke laid one of the bricks carefully on top of the fresh mortar. Aside from the hatred, he felt used and humiliated.

'I liked you, too. I still do. I respect you. What you've been able to do. But all this nonsense can't be allowed to continue for much longer. I know you don't intend to leave us down here. That would be too monstrous. You've been waiting for my former friends to abandon me and now that's happened. Please, Pyke. I can give you anything you want. *Anything* at all. Any amount of money you ask for.' Pyke noted the first trace of panic in Gore's voice with a certain grim satisfaction.

'Can you give me my wife back?' When Gore didn't answer him, Pyke laid another brick and added, 'How does it feel to know people you've supported and backed for years, men you've counted as your friends, have abandoned you in your last hours of life; have not just abandoned you but have conspired to hand you over to me on a silver platter? That can't be a pleasant thought.' He felt a sadistic pleasure in what he was doing and despised himself for it.

A few minutes later he had added another layer of bricks to the wall. The gap was down to a few inches.

'You may have bankrupted your old bank but that's as far as they'll allow this to go, Pyke. You'll never bring down the system. Gore's will endure and very soon men and women will be able to travel from London to Birmingham in less than eight hours for just a few shillings. Imagine that. Eight hours. The world will never be the same again.' Gore was yelling now, his voice echoing around the enclosed chamber. 'And when it's finished that railway will be a monument ... *to me.*'

Pyke added another row of bricks and then another until he had only one more row to build before the tomb was complete. He smeared a thick paste of mortar on top of the wall and took his time placing each brick, forcing some of the mortar into the gaps at the sides and between the top of the bricks and the stone ceiling. It was demanding work and he was sweating by the time he had just one final brick to slot into place. He was standing on tiptoe on the top rung of a wooden ladder and had to strain to get as close to the small hole as possible. '"What's called the splendour of the throne is nothing more than the corruption of the state; it's made up of a band of parasites living in luxurious indolence." I found that written in Emily's diary. It's a quote from Paine's *The Rights of Man.*'

Gore tried to say something but once Pyke had forced the final brick into its place, he couldn't tell what it was. He smeared the rest of the mortar across the join between the bricks and the ceiling, climbed down the ladder and wiped the sweat from his forehead with a handkerchief. The candle in the lantern had almost burnt down and Pyke guessed he had only another five minutes at best before the light went out. Gore was screaming now but they were too far down in the belly of the old building for his cries to disturb Felix. Pyke gathered up his tools, picked up the lantern and started off along the narrow passageway, having to duck his head slightly because the ceiling was so low. By the time he had passed through the first door and bolted it, Gore's screams had evaporated into the air, and just as Pyke made it to the top of the stairs, the flame in his lantern flickered and died.

EPILOGUE

The winter that year was the coldest anyone could remember since the Thames had frozen over and Pyke and Maggie Shaw still believed the world held out possibilities for them. Pyke didn't see any more of her after walking away from her with Felix, and he heard later she had sold the estate and moved back to France, where she'd married into the aristocracy.

The furore unleashed by Pyke's actions towards both the Grand Northern and the entire financial system started to abate only once the prime minister, Viscount Melbourne, announced a series of measures, including a substantial investment of government money, to bail out shareholders and prop up the ailing company while the damage was assessed. Surveyors reported that the devastation caused by the blasts would cost the best part of two hundred thousand pounds to rectify. The Grand Northern was eventually taken over by one of its competitors, the Northern and Eastern, but even with a new board in place and bolstered by new sources of capital, the first trains didn't run on its tracks for another two years, and even then the fledgling railway terminated at Bishop's Stortford rather than Cambridge. Morris's railway, which was to have stretched one hundred and eight miles from London to York, had barely limped over the Middlesex border into Hertfordshire. To no one's surprise, the Birmingham railway fared much better; the first section was completed by the end of the following year and at an official ceremony to mark the opening of the line between Camden Town and Boxmoor, a memorial was unveiled to commemorate the sudden demise of its founder and chairman, Abraham Gore, who, according to the plaque, had died from an unspecified illness some time in the previous winter. Nonetheless, the railway fever that had gripped the country for the middle years of the 1830s ran out of steam, perhaps as a result of the losses investors had incurred during what become known as the 'Grand Northern debacle', and as the economy slowed and then slipped into recession, only a handful of new railways were proposed and built in the final years of the decade.

Pyke's war against the railway had resulted in many casualties but intervention on the part of Melbourne's government had propped up the share price to the extent that the losses suffered by ordinary investors were, on the whole, small.

Once the navvies had been paid, Pyke and Red had parted on good terms and, just as Pyke had promised, no one was ever arrested or charged for the devastating attacks on the railway tracks and the subcontractor's warehouses. The sudden, brief rise of Captain Paine lit the fuse for some radical activity in the capital and its outlying areas but he was quickly forgotten about, or rather passed into folklore. For a while afterwards, Pyke heard different versions of the ballad of Captain Paine being sung in the streets and in pubs, and he always found that its lilting melody and plaintive words brought a welcome lump to his throat. But radical activity didn't peter out after Emily's and Jackman's deaths. Quite the opposite, in fact. In London, a plethora of Jacobin associations based on the Wat Tyler Brigade were established, particularly in the East End, trade unions saw their numbers leap, and agitation for political and workplace reform eventually resulted in the establishment of a set of demands put forward by a new movement whose advocates became known as Chartists. Pyke followed these developments with interest but played no part in furthering their cause; and no one ever found out that Captain Paine had been a woman. The Duke of Cumberland also never found out how close he had come to seizing the British throne and when, two years later, and just a few months after she had come of age, Victoria became queen, Cumberland was crowned King of Hanover, where, under Salic law, a female ruler was not permitted. Though Pyke had had no further contact with the princess, he had been interested to learn that one of her first acts as queen was to banish Conroy and her mother from the court for ever. Pyke saw Kate and Milly Sutton a few times after they'd returned to London. At Princess Victoria's insistence, a good job was found for Kate in the King's Palace and she was able to support herself and her sister from what she made. In the short time she'd stayed at Hambledon, Milly had developed a fierce attachment to Pyke, and it was only after he had promised to visit them regularly in their new quarters that Milly had agreed to go with her sister.

In order to smooth things over with Ned Villums, Pyke paid a visit to his associate Barnaby Hodges at his gaming house on Regent Street and told him about the money Jem Nash had blackmailed from Morris and which could be retrieved from beneath the floorboards of Nash's lodgings in Fulham. Pyke's former colleague and henchman, Townsend, died that winter, too. Pyke paid for his funeral and made sure that the grave was adorned with a headstone bearing his name and dates. He didn't know anyone else at the funeral and left without introducing himself. On his way back to Hambledon, Pyke thought about his association with Townsend and wondered why, though they had known each other for fifteen years, they had never been friends.

During that first winter after Emily's death, Pyke took long walks with Felix and Copper in the grounds of the estate and spent time in the field where she had been buried, a picturesque spot in the shadow of oak and sycamore trees. It was only during those months that Pyke felt he got to know his son for the first time, what he thought and felt about the world, and it relieved him to discover that a keen, unsentimental intelligence lay behind his frail appearance. One night, soon after the servants' return to the hall, Felix had complained of hearing noises coming from somewhere below him and, though Pyke knew for a fact they couldn't have been made by Gore, he paid one final visit to the tomb he had built deep under the cellar, only to be greeted by a long, unedifying silence. That night he, too, had heard the voices, and for a while he truly believed that the banker's ghost had returned to haunt him. After that, Pyke encouraged Copper to sleep on the floor beside Felix's bed, and soon after that the lad and the slobbering mastiff were inseparable. It never ceased to amaze Felix how a dog as large as Copper could walk and even run using only three good legs.

Taking a rest from his business, Godfrey often stayed with them at the old hall and entertained them with gruesome stories of criminal wrongdoing. He would tell the stories in such a way that, by the end, even Felix and Jo were cheering for those who faced the scaffold. Though he knew that Emily wouldn't have approved, Pyke felt it was somehow still appropriate. By the time spring finally came, the once plentiful wine cellar had been nearly depleted.

But those first few months after Emily's death were also the worst of times. After Felix and the servants had retired to bed, Pyke would roam the dark passageways of the old hall with only his memories and laudanum to comfort him. Unable to sleep, he would pass silently through the house, trying to remember happier times: when he'd first met her, in the drawing room as she had played the piano, apparently unimpressed by his appearance; when she'd risked her own life to help him escape from the condemned block at Newgate; and the first time they had kissed, though now he couldn't remember where it had been. He remembered their marriage, an intimate affair in which her desire to keep her family name had been matched by his desire not to reveal his first name to her. He also remembered their arguments, but even these brought him some comfort. Emily had always been as obstinate as him. It was what people loved about her. Her passion lit her up from the inside and made people want to know her. Her passion, her grace, her playfulness and her intelligence. Shortly after her death, Pyke had given up the house in Berkeley Square a full eleven and a half months before the lease was due to expire. Emily hadn't known the house and he wouldn't have felt right about moving there. In fact, spending time alone in the old hall finally taught Pyke to appreciate it and, in a cruel twist, it was only once he had started to feel at home there for the first time that a lawsuit was brought against him by a distant relative of Emily's father, claiming that now Emily had died, the estate and its title should revert back to him. Pyke instructed the best solicitors in London and spent tens of thousands of pounds fighting the case, but even a year later the matter had still not been resolved.

The famous Florentine consort, Niccolò Machiavelli, once wrote, 'I believe it is probably true that fortune is the arbiter of half the things we do, leaving the other half to be controlled by ourselves.' In the days and months following Emily's bloody death and the wilful devastation that had ensued, Pyke thought often about Machiavelli's claim and while it sometimes struck him as outrageous prevarication, more often than not he saw its truthfulness. Pyke had done what he had done, and while those actions may have led to the death of his wife, fortune, too, had played its hand, and fortune, as it always did with men who took risks and imposed themselves on the world, would shine on him again.

AFTERWORD

It would be misleading in the extreme to pretend that a novel founded upon the imposition of an essentially twentieth-century form – the hard-boiled detective novel – on to a much earlier historical period carries any real degree of historical accuracy. More particularly, the demands of the genre have necessitated some gross tampering with the so-called historical record. The Grand Northern is a wholly fictionalised railway; there were plans to build a line from London to York in the early 1830s but the fledgling company never received Parliamentary approval. The London and Birmingham railway *was* incorporated in 1833 and the railway would have been under construction at the time my novel is set, but while there were examples of skulduggery and sharp practices on the part of some less scrupulous railway proprietors across the sector, there is no evidence to suggest that the affairs of the London and Birmingham railway were anything less than carefully managed. Abraham Gore is a fictional creation and is in no way intended to resemble the real chairman of the London and Birmingham railway, George Carr Glynn. On the other hand, Ernest Augustus, the Duke of Cumberland, is very much a real figure and while there is little or no hard evidence to suggest that he ever actively plotted against his niece, Princess Victoria, the fears at the time that he might try and seize the throne for himself were pervasive and genuine. In fact, he was called upon to defend himself from these charges in front of a House of Commons select committee chaired by the radical MP Joseph Hume. Likewise, Sir John Conroy was, indeed, the comptroller of the Duchess of Kent's household, and while there is no evidence to suggest that he deliberately exacerbated the princess's illness during the autumn of 1835 by introducing substances into her food, he did try to exploit her illness during an elongated stay in Ramsgate, by trying to persuade her to sign a document appointing him as her private secretary when she became queen. Victoria duly resisted his overtures and when she became queen in 1837, Conroy and her mother, the Duchess of Kent, were cast off into the wilderness.

In spite of the novel's largely fictitious basis, it would be equally churlish to pretend that some degree of verisimilitude isn't absolutely central to the project of historical fiction. In order to try and create a milieu that might have existed in the mid-1830s, I am indebted to the following (by no means exhaustive) list: Rick Allen, *The Moving Pageant*; Michael Alpert, *London 1849*; Arnold and McCartney, *George Hudson*; Felix Barker and Peter Jackson, *London*; Kellow Chesney, *The Victorian Underworld*; Mordaunt J. Crook, *The Rise of the Nouveaux Riches*; Giles Emerson, *Sin City*; James Epstein, ed., *The Chartist Experience*; Michael Freeman, *Railways and the Victorian Imagination*; Norman Gash, *Reaction and Reconstruction in English Politics*; David Goodway, *London Chartism 1838–1848*; Francis Grose, *The Vulgar Tongue*; Tristram Hunt, *Building Jerusalem*; Peter Jackson, *George Scharf's London 1820–1850*; Elizabeth Longford, *Victoria R.I.*; Michael Patterson, *Voices from Dickens' London*; David Pearce, *The Great Houses of London*; Liza Picard, *Victorian London*; Robin Pringle, *A Guide to Banking in Britain*; Pamela Sambrook, *A Country House at Work*; Jack Simmons and Gordon Biddle, *The Oxford Companion to British Railway History*; John Wardroper, *Wicked Ernest*; Frederick S. Williams, *Our Iron Roads* and Cecil Woodham-Smith, *Queen Victoria: Her Life and Times Volume 1*. In addition the following websites have provided me with much useful background information: http://www.oldbaileyonline.org & http://www.victorianlondon.org

I would also like to thank the following people at Weidenfeld & Nicolson for their hard work in helping to bring this, and the first book in the Pyke series, to fruition: Kelly Falconer, Emma Finnigan, Susan Lamb, Mark Rusher, Kate Shearman, the whole sales team and, most of all, Helen Garnons-Williams for her patience, creativity and diligence during the editing process. In addition, thanks to Dave Torrens at No Alibi's book shop in Belfast, Luigi Bonomi, my agent, and Sean McCartney for his helpful pointers regarding the birth of the railways. Most of all, though, I would like to thank Debbie for her love, advice and tireless support during the writing of this book.